PORT ANNA

A Novel

Libby Buck

SIMON & SCHUSTER
New York   Amsterdam/Antwerp   London
Toronto   Sydney   New Delhi

Simon & Schuster
1230 Avenue of the Americas
New York, NY 10020

First Simon & Schuster hardcover edition July 2025

SIMON & SCHUSTER and colophon are registered trademarks of Simon & Schuster, LLC

For information about special discounts for bulk purchases, please contact Simon & Schuster Special Sales at 1-866-506-1949 or business@simonandschuster.com.

The Simon & Schuster Speakers Bureau can bring authors to your live event. For more information or to book an event, contact the Simon & Schuster Speakers Bureau at 1-866-248-3049 or visit our website at www.simonspeakers.com.

Interior design by Wendy Blum

Manufactured in the United States of America

10 9 8 7 6 5 4 3 2 1

Library of Congress Cataloging-in-Publication Data

Names: Buck, Libby, author.
Title: Port Anna : a novel / Libby Buck.
Description: New York : Simon & Schuster, 2025.
Identifiers: LCCN 2024041715 (print) | LCCN 2024041716 (ebook) |
    ISBN 9781668060070 (hardcover) | ISBN 9781668060087 (paperback) |
    ISBN 9781668060094 (ebook)
Subjects: LCGFT: Romance fiction. | Novels.
Classification: LCC PS3602.U262345 P67 2025 (print) | LCC PS3602.U262345 (ebook)
LC record available at https://lccn.loc.gov/2024041715
LC ebook record available at https://lccn.loc.gov/2024041716

ISBN 978-1-6680-6007-0
ISBN 978-1-6680-6009-4 (ebook)

For my mother, Kate, and her sisters, Alice,
Louisa, Dodie, and Eleanor.

There is no house
Like the house of belonging.

David Whyte

PORT
ANNA

PROLOGUE

A MOUNTAIN OF THICK, DARK WATER GATHERED AND rose, a froth of white curling at the peak. For a second, it paused, undecided, but then she leaned forward and held her breath, and it came to claim her, pulling her from the ledge into darkness. The frigid sea impaled her small body, her outstretched arms like those of a pale sea star. She spun, weightless, thoughtless, while, above her, the Atlantic hurled itself at the rocky shore.

Below, a fat swell grew, lifting her from the depths. Her face broke the surface and she gasped. Sleet stung her eyes and cheeks. In the distance, the lighthouse bellowed, its beam sweeping overhead. She leaned into the sound, but her limbs were too frozen to respond. If only she could reach it, all would be well. If only she could swim against this great muscle of ocean.

A wave slapped the side of her head, and seawater filled her mouth and nose. Another, larger than the first, held her under once more. Bubbles swirled as her lungs began to burn. Her skull ached, the cold punching her eardrums. Everything ached with desperation, her thoughts too jumbled to understand any directive other than "Breathe," and yet she couldn't. The sea gripped her ankles and pulled. She slid into the deep, farther, farther, and farther still until the pressure forced out all remaining air.

She drifted from her bones.

This would be her ending, then. No fairy tale, no dreams come true. Sorrow wrapped itself around her, and she reached for it. Water claimed her tears. All fell quiet, so quiet, and a vast peace took hold. Seaweed brushed her face in welcome.

Yet, just as everything was almost extinguished, a dark shape lunged from the gloom.

And a pair of eyes, black as pitch, found hers.

PART ONE

ONE

GWEN DID NOT WAKE WHEN THE LOBSTER BOATS ENTERED the cove at dawn, engines thrumming and radios blaring classic rock. Above the din, the helmsmen yelled at their crew, and still she remained dreamless in the creaky old house, cocooned in yellowed linen. She didn't note the rising sun, either, a sliver of light that, just after six, edged past the partially closed blind toward her exposed foot. The warmth crept up her calf, with designs on her thigh, its progress arrested only by a faded curtain. She snored softly on, her hands clasped between her knees, forehead puckered in concentration.

At seven, the kitchen door opened. "Hallooo?" a voice said.

Gwen shivered, and her eyes fluttered open at last. A veined ceiling came into focus, the knots in the wood darkened with age. A beat passed before she remembered crossing the state line just after midnight. *Welcome to Maine, the Way Life Should Be.* Three hours later, Periwinkle Cottage had appeared, its silvered shingles gleaming in the moonlight.

"Halloo?" The voice grew closer. "Who's there?"

A shape darkened the doorway as Gwen sat up, blinking, a hand shielding her eyes.

"Gwen?" Mrs. Condon stared, astonished. "Is that you?"

Gwen nodded, unable to speak.

Mrs. Condon raised her hand to her mouth. "My goodness. My goodness." She said this over and over again.

Gwen's throat clamped shut, a hard knot that wouldn't move.

"I can't believe it." Mrs. Condon wiped her face with her wide palm. She sat down heavily on the bed next to Gwen and pulled her close. "Aren't you a sight for sore eyes. Yes, ma'am, you are. Little Gwennie. All grown up. My goodness."

Gwen buried her head in Mrs. Condon's shoulder and wrapped her arms around the old woman's waist. Her faded dress smelled of Tide and bleach. "I'm so happy to see you," she managed.

"I'd just about given up hope, dear." This she pronounced *dee-ah*. "It's been so long, I thought that you'd never come back."

Gwen couldn't let go.

"And, after what you been through, I can't say as I blame you. But still . . . Well, I couldn't believe it when I saw the North Carolina plates. Thought it was my imagination running away with me."

A shadow fell across the bed. "Donald, Donald," Mrs. Condon said. "Look, it's our girl. She came back after all this time."

Gwen smiled at the large man in the doorway. Hair sprouted from his head and chin, yellowed dandelion fluff that reached his chest. He removed his small round glasses and wiped them, his forearms stippled tan and brown by the sun. "Goodness," he said, his voice graveled by years of smoking. "We are mighty happy to see you, child."

These were more words than Gwen had ever remembered him saying.

"I'm glad to be back," she said. And, for a moment, she meant it.

Mrs. Condon leaned toward her. "A few weeks ago, I could have sworn I saw you as a girl standing at the edge of your woods. Just like old times. But, of course, it wasn't anything. Just me being sentimental, I guess. Or getting old."

Gwen smiled. "Never."

"I would have had the place ready if I knew you was coming."

Mr. Condon nodded. "Aye-yuh." He crossed his arms over his belly, tucking his palms into his armpits.

"Oh," Gwen said, her face heating with embarrassment. "I should have called. I'm so sorry."

"That's okay." Mrs. Condon patted her back. "It's not important." She released her hold and sat back. "After all this time. All grown up."

Gwen shook her head. "I'm not so sure about that," she said. Her mad dash up 95 didn't seem like something a sane forty-year-old would do.

Mrs. Condon reached forward to touch the shock of white at Gwen's temple. "I'd forgotten about this," she said. "It suits you now, you know."

Gwen looked at her feet on the old rag rug.

"Can we bring you anything? Some breakfast? Donald here can go to the store."

Mr. Condon grunted.

"I'm good, thanks." She'd remembered the essentials: coffee, a jar of peanut butter, and a handful of PowerBars to get her through the long drive. She stood.

Mrs. Condon followed her into the kitchen. Gwen pulled the hefty Mr. Coffee, circa 1983, from the cabinet. "You sure?" she asked.

"I promise." The pipes groaned when Gwen turned the tap.

Mrs. Condon laughed. "Oh no, dear, the water's shut off. I'll call Jess to turn it back on."

Gwen froze.

"You remember my nephew, don't you?"

A woodpecker landed on the branch just outside the kitchen window, tapping, testing the pine for soft spots. Gwen had once read—she could no longer remember where—that woodpeckers curled their tongues into their heads to protect their brains against the blows. "Yes," she said softly.

"He'll be glad to see you, too," Mrs. Condon said, opening the back door to the driveway.

Gwen gripped the coffee mug, her mother's. *Not a Morning Person*, it said.

Mrs. Condon turned. "You know about that hot tub, right?"

"Hot tub?"

"Out there." Mrs. Condon pointed toward the woods.

Gwen peered out the kitchen window, spying the edge of a vinyl-covered cube on the ledge.

Mrs. Condon shook her head. "The Misses threw a fit, stomping and banging. Scared your dad so badly he pulled out of here and never came back."

Gwen's jaw tightened.

"Ask Jess to cart it off for you when he comes by. He'll give you a good price. But best to do it before the season gets too busy. Last year he was turning jobs down, he had so much work."

Mr. Condon ran a hand down his beard, nodding.

Mrs. Condon said, "Now that you're back, it's gonna be a great summer." *Summah.* "Mark my words." The screen closed behind them with a bang.

Gwen waved as they walked past the garage toward their house at the end of the lane. What did Mrs. Condon mean by a good price? What would it cost to haul an old hot tub away?

She swore as she crept across the pea gravel from the kitchen door to the driveway in her bare feet to grab the remains of a Pepsi bought just after two a.m. at a lonely convenience store. The inside of her car smelled like the burrito she'd eaten and the soda was flat and nasty, but she desperately needed the caffeine. In the kitchen, she poured it into a cup and walked through the living room to the porch.

When she opened the front door facing the water, the ocean exhaled a warm, briny breath. Gulls flew over the glassy sea, their white bodies gleaming. One dropped its meal on the rocks below, the clam shattering on impact. The bird shouted as it swooped to collect its prize. A lobster boat chugged across her view, heading back toward town, its wake like a vanilla ice-cream soda. Gwen waved even though the boat was too far out for the crew to see her.

For the first time in a long time, she wanted breakfast, a real breakfast, eggs, bacon, thick slices of toast slathered in butter. Dumping the last inch of soda into the empty flower bed, she reentered the cottage on tiptoe, catching the screen with her heel before it could slap into the frame.

When she reached for her car keys, a crash caused her to jump.

Gwen stopped moving and shut her eyes, bracing herself for what would surely follow. "I'll be back soon," she called to the house.

The attic joists creaked and popped. The walls cracked. The Misses were annoyed, and they wanted answers. *Where have you been? Why has it been so long?*

There was too much to explain, and all of it hurt. Gwen slid on her shoes and ran to her car.

TWO

THE ROAD BLURRED SLIGHTLY AS GWEN ROUNDED THE bend into Port Anna, past familiar front yards stacked with lobster pots, Ford F-150s hunkered in their driveways. At the bend into town, the steeple of the Congregationalist church rose dramatically above the tree line. Dedicated to those lost at sea and the lifesavers who'd tried to rescue them, the single stained-glass window included the name of Anna Vale herself, the town's namesake and patron saint. Every first of May, on the anniversary of her death, the local chapter of Odd Fellows placed a bouquet beneath. This year's wilted version still sat there, two weeks later.

Captains' houses lined Main Street, a row of whitewashed façades facing the bay. Oak trees shaded the yards, their heavy branches drooping over the sidewalk. Even before Gwen's family had arrived, most had been converted into bed-and-breakfasts, a few into galleries that sold paintings of the Maine coast, sculptures whittled from granite, and jewelry made of sea glass. These all closed in winter, only to creep back to life in spring. One or two had already had *Open for the Summer!* posted out front.

At the bottom of the hill, the sign outside the town library announced a lecture series sponsored by the tiny bookstore next door. When she was a young girl, this had been Gwen's favorite outing. She and her younger sister

Molly would run through the stacks untethered, plucking books at random. Volumes crammed every shelf and surface, many even stacked on the floor, a maze they had to navigate to reach the children's section. A big chair in the corner welcomed them once they'd found something they wanted. Gwen fought the urge to pull into the parking lot. She needed groceries, not another paperback. And she wasn't ready to confront a memory of Molly on her lap, thumb in her mouth.

On her right, the Black Anchor Restaurant had a new neon sign: *We Serve Breakfast.* The enormous anchor out front—salvaged from a three-masted schooner—shone with a new coat of paint. In high season, the line would stretch down the block, everyone waiting for a triple-decker cheeseburger or lobster on a lightly buttered, toasted hot dog bun.

The Inn at Blueberry Hill around the corner had a fancier menu but wouldn't open until June. A wooden sculpture of a giant squirrel directed traffic toward the parking lot, its other hand raised in greeting. Gwen returned the gesture, smiling. So much had changed for small towns in the past twenty years—transformed by shifting jobs and global pressures—but not Port Anna, the village at the edge of the world.

As she hit the brakes and coasted downhill, a huge pickup truck appeared on her tail. Before she reached the bottom, she pulled onto the shoulder and inhaled sharply as it passed, the driver gunning his engine to demonstrate his impatience with summer people who don't know how to drive. She wanted to shout that she was no from-awayer, no matter what her license plate said, but he was gone before she could open her mouth.

———

DRINKWATER PROVISIONS SAT between the ferry dock and the public landing. The weathered façade had darkened, and paler shingles marked an addition out back, but the sign over the door remained unchanged: *Groceries and Ferry Service to Snow's Island (twice daily unless there's weather or the captain prefers to go sailing).*

The familiar bell tinkled when she stepped inside. Walter Drinkwater sat behind the counter. His hair had thinned and there were grooves etched into his forehead. He raised an eyebrow. "Heard you was back."

"I am," Gwen said. Mrs. Condon evidently had the town on speed dial.

"Been a while."

"Twenty-three years."

He nods. "Aye-yuh. That's quite a while."

The shopping cart's wheels bumped over the wooden floorboards. Because she had no plan, she grabbed random items from the shelves: sugar and salt, ketchup and pasta, but also a king-sized bag of Milky Way candy bars and frosted oatmeal cookies, things she hadn't eaten in years. The eggs and bacon were encased in the refrigerated section, half-hidden behind clear plastic strips.

Walter watched her. Behind his head, artfully faded sweatshirts hung on clothespins. *Maine*, one read; another, *Port Anna, Est. 1842*. A few sported the town mascot: a mermaid, hair wild, her thick tail wound about the lighthouse.

Gwen unloaded her items onto the counter.

Walter cleared his throat. "House account?" he asked, opening a three-ring binder to the page marked "Gilmore."

Gwen raised her eyebrows. "It's still active?"

He looked at her impassively. "No one called to close it."

"Sure," she said, laughing. "Thanks."

Someone called from behind her, "Gwennie?"

She turned to find a couple staring at her. The man raised a pair of gold-rimmed aviators for a better look. "Is that you?"

She exhaled. "Hugh." His thinning hair, carefully gelled into place, had faded from its youthful copper, but he was still slender, his skin bronzed and polished.

He smiled. "You're back."

"Yep."

He held out his arms.

A beat passed before Gwen stepped forward, the memory of his last hug

13

so strong it made her dizzy. He pulled her close, her cheek against his chest. She held her breath, heart thumping at her ribs, until he released her.

"I read about your mom in the paper. I'm so sorry."

Gwen waved a hand, swallowing the stone in her throat.

His companion stepped forward, hand extended, a wide smile spread across her face. Her teeth gleamed, too white. "You're Gwen Gilmore," she said. "I'm Janet. Janet Riggs. I've heard so much about you. I own the real estate agency in town. Well, one of them anyway. I can't tell you how many times people have asked me about your property." Her tone rose, a question embedded in her introduction.

Gwen took a step back. "I'm not interested in selling."

The smile dimmed. "I understand. Family home and all that. But if you change your mind"—she leaned in too closely, coffee on her breath—"you know who to call."

"I'm not interested," Gwen repeated.

"Sure, sure." Janet reached into her oversized purse, pulled out a card, and handed it to Gwen. "I can get you a great price. Especially now that the lighthouse is a designated historic landmark."

Gwen stuffed the card into her pocket.

Hugh cleared his throat. "Staying all summer?" he asked.

"And beyond."

"Interesting. You plan to winterize, then."

"I'll be fine."

"Of course you will." He lifted two bottles of unsweetened iced tea and a bag of sandwiches toward Walter. "Add it to the bill?" He smiled at Gwen. "Come for a sail sometime, yeah?"

She nodded.

"See you later, Gwen," Janet said as she trotted out the door behind Hugh.

Walter's eyebrows lifted as he punched numbers into his register, pushing her items to the back of the counter. "Got bags? State says no more plastic and I have to charge for the paper."

Gwen shook her head. They were still full of her clothes and books.

"I got some used ones here, I think." He pulled rumpled bags from a drawer and handed them to her. "If you have some time, you should go see the old man. He was right fond of you."

Gwen stopped bagging. How could Ralph Drinkwater still be alive? As a child, he'd seemed ancient, his mouth emptied of teeth, a handful of white hair plastered to his bare head. When Gwen came shopping with her mother, he'd lifted pieces of penny candy from glass jars, hard straws of raspberry licorice, and gummy caramels wrapped in stiff cellophane, handing them to her as he smacked his gums. "You don't have to eat it," her mother would whisper into her ear beforehand. "Just say thank you."

Walter lifted his chin in the direction of town. "He's living up that way. The new condos near the post office," he said. "Been there a few winters now. We moved him when he couldn't manage the woodstove anymore. He doesn't get about quite as well as he used to, but he's still sharp. Talks about your mother now and then." He shakes his head. "Your sister, too, when she was just a little shaver. Such a shame."

Gwen said quickly, "Yes, thanks, Walter. I'll stop by." She grabbed her bags and left, stubbing her toe on the threshold.

THREE

GWEN HAD A PICTURE OF THE DAY HER FAMILY FIRST SAW
the cottage inherited by her father. Hair ruffled by the wind and salt, her
father beamed at the camera. Gwen's mother, Liza, willowy, redheaded, held
one hand to her swollen belly: Molly. Gwen, a skinny eight-year-old, held
the other. From the dormer window above their heads, a silvery light flashed
in the shape of a hand.

Soon afterward, the noises began, startling the new owners. The Misses
Elizabeth Gilmore and Judith Whitehead, the lifelong partners who had built
Periwinkle, banged doors and cabinets and caused the walls to creak. *Who are
you?* the cranky women wanted to know.

"We're your relatives," Gwen's mother had said to the ceiling. "And we
love your home." She'd repeated this day after day until silence fell.

Because the house had come fully furnished—all artwork, letters, linens,
and plates included—Gwen grew to know the Misses well. From the photograph albums, she knew they liked to swim every day, wearing funny bathing
costumes, dipping into the still-freezing June water. One July, they adopted
a pair of kittens. Their nephew came to visit with his new wife and baby. As
Gwen carefully turned the pages, they hovered nearby, brushing the wall.

She read their books, some annotated in a spidery script, and folded their towels. In the evenings, her family rocked on the porch, watching boats pass by, their sails aloft, just as the Misses had done. Sometimes the women left their attic to sit beside them, softly tapping the siding.

When Molly arrived, the Misses passed through the rooms on tiptoe. Gwen felt them as a whisper, creeping past the baby's door, afraid to wake the golden-haired girl. Little Molly learned to crawl up and down Periwinkle's wooden stairs, scooting on a diapered bottom. Like all who met her, Molly enchanted them. They chuckled when she shouted for her "Winnie," and didn't protest when she pushed a plate from her high chair, shattering it.

As Gwen and Molly grew, they added new treasures to the cottage, and the Misses made room. Silvery driftwood, pieces of white-ringed granite, and Molly's art projects sat on the mantel. Moth-eaten sweaters, T-shirts, and old bathing suits remained folded in the drawers all winter, waiting to be reclaimed in June.

———

AFTER BREAKFAST, GWEN left the greasy pan in the sink. Without water, it was impossible to wash anything. But she could dust. It was time to wake Periwinkle from its long slumber. She pulled frayed sheets from the furniture, sneezing. Arms full, she opened the door to the laundry room with her elbow. The window over the machines was cracked open, the lock broken long ago by a teenage Gwen, sneaking in after curfew. She tried to force it shut, but the wood had swollen and refused to fit inside its casing. She left the sheets on the washing machine and shut the door.

The ancient vacuum wheezed as it sucked up years' worth of dirt from the rugs and upholstery. Spiders scurried for the door when she moved the sofa, leaving behind cobwebs thick as gauze. Rags accumulated at her feet as she wiped the mantel and shelves, gently polishing the family photographs streaked with dust: annual portraits of her and Molly on the porch steps, the earliest dated to the summer before Molly could walk. But the collection of Molly's sea creatures that used to nestle between the frames had vanished.

Gwen checked the cabinet under the stairs where the art supplies—packages of googly eyes, pipe cleaners, and beads—had been stored. These had trailed after Molly like breadcrumbs through the woods. But the shelves were empty. Behind the bookcase, an impressive collection of dust bunnies floated away when she breathed on them, but no crazy-looking crabs with pasted-on eyes were hidden there, either. The closets in the kitchen and laundry room likewise yielded nothing.

Blinking grit from her eyes, she returned to the task at hand. Beneath more sheets, the dining room table gleamed. She straightened the whitewashed chairs, one splotched red where Molly had gripped the edge with cherry-stained fingers. Even after so much time, the whorl of her thumb pad was still discernible.

Gwen sat on her heels. She'd lived in grad-student housing with IKEA furniture for so long that she'd forgotten how much of themselves a person could leave behind. Even a very small person.

She placed a fingertip on the stain. That little thumb had once gripped Gwen's fingers so tightly.

A bang on the back door caused Gwen to fall backward. "Gwen? You home?"

She scrambled to her feet.

Jess Chapin's dark eyes searched her face, his expression so concerned she stepped backward. He didn't seem quite real, yet here he was again, the boy with the long nose and the quiet voice, the boy she snuck out of the house to meet, her first crush, her first kiss.

"Hi there," he said.

How did he look the same? No furrows indented his eyebrows; no creases lined his cheeks; and he was still wearing jeans and a soft flannel shirt. Only a speckling of salt in his dark hair revealed his age.

"Aunt May said you needed me to turn on the water?"

"Oh yes. Please."

They stood looking at each other, uncertain of their next steps. Jess scratched his head under his hat. He wore a wedding ring.

He asked, "You doing well?"

"Sure," she said.

"Glad to hear it."

He smiled.

The last time she'd seen him, she'd had the taste of his mouth in hers, the scent of his deodorant on her clothes. "I saw Hugh at the store. He looks good."

Jess shifted his gaze, a tic in his right eye. "Yeah. His father died a few years back and left him the house."

"Is that right?" The Fox estate had included the longest stretch of water-front property in Port Anna, and a huge shingle-style house overlooking the harbor to boot.

He shrugged. "About that water connection?"

"Do you know where it is?"

"I remember."

Gwen watched him walk away. His pants still hugged him in all the right places.

His voice sounded muffled from the laundry room. "Do you know you have an issue with this window?"

"I broke that years ago."

He chuckled as he moved the old machines aside. "Well, summer's fine, but come fall it could get mighty cold in here. You need some help winter-proofing, insulation or whatnot, you give me a call, yeah?"

She shrugged, noncommittal. Jess had sometimes made promises he couldn't keep.

"Open the taps," he said.

In the kitchen, the water hissed and spat as it gathered pressure, drizzling cloudy liquid into her greasy breakfast pan.

"Give it a while," he said. "The antifreeze will clear soon. You're lucky the pipes are still okay." He shoved the washer back against the wall and slapped his fist to the open window, forcing it back into place. "There," he said.

He was halfway out the door when she said, "Wait. What do I owe you?"

He shook his head without looking at her. "Nothing, Gwennie. Not a thing. It's good to see you."

Up the lane, Mrs. Condon's dogs started barking as soon as he started his truck.

"You, too," she said to the empty driveway.

Over the next few hours, she uncovered the pine dresser in the downstairs bedroom and pulled open the sticky drawers. Despite the mothballs, her father's plaid shirt fell apart when she removed it. Under the sink, a collection of long-expired medications bore his name. *Coumadin*, she read, and *Plavix*, both prescribed after his first stroke. She threw the useless bottles in the trash along with the crusted containers of lotion and shampoo. It took a while to scrub the green ring from the bathtub.

Meanwhile, the attic joists popped.

"I'm working as fast as I can," she muttered to her impatient ghosts.

Beneath mildewed life preservers, she found Miss Gilmore's portrait wrapped in a trash bag.

Miss Whitehead had painted Miss Gilmore as she sat under the window, reading just before sunset, the light golden and warm. The paintbrush dipped, dragging white highlights into the tendrils at the base of her neck. Yellows caressed her hand, and a sweep of blue followed the curve of her body. The date on the lower right corner read *1971*, more than fifty years into their relationship.

"How did you end up in here?" Gwen asked the air.

A kitchen cabinet slammed.

Gwen carried the painting into the dining nook where it belonged. Someone had replaced Miss Whitehead with a Mary Cassatt poster of angelic children playing in the sand. When Gwen removed the faded picture from the wall, a relieved sigh swept through the room, a whisper of gratitude.

Soon the scent of pine and lemon oil filled the cottage, every surface clean, the fire laid with the last few logs left in the woodshed. Everything looked as it once had, as if time had rolled backward and erased all her mistakes and missteps. The light slowly crossed the floor, warming the wide oak boards. Gwen stretched her toes and laid her head against the sofa, listening to the tide splash the ledges out front. In the attic, the insistent Misses thumped the walls.

Finally, she had no choice but to climb the stairs. On the way up, she wiped the dust from a seashell mosaic, her mother's favorite piece. Once it was clean, the colors returned, blues of a winter sky and pinks the shade of a baby's lips. At the top, she straightened the hooked rugs and swept the floor.

Propping the broom against the wall, she opened the door to her old room. Concert tickets, detritus from the beach, a beer bottle, and some wine corks littered the carpet like she'd left it suddenly, her teenage self frozen in that moment.

She picked up an old favorite T-shirt from the floor. Green and white, embellished with an image of the town's mascot, it read *Mermaid Fest 1995, Dance with the Fishes*. There was a tear in the shoulder that she didn't remember, but it had been a long, long time since she'd worn it. She folded it and put it back in the chest.

The view from the dormer window reached the offshore ledges. Beyond, the water glittered. Glaciers had carved the coast of Maine into its distinctive ragged shape many eons ago. In Port Anna, the ice dug sharp teeth into the rock like a deeply tined fork through butter, creating a series of granite walls separated by trenches. The first of these rose two hundred yards from the berm in front of the cottage. At low tide, the ocean pulled away from the face closest to shore, revealing seaweed-fringed boulders and scurrying crabs, but on the other side, the cliff dropped into deep water, creating swift currents between it and the next granite ledge. The third—the farthest area—stretched for over a mile, reaching around the corner and into the depths. Most of the time, it hid, but on a full moon, at dead low, a slick length of brownish gray reminiscent of a whale's back revealed itself, a menace waiting to reduce a keel to splinters. The lighthouse just beyond the point, unseen from Periwinkle's front porch, had been built to warn unwary sailors of its presence.

Winter storms tended to deposit all kinds of treasures at the foot of the ledge out front: lengths of rope with frayed ends, bait bags still stuffed with rotting bits, rubber gloves, suspenders, and plastic bottles. Gwen had even found a baby doll, her face bleached, washed overboard by the wind.

Molly had claimed it, scrunching her little freckled nose. "Mise," she'd shouted, her word for *mine*.

"You're a little *mise*," Gwen had said, tickling her chin.

The walls murmured, a soft rustling.

There was, of course, one more room. She paused, forehead on Molly's door, gathering her courage. After a minute, she turned the knob with a sweaty palm.

The house stilled, and even the dust motes stopped circling.

Nothing had been moved. Nothing had changed. The small table was set for tea, the chair pulled aside, expectant. Teddy bears faced the door from the open toy chest, their glassy eyes flashing. In their midst, the bleached doll stared at Gwen, her blue eyes wide. Gwen struggled for breath, her heartbeat unsteady. She stooped to retrieve Molly's hairbrush, the only thing on the floor. Pale golden strands still clung to the bristles. She carefully replaced it on the dresser.

A small strawberry dress and matching hat lay on the bed, waiting for a child who would never return.

How could you? The words, her mother's, popped into her head. *How could you?* The question ricocheted, doubling its volume until her skull hurt.

She retreated, quietly shutting the door.

The old pine railing wobbled as she ran down the stairs. In the living room, she threw open the front door facing the sea and clattered down the sun-bleached steps, past the crescent of scraggly lawn and up the berm of shoreline rocks. Small stones slid underfoot, and she teetered before she reached the boulders crouched at the lip of the first ledge. Heart racing, she balanced atop the largest, careful to avoid slipping on the seaweed, and hauled herself onto the flat expanse of granite.

On the other side of the ledge, at the drop-off, she faced the ocean. As a child, when her mother wasn't watching, she had bounded across the eight-foot gap like a gazelle, but no longer. She crouched awkwardly, gathering her strength, before leaping. She stumbled onto the second and much larger ledge, a dark granite that sloped slowly downward. In the center, a wide stripe of quartz looked like a river meandering toward the sea.

She sat at the top of the incline, bone on rock, eyes on the rising tide. Below, at the rim of the ledge, water eddied and swirled. She inhaled slowly, her hands pressed into the stone. An old barnacle, yellowed and knife-edged, bit into her thumb. It hurt just enough to muffle her mother's voice. *How could you?* She pushed until the skin broke.

FOUR

THE FOLLOWING MORNING, GWEN WALKED INTO THE
Port Anna post office past a row of old Volvos and planters filled with gera-
nium and petunias. A bulletin board near the counter bristled with flyers.

*Bach on the Beach, a fundraiser to support the summer music festival, June
21st,* one announced. Another invited everyone to a pick-up soccer match
every Friday at the park. A photograph of a teenager peeked from beneath the
collection. *Do you know me?* Gwen read. *The Portland Police need help locating
Shania Farrow, age 15. Last seen at the Irving gas station in Port Anna, April 15.*

Her gap-toothed smile, tentative below heavy eye makeup, was familiar. Some of the young women who used to come to Gwen's office hours
had looked much the same, smothering dark circles beneath cover-up, their
voices hesitant. "Too much going on," they'd begun with thin confidence.
The real reason for the visit had never tumbled out until a solid half hour
or more into the conversation. The specifics varied: maybe alcohol, maybe
a celebration—storming Franklin Street after a big win—or both, and then
everything upended, their bodies no longer their own, emotional scaffolding
dismantled in the aftermath. *Hand it in when you can,* Gwen would say, her
heart aching. *You have until the end of the semester.* Afterward, she shut the
office door to cry.

"Can I help you?" the postman asked from behind a pane of plexiglass, a remnant of the pandemic. The chubby man, his white hair cut short, wore a feather earring that swayed when he moved.

"I was hoping to rent a box."

"Well, I've got a few." He laughed. "What's the name?"

"Gilmore, Gwen Gilmore. We used to have number forty-five."

He looked up at her, eyebrows raised. "Periwinkle Cottage?"

"Yep."

"Always did like that mother of yours. She still with us?"

Gwen paused. "Alzheimer's."

"Wicked disease," the postman said, shaking his head. "My condolences. Box forty-five it is." He handed her a set of keys.

She turned to leave.

"Wait a sec. Been saving your mail for you."

As he walked away from the counter, Gwen leaned in for a closer look at the picture on the flyer. Pretty, sharp-featured, hair cut into a shag.

The postman returned carrying a heavy box overflowing with catalogs. "So sad," he said, when he saw her examining the flyer. The feather earring dangling from his right ear trembled as he shook his head. "Lord knows what's happened to her."

Gwen stiffened. She didn't want to talk about lost girls, tragic girls, little girls taken too soon.

"I got a teenager myself. Can't think what I'd do if she ran off. Of course, you know, some days I'd think that was just grand, a break from the drama. But still . . ."

In her pockets, Gwen's hands shook. *Stop*, she thought, *please, please stop.*

But he kept speaking as he pushed the box forward. "Maybe she'll turn up yet."

Gwen's hip buckled a bit under the weight.

"You can probably dump most of it in the recycle bin over there." He pointed to the corner. "But it's probably best to check through it, just in case."

"I'll take it home, then. Thanks." Another sorting project, just what she needed. Turning, she ran smack into another customer. "I'm so sorry," she said.

"Gwen." A thin man in khakis and a pressed shirt, fair hair cut very short, smiled at her.

She laughed. It was impossible to go anywhere without bumping into someone she used to know. "Aidan."

"Welcome home."

"Oh, come on, AK. You can do better than that," she said. "What about one of your world-famous hugs? I've missed those."

"You've got your hands full," he said, arms at his sides.

"Oh." She frowned at the box, her happy bubble deflated. *Things change.* "This is just the tip of the iceberg. Twenty-some years of neglect leaves a pretty long to-do list."

"The cottage needed some tending, did it?"

"The spiders had decided it belonged to them."

"Nasty little squatters. Lucky for you, you can kick them out."

"Where are you these days?"

"I live in Bangor. I just came to see my mom at Parker Ridge. She's pushing ninety now and doesn't get around well anymore."

"I know how that is." She shifted the heavy mail to her other hip. "Jess seems well." Aiden and Jess had been best friends since preschool and insep-arable as teenagers.

Aidan looked at his feet and sniffed. "Yep." Anger rippled across his face as he lifted his chin toward the mail in her arms. "You better take that to your car before you drop it."

Gwen blinked in disbelief.

"Maybe I'll see you in another twenty years," he said.

She stuttered in confusion. "But . . . I'm staying."

He rolled his eyes. "Right. Summer people always think it would be nice to move here and live like a local. But then winter comes and, *pfft*, they're off to Florida. It takes more than youthful memories to build a life here, Gwen." He shuffled to the counter before she could say anything else.

After unlatching the back of her Subaru, she discovered the box wouldn't fit. She moved the suitcases she hadn't yet unpacked, shifting books, orange jumper cables, and an old Target bag filled with God knows what. Even then, it took all her weight to make the hatch click shut.

In the front seat, she gripped the steering wheel. Aidan had always been the peacemaker, the one who stepped in when his friends argued. Hugh had been the risk-taker—staying on the island past sunset, paddleboarding outside the harbor's mouth where the current picked up, or jumping from the tallest rock in the quarry. Jess had hated how Hugh could talk Gwen into joining him, laughing as she leaped. But Aidan's calm voice and quiet earnestness could soothe Jess's anger, and, at times, deflect some of Hugh's worst impulses. Everyone had trusted him. The Aidan she'd seen in the post office lobby bore little resemblance to the boy she'd known. He'd disappeared, replaced by an unpleasant, angry man who wanted to provoke arguments.

Nothing stays the same, she reminded herself. *Nothing*. She should know that better than anyone.

From her vantage point at the top of the hill, she could see all the way to the mail-boat pier. The Goose Island ferry was unloading passengers and crates, the men in Carhartts and boots, a handful of early tourists in pastels and ironed shorts. They milled about, chatting, getting in the way of the workmen. In the distance, a bank of fog gripped the horizon, blanketing the Camden Hills and the islands beyond. In an hour, it would reach Port Anna, and all the shivering visitors would flock to Drinkwater's for sweatshirts and windbreakers.

———

SHE STARTED THE car and turned up the hill, away from town. New condos lined the street just past the graveyard, a stretch of identical structures attached at the hip, the vinyl siding so new and shiny that the units looked more like Legos than homes. She pulled onto the shoulder and got out.

Walter had failed to tell her which one belonged to his father. On the corner, a shadow passed in front of a window. She rang the doorbell.

A man came to the door, scowling. He wore a ripped shirt and jeans, both streaked with blue. There was a smudge on his nose and another on his forehead. "What do you want?" he barked, his accent Spanish. "I do not want knives, wrapping paper, or cookies."

Gwen raised her hands in surrender. "Wow. Okay, then," she said. "No cookies for you."

"What do you want?" he repeated, but without the same vehemence. A shock of white hair fell forward. He pushed it back into place with paint-stained fingers.

"I just . . ." Gwen stopped speaking. His eyes glittered, a kaleidoscope of green and brown. They were like sea glass, colors softened by sea salt and the tide.

His eyebrows raised. "You were saying?"

"I . . . I'm looking for Ralph Drinkwater."

He pointed. "That way. Number Seven."

"Thanks." She backed away, tearing her eyes from his, and looked toward Number Seven, two doors down. "I'm sorry I bothered you."

"Hey," he called out. "I didn't mean it. I like cookies. Come back if you have cookies."

"Not a chance," she said.

Ringing the bell for Number Seven, she heard shuffling, a slow advance to the door. It creaked open.

"Gwennie." Old Man Drinkwater's eyes crinkled. "Walter said you might stop by. Come on in. I'm making tea." His gums shone when he spoke.

She followed him inside. He moved slowly, his thin frame hunched.

Beige wall-to-wall carpet covered the floor, a perfect match for the wall color, a drab shade of putty. An ornately carved Victorian table dominated the living room, heavy-footed and ponderous, heaped with books. A pair of orange corduroy La-Z-Boy chairs faced an enormous television.

"Walter thought it would keep me company, but I can't stand the thing," he said. "Eight thousand channels, and it's still an idiot box."

Gwen laughed. She didn't like television, either. When her mother had first arrived at the nursing home, the nurses had run *Titanic* on a loop, the sound turned up to fill the silence. Watching the boat slowly slide into the water, her mother had grown agitated, and Gwen had begged the supervisor to turn it off. They'd compromised with the Nature Channel. The writing was still mediocre, but at least the images were prettier and no one drowned.

Mr. Drinkwater fussed with a tea bag, trying to unhook the paper from the string. "My grandson likes to come over and watch the soccer. So it stays." He poured hot water into a teapot and put mugs and a box of Girl Scout Thin Mints on a tray. When he returned the kettle to the stove, his hand shook.

Gwen reached for the tray. "Let me," she said, picking it up.

They sat by the window. He spoke about his retirement from the store. He said he missed the folks, but not driving the ferry in winter. "Started slipping on the ice. So I let Walter win the argument, and here I am. Staying warm in a condo with a huge TV, living the dream.

"How's the cottage?" he asked, lisping a bit as he bit into a cookie. "Has there been much damage?"

"Some," Gwen said. "But Periwinkle is still in pretty good shape after all this time."

"Good to hear. I was a bit worried, knowing no one was living there. Things can happen to a house, you know, especially when the weather comes. We had a terrible winter last year, a dumping of snow, and an ice storm in March. Lost a boat off the coast near Matinicus. Shouldn't have been out in those conditions." He shook his head. "But those young ones, they think they know it all. Such a shame." He sighed. "So, dear, what have *you* been up to?"

"Short version or long?"

"Short, dear." He poured a cup of tea and handed it to her. "I'm old."

Gwen took a sip of the too-hot liquid, burning her lip, before setting it down. "I moved to North Carolina for grad school fifteen years ago to be close to my mother and stayed. I taught there until a few weeks ago."

"Why the past tense?"

"I guess you could say I needed a change."

"Are you writing?"

"No, sir." Not even in a journal.

He smacked his lips. "Always thought you'd be a writer. I think I still have the book you young ones put together for the library fundraiser. Of course, I don't know where anything is anymore."

"Don't worry."

"You seen Jess? Part of your pack, wasn't he? Back when."

"Sure was."

He patted her hand and placed a Thin Mint in her palm. "Had the world by the throat, didn't you?"

Gwen nibbled at the chocolate; she didn't need to answer. *Things change.*

"Never mind, deah. We all gotta grow up some time."

She nodded. "Guess so."

"You'll come to the concert, won't you?"

"Concert?"

He gestured toward the water. "At the park . . . you know. The start of summer." Mr. Drinkwater's eyes blinked slowly, fighting sleep. "Everyone goes. People will want to welcome you back."

"Wouldn't miss it, then." She placed her cup on the tray. "Can I take this back into the kitchen before I leave?"

"No, no. I'll manage. I'm going to sit here awhile longer. It's good to see your face."

FIVE

A DENSE FOG ROLLED ACROSS THE BAY AND SWADDLED the peninsula in a curtain of white, refusing to leave. Over the course of a week, it crept onto porches and slid through cracked windows. It muffled the cries of the circling gulls and stilled the growl of boat engines. Only the lighthouse horn broke through, calling across the water, warning of danger ahead.

Gwen nursed endless cups of tea, eating whatever she could find in her cabinets, bundled in sweaters, afraid to use up the last remaining logs of her father's firewood. Her cell signal dropped to zero. She reread the Misses' books and thumbed through the old albums. Her old life drifted away, less real every day. She could no longer recall why her research into feminist theory or Victorian women or semiotics had ever seemed urgent. She forgot the names of colleagues and friends and students. Even Guy—the boyfriend-who-she-thought-would-be-fiancé—slipped away. Memories of their conversations, including the last and most painful, dissolved, swallowed by the fog at her doorstep.

The years rolled backward.

In the quiet, Molly's hummingbird trill rolled down the steps. *Winnie!* Her feet thumped the steps as she jumped up and down, clutching her Mermaid Barbie with the translucent tail. *Let's play. Let's go the beach.*

Their mother stood on the porch, calling, *Come on, girls, it's time for supper.*

Their father ruffled their heads on his way to make a cocktail. *Good day, little ones?*

After dinner, Gwen plugged in the old CD player, and music filled the cottage: The Beach Boys, Madonna, and Jimmy Buffett. Molly shouted, *Turn it up,* so they could dance, jumping and waving their arms overhead until their mother stopped them. *You're going to make yourselves sick,* she warned, laughing.

Gwen closed her eyes and danced to the same songs, the old floorboards creaking loudly, no one to stop her anymore.

The soundtrack played over and over, a lullaby.

When the fog moved on at last, cell signal returned, and the confirming salvo from the English department landed in her inbox. *Ms. Gilmore, Pursuant to the complaint filed by Ms. Lyall Cunningham, we feel we have no choice but to recommend your termination.*

The music ground to a halt, and the reality of her situation returned.

When the dean had called Gwen into his office to discuss Lyall's grade, she'd known what was coming. But, as she turned to leave, he assured her the final decision would come from the chair of the English department, Phillip Melborn. For a few hours, Gwen had hoped that Phillip would stand up for her. By nightfall, though, she came to her senses and packed her bags, shoving clothes into suitcases and books into boxes.

She'd attended grad school with Phillip. Despite an Ivy League degree and a tendency to lecture about the latest academic trends, he'd failed his Ph.D. exams—twice. This might cause a reasonable person to buckle with humiliation. But the dean had a soft spot for suck-ups, and Phillip had a lot of practice licking boots.

Gwen should have considered this when she refused to change Lyall's grade.

"I earned an A," Lyall had insisted.

"You neglected your footnotes. That's considered plagiarism," Gwen said. "Redo it for half credit or fail."

Lyall bounced from her chair, indignant. "I'm going over your head."

"Fine," Gwen said to Lyall's back, assuming that the dean and his chair would take her side, as the instructor of record. Yet, she'd committed one of the great academic cardinal sins: neglecting to connect Lyall's last name to the newly christened Cunningham Stadium. So much for the years of academic servitude, the committees she'd sat on, the recommendations she'd written, the endless faculty meetings. Lecturers were cheap, paid by the class. Also, disposable. They'd replace her in a nanosecond, plucking another recent, broke graduate student from the vast pool of eager faces. Rinse, repeat.

Thank God that Michaela, her boarding school friend, now the principal of Peninsula High, had offered Gwen a lifeline.

"Fuck them," she'd said. "We'll find something for you here. There's an opening for an AP lit teacher."

In the meantime, Gwen would have to watch her expenses, but at least there was no more rent to pay, no more mother to support. Unless something unexpected arose, she'd manage until school started.

The email ended with as little grace as it had begun. *Please return the keys to your office. Your final paycheck will be delivered electronically.*

"Fuck them," Gwen repeated as she shoved the swollen envelope through the slot at the post office.

———

WHEN GWEN RETURNED to the cottage, the still-unopened box of mail squatted on the table, accusatory. She'd put off sorting it for a week, indulging in a fantasy that didn't include adult responsibilities. "Just get it over with," she lectured herself.

She tossed envelope after envelope addressed to her parents in the trash, all of it junk—requests for donations from the local hospital, the library, and the private school serving peninsula children. Darling's Dealership in Bangor sold used Fords for cheap! Best price in Maine. And then, at the bottom, out came a receipt for a hot tub. Her father had paid two thousand dollars for it, and in the same year, Gwen stretched a single jar of peanut butter, scraping the plastic as clean as her checking account.

Two thousand dollars to destroy Molly's special place.

Anger raised the hair on her arms. She stood so quickly her chair fell to the floor. Trash bin in hand, she shoved the screen open with her shoulder and went outside to the fort.

When Molly was four, Gwen had cleared the undergrowth from the flat ledge that ran under the house, stopping at the edge of the woods behind the kitchen. Using a cache of debris from the garage, some old shingles and window frames, she'd constructed two bedrooms and a living room. Old linoleum remnants became beds, and plywood turned into tables. Sea glass and polished shells found on the beach decorated the tree roots. Her proudest accomplishment had been the fireplace built of wood scavenged from the cord behind the garage. Molly had glued mosses and wishing stones to the mantelpiece and declared it was perfect.

When they had finished furnishing it, Gwen smuggled out plastic glasses and cans of soda for "tea." Molly, delighted, made pine cone cookies topped with rugosa petals. They spent hours in the clearing, so wrapped up in their play they didn't hear the calls for supper. It had been their little haven.

Yanking the bird-shit-streaked hot tub cover aside, Gwen upturned the trash. The mail fell, a wave of white paper spattering the pale blue plastic. In the kitchen, she found matches and an old bottle of accelerant. Careful not to spill, she squeezed the contents into the tub and tossed in a match.

Flames burst from the interior, a billow of black smoke and brilliant red. Her lungs burned as sparks and bits of paper floated into the air. The smell clawed her throat, and her face heated, but she stood and watched as the scraps turned to ash.

At sixteen, Gwen had lost her fascination for their fort. "Winnie, *pleeeaaase* come play with me," Molly had begged, tears running down her freckled cheeks.

But Gwen had patted her head distractedly. "Sorry, mushroom, got places to be." A pickup truck filled with other teenagers waited for her, Jess grinning from the driver's seat, Aidan beside him. Hugh, already shirtless, sat in the back.

Gwen had left Molly behind, that lovely child who only wanted to play with her sister. Her blond curls had sparkled in the sunlight. Her little face had wrinkled when she laughed.

Gwen's brain screamed, *How could you?*

When the fire died, she peered over the lip at the smoldering remnants. The heat had scorched the plastic, darkening the interior from blue to black. The hot tub was still an ugly squatter, but somehow she felt better. As it turned out, revenge tasted pretty good served up hot, too.

Above the tree line, silvered clouds streaked with pink caught the evening light, a mackerel sky. She watched the shadows slowly gather and move toward the spiked firs. She'd dreamed of this many nights, a thousand miles away: the long pause at dusk as Maine gratefully opened her arms to the night. The sun shrank, the ocean calmed, and stillness settled on the earth. In the distance, a loon called to its mate.

And a small voice rolled across the ledge, landing at Gwen's feet. *Stay with me.*

SIX

"BACH ON THE BEACH" WOULD OPEN THE SUMMER CON-
cert series at five p.m. sharp. Gwen sprayed on bug repellent, stuffed some
cash in her front pocket, and grabbed a jacket. In June, once the sun went
down, the temperature could drop quickly.

The park was crowded: parents grouped around the play structure,
kids running, and middle-aged women pushed the elderly in wheelchairs.
Mr. Drinkwater sat on a bench, blanket tucked around his knees, deep in
conversation with an older woman. Teenagers raced from the parking lot,
hoping to shake off watchful eyes.

A handful of people stood on wet gravel before a makeshift stage while a
string quartet played. The melody wound through the crowd, mingled with
voices and the waves, and drifted toward town. The cellist played with his
eyes closed, swept far away, his instrument moving with his body. The melody
rose and fell, crescendo, trills, decrescendo, then crashed, taking Gwen along
with it. Classical music was all she had listened to in the months after Guy
left her. Anything else had made her skin crawl.

A hand touched her elbow, and she jumped.

Jess stood beside her. "Sorry. I didn't mean to startle you. I just wanted
to introduce—"

The man at his side interrupted. "You're Gwen," he said eagerly. "I've heard so much about you. Jess here"—he elbowed Jess, grinning—"says you guys were great pals many moons ago. I'm Steven." He was tall with ash-blond hair and cheekbones so sharp they could cut paper.

Gwen smiled. "Nice to meet you."

Jess looked at her with a pleading expression. Was he trying to set her up?

"I'm Jess's husband," Steven said.

Gwen's eyebrows rose. A visceral memory returned—Jess's hands on her waist, her legs around his—and her stomach flipped. She started to say something, anything, but nothing came out, her thoughts too disorganized to make sense.

Steven turned to Jess. "You didn't tell her."

Jess sighed. "When was I supposed to tell her?"

"Oh, I don't know, sometime in the last decade, Jess."

"She hasn't been here for more than twenty years, Steven. We had maybe a two-minute conversation when I turned on her water."

Gwen searched Jess's face. Steven opened his mouth just as Gwen's brain came back online. Her words tumbled out. "He's not lying. We haven't spoken in years, Steven." She took a breath. "Congratulations. How long have you been married?"

Jess cleared his throat. "Five years."

"And together five before that," Steven added.

She said, "I really am happy for you, and I am sorry I hesitated to say so. I was just surprised. Can we start over?"

Jess and Steven held each other's eyes, an intimate exchange passing between them.

Guy had been her live-in boyfriend for more than four years, her longest relationship, but they'd never communicated like this, not even once. At first he'd whispered all kinds of sweet words, so many promises on his lips. A house, a dog. A child. But when she asked—begged, really, her face slick with snot and tears—he'd said no, *Never*, and the contempt on his face knocked her backward. She hid in the kitchen as he packed his bags, his face pinched with anger. Months later, a mutual acquaintance told her the news—new partner, new baby, new job—leaving Gwen staring at the floor, her future shattered on a dull gray carpet.

A long minute passed before Steven turned his face to Gwen. "Hi, I'm Steven Bowditch, Jess's husband, and I'm happy to meet you finally, Gwen."

Gwen took his hand. "Hi, Steven. Nice to meet you, too."

A beat passed before he shrugged toward the stage. "How do you like the music?"

"Oh," Gwen said. "It's amazing."

"The pros who come for the summer festival always complain about how the ocean air messes with their tuning, but you know what, the music does sound incredible, bouncing off the water." He took a sip from a Solo cup.

"Where'd you get that?" Gwen asked, grateful for an excuse to step away.

"The kiosk is over there." Steven pointed toward the park's edge.

Jess cleared his throat. "You'll come back?"

"Sure," Gwen said, already walking, her feet unsteady beneath her.

She hadn't thought she'd pick back up again with Jess—it had been a teenage fling, nothing more, and besides, she had no interest in another relationship. And yet, the news registered as a shift, a loss. Bereft, that's the word. She was bereft, another part of her life set adrift.

A couple stood at the head of the line, at least two beers each under their belts. The man struggled to insert his credit card into the mobile reader. Irritation climbed up Gwen's spine as she watched him fumble.

"Sorry," he mumbled. He dropped his wallet.

A man reached down to grab it. "Better stow that in your pocket," Aidan said to them as he handed it over. The woman pulled on her companion's arm, the beer sloshing as they walked away.

"Hey," Gwen said, waving.

Aidan nodded. "Nice night, huh?" The music wafted across the water, a rendition of "Somewhere Over the Rainbow."

"I was just talking to Jess and his husband." She pointed toward the stage. "Come join us."

Aidan stiffened, the smile wiped from his face. "Why would I?"

Gwen's mouth opened. *Because you're best friends*, she thought. Her mother had called Aidan and Jess the "odd couple." One dark-headed, built like a linebacker, the other elfin and fair, but they shared the same sense of humor, the same gentle smile.

"That was a long time ago." His voice was hard. "And here I had told myself that things would be different . . . Hugh's over there, too, isn't he?"

"No—" she began.

A string of curse words ensued as he shook his head, ending with, "Damn master manipulator."

"Hugh?" *A master manipulator?*

"You gotta hand it to him, he's a fucking genius," Aidan said. He stepped away from the line and threw his empty beer cup into the trash barrel. "Later," he said to Gwen over his shoulder.

Gwen's head reeled. *A genius?* Hugh had always been competitive, sure, but he'd also had a habit of doing things he shouldn't: stealing road signs, breaking into the yacht club after hours, sneaking onto boats at midnight with girls. He'd even made a play for Gwen once, coaxing and cooing, his eyes all mushy, but she'd explained, removing his hand from her hip, she wasn't interested.

"What's your pleasure?" the server asked.

Gwen shook away the memory of Aidan's angry face and squinted at the kegs. "I'm not sure."

"I'll give you a taste of the IPA." He poured a measure into a cup and handed it to her.

She sipped. "That's great, thanks."

Behind the beverage tent, the moon rose, huge and neon-white. Loud laughter rippled from a gaggle of teens gathered near the seawall. The music built to a final flourish. After the last note, the cellist dropped his hands to his sides, and the musicians stood, bending as the crowd clapped. The teenagers whooped—she suspected less in appreciation for the classical performance than for its end.

She found Jess and Steven in conversation with someone else.

Jess smiled as she stepped into their orbit. "Oh, Gwennie, good, you're back. Have you met Leandro Vasquez?"

When the man turned, kaleidoscope eyes met hers. She stifled a gasp. Leandro smiled at her. "Oh, we know each other," he said. "She tried to sell me cookies."

Gwen blinked, and then she grinned. "Oh, no, I didn't. I only sell cookies to nice girls and boys."

"Cookies?" Jess asked, looking confused.

Leandro continued, "She came to my door with cookies, and I am afraid I was quite rude."

Gwen said, "Yes, you were."

He bowed. "I apologize for my behavior. Sometimes when I am working, you know"—his hand made circles above his head—"I get a little crazy."

"And you yell at poor lost strangers."

His eyes flashed. "Not when they have cookies."

"Well, I had snickerdoodle and chocolate chip—but you chased me away. So no cookies for you."

"And if I ask nicely?" Leandro said, eyes shining with mischief.

"That depends. What are you offering in exchange?"

Steven interjected, "Soooo . . . Gwen, what do you do when you're not selling cookies?"

"I teach literature." She sipped her beer, wetting her lips, determined to savor the entire six-dollar cup.

"You were going to be a writer," Jess said, a wrinkle between his eyebrows.

"Yeah, well, I learned as an undergrad there were others far better at it than me," she said. "And it pays the bills. Most of them anyway."

A crash from the stage ended the conversation.

"Here we go," Leandro said. "The Pan-Tones." He drew out the syllables with a flourish.

The band hauled metal cradles and black cases that resembled oversized hatboxes up the steps, dropping them onto the wood. They leaned over to unzip the boxes and removed what Gwen first mistook for hubcaps. Then she laughed. "Steel drums?"

Leandro said, "Just wait. This is fantastic."

Tie-dyed fans lined up in front of the stage, followed by the gang of teens, all jumpy with excitement. A weed-scented cloud wafted past. As soon as the bandleader stepped to the front and raised his arms, the crowd began to whoop and clap. A note sounded, and a blanket of bell-like chiming engulfed the shoreline. People began to dance, arms flapping.

Gwen grinned at the spectacle, wonderful and bizarre all at once, the cold, wet ground beneath her feet and the imaginary scent of rum in her head.

"It is intoxicating, no?" Leandro said.

She watched the dancers spin, many with eyes shut. "It looks like a Grateful Dead concert."

"I'm going in," Steven said to Jess. Jess put his cup down, and they entered the fray of bodies moving to island music.

Leandro stood next to Gwen, his white T-shirt almost touching her jean jacket.

"You are a writer, yes?" he said.

"Not anymore."

"Why is that?"

"I answered that question."

His head tilted. "I am not sure that I believe your answer."

"Not much for small talk, are you?"

He sighed. "True. I am not, Cookies." He leaned toward her. "Would you like to dance?"

She stepped backward. "No, thanks," she said.

Leandro pushed a shock of white hair from his forehead. "Drinking is not much fun without a little dancing." His eyes glittered, laugh lines crinkled.

Her heart skipped a beat when he held out his hand, the wide palm streaked with blue paint. Its warmth would swallow her, and then she'd land where she always had, on her ass and alone.

"I'm not into fun," she said. She drained the rest of her beer onto the beach, a gentle stream washing the shells and small rocks, and turned away. Her steps fell on the half beat, discordant with the great steel drums. She could feel Leandro's eyes glued to her stiff back all the way to the parking lot.

SEVEN

STEAM CURLED IN THE CLEAR MORNING AIR. GWEN SET
her coffee mug on the porch railing. Seals basked on the second, half-submerged
ledge out front, a crowd of slippery bodies, their tails lifted with pleasure. The
newborn pups stayed close to their mothers. One, her fur mottled white and
gray, watched Gwen carefully.

"Don't worry," Gwen said. "I'm not going to bother you. You can stay
right where you are."

She closed her eyes and lifted her chin to the sun. Today would be warm,
hot by Maine standards.

"Hello," she heard.

"I'm on the porch," Gwen said. She edged closer to the porch railing,
peering around the corner.

Mr. Condon appeared. Red suspenders held up a pair of old jeans, and
his faded T-shirt read *Blackflies, Defenders of the Wilderness*. He stopped in
front of Gwen and looked up.

"Me and the missus thought you might need this." He passed the box
up to her.

She opened the lid. Inside, there were flashlights and candles, a first-aid
kit, and an emergency blanket, the Mylar bright in the morning light.

"You never can tell . . ." His voice trailed away. "Might look like summer now but . . . you just never know."

"Oh, I know. The season only lasts six weeks." Her parents had often repeated this to each other, shaking their heads. Gwen was an adult before she realized how quickly six weeks flew by. "I'm going to need another cord of wood soon."

He wiped his forehead with a bandanna and nodded at the flower beds that lined the front of the cottage facing the sea.

The decking creaked as Gwen leaned forward following his gaze. A small stand of lupine pushed upward, pale leaves unfurling, but all the other perennials—the echinaceas, daisies, delphiniums—were gone, swept away by neglect and the winter tides.

"Your mom . . ." He stopped.

"Yes, sir, she loved the garden," Gwen said. The beds that faced the driveway, on either side of the kitchen door, looked equally as terrible.

He stuffed his bandanna back into his pocket. "Well, sure am glad you're back, Gwennie." He waved and walked away, his joints so stiff they almost audibly creaked.

"Thank you, Mr. Condon," she said to his retreating back.

Gwen found the tools still in the garage, the shovel sewn to the wall by an army of zealous spiders. Her mother's gardening gloves, covered in dust, sat on a shelf by the door. She slapped them against her thigh before putting them on, shaking loose the remains of a few shriveled insects. Returning to the sunlight, she sneezed and coughed.

The soil resisted her efforts, the dirt caked and hard. Gwen struggled to push the shovel's nose into the earth, forcing it past a layer of salted turf, but she only managed to bring up handfuls of topsoil laced with shell and stone. At this rate, preparing the beds would take a week. How had her mother made this look so easy? She raised the shovel above her head and brought it down with all her force. The metal landed on the ledge that ran underneath the house only inches beneath the compacted soil. The resulting thwack snapped the handle and knocked her off-balance, her arm vibrating from the shock.

She rubbed her wrist to ease the lingering static. Granite might offer the perfect foundation for a house at the edge of the sea, but it definitely made gardening a challenge.

Not a single cloud crossed the big Maine sky all morning as Gwen worked the salt-encrusted earth with her truncated tool. Her arms ached, and sweat ran down her back, but the sun was warm, and she liked the way her muscles felt used and useful. It had been ages since she'd undertaken a project like this—the rental in Chapel Hill had discouraged tenants from doing their own landscaping—and she was surprised by how much she enjoyed the loamy smell of overturned soil, even though the stones and roots fought her all the way.

At midafternoon, she stood back and smiled at her progress. She wiped the hair from her forehead, and the dirt streaking her arms left a fat smudge behind. She slapped at a blackfly on her neck. Another landed on her forearm, and she swatted at that one, too. The breeze that had kept them away since morning had stalled. She waved her arms around her head, hoping to chase them off, but they were persistent little buggers. She couldn't decide if they were better or worse than the swarms of mosquitoes that took over North Carolina in the summer.

From the roof, a crow squawked loudly, over and over, until Gwen turned.

A figure stood on a rock at the spot where the coastline rounded a corner toward the lighthouse. It was far enough away that she could only see an outline of a person staring into the rising water as if getting ready to dive in.

"Hey," she yelled. She ran one hundred yards up the rocky berm, slipping and waving. The broken shovel swung as she tried to get the person's attention. "Hey," she said again, "that's not safe!"

The head lifted, looking in Gwen's direction. Gwen moved carefully down the berm to the boulders at the lip of the first ledge, gesturing wildly toward land. "Go back," she shouted. "You can't swim there." The ocean near the lighthouse might look calm in good weather, but it hid unpredictable and fast-moving water. Even in August, when the water temperature finally rose to sixty-five degrees, hypothermia could set in within fifteen minutes. "It's not safe," Gwen repeated, standing on a boulder and pulling herself onto the ledge. She waved the shovel again as she moved closer to the sea.

The figure remained undecided for a moment before turning around and leaping back onto the rocks that led around the corner to the Port Anna lighthouse.

Gwen waited to exhale until the person rounded the corner to safety.

A wave rolled over her feet, filling her shoes. She jumped backward. "Shit." The shovel slipped from her sweaty hands and slid into the deep water. She leaned forward to grab it, but the drop-off was too steep. The ocean had claimed it. "Shit!"

Walking up the path toward the house, she left wet footprints behind.

At the hardware store, a teenager helped her lift the new shovel onto the counter. "Doing some gardening, then?" he said, eyes on her dirty jeans. "Or burying a body?"

"That's my secret."

He grinned with slightly crooked teeth. He was younger than her former students, but not by much. "Either way, plant sale is at the end of the month."

"Thanks," she said, adding, "And I'll take a newspaper."

He nodded sagely, his finger to his nose. "Ransom notes."

She tapped her nose, too. "I like the classics."

His name tag read *P. Drinkwater*.

She asked, "Are you related to Walter?" There was a resemblance in the heavy eyebrows and the round chin.

"Parker." He reached across the counter, and Gwen shook his hand, his grip tight and strong, his blue eyes direct. "Walter's my dad."

"Gwen Gilmore. So nice to meet you. I hear you like soccer. I saw your grandfather's big TV."

His face brightened. "Do you play? We have a pick-up game every Friday evening."

"Not since I was very, very small."

His shoulders drooped. "Too bad. We need more players."

Half of the kitchen cabinets stood open when she returned to the house. She put the shiny new shovel and the newspaper on the table and pulled out the peanut butter.

Stuffing a sandwich into her mouth, she checked the want ads. Whatever Jess would charge to haul that hot tub away, it wasn't in her budget. Although neither were shovels.

She almost laughed at the salary offered for a teacher at Bangor High. Guy had warned her the university's English department was taking advantage, relying upon her loyalty to the institution and her affection for her students. Without tenure, she'd received no benefits, no health insurance, no promises of sabbatical.

And, it seems, she'd been vastly underpaid.

Beneath the listings for janitors and nursing home staff, the *Port Anna Packet* also sought a freelancer to take on long-term projects. Deep in her belly something unfolded. *I'm not qualified,* she told herself, smothering whatever it was that had suddenly rippled to life. It had been years since she'd written anything but academic papers or recommendations. Her older stuff was stale and irrelevant now, and besides, her undergraduate adviser hadn't liked any of it. She flipped the newspaper shut.

"Yoo-hoo." Mrs. Condon smiled at her through the screen. "I have something for you."

Gwen opened the door. "Oh my goodness. You and Mr. Condon spoil me."

"I forgot that I'd stuck this under the sofa bed." Mrs. Condon pointed to the box at her feet. "That summer, when your dad came up all by himself and said he wanted to fix the place up so he could rent it, he started to clean out closets and get rid of things, but the Misses didn't let him get very far. Anyway, I found these in the garage."

Gwen opened a flap. Molly's painted rocks stared at her, one of the crab's plastic eyes askew. Beneath the newspaper, photographs were neatly stacked atop the rest of Molly's creations. Gwen reached for Mrs. Condon's forearm and squeezed, the skin warm, the muscles ropy beneath Gwen's fingers. "Thank you," Gwen said.

Mrs. Condon covered Gwen's hand with her palm. "Yeah, he went a little crazy that year. Can't say as I blame him. Poor man." She shook her head.

After Molly's death, Gwen's father shrank; his skin loosened more and more each year until it hung from his bones.

"Well, you have fun putting those back up, dear," Mrs. Condon said as she turned to go. "Might remind you of some good times."

Smiling, Gwen carried Mrs. Condon's box into the living room and carefully arranged the contents where they used to sit—crabs on the mantel and pictures on the shelf. Molly, in her strawberry hat, grinned, gap-toothed.

A photograph of her father's boat, the *Liza G.*, emerged last. Gwen sat on the stern, her eyes fixed on the three boys on the cabin top—Jess in the middle, hat obscuring most of his face; Hugh, oiled up and camera-ready; and Aidan, grinning, his braces flashing.

As she held the picture in her hands, the recklessness of that summer returned, a rush in her belly. There was salt on her skin and bonfire smoke on her clothes. The taste of beer, warm and yeasty, filled her mouth. Her body stirred where Jess had once touched her, her face lifted to the night sky, gulping at the air, the stars, the dark trees, and begging for more. She'd wanted more of everything, more hours in the day, more laughter, more sunshine, more of the wildness promising her that life was wonderful and filled with joy.

She wanted it still, her desire so ferocious it took her breath away.

A gust blew through the open window, and the kitchen door slammed decisively shut. She jumped, almost dropping the photograph. The second-hand euphoria ebbed, leaving an emptiness behind.

You're an adult now, she reminded herself. *Grow up*. She left the picture face down on the shelf.

EIGHT

THE FOLLOWING DAY, JUST BEFORE LUNCH, A BLACK CAR, buffed and polished, rolled into Periwinkle's driveway, the chrome so shiny it gleamed. Next to it, Gwen's Subaru, covered in pine tar and a layer of pollen, looked pitifully untended.

The door opened, and out stepped Hugh Fox, wearing a Gucci belt and a pair of suede driving moccasins. Her former students would have called this display "bougie." Or maybe "basic." She never had figured out the difference between the two.

She opened the door. "Good morning."

He stepped gingerly onto the path. "Wow, this place hasn't changed much."

"No one has been around to change anything." The Misses tapped a window upstairs in contradiction.

Hugh didn't notice. He pointed to the churned-up soil bed beneath the kitchen window. "Looks like you have giant groundhogs under your house. Any foundation damage?"

"I'm getting ready to replant it." She didn't add that she was waiting for the plants to go on sale.

"Good day for it."

"What do you know about gardening, Hugh?"

53

He grinned. "Blue flower, white flower. That's what I know. Listen, come over next Sunday. We'll go sailing. Two-ish?"

She started to refuse—she had a garden to plant, and an AP lit textbook to digest before her meeting with Michaela in August—but then he grinned at her, and suddenly she was fifteen again, adrenaline pumping through her veins. "Sounds great," she said.

She regretted her answer as his car pulled away; the wide tires hushed the gravel, a tribute to their price tag. What would she talk about with a man like that for a four-hour sail? Her failed career? Her failed relationships? Maybe it would rain. The forecast wasn't calling for it, but Maine's weather was unpredictable. She did a little dance in the kitchen, begging the gods to send a torrent so she could bail. The washing machine danced along, pounding the floor until a buzz indicated the end of the cycle.

A few hours later, once again bent over the flower bed, she heard another "Hello?"

Steven peered down at her, one hand cupping his eyes. He handed her a foil-wrapped package. "Banana bread, my specialty. Jess says it's making him fat, as if he ever has to worry about his weight. I swear that man can eat a horse and still look good."

The loaf was still warm.

He squared his shoulders. "I'm sorry about the other night. Every couple has their stuff, and I guess we paraded ours in full view at the concert."

Gwen blinked, color rising. Wasn't she to blame for the awkwardness?

Steven continued. "Jess had a whole life before I came into the picture, all kinds of friends and family, things I never had until we met. We've been together for more than ten years and married for five, but I still get anxious that I'm not welcome sometimes. I didn't mean to take it out on you. Even if you were my husband's high school sweetheart."

Gwen took a breath, relieved. "You didn't, not at all. I was just caught off guard, you know?"

"Friends?"

She took his hand. "Friends."

He nodded toward the kitchen door. "Can I take a look? I've heard a lot about this place."

She opened the kitchen door.

Inside, he spun around very slowly, noting every detail: the baskets above the cabinets, the copper-lined bar, the wide-planked floor, the pebbles and sea urchins on the windowsills.

In the living room, he nodded. "Very shabby chic. I like it."

Gwen chuckled. "I had nothing to do with it. It's always been like this."

"So Maine-ish. A Sister-Parish-meets-accidental-hoarder vibe."

"I'm flattered, I think."

"Jess said Periwinkle was great. He's right. Good energy. Anyway . . . if you're not busy, we could go for a walk?"

She hesitated.

"I won't keep you long, I promise. Please say yes. I'd like to get to know you, Gwen Gilmore." Steven's face was serious.

After a second, she said, "Okay." Flower beds and textbooks be damned.

She pulled on socks and dirt-stained running shoes while Steven inspected the bookshelf.

"Robert Louis Stevenson," he said. "I plowed my way through all of those when I was a kid."

"I've read just about everything on that wall."

"Jess says the house is haunted."

"If you stick around long enough, you'll hear them." In response, the Misses gently thumped the floor above their heads.

Steven looks surprised. "Who is it?"

"The two women who lived here."

He grinned conspiratorially. "You know what they say, don't you? 'There's bound to be a ghost at the back of your closet / No matter where you live.'"

"Oh my gosh. The Mountain Goats! That's a North Carolina band. You know that music?"

"I've been into alt everything since way back. So tell me about your ghosts, Gwen Gilmore."

"My father's great-aunt, Elizabeth Gilmore, and her colleague, Judith Whitehead, both professors at Bryn Mawr, classics and history, I think. They bought the land in the twenties and built the cottage shortly afterward. They spent summers here for more than fifty years."

Steven tipped his head backward and laughed. "Go, lesbians!"

They both looked up when a resounding thud came from the ceiling.

Gwen grinned. "You scared of ghosts?"

"Not these two," he said. "They're my people."

Another thump followed.

"Hello," he said. He moved closer to the stairs and pointed to the mosaic on the wall. "That's so cool. It's called a 'Sailor's Valentine.' Old mariners used to commission them in the Caribbean for their girlfriends back home. They're exceptionally hard to find now, especially ones as nice as this."

Inside the deep octagonal frame, tropical shells were arranged in a spiral, each overlapping the other, a flower that radiated outward from a heart of tiny pink mother-of-pearl. The effect was tactile and magnetic, dizzying and heady.

"It was my mother's favorite," Gwen said.

The walls whispered as they walked to the door.

———

THEY TURNED LEFT out of the driveway, Steven narrating his life story. A fifth-generation Mainer and the youngest of eight, Steven was bookish and quiet. No one paid much attention to him when he was young.

"That's hard to imagine," Gwen said, huffing.

Steven, in contrast, hadn't broken a sweat. "Well, I wasn't the same person back then. I was used to being ignored. Once, on a family trip up north, they left me at a gas station and didn't realize it for sixty miles."

"Weren't you worried?"

"I knew they'd figure it out eventually. The convenience store owner felt sorry for me and gave me a grape soda. I wasn't allowed to have it at home—my parents were Christian fundamentalists and organic farmers. I was bouncing off the walls by the time they picked me up."

He didn't speak to his parents anymore, not since he came out in high school and they held an exorcism in response. Steven rolled his eyes. "Don't get me started on the crazy-ass shit they tried," he said.

Gwen didn't.

A bus painted with images of pine trees and lobsters barreled down the road, and they had to step into the woods to let it pass.

"Tourist season," Steven said. "Buckle up. No parking at Drinkwater's, and you'll need to order ahead at the Black Anchor if you don't want to wait an hour for a lobster roll."

"That bad?"

"Port Anna was 'discovered' during the pandemic. All the big-city people hoping for some fresh air. But at least we now have reliable internet."

"Do we?" She had none.

"No one is going to string fiber down your long driveway, but the library has a great connection. You can get service from the steps outside even when it's closed."

The sign for the Port Anna lighthouse appeared. Steven stopped abruptly and cussed under his breath. "I'm so sorry. I was on autopilot." He took his sunglasses off to look at her.

He knows. Of course he did. Port Anna was a small town, gossip its currency. By now her story had become legend, the girl who lost her sister to the sea.

Steven reached for her elbow. "Come on, let's turn around."

Gwen looked at the gate. Buses crowded the parking lot, disgorging the tourists who'd come to see the Vales' unusual home. Unlike other lighthouses dotting the Maine coastline, the one in Port Anna was only a squat tower with no house attached. The keeper lived in the tall, rounded room, furnished with a bed affixed to the wall, a table, and a woodstove. Folklore held that Anna was left on the rocks by the door, only days old, and the old keeper had raised the quiet child by himself, teaching her the art of lifesaving. By the age of sixteen, she knew how to shoot rockets at the stranded vessels and how, if the ropes missed their targets, to dive into the surf and bring the stranded to safety. It had taken enormous courage and physical strength, something a woman in those days was said to lack. And yet, she'd rescued more men than any other keeper on record.

By the time Gwen's family arrived, though, Anna's duties had been replaced by a computer and the abandoned building had found other uses. Gwen and her friends jimmied the lock and turned it into their hangout, a place away from adult eyes. They played card games and lit bottle caps and cigarettes, leaving behind a cache of empty beer cans, old Doritos bags, and a futon slumped in the corner that saw more than its fair share of action. They'd left their childhood there, too, washed away along with Gwen's baby sister.

Steven took her arm. "Let's go."

They started again, in the other direction, walking in silence. Gwen's dizziness refused to pass until the sign for the lighthouse was well behind them. She needed a change of subject, anything that didn't raise the specter of Molly's death. In desperation, she landed upon, "What do you do for work?"

Steven cleared his throat. "I'm gainfully employed as a glorified secretary at the real estate office."

"For Janet Riggs?"

"You know her?"

"She wants to sell my house."

"And you don't want to?"

"Definitely not."

"Oh, lordy. Once she gets an idea in her head, she can be pretty pigheaded, but don't worry; she'll leave you alone eventually."

At the top of the hill, they stopped. Steven gestured toward the horizon, the bright sun painting the ocean in shades of bronze and copper. "Look at that."

A line of cars edged toward the ferry's loading dock, a flock of summer folk headed to Goose Island.

"Too many people," Steven said.

"It must get kind of lonely in the winter, though?"

Steven looked at Gwen. "Yes, the winters are long. And cold. And dark. But there's so much beauty, even when it's frigid and barren. I'm happiest when I drive home and there's not another soul on the road. Being alone doesn't always mean lonely." He smiled and tilted his head. "I live here because I want to."

An eagle flew overhead, wings stretched wide. It circled once and dove into a copse of fir trees.

"Would you look at that," he said. "Who'd want to be anywhere else?"

He turned to Gwen. "Why are *you* here?"

She opened her mouth, but nothing came out.

"Reconnecting with your childhood? Nostalgia? Searching for the rom-com ending? Love in a small town?"

"No." She stared across the water and shivered. "God, no." When the rug had been ripped from beneath her feet, she needed someplace solid to stand, and Periwinkle had been built on a granite ledge. "It's where I need to be," she said at last.

He looked at her for a long minute. "You know what they say, don't you? That wherever you go, you take yourself."

"I'm not running away. If anything, I ran toward something."

On the way back, he was quieter, as if he knew he'd touched a nerve. Gwen, to fill the void, asked more questions about his family.

Steven told her he was in touch with one sibling, a brother who lived near Jackman, not far from the Canadian border, population around 850. "And that's the big city up there. He lives in a cabin without electricity, working as a fishing guide in the summer and moose hunting in the winter. Can you imagine? Ugh."

When they turned into the driveway, he hopped over a pothole and stopped. He rotated his foot one way and another, squatting tentatively.

"Are you okay?"

"I tweaked my knee a few weeks back, and it's still funny. Jesus, the game is going to be rough."

"Game?"

"Pick-up soccer. I promised Parker Drinkwater I'd play. That kid makes such a sad puppy face that you can't say no."

"He tried to talk me into it, too."

Steven reached down and rubbed his kneecap. "And yet you weaseled out of it."

"Look at me." Her T-shirt was soaked with sweat, but Steven still looked fresh. "Not an athlete."

"Come anyway. There's beer."

"Well, if it's beer on offer, then okay."

He stopped at his car and looked at her. "Let's do this again, okay?"

Something flashed in the upstairs dormer, the Misses hovering. Gwen smiled. "I'd like that," she said.

NINE

BY THE TIME GWEN TURNED TWELVE, HER MOTHER HAD
hiked every trail on the peninsula, a pair of binoculars slung around her neck.
She kept a log of all the birds she'd seen, alongside her fanciful descriptions.
Black-capped chickadees and tufted titmice, she said, had plump little bodies that resembled a child's stuffed toy. Cormorants, with their heavy wings
outspread, looked like caped Avengers; and scoters, with their cartoon eyes,
were comedians. Falcons, on the other hand, only appeared to the reverent,
and Liza had been willing to wait.

Unlike her mother, Gwen hadn't had the patience to sit silently in the woods,
eyes straining. She hated the wet feet and cold bottom that came with the
admonishment to *sit still*. Now that she was older, though, she better understood.

Out Periwinkle's kitchen window, a sparrow trilled, and beneath, a dark-eyed
junco pecked at the ground, its head moving so quickly it was hard to follow.
Several argumentative crows sat atop the hot tub's vinyl cover, so shit-streaked
it resembled a bad Jackson Pollock. They squawked at one another, ruffling
onyx feathers as Gwen stuffed the last of Steven's banana bread into her mouth.

Behind the maple, something moved, stirring the violet heather growing
at the forest's edge. Gwen leaned over the sink for a better look, hoping for
an owl or a hawk—beautiful creatures that were also savage hunters.

Instead, a flash of red in the brush startled her. Too big for a bird, it darted into the woods.

She left the kitchen. Skirting the hot tub, she walked to the edge of the woods where the ledge sank beneath a thick cushion of leaves and springy moss.

"Hey," she yelled. But the forest muted her voice.

The air was cool beneath the dark branches. Mosquitoes buzzed at her neck, and a chipmunk scampered up a large pine. Nothing else stirred. She must have been mistaken, confused a woodpecker for a human as it flitted from branch to branch in search of food. Their crowns were speckled red, and she hadn't been wearing her glasses.

She waited a few more minutes until her phone pinged and a text from Steven appeared. *There's a soccer game tonight*, he wrote. *We need a cheerleader!* A string of emojis, bullhorns, and dancing girls followed. *Not on your life*, she responded. *But I'll come for the beer.* She turned away from the silent trees.

When Gwen arrived, the players were already on the field. Parker bounced in place, shaking his hands, a bundle of adolescent energy. He grinned when he saw her and touched his nose.

She touched hers in response and pointed at the goal. "Bury 'em," she said.

Jess appeared at her elbow and handed her a beer. "Hey, hey, this is a friendly game." He pointed to the opposite side of the field. "And you see that guy over there? On the other team? Waving? That's my husband. No burying allowed. I like being married."

Parker saluted. "Yes, sir."

Steven waved toward her with one hand; the other held his left foot, stretching his quad. Behind him, another player bent a white head over his thighs, a stripe of blue paint on his knee. Gwen inhaled when she recognized Leandro.

Down, girl, she thought.

"You okay?" Jess asked.

"All good." She took a sip. This one, she swore to herself, would not end up on the ground.

Walter stepped onto the field, whistle around his neck. "Everybody ready?"

The younger players held up their thumbs, and the older ones groaned. Leandro shouted, "Bring it on, ref," his voice like a song.

Walter blew the whistle. The players shouted directions at one another as the ball bounced up and down the field. So did the spectators, clumped along the sidelines. "Pressure, pressure . . . who's there to help him? . . . First touch, first touch . . . Nice!"

The ball whirred overhead and slapped the goalpost before bouncing back onto the field. Steven ran toward it.

"I can't watch," Jess said. "He's going to blow that knee out again, I can just feel it."

"I don't know, Jess. He seems in control to me."

Steven's feet moved so quickly that he looked like he was dancing. The other player fell away just as Steven booted the ball toward the goal. The crowd gasped. But the keeper grabbed it before it reached the net.

"Did he score?" Jess asked, eyes averted.

The goalie kicked the ball high into the air. It lofted upward in an arc and landed at Leandro's feet. "Not yet."

Jess held his hand at his temple to keep from seeing the field. "I hear you had a nice walk."

"We did."

"Steven wanted to get to know you. And . . ." Jess shuffled his feet. "I'm sorry about springing that on you the other night. I should have called before or something . . ."

"We're good, Jess. Seriously." She touched her beer to his. "No worries."

He smiled at her, the care in his expression filling a hole in her chest.

She took a breath. "I do have a question, though."

Jess raised an eyebrow. "The answer is yes."

"Yes?"

"You're wondering if my feelings were real, and the answer is yes. I honestly cared for you, Gwen. Still do."

"So, I wasn't just—"

"Nope." He grinned. "Although I did also have a little crush on Aidan."

"Oh, join the club. Everyone had a crush on Aidan. He was always the sweetest."

"Yeah," Jess said sadly. "Yeah, he was."

"I've seen him a few times. Granted, it was only for a minute, but . . . he changed."

Jess dug a toe into the dirt. "His family signed away a big chunk of land a while back. He never got over it."

"You mean the lobster pound? The one in Portland?" Her family had stopped there twice on their way up the coast.

"That's it." He tipped his beer back and swallowed long and hard. "It happens all the time. Waterfront properties that used to be working docks and fisheries have been converted into second homes and restaurants. Locals can't compete with the rising property taxes. So they sell."

"I'm sorry to hear that."

Jess shrugged. "Stuff happens, things you can't control. And then you wake up one day, and everything has changed."

"I wouldn't know anything about that," Gwen deadpanned.

"Right." Jess laughed awkwardly. He wiped his forehead. "Jeez, it's humid."

Leandro ran past, sweat pouring down his cheeks.

Jess waved his beer at the field. "Speaking of hot."

Gwen smiled. "How do you know him, exactly?"

"I delivered a big order of granite when he received the Lighthouse Grant a few years ago."

"He's a sculptor?"

"He paints, too. I gather he has a fancy gallery in New York. At the moment, he has me collecting metal sheets for a project."

Leandro raced to the ball. A player fell. Leandro leaped over him and sent it hurtling toward Parker, who scored. Jess whistled. Gwen clapped. "Impressive," she said.

"He's a little intense for some people, but I tell you what, he gives a hundred and ten percent all the time, every time. At least when he's here. He's gone a lot."

The rest of the half slid by as they drained their beers, Jess flinching every time Steven controlled the ball. Parker scored once more and jumped into his teammates' arms. The team collapsed onto the field.

Just before the whistle blew, Gwen said, "I saw Hugh, too. He wants me to go sailing with him on Sunday."

"He always had a thing for you."

Gwen shook her head. "It's not like that."

Jess hitched a shoulder.

"He must have someone he's interested in. That's a big house for one person."

"He imports his entertainment now."

Gwen raised her eyebrows.

"Rumors, mostly. But I will say he treats this place like a playground, setting off fireworks, making too much noise on the harbor when everyone else has already gone to bed. He bought himself a big Hinckley a year back. Zips all around the bay in that thing, women on the bow."

"Why would he take me sailing, then?" She pointed to the streaks of white at her temples. "I'm way too old for him."

"You're the one that got away."

"That was a long time ago, Jess."

"Maybe. He never did take no for an answer. I bet he keeps trying."

The whistle blew for halftime. Steven headed for the bleachers, limping slightly.

"I'm going to grab him some ice," Jess said. He took off at a lope.

The air was soft, the ground still warm from the afternoon sun. She sat, running her hand across the grass, the blades tickling her palm. A few yards away, Jess knelt, holding an ice pack to Steven's knee.

"Cookies!" Leandro sprinted toward her, pushing wet hair from his eyes. He plopped onto the grass beside her. He smelled of cedar and turpentine. "Hello."

His eyes shimmered, shades of topaz and green, and, just like that, she was caught. He smiled, his hand extended. His palm swallowed hers. "I am sorry I caused you discomfort the other night," he said.

Her stomach contracted at the strength of his grip, the calluses at the base of his fingers. "It's okay."

He gulped his water, breathing gently. He still had blue under his fingernails, more spattered on the dark hair covering his legs. "I sometimes say more than I should," he said. "Truly, I only wished to dance with you. Nothing else."

"I understand," Gwen said.

The whistle sounded the end of the break. Leandro stood. She waited for him to run back onto the field, but instead he leaned forward. "Always a pleasure to see you, Cookies," he said.

She watched him walk away, adrenaline racing through her body. The rest of the game passed in a flash. People ran up and down the field; they shouted and groaned, and Gwen took in none of it. As soon as the game whistle blew, she jumped to her feet and headed toward the car. If he came and spoke to her again, she might say something stupid like, *Come home with me.*

"Ms. Gilmore!" A breathless Parker appeared at her side. His dark hair was plastered to his head, his cheeks splotchy. "I'm glad I caught you."

Gwen leaned forward and whispered, "Don't tell me. You need my shovel?"

His brown eyes twinkled. "Not a shovel. Witchcraft."

Gwen raised her eyebrows and nodded. "That depends. Are we turning someone into a toad?"

"You guessed it. My guidance counselor."

"We'll have to wait until the dark of night. Meet me at the cemetery in an hour. Bring a cat and some eye of newt."

"Eye of newt," he said. "Nice. How about toe of frog?"

"Of course. Old school is the only way to go."

His teammates shouted his name from across the parking lot. "Sorry," he said. "I have to run, but, seriously, my dad has this idea that you might be able to help me with my college applications. I have to write a bunch of essays, and my counselor doesn't have time."

"And your dad told you to ask me?"

"He says he'll pay you."

Gwen's heart jumped.

Parker shifted his weight from foot to foot, anxious to be on his way. "Please?"

"You've got a deal."

TEN

THE FOX HOUSE, NAMED AYR-Y-LEE, SAT AT THE MOUTH of the harbor, a large turn-of-the-century shingle-style "cottage" with ten bedrooms and a pool. Hugh's father had installed a jetty to accommodate a deepwater dock, much to the dismay of his neighbors and the outrage of local environmentalists. A boating enthusiast, he'd owned an entire fleet, motor and sail, each vessel more beautiful than the last, all the hulls painted a matching dark green.

That morning, Gwen had rolled her eyes at the bright blue sky, kicking herself for agreeing to the sail. She'd run the vacuum cleaner and swept the porch to pass the time, and, when there was still no hint of bad weather, she finally packed a boat bag—windbreaker, hat, sunscreen, sunglasses—and changed into shorts.

She pulled into the circular driveway and parked behind Hugh's shiny car. The front door opened and Hugh appeared, wearing shorts and a pair of L.L.Bean moccasins. "Come on in," he said. "I need to grab the cooler."

She stepped into the foyer. A checkerboard floor led directly into a living room that spanned the width of the house. Above the fireplace hung a loosely rendered depiction of the coastline in shades of blues and greens. The chairs and pillows echoed the color scheme, carefully arranged around a matching pair of white sofas. Beyond, a wall of windows faced the harbor.

Gwen walked to the center of the room, where photographs in matching silver frames crowded a table. She recognized herself seated on a log, a campfire burning. Jesse, Hugh, and Aidan had their arms around each other.

"Ready?" Hugh held the door.

She followed him across the expanse of grass. A crescent of perennials edged the lawn in shades of purple and blue, not a weed in sight. The Hinckley was tied to the dock, its lines curled into spirals, rubber fenders covered in navy terry cloth. Hugh headed toward a small sailboat behind the yacht, a classic Herreshoff whose brightwork reflected the sun.

"She just came out of storage last week," he said. "The yard is running behind."

He gestured for her to climb aboard. She sat on the wooden planks, back against the gunwale.

"You sail a lot?" she asked.

"As often as I can. I'm planning to race the Atlantic Nationals in August." He unlaced the sails. "I need crew. Any interest?"

"Not unless you want to lose," she said.

Even when they were kids, Hugh had to be the best at everything—and sailing was the ultimate competitive sport on the Maine coast. An unforgiving coastline and unpredictable wind made for conditions that only the best could navigate well. Races excited a surge of testosterone, and the skippers' type-A personalities rendered them unhappy with anything less than first place. Hugh fit the mold.

He peered at her from beneath the boom. "You don't remember how to do this?"

"Not really," she said. "Only the capsize test." That dreaded day in the summer when they had been expected to turn their boats over and right them again. Hugh had managed it in ten minutes flat. She'd swallowed mouthfuls of water and came up spitting and coughing.

He grunted as he raised the sail. "It'll come back to you. It's like riding a bicycle." He flashed a smile.

"I don't love that, either."

They glided across the harbor. The only sounds were the snap of the sailcloth and the rush of sea on the hull. Gwen reached into the cold water and let it lap her fingers.

Hugh kept up a patter, talking about work—real estate development, specializing in properties around Boston—and food. He bought a lot of wine at auction. "God, one crazy night we got into the Beaucastel and, poof, there went several thousand dollars." He laughed.

Gwen had never heard of the Beaucastel vineyard. She pictured a crumbling estate above fields of lavender, grapes hanging heavy on espaliered vines.

They passed through the field of boats swaying on their moorings and headed toward the buoys that marked the channel out of the harbor. Even though the tide was falling, Hugh made straight for the bay, ignoring the red nuns, the navigational aids that outlined safe passage. Only the most confident of navigators took this route; rough boulders hid beneath, waiting to grab the keel and capsize the boat.

They passed through unscathed, and Gwen exhaled.

"Here, take this." He handed her a rope. "The sail's luffing," he told her. "Pull." Thankfully, she remembered how to cleat, wrapping the line in a figure eight. As they tacked, he said, "Ready about, hard-a-lee," and she ducked her head under the boom, switching sides. The sailcloth tightened, and the boat leaned, the water only inches below the gunwale.

Hugh said, "That's better." He reached into the cooler and retrieved a bottle of rosé. "Do you like Bandol?" he asks.

"Of course," she said. "It's a board game, right?"

"Funny. It's my favorite summer wine." He poured it into insulated tumblers emblazoned with an anchor above *Ayr-y-Lee*.

She looked at the water to keep from rolling her eyes. Bougie or basic? Somehow, those glasses were both.

"Cheers," he said. "Welcome back, Gwennie. You were gone way too long."

"Thanks, Hugh." She took a sip. It was delicious, a pleasantly fruity taste that wasn't too sweet. "I couldn't help noticing the photograph of you, Jess, and Aidan in the living room."

"Yeah, good times."

"So, what happened?"

Hugh shrugged. "Life, I guess. We're still friendly. Jess does some work for me from time to time, but, you know . . . we just drifted apart. It happens. Things change."

Everything except this coastline, she thought. Granite stayed put.

Hugh said, "It must have been hard to come back."

Her hands tightened around the navy tumbler, her fingers pale.

"I never thought I'd see you again." He paused, clearing his throat. "Elephant in the room, so I guess I'll acknowledge it. It took courage for you to come back, Gwen."

"There's no need—" She didn't want to go there, but Hugh was undeterred.

"I wish I could have done something. I really do. I want you to know that."

"You did what you could," she said.

"I just didn't want you to think I'd forgotten. This will sound strange, but, in some ways, I'm really glad I was there with you. What happened changed my life. It shifted my perspective and gave me a focus I didn't have before. Things change so fast; you have to grab life when you can. Everything I've done since then—school, job, charitable work, all of it—has been with that in mind."

She took a deep breath and held it.

He sat back, satisfied. His monologue continued, this time focused on his philanthropy. He provided sailing gear and lessons for underfunded school districts. Evidently, being on the sailing team offered valuable lessons on competition and motivation, preparing the next generation of Ivy League–educated financiers and bankers.

Gwen stopped listening. The wine went to her head, a pleasant buzz.

"What's the plan now?" he asked.

She stiffened, her happy calm shattered. "A position at the high school."

"Isn't that a step down for you? What about Orono?" The University of Maine's flagship campus was only a one-hour drive away. "I can make some calls."

"Please don't."

He raised his eyebrows. "So you just plan to stay and live in the cottage, teaching far beneath your pay grade?"

"I never finished the Ph.D., Hugh. Colleges don't want me. High school is a better fit."

"Okay, so it's a no to the University of Maine." He switched tactics. "Is that cottage safe in the winter? Temperatures drop below zero here. And the windchill can be pretty fierce."

"I know that."

He paused a moment before he spoke again. "Janet can get you a great price. You'd have choices then—maybe go back to writing. It's prime land, deep water, backs up to the lighthouse park. You could buy whatever you want in town. Something with HVAC, for instance. The new condos up the hill from the post office are nice."

"Fuck, no. What is it with Janet? I'm not selling, and I don't want to live in a condo." She'd been there, done that.

He kept his eyes on the water. "That's a valuable piece of land, Gwen. If you need money, there are ways to leverage that."

"I have enough debt as it is, Hugh. Eight years of grad school . . ." She shrugged as if the hole in her bank account didn't matter.

"Well, if you need help, I'm happy to sort things out for you."

"I'm doing fine."

"Sure you are. Still, it's nice to be needed." He shifted the tiller, and they both ducked as the boom passed overhead. His face came within inches of hers. She could smell his cologne and the wine on his breath. It was so familiar she didn't pull away. He lowered his sunglasses. His eyes met hers.

"Hi there," he said, his face filled with joy and an ounce of the old mischief.

She smiled back. "Hi."

The wind blew his hair off his freckled forehead. There was a smudge of sunscreen at his temple. She reached up and rubbed it in. "Wouldn't want you to get sunburned," she said.

He took her hand. "We could head for the Falls and you could jump off the bridge."

Gwen pulled back. "I'm not that girl anymore."

He frowned. "Of course you are. You're the girl who's game for anything."

The words sent a spike into her heart, a rush of longing.

"No." The wild girl was also the one who'd destroyed her family. "Not anymore."

He retreated, sliding his back against the gunwale, and looked at the sky. "We should head back," he said. "I have friends driving up from Prouts Neck for dinner."

Of course he has friends in Prouts Neck, one of the fanciest addresses in the state.

"Join us?" he said. "You'll like them, and they'll like you, too. It'll be fun—a welcome-back dinner."

She did a mental inventory of her cabinets: a can of black beans and tortillas. She knew what she'd have for dinner, and it wouldn't come with a side salad and sparkling water.

"My treat." He looked so earnest that, against her better judgment, she said, "I'd love to."

ELEVEN

WHAT EXACTLY SHOULD ONE WEAR TO A DINNER WITH friends of Hugh's? The only things in the "yes" pile were the navy skirt and ivory blouse she'd worn to every departmental event, both hopelessly wrinkled. The iron was rusted, and the cord frayed. She plugged it in impatiently, running the warming metal over the faux-silk. When it started to smoke, she knew she was shit out of luck; she'd have to show up looking like the raggedy cousin.

She pulled on the half-warmed blouse and the creased skirt, hoping her jacket hid both. Concealer and lipstick would have to do the rest.

At six thirty, the Inn's parking lot was already full, Suburbans and Audis from New York and Massachusetts stuffed into every space, even those marked *Compact*. Circling twice, she settled for a spot on the street and rushed to the front door.

Once inside the lobby, she slowed, struck by the decor. Her family had eaten here every year, a final goodbye-to-summer celebration, her parents sipping martinis, Shirley Temples for Molly and Gwen. In Gwen's memory, the Inn at Blueberry Hill had seemed an extension of Periwinkle, an eclectic combination of antiques and thrift-store finds. The change was dramatic; the rag rugs were gone, and the strawberry wallpaper had been stripped away, replaced with shiplap-painted cream with ash-blue trim. A dramatic arrangement of flowers sat atop an antique Biedermeier table so highly polished she could have used it as a makeup mirror. Maps of the peninsula hung on the walls, the town of Port Anna depicted as a mermaid waving a trident.

The receptionist pointed her toward the bar.

Hugh and his friends were already seated by the fireplace. He stood when he saw her and buttoned his jacket. His hair was gelled to his head, wet and unmoving. "Welcome," he said, and kissed her cheek. He was cocooned in cologne, bay rum, spicy, overwhelming.

"Hi," she said, stepping back for some air.

His guests were named Crys and Scott. They volunteered that they lived in Massachusetts but summered in Prouts Neck, a little more than two hours south of Port Anna. Crys's forehead was smooth, dewy, as if she'd never had a single care—or, for that matter, a single emotion. But she held Gwen's hand as if they'd been friends for years. "So lovely to meet you," she said, smiling.

Hugh ordered a bottle of Chablis and two martinis. "Dirty," he told the waiter. "And two olives."

"I like mine the way I like most things: extra-dirty," Scott said, laughing at his joke.

"Oh, my man," Hugh said, shaking his head.

Crys leaned conspiratorially toward Gwen. "Boys," she said.

Men, Gwen thought. *Grown men.*

The enormous diamond on Crys's left hand flashed as she tucked a strand of blond hair behind her ear. "I love your look," she said, touching her temple. "It's so unusual. Did your hairdresser come up with it? Or you?"

"I wish I could say it was planned." Gwen looked at the wall of books behind Crys's head. Maeve Binchy and Danielle Steel. "I woke up, and there they were, two streaks of white that weren't there before."

"Must have been quite a shock."

"Not really." The morning after Molly had washed ashore, Gwen woke to find she'd grown old overnight.

She sank back into the generous leather chair, Chablis in hand. Crys hadn't meant to step on a land mine. She'd just wanted to talk about hair.

Crys and Scott took turns with stories about their summer, the trips they'd taken, and those they planned to take. "Four weddings in May," Crys said, eyes wide. "Can you imagine?"

Hugh commented on last week's race. One boat had collided with another, sending one of the crew overboard. "I haven't heard language like that since I played hockey for St. Paul's," he said.

Gwen drank her wine.

Scott refilled her glass. "Hugh tells us you're a professor?"

She looked at Hugh, biting her tongue.

Scott added, "He credits you with lighting a fire under his lazy ass, you know."

"Really?"

Hugh said, "I told you. You changed my life, Gwen."

Her chest tightened. From far away, she heard herself screaming at the paramedics, Hugh's hands on her shoulders. "Excuse me," she said. She walked unsteadily down the hall to the bathroom.

She shut herself into the stall and leaned her forehead against the cool wall tile. Why on earth had she agreed to this dinner? Because she hadn't wanted to eat canned beans? She fanned her shirt to dry the sweat gathering under her armpits.

The door to the bathroom opened, and high heels clicked on the floor. "Do you feel okay?" Crys asked.

Gwen sat up and took a shaky breath. "Just a little overheated."

The water ran. "Didn't you go sailing today? Probably got too much sun. I always feel a little off after a day on the water. Plus, it makes you so hungry."

Gwen silently begged Crys to leave, but the high heels didn't move.

"I'll wait for you," Crys said.

Gwen suppressed a groan. "I'm coming." She flushed the toilet unnecessarily and stepped out to wash her hands.

Crys smiled at her in the mirror, her eyes the same shade of aqua as her starched linen blouse, the pleats perfectly aligned. "Ready?" she asked.

"Sure." Gwen splashed water as she turned off the tap, leaving a splotch the size of Rhode Island on her front. She followed Crys, arms crossed over her chest. In the bar, she picked up her wine and drained the glass.

"Mr. Fox." A woman appeared, holding thick leather menus. "Your table is ready."

Gwen stood with the rest of the group, arms still wrapped around her torso. Someone waved to Hugh from a corner table.

"That's what is so lovely about a small town," Scott said. "Everyone knows everyone."

"And everyone thinks they know everything," Hugh added, sitting down.

Scott tapped Hugh's arm with the back of his hand. "People all up in your business, Hugh?"

"Someone"— Hugh waved a hand toward the dining room behind them— "sent the police to my house earlier this summer, asking questions about a girl."

"Harboring fugitives, are you?"

"If you can call my niece and her buddies fugitives. They've been up almost every weekend, working on their suntans."

Gwen read the menu. A piece of paper listed the specials: lobster ravioli with clarified bacon butter and crispy sage, halibut on a bed of sausage and leeks, and a fillet, dry-aged and coffee-rubbed. The prices made the hair on her arms stand on end. The wine list in Hugh's hands was longer than her unfinished dissertation. He flipped through it, speed-reading.

Crys and Scott talked about tennis matches, their family game. Crys played competitively.

"A real ball-buster on the court," Scott said, chuckling.

Their three daughters played, too, evidently. Gwen pictured them: a quintet of blondes wearing matching outfits. During the school year, they traveled all the time to USTA matches. Of course, the pandemic put a halt to that.

"Gosh," Crys sighed, "we had a few glorious months at home playing family round robins—but then the tournaments resumed, worse than before. All the college-bound kids were eager to show off their skills and attract the attention of recruiters. And so many of the older undergraduates stayed on to play a fifth year that the competition for an athletic scholarship ratcheted to an all-time high."

Gwen had seen the results of the crunch in the exhausted faces of her students. In the years post-Covid, the leaves of absence had skyrocketed. The university had instituted mental health days—although sporadic free days did little to ease the pressure.

"As if it weren't hard enough already for a white kid from Massachusetts." Scott shook his head.

Gwen looked at Hugh, who was methodically buttering a roll as if it were his job.

"When are you going back to North Carolina?" Crys asked.

"I'm here permanently." Gwen braced herself for what would come next.

"Good for you," Scott said. "Not sure I could stomach the winters, but I've often thought it would be wonderful just to step out of the rat race and retire in 'Vacationland.'"

"Well, I'm not retired. I'll be working."

Crys clapped her hands. "That's right, you're a writer. I love to read," she exclaimed. "Do I know anything you've written?"

Gwen opened her mouth to explain for the millionth time, but Hugh stepped in. He volunteered a short story called "The Mermaid's Tale."

Crys looked deflated. "I'm sorry, I haven't read it."

"I'd have been surprised if you had," Gwen said. How could Hugh have known about that? The journal had a tiny circulation, mainly to libraries.

Hugh looked up at her. "I loved that piece."

"That's very generous," Gwen said, shifting in her seat.

Crys leaned forward. "I wish I could read it."

Gwen started to shake her head.

"Of course," Hugh said. "If I can find it, I'll send it."

What would a woman like Crys make of Anna Vale's story? Gwen pictured her saying, *See, you can do anything, just like that Anna,* to her daughters as she brushed their hair into tight ponytails and sent them back onto the court in perfectly starched tennis whites.

The food arrived. On Gwen's plate, the pink lobster glistened through translucent ravioli, fried sage leaves curled on top. It was almost too beautiful to eat, but when she inhaled, the scent of bacon opened her stomach, and she dove in.

"I know, right?" Crys picked up her fork, too. "It's the water. It makes you starving."

Gwen concentrated on her food as Scott and Hugh talked about work, a project that had massive cost overruns due to a squad of teenage squatters. The contractor had forced them off the property many times, but they kept coming back, spray-painting the sidewalks and half-built foundations. *Capitalist Pigs*, they'd written. And *Get Off Our Lawn*.

Gwen swallowed a giggle.

Scott looked at her. "What?"

Poor kids. "They're just young and stupid."

Hugh rolled his eyes. "They're not coming back. I spoke to the cops. They already rounded some up and charged them with trespassing and vandalism."

Gwen drained her glass, and Scott poured her some more. The wine Hugh had picked was golden and soft, sliding down her throat.

By the time dessert arrived—crème brûlée for Hugh and a berry crumble for Scott—Gwen realized she was drunk. When Crys had pointedly run a hand over her nonexistent belly, Gwen hadn't ordered a dessert either. Her head was blurry, and the world seemed to wobble. She watched from a distance as Hugh paid the bill, Scott protesting ineffectually.

Crys disappeared to the "little girls' room." Gwen wondered if Crys talked like a child all the time.

Scott watched his wife walk away. "It'll be a solid half hour. What do you gals do in there?"

"Witchcraft," Gwen said. She downed the rest of her wine.

Hugh and Scott looked at her, speechless.

On the way out, the mermaid on the map near the entry looked ridiculous, her smile silly, her thick tail cartoonish. Anna Vale had been a legend, a powerful woman who'd pulled grown men from churning seas, not an adolescent with prepubescent breasts frolicking in the surf.

The front steps proved challenging. She stumbled and almost fell.

"Too much sun," Crys said. "I told you it can be dangerous."

Hugh said, "Why don't you ride with us?"

Gwen sat in the back, pressing herself against the car door, ready to bolt as soon as they turned into her driveway. But the child locks were engaged.

Crys cooed over the cottage. "So charming, vintage Maine. Isn't it, Scott?"

He agreed. "Cozy."

Hugh opened the door. Gwen stood up, swaying a little.

"Bye," she said. Walking toward the house, she knew she was weaving. She should have been embarrassed, but instead she felt pleasantly light, floating. *Alcohol*, she thought, *is Botox for the soul.*

Hugh couldn't unstick the screen door.

"I don't think they like you," Gwen said, taking over. Her tongue felt thick, a little unmanageable.

Hugh followed her inside. "Why are all the kitchen cabinets open?"

She waved her hand. "Oh, it's just, you know—the Misses." She'd developed a slur.

"You mean the house is actually haunted? I thought it was a myth."

"I thought you liked scary things, big guy."

A clunk sounded in the laundry room, and Hugh flinched. "I don't like things I can't see."

In the bedroom, he helped her with her jacket—she couldn't quite get one arm out—and folded down the quilt for her to climb inside. From the pillowy darkness, she felt the brush of his hand on her neck.

"Good night, Gwen," he whispered. "Call me tomorrow."

———

IN THE MORNING, her head pounded, and her stomach refused to settle. The Misses were restless, dragging things through the house, bumping the walls. She put the pillow back over her head, hoping sleep would dissipate the hangover, but the banging kept her awake. After an hour, she gave up.

She tried to eat, but nausea forced her back onto the mattress. The cycle repeated itself. It was noon before she could consider retrieving her car from the restaurant parking lot.

Embarrassment flooded her system. Hugh expected her to call, but she didn't want to see him. She'd slurred her words, eyes at half-mast. *What a way to make an impression.* She didn't expect to see that couple again, but still, the waitstaff had seen.

She crept on hands and knees to find her phone.

She tried Jess first. He was working in Castine. Steven was in Surrey with Janet. She even called Mrs. Condon to beg, but she was off to Sam's Club in Bangor.

"I'm sorry. You know I'd help you any other time."

"That's okay," Gwen said, the heel of her hand pushed against the bridge of her nose.

Mrs. Condon, ever chipper, kept talking. "Oh my, did you hear the dogs last night? They went crazy at about midnight, barking like it's the end of the world."

"I slept through it."

"Good for you. It must have been a fox. There's a den near the lighthouse. I've seen them crossing the road at night, a pack of kits following behind. Big, she is. I've heard her screaming, too. It sounds like someone's dying."

"I'm sorry, Mrs. Condon, I have to run." She needed another Tylenol.

"Well, good luck with the car, hon. If you still need a ride this evening, I'll help you then."

"Thanks. I'll let you know." She couldn't leave that car there all day.

She covered her eyes with her hand. Why on earth had she let Hugh pour her that last glass? It had looked so pretty—a lush gold-tinted orange in the candlelight, like toxic liquid sunshine.

Her phone lit up.

Hugh's voice said, "I have a spare half hour right now. I can pick you up."

She pushed herself up onto her elbow. "Now?"

"I have to get on the road soon. Work is calling."

"Right. Wouldn't want to keep Scott waiting." She put down her phone and got up to wash her face. The dark circles under her eyes revealed just how terrible she felt. She rubbed on some cover-up and pulled her hair back.

She was standing in the driveway when Hugh arrived.

He nodded toward the hot tub. "Who put that in?"

"My father. It was never hooked up."

"Too bad. It was a good idea."

Gwen sighed as she got into his car. "I need to get rid of it."

He stared at the backup camera as he eased from the driveway. "Jess can do that for a few hundred dollars."

"Mm." She looked out the side window, fist to her mouth.

He moved slowly down the driveway, careful with the potholes. "I could repurpose it. People like hot tubs in their backyards."

"It's damaged."

"Ah, well, then." He shrugged. "Still, if you need some help . . ."

"I'll figure it out, Hugh. You don't need to worry about me."

"If you say so." He stared straight ahead.

"Thanks for dinner," she said. "And for driving me home. I guess I didn't realize how much I was drinking."

"No worries. It happens. I wouldn't have insisted that we get the car right away, but I have to be in Portland by four. Scott and I have to check on a property there."

"Portland? I thought you were based in Boston."

"We're expanding into the Maine market. Things are hot up here right now, and there is a lot of demand for second homes. Portland is the test: a big piece of property north of downtown, with plenty of waterfront. We're building high-end condos with a marina."

"Wow," she said.

"Wow is right. Everything sold before we broke ground, but now we're running behind schedule."

Gwen turned to face his profile. "Are you thinking of coming up this way? To Port Anna?"

"Maybe. If the right opportunity arises."

"A development with cul-de-sacs and matching siding?"

"I'd like to think I can do better than what you're describing, but, yeah, sure, why not? People like them."

"Huh." In the fifteen years she'd lived in Chapel Hill, she'd watched the farmland surrounding the town slowly disappear, eaten up by soulless McMansions with enormous kitchens and bonus rooms. Builders had slapped every facing material possible onto the exteriors: brick, stone, and wood, as if the excess itself represented luxury. Why anyone would want to live in a house so completely lacking in architectural integrity, and no respect for the land, baffled her.

"You know, Gwen," Hugh said after a beat. "There's no need to be sanctimonious about this. Tourism is one of the biggest drivers of Maine's economy. And what do you think will happen when the lobster migrate north? The water is warming; it's already started. No one wants their kids to leave the area, but they'll have to if there's nothing here for them to build a life. Construction means good-paying jobs, and second homes bring needed dollars to the community without requiring services or expanding the school system. So don't be such a NIMBY."

Georgian homes in varying shades of white lined Main Street. Generously proportioned and solid, these attested to the seafaring fortunes that built them a hundred years ago. Hugh pointed to the largest, a *For Sale* sign swinging out front, Janet Riggs's smiling face prominently displayed. "This one is lovely, sure, but who can afford the upkeep? It has to be repainted every five years in this climate. And Maine's population is aging. They can't go up and down steps in a house like that. Not to mention the bathroom situation."

"Mr. Drinkwater had to move," she acknowledged.

"Exactly my point." He pulled up alongside her Subaru.

"Thanks again, Hugh."

He touched two fingers to his forehead. "Sayonara," he said. "I'll see you in a few weeks."

She nodded noncommittally. Spots appeared in the periphery of her vision. She needed to get home.

"Hey, Gwennie."

She turned.

"I'm sorry about Scott. I know he can be a Neanderthal," he said.

She watched him drive away. *Now, that was unexpected*, she thought. Hugh wasn't the elitist asshole he appeared to be. And she'd ruined his dinner—with a business partner, no less. Why couldn't she behave like a grown-up? Her body flushed with embarrassment.

How could you?

On the way home, her eyes began to shimmer. By the time she found the bed, a spike had driven through her right temple. She curled into a ball, knees to her chest. If she could lure her sister from the sea, Molly would fit there, her small back curved into Gwen's belly, sisters comforting each other. Weary tears wet the pillow.

TWELVE

IN THE MORNING, HANGOVER GONE, GWEN STOOD ONCE again at the kitchen window, a cup of hot, mud-colored water masquerading as coffee in her hand. She glowered at the ugly hot tub, willing it to disappear.

Hugh had said it would cost a few hundred dollars to haul it away.

In other words, a lot of college essays. *Hey, kid*, she texted Parker. *You ready?*

Bubbles appeared as he typed his response. *A zombie apocalypse?*

She laughed. *Your application.*

Right, he said. *I'm free at 1.*

Great, Gwen responded. *Where?*

Anyplace. I have wheels. He sent an emoji of a bicycle.

The store? I have to resupply anyway. She'd eaten the beans the night before and run out of practically everything else, even the tub of peanut butter she'd thought would last the month. Soon she'd be reduced to eating the contents of the candy drawer.

When she put down the phone, a crow landed on the tub and croaked. A second joined him, feathers gleaming in the morning sun. Both hopped about before depositing a stream of white atop the cover. Gwen laughed. *Exactly.*

As they lifted off, voices raucous, a tree trunk shifted.

A girl appeared. She looked almost transparent, thin and pale. A wraith. She stared intently at Gwen through the window.

For a moment, Gwen couldn't move. Her lips parted, but her tongue could not form words. Her heart coiled into a tight knot. In the days following Molly's death, Gwen had strained to hear the slap of wet feet in the hallway. Surely Molly didn't want to stay in that vast, empty ocean by herself. Surely the Misses wanted her company. But Molly had never emerged, no matter how desperately Gwen had prayed.

Gwen dropped her coffee mug into the sink and ran out the door. When she reached the forest edge, though, the apparition had vanished.

Gwen screamed, "Molly!" Her eyes scanned the dense woods for a sign. "Molly!"

She had to follow.

The air stilled, and the light dimmed beneath the dense canopy. She shoved her way past spindly pines and heavily branched fir trees, her breath ragged. Branches slapped her face. Without a path, the tangles of undergrowth and uneven ground made progress difficult. She broke spiderwebs with her arms, her feet crunching mounds of reindeer moss and lichen and stumbling over the snaking roots that gripped boulders. Her eyes watered as she strained to catch sight of the ghostly child.

As she yelled for her sister, the crows screeched overhead, echoing her desperation.

Feeling her way past a huge rock, she almost stepped on an old stove, half-swallowed by undergrowth. *Careful*, her brain warned. The metal edges had eroded, the rusted lace as sharp as a knife. A few steps beyond, she found a stake pushed through the loam, a tangle of rope attached. A circle of stones suggested the remains of a firepit as if someone had once cooked and slept here, hidden from the world.

In Maine, such places weren't unusual. When Gwen was young, people had spoken about a woman who lived off the grid near the mountain, on the other side of town. Every few weeks, she hiked to Drinkwater Provisions on callused feet. Gwen had once seen her from the car, disappearing into the forest.

"Where does she go?" Gwen had asked her mother.

"Who?" Her mother, distracted, had been biting her nails.

"That person." Gwen tapped the window.

"I'm not sure, honey. But don't fret. She knows how to take care of herself." Her mother's voice had sounded unconcerned.

But Gwen had worried. Did the woman have enough to eat? How would she survive the winter? Gwen had pictured her huddled over a fire, draped in blankets, conjuring spirits for company. The image had made child-Gwen shiver. No one should be that alone.

After Molly's death, the fear rebounded. Like that old woman, her sister had disappeared. Taken by the tide, no one to play with, no one to talk to. Desperate, Gwen went looking for Molly in her dreams. And she found her there, her presence so vivid that Gwen woke sobbing with relief, so happy to see Molly no longer blue and wet, no seaweed tangled in her hair. Gwen's sleep became more important than her homework and extracurricular activities. Weeks passed in a twilight haze. Every night, they played in the fort, hunted for fairies, and read picture books, Gwen holding Molly's little hand.

Eventually, though, Molly drifted away, lured to other, unreachable shores, and Gwen stopped sleeping. She roamed in the dark, hoping exhaustion would bring Molly back. Alarmed, her mother took her to a doctor, who prescribed sleeping pills. Gwen had taken them eagerly, but they hadn't helped. Molly had never returned.

Come home, Gwen had begged. *Please, please, please.*

"Please, come home," Gwen said aloud to the trees. The pain in her chest made it hard to breathe. "Please?" she said again, quieter this time.

The woods refused to answer.

She held on to a rough wall of granite, easing her body between the boulder and an old oak, the roots deeply splitting the rock. On the other side, the ground gave way, and Gwen fell. Her outstretched palm found something sharp. It took a moment for the pain to register, but when it hit, it was awful, driving up her arm. Instinctively, she pulled her wrist to her chest. The sharp tip of a nail, old, rusted, had poked through her hand. It looked so foreign, so *wrong*, it turned her stomach. She found the other end embedded in her palm and yanked. The pain intensified, angry and destructive. A sound escaped, a strangled cry that went nowhere in the mossy woods.

She stared at the enlaced branches overhead, dark runes she couldn't read. What had she done? She'd chased her dead sister into the Maine woods, that's what. Even to herself, she sounded crazy.

She shut her eyes. Fury gathered behind her closed lids. How could she have been so stupid? Wherever Molly had gone, she didn't want Gwen to follow. Gwen knew that. She'd known that for years. *Shit.* Her thoughts compressed, squeezed by the pain that radiated from her palm to her shoulder. Through the stream of *Shit, shit, shit*, she heard her mother: *Come on home now, girls.*

Gathering herself, she rolled onto her back and pulled her foot from the hole, still holding her wrist. Dirt and bits of moss filled her shoe as she stood. Her hand throbbed, a drumming that radiated through her body. Her ankle hurt, too, when she put weight on it. It took a long time to reach the house.

The cabinet beneath the bathroom sink was empty. Not a single bandage or gauze, no Bactine or Neosporin. Turning on the hot water, she eased her palm beneath the flow, flinching at the pressure. Blood and dirt ran into the sink. When she couldn't take any more, she dabbed the wound with a towel. Her entire hand was now inflamed, her fingers like pink sausages. Her father's old T-shirt, secured with duct tape, served as a bandage. She limped to the car, eased herself in, and drove to meet Parker.

The spots in front of Drinkwater Provisions all taken, Gwen parked in the lot reserved for the ferry. She broke into a sweat climbing the steps to the Drinkwaters' apartment above the store, her ankle groaning, hand pounding. She was breathless by the time Parker opened the screen door.

"Come on in," he said. The table was set with paper, pencils, a computer, and a box of Thin Mints. "Grandpa says you like cookies."

She laughed. "Your grandfather is right."

"What happened?" He nodded at her hand.

"I went for a walk in the forest and took a tumble. It's fine."

"Ouch. Can I get you a better bandage?"

"This will do." At his concerned expression, she patted his arm. "I promise. It's not that bad. I'll buy some gauze after our meeting."

He opened the box of cookies and passed it to her. "You should be careful walking off the path. People get lost in the Maine woods all the time."

"So I've been told. Here." She passed the cookies back to him. "Sustenance for the battle."

"The zombies. We need sugar to fight them off."

"I think it's the mint. They hate the smell."

"Good to know, good to know."

"Tell me about your college plans," she said. The heat made her hand itch, the fingers too swollen to fold.

"Dad wants me to do the stuff he never got to do."

"I see. Why is that?"

Parker's face scrunched as he thought. "He says that even though driving the ferry seems fun, it gets really boring, and he thinks the store's not enough for me."

"What do you think?"

He hitched a shoulder. "College would be cool, I guess. If it's not too far away."

She leaned forward. "You're in luck. New England has more colleges than almost anywhere else in the country."

"Yeah. Orono's close."

"It sure is. So are Colby and Bates."

His face brightened. "Mr. Kemble mentioned those, too."

"Aidan's your counselor?"

"Yeah. You know him?"

"When we were kids." *People change*, she reminded herself. "Any idea what you want to write about?"

He shrugged. "Dunno." He stuffed two Thin Mints into his mouth. Gwen did the same.

"Soccer?" she asked.

His eyebrows lifted skeptically.

"You can write about anything you feel passionately about. I read an amazing essay once about baking bread." The author had described the smell of the yeast, the feel of the dough, and the beauty of creating something that fed both body and soul. "All you have to do is love your topic."

Parker's smile made her forget about her hand. For two hours, he described his love for the "beautiful game," the theatrics, the calculus, and the way the players communicated. When they finally stood, Gwen's ankle protested. She leaned on the table until she felt confident enough to walk.

"You okay?" he asked.

"Sure," she said.

"Oh, I almost forgot." He stepped into the kitchen and returned with a brown bag. "Grandpa said to give you these."

She peeked inside and laughed. "He used to give me caramels when I came into the store." Thankfully, Mr. Drinkwater never saw her spit them into her mother's hand.

When she reached the car, a text from Jess waited for her. She fumbled with the phone, her left hand slow to react. *Come for a drink tonight. 6 p.m.*

Her stomach fluttered. *I'll be there*, she said.

At home, she gingerly unwrapped the T-shirt. The bruise was impressive, purple and black, and the wound's edge looked ominous, pale yellow and crusted.

It needed an antibacterial wash. She found some in Mr. Condon's gift box shoved under the kitchen sink: tape and gauze, and much more: a flashlight and flares buried beneath the Mylar blanket.

Her head spun as she poured the iodine over her palm, gasping. *Shit, that hurts.* She gripped the sink until the worst passed. Still, it took another five minutes before she could face wrapping the hand. It took even longer to button her favorite shirt, and she ground her teeth in frustration. Whoever had said practicing tasks with the less dominant side was good for the brain was an idiot. When she was in the car, her palm sent waves up her arm, insistent. She elevated it above her head, an alien thing best kept at a distance.

Steven and Jess lived on the other side of the harbor, on a bluff overlooking the bay. Swells broke on the cliffs below. Gwen struggled with her seat belt. When she finally unlocked it, she heard, "Hey."

Steven stood in the doorway, holding a martini glass. "Coming in?"

"What a beautiful spot you have," she said, limping to the door.

"What have you done to yourself?"

She waved her good hand dismissively.

He handed her the glass. She swallowed a big slug of the Cosmopolitan, praying the vodka would have a numbing effect.

"Happy summer," he said, raising his glass of water.

"Thanks." She took another sip. "Wow," she said softly, taking in the room. The ceiling in the entry rose double-height. Wrought-iron stairs twisted upward, hugging the wall. A compass inlaid in the wood beneath her feet told her she was facing north.

"Isn't it great? Jess's uncle left the house to us eight years ago." His gaze shifted to her hand. "What happened?"

She looked down. Blood stained the bandage. "I fell," she said.

"In here," Jess called from the next room. "Come on in."

Late-afternoon light poured through two bay windows. A pair of wooden chairs and a deep sofa faced a fireplace. The shelves behind were filled with objects: glass vases, Staffordshire dogs, cloth-bound books, old glass fishing floats, and a porcelain doll dressed in calico. A collection of folk art, still lifes and landscapes, hung on the opposite wall, arranged gallery-style.

Jess said, "Steven really likes flea markets."

She sidled up to the mantelpiece, admiring a china duck and a pair of antique wooden trains, fraying strings still attached. She pictured a small child pulling these across a wide-planked floor.

"You're hurt," Jess said.

"Just took a tumble in the woods. It's nothing."

A thump from the far side of the room made her turn her head. A Maine coon cat, brindled and enormous, was headed her way.

"Meet Miss Kitty," Steven said. He picked her up and kissed her head. "She runs the house."

Gwen sneezed. "Allergies," she said as Miss Kitty jumped from Steven's arms and made a beeline for Gwen.

"I'll lock her up," Jess offered.

"Please don't. It's her home." Miss Kitty purred as she weaved between Gwen's legs. Her fur stuck to Gwen's white jeans.

"Aww," Steven said. "You made a friend."

Gwen's throat began to itch.

"Let's go to the porch." Jess opened the side door, a platter in his left hand.

They sat facing the ocean. The bronzed late-afternoon light made the rippled sea look like moiré taffeta.

Jess sliced Brie and smeared it on some water crackers, adding a dollop of caramel-colored jelly. "It's onion jam," he told Gwen when he passed her the plate. "Steven made it last winter."

Gwen spilled her martini as she reached one-handed for the platter.

"Let me see that," Steven said, taking her glass. He held her wrist gently and unwrapped the bandage. Gwen averted her eyes.

Steven inhaled sharply. "Gwen, this looks really bad."

"Hello." They all turned. Leandro's head poked around the doorframe.

Jess jumped up. "Come in, come in. Let me get you a drink." They disappeared into the kitchen.

Gwen took another sip. "Steven?"

"Yes?"

"Is this a setup?"

He grinned. "Maybe?"

On the other side of the bay window, Miss Kitty jumped onto the bookcase, staring at Gwen through the glass with big green eyes. She sat on her haunches, her gaze unwavering. "I don't need a date," Gwen said.

"Ghosts aren't the best company, you know."

"I beg to differ." They made few demands and made comforting noises when she was sad. Who could wish for more?

Jess and Leandro reappeared, chilled glasses in hand. Jess said, "I have more salvaged tin from the barn we tore down. Do you want it?"

Leandro nodded, eager. "Yes, I would very much like to have it. This project has become quite complex."

Gwen reached for a cracker.

"Hello there," Leandro said to her. He looked at Steven and pointed at the plate. "But this is not cookies. I thought I mentioned that she likes cookies."

Gwen started to laugh, but her mouth was full of cheese. Her shoulders shook instead.

His eyes shone amethyst and hazel, twirling, and she almost choked. How did he do that? It was like peering into the night sky, a maelstrom of glimmering stars.

"Gwen?" Steven touched her shoulder.

"Yes?"

"Leandro asked if your hand hurts."

She looked down at the stiff, swollen appendage that no longer felt attached to her. "I think it's numb."

Leandro leaned over, assessing the wound. "You are a very tough cookie, my friend. Your hand is very unhappy."

Steven asked, "When was your last tetanus shot?"

Gwen shook her head. When had she last seen a doctor? Years, probably.

The men all looked at one another. Steven stood up. "That's it, we're going," he said.

"Going where?" Her voice sounded distant.

"To the urgent care, Gwen. That needs medical attention. Come on, I'm driving." He reached down and took her elbow, lifting her to her feet.

Her brain too fogged to argue, she let him guide her to the truck and buckle the seat belt. She rested her head against the seat as they drove to Ellsworth.

When they walked in, an older woman smiled from the front desk. Gwen let Steven explain. He filled out the paperwork as she looked on, holding her stiff hand in her lap. "Your insurance card?" he asked.

"I don't have one."

"No insurance at all?"

She shook her head. When Guy left, she'd had choices to make. Paying rent meant health insurance had to go.

Steven filled out another form, and a nurse ushered them into a room. The tiled floor looked slick and cold. A finger of worry poked her ribs. What would they charge for stitches?

A howl of pain echoed down the hallway as the doctor opened the treatment room door. Gwen and Steven both jumped at the sound.

"What was that?" Steven asked, aghast.

The doctor, his nose in Gwen's chart, said, "A kid having a rough day." He reached for Gwen's hand. "And what have we here?"

"I fell on a nail."

He took his time, poking and prodding her palm, Gwen flinching.

"Huh," he said. "You probably needed stitches, but I can't sew this up now. There's a risk of infection."

Holding her hand over a basin, he flushed saline solution into the wound. Gwen tried to breathe. "I'm going to need to X-ray this," he said.

Alarm bells grew louder. "Are you sure?" she squeaked.

"There might be a foreign body in the wound."

Gwen bit her lip. Steven reached for her other hand and squeezed. "It'll be okay, hon. We'll figure it out."

How? The question grew, a balloon squeezing her lungs. It filled her chest as the nurse carted her away to the X-ray machine and gently flattened Gwen's hand on the plate, a beached orca unable to move.

A half hour later, the doctor returned. "There's something jammed in there," he said. "Looks like a pebble." He gave her a shot for the pain, waited a few minutes before it kicked in. *Cha-ching, cha-ching,* her brain repeated as his tweezers sank into her palm. She couldn't feel anything, but she winced at the pressure.

Steven rubbed her shoulder. "It's okay, it's okay," he whispered.

"Aha," the doctor said, holding a sharp-edged piece of granite. He dropped it into a metal pan with a clink. "I'll let the nurse patch you up."

The nurse wrapped the hand in yards of gauze. She told Gwen to check for signs of infection and take all the prescribed antibiotics, even if the hand looked better. Also, Gwen probably needed physical therapy. Would she like a referral? When Gwen shook her head, the nurse handed her a photocopied sheet with directions. Finally, she gave Gwen a tetanus shot.

"Don't worry," Steven assured the nurse. "I'll check on her." He held on to Gwen's waist as they walked to the car. She closed her eyes, worn out, worry and exhaustion draining her. The car shimmied once they reached Periwinkle's driveway, and she opened her eyes. Jess stood next to her Subaru.

"Couldn't leave you without a car," Steven said, waving away her gratitude. "You'd do the same for me, I'm sure."

"Should I come in with you?" Jess asked.

Gwen shook her head. She thanked them both and assured them she was fine. Honestly. She'd have some dinner and go to bed. They backed out of her driveway, waving.

She stumbled into the kitchen. Everything hurt, her head, her hand, her ankle, her heart. Her stomach rumbled, demanding. She opened the fridge and peered inside. Empty.

"Fuck," she shouted. "Fuck, fuck, fuck." Excited about the cocktail party, she'd neglected to buy groceries. She opened the candy drawer and reached for a fun-sized Milky Way. It crumpled in her fingers, only a loose wrapper. "Fuuuck," she yelled one more time. All the good candy bars were gone; only Mr. Drinkwater's awful caramels were left.

She slammed the drawer shut, and the knob fell to the floor.

THIRTEEN

SUNLIGHT STREAMED THROUGH GWEN'S OPEN WINDOW, piercing the thin membrane of her eyelids. She bolted upright, gasping, on the verge of tears. Her dreams had been filled with small girls lost in the forest, running, falling, and hurt. Adrenaline surged as she pulled on her clothes, shoving her arms into a T-shirt and feet into sneakers. She sprinted for the car, her injured hand screaming. She held it to her chest, the tires squealing in reverse, barely missing the corner of the garage.

Gwen had so longed for a visitation from her long-dead sister that she'd neglected to note the ghost girl's dark hair. Molly had been freckled and blond. And somewhere in her dream, she knew she'd seen that face before.

She barreled down the road into town. The post office parking lot was empty. Inside, she went straight to the bulletin board, scanning the reams of stapled announcements.

"Can I help you find something?" The postman's earring swayed when he tilted his head.

"The poster for the missing girl," she said. "Is it still here?"

"Oh, that. We have a sixty-day policy on notices. Why?"

"Do you still have it?"

"Depends. Check the lobby recycling."

Gwen rummaged through flyers and envelopes, folded newspapers and discarded letters. The Pan-Tones had performed last week in Surrey, and the building supply store was having a sale. Customers sidestepped the pages piled at her feet, shaking their heads as Gwen tore through the bin. Halfway down, she found it.

The pixie-faced girl looked up at Gwen, eyes outlined in black, a faltering smile on her lips. *Trying to be brave.*

"Shania," Gwen said softly. "Shania Farrow."

"What's that?" the postman shouted from behind shelves of boxes and letters.

"Her name is Shania."

"Aye-yuh," the postman agreed, emerging. "You seen her?"

"Maybe," Gwen told him.

He leaned on the counter. "We never had a situation like this before. Sure, teens get into a mess of trouble, drinking beer or smoking weed, some petty crime, maybe—but a runaway, that's whole 'nother thing. Sounds like a mess. You calling the sheriff?"

She made a noncommittal noise.

"Thing is, you don't know why she ran, do you? Could be almost anything."

Gwen chewed her lip. The girl was probably frightened and hungry. And lonely. "I could have imagined it," she said. "I didn't get a good look."

"Right," he said. He disappeared behind the stacks again.

She stuffed the recycling back into the bin, took the page, and pointed the car down the hill to the grocery store.

The girl had been in the woods since May. Months on her own, scrounging for food and shelter, she'd likely eaten nothing but junk, living on Milky Ways and whatever else she'd found in Gwen's poorly stocked kitchen. A growing teen needs more than candy.

The smell of knotty pine and molasses, stirred by the heat, filled Drink-water Provisions. Parker waved from behind the counter.

"Terrible humid," a woman said, fanning herself.

100

"Yep," Gwen agreed, reaching her good hand for some bananas and oranges. She added whole wheat bread to the cart, followed by granola and a handful of energy bars with added protein.

"Will you be making pizza tonight?" someone asked Parker. "I can't bear the idea of cooking."

"No, ma'am. Dad says we're not turning the oven back on until the temperature drops. You could try the Inn," he said helpfully. "They serve pizza."

"And they charge double the price." The woman jerked the door open, and the entry bell clanged.

"Yikes." Gwen heaved the full basket onto the counter. "Heat makes everybody grumpy."

Parker grinned. "Perfect weather for sleeping outside, though." He slid her groceries across the scanner.

"You're camping? Hart's Island?" A short boat ride away, the island belonged to the Peninsula Conservancy.

"Nah, we're headed to the lighthouse. All boats spoken for today."

"Be careful, will you? No swimming, okay?"

He raised a hand to his forehead in mock-salute. "Yes, ma'am."

Parker pushed the account book across the counter.

Gwen gulped at the total, struggling to write her name with her left hand.

"Oh my gosh," he said. "I forgot you hurt yourself."

"The doctor took care of it last night. All good now."

He shook his head. "You should know better than to feed vampires." He took a mint from the open bowl by the counter and handed it to her. "I hear they hate the smell of these."

Gwen popped it in her mouth. "Silly boy. You know perfectly well that vampires hate garlic."

He raised his hands in resignation. "We're fresh out of garlic mints, ma'am. So sorry."

Back home, she added some clothes and an old raincoat into a shopping bag. Wearing rubber boots, she opened the kitchen door, edged past the hot tub, and stepped into the woods. She walked slowly, more careful with her footing this time. Picking her way through low branches with her good hand, she scoured the ground for footprints in the deep moss. The air thickened and sweat dripped down her nose. Mosquitoes buzzed her head. Next time she should remember to bring bug repellent; the poor girl was likely covered in bites.

She passed the rusted stove and the circle of wooden stones, giving the granite boulder a wide berth after yesterday's debacle. Hand throbbing, she edged through a grove of pines. Above her head, crows squawked and black-capped chickadees twittered, warning of the giant invading their territory.

In a clearing, she found a pile of Milky Way wrappers. She'd bring a toothbrush next time, too.

She put the plastic bag on the ground and stuffed the trash in her pocket.

"Shania?" she said, scanning the trees.

The forest didn't move.

"I'm Gwen."

She turned in a circle, looking.

"I'm sorry I scared you yesterday."

A red squirrel peered down at her, teeth bared. He began to chatter in warning.

"I brought you some food and a jacket," she said. "Let me know if you need anything else, okay?"

No response.

"I'm not going to call the police. I just want to make sure you're safe. I put my contact information inside a Ziplock baggie and some paper to write to me if you need anything."

Still nothing.

"Right. Well, you know where I live."

The trees kept a close watch as she made her way home.

In the bathroom, she swallowed two Advil and limped to the kitchen, her ankle still swollen and sore. With a glass of ice water in hand and a book under her arm, she went to the porch, hoping for a breeze. She propped her foot on the railing, a coolish dish towel wrapped around her lower leg. She opened the first page, and Anne Morrow Lindbergh's familiar voice replaced the silence. Honeybees buzzed, looking for the flowers she had yet to plant. At her back, the house creaked contentedly.

An hour later, her eyes closed, and her head dropped to her chest.

"Cookies?"

Chair legs scraped the porch as Gwen jerked into consciousness. Both the book and towel fell to the floor. "Huh?" she grunted.

Leandro stood in the yard below, looking up at her, hand shading his eyes. "Hello," he said.

"How—" She wiped the drool from her mouth, blushing. "How did you find me?"

His teeth flashed in the sun, bright white and straight like his hair. "A little bird, perhaps."

"A little bird," she repeated. *Steven*, she thought.

"Yes," he said. He stepped into the shade, topaz-green eyes on her face. "He told me you want company."

"No, I don't," she said. *Shit.* Why had she chosen today to put on her rattiest shirt and stained shorts? She looked flea-bitten and bedraggled, like something a cat spat out.

"And you dressed for our outing," he said, pointing to his pockmarked blue-and-brown shirt. "We match."

"Outing?"

"Yes," he said. "We are taking the boat."

"The boat." She sounded like an idiot.

He pointed to the horizon. "It's too hot to stay on land. And I have to check on my work."

Gwen's skin prickled, hungry for a cool breeze. She said, "Let me get some sunscreen."

She grabbed the bottle from the bathroom shelf, refusing to look in the mirror, and shoved it into a canvas bag. On the way out the door, she pulled her sunglasses from her purse and put them on.

He was waiting by his car.

She lifted the glasses above her eyebrows for a better look and grinned. "An El Camino?"

"At your service." He bowed.

She got in, laughing. "I haven't seen one of these in years." Her knee bumped an eight-track player screwed underneath the glove compartment. His arm grazed her stomach as he reached across her to open it.

"Here you are," he said, handing her a box. "For the hand, so that it does not get wet."

Gwen pulled out a plastic glove designed to fit over a bandage. "That's so thoughtful."

The engine started with a deep rumble. Leandro chuckled. "This car, it is fantastic, no? I saw it parked beside the Port Anna garage. I had to beg the owner to sell it to me."

They lurched down the driveway. When he turned, Gwen had to grip the seat to keep from sliding into him.

They parked in the ferry lot and crossed the hot asphalt to the town dock. Heat rose through the soles of her sneakers as she clattered down the metal ramp to the floats. Only a single boat remained tied to the dock.

"Everyone had the same idea," she said.

"Perhaps," he said, uncleating the skiff. "But they aren't going where we are going. Climb in." He eased the boat away from the dock.

She sat back, her mummified hand in her lap.

"We're off," he said, pointing the bow toward the green can at the mouth of the harbor. Within seconds, a rush of wind cooled her face.

Once they were through the no-wake zone, he pushed the throttle, and the boat leaped forward. "Where are we going?" she shouted over the engine.

He winked at her. "This is a secret."

"Okay. I'm game." She settled into her seat in front of the console, facing the wind. The boat skimmed the water, bouncing slightly, the speed exhilarating. She closed her eyes and lifted her chin like a dog with its head out a car window. They passed the commercial dock where lobstermen in bibs and gloves unloaded their catch, dumping angry crustaceans into plastic floating tubs called cars.

Hart's Island appeared on their right, a host of small craft anchored in the cove. People in hats and bathing suits stood hip-deep, beers in cozies. Children paddled in arm floats between them, splashing. One of the adults waved to Leandro, who returned the gesture.

"Not much farther," he told her.

They rounded the bend, keeping the nun to port. Brightly colored lobster pots dotted the water, confetti spread across their path. Leandro bobbed and weaved to avoid them, Gwen holding on to the gunwale as the boat swayed. Fifteen minutes passed before a small island emerged from the haze ahead.

Leandro slowed. "You see, a mirage," he said. "It is an effect of the heat on the water. The shoreline is doubled."

She squinted at the bright glimmer of cliff reflected in the still ocean. "You mean the shore looks bigger than it actually is?"

"Precisely. It's an illusion, a fata morgana."

"Sounds like a fairy tale," she said.

As they approached, the apparition dissolved. What she'd thought was a cliff was a sand beach. It was such a rare sight in northern Maine that her mouth dropped open. "How did you find this place?"

"This is private. The owner collects my work, and he lets me use it for projects from time to time."

The bow gently nosed ashore. "Madam," he said. "Your oasis."

Gwen took off her shoes. He helped her over the side of the boat, hands at her waist. The salt pinched her sore ankle, healing. She could stand here all day, letting her toes grow numb.

She reached into the water with her good hand and splashed her face.

When she looked up, Leandro was watching her. "Wonderful, no?"

She grinned. "Yes."

"Come, come," he said, walking onto the beach.

He led her toward shore, both of them stepping carefully to avoid sea urchins and discarded barnacle shells. Gwen stopped and reached down.

"Look," she said, pulling up a dark sand dollar, still alive; the sueded surface glistened, a silvered eggplant.

He leaned in. "That color," he said. "So beautiful, and it's already fading."

She opened her fingers, and the creature settled again on the ocean floor. She pushed through the clear water, pausing to retrieve blue-gray shells and a trove of smaller whelks, pale yellow and white. They emerged from the sand by the handful. Molly would have made something wonderful with them. Gwen stuffed them in her pocket on top of the Milky Way wrappers she'd forgotten to throw away.

On the beach, her feet sank into the warm sand. She limped forward, struggling to keep up with Leandro, sliding, feeling like a cartoon character trying to run.

Around the corner, they entered a second cove. Leandro walked into the sea, shifting seaweed aside with his hands as if he were dancing. When the water reached his thighs, he stooped and pulled at something heavy.

"Can I help you?" She waded in.

He handed her a rock, a rounded stone of gray granite. "Hold this." He lifted a second one, darker gray and shot through with a vein of pink, followed by a third, and then a fourth. Gwen rested them on her forearm, squeezing the stones against her torso.

"Agh, come on, you," he said, pulling. "It is asleep and does not wish to wake." He heaved, and a large sheet of metal, four feet wide with rounded edges, finally rose from its bed. He grabbed it on both sides and carried it to shore, Gwen following behind.

"It is alchemy, no?" he said.

She squatted, tipping the stones onto the sand beside the piece. Traces of blue and red webbed the mottled surface, both color and metal transformed.

He lowered himself next to her, his shoulder almost touching hers. "It's a wash of marine paint. Each is different. Then I carried the panels out here and sank them. I let Mother Nature help, you see?" He pointed to a particularly corroded area. "She eats the color, chews the metal."

Gwen tilted her head. Salt crystals pushed the color aside, creating wave-like patterns.

"I think of it as a study of time and elements, of chance and deliberation, the way nature reclaims." His *r*'s rolled, a song. "Water changes things. It shapes rocks and coastlines, sculpts the land. I wanted to do something to capture that power but also to suggest that nothing ever lasts."

"But surely artwork is meant to last. Museums definitely care about that."

"Of course they do. But they are wrong. Even oils change over time, no matter how many conservators try to stabilize them. Van Gogh's blues used to be purple. Look, even now, as the metal dries in the air, see what happens?"

Gwen leaned in. The colors, vibrant when they were wet, had faded, laminated beneath a crystalline web.

He said, "There are chemicals in the atmosphere and in the water, some natural, some man-made. Salt, of course, but also phosphate and calcium. And then there are the things humans dump into the ocean, bleach and solvents, which are toxic to marine life. All of these affect the pigments." He stood. "Come. Let's see the others."

They returned to the water and pulled a second sheet from the bottom. It was different, the swipes of color more evident, the metal less corroded. "You see," he said. "The result depends upon the concentration, how the tide moves the elements in and out of the coves."

They repeated the exercise a dozen more times, each panel completely different from the one before. One was almost denuded of paint, the residue of ocean arranged in geometric patterns.

Gwen said, "They are beautiful."

Leandro looked at his handiwork. "The sea can be damaging but also healing." He carried the panel back into the water. Gwen retrieved four stones that she'd left on the sand and handed them over.

He rested his ear on the water as he adjusted the rocks, anchoring the panel in place. "I have also been thinking this project embodies another theme: how humans try to destroy themselves." He stood up, his hair dripping.

"Like the chemicals we dump? The tankers spilling fossil fuel?"

"Yes, but also the self-destruction we carry inside of us."

"You mean emotionally?"

"Of course. Guilt, fear, self-hatred. The tools we use to inflict harm."

They sat in silence, watching the last metal plate transform in the air, colors flickering in the bright sun. Her hand moved, wanting to feel the crunch of salt on her fingertips.

He held out an arm to stop her. "Please don't. It's so fragile, this work. The oils on your hand will change it."

"I'm sorry."

"You're right, of course, the work is very tactile. People will want to touch, and it will make my gallerist crazy."

He carried it back into the water and sank it. She waded out, too, and passed him the stones. Finished, he dove beneath the surface, emerging thirty feet away. He splashed her. "Come on in," he said. "The glove will keep your hand dry."

She backed up, shaking her head. "I don't swim."

He paddled toward her, concerned. "What is this? No dancing, no swimming? These are two of the great human joys."

Seaweed brushed her legs, sweeping back and forth with the current. Mermaid's hair, face turned into the depths, weeping.

He stood up, facing her, his kaleidoscope eyes spinning. "Are you afraid of the water?"

"No . . ." She held her good hand at her side, fist clenched. Of course she was afraid of the water. "I just don't like to swim."

He touched her shoulder. "Forgive me. I am careless sometimes."

He pulled the boat to the shallows. He held her waist as she swung her leg over the side and pulled herself in. He pushed the stern into deeper water before lifting himself over the gunwale, landing with a thud. As they drifted away from the cove, he pulled a towel from the rope locker to dry off, shaking his white hair like a dog after a bath.

He grinned. "Today is a good day." He was tan, his nose a little red, his hair tinseled in sunlight. Moving toward the bow, he came to sit beside her as they watched the island float away. Tiny waves lapped the hull, encouraged by the late-afternoon breeze. Leandro said nothing, unafraid of silence.

There was an exhale to starboard, a chuffing noise.

Leandro raised a finger to his mouth. "Shhh," he whispered, pointing. "Look who came to see us."

Gwen leaned forward.

A seal stared back at her, wet eyes unblinking, her own face reflected in the wide irises.

"She's lovely, no?" Leandro said, his voice barely audible.

Gwen looked into his magic eyes and mouthed a question. "She?"

"Too small for a male."

The fur, dark gray speckled with brown, shed droplets of water. White whiskers twitched, nostrils opening and closing with each breath. The creature was both human and not, utterly alien and yet completely familiar. Something passed between them, a sort of recognition, as if she'd once been like Gwen but then had chosen to shed her skin, seeking the cold darkness, the secret places where tiny octopuses and vermilion sea stars hid.

"Oh," Gwen said. She felt the wet warmth of Leandro's body at her back. He made a sound, a small *hmm*, a vibration that caused the seal to blink. She slipped back into the ocean, the water closing over her head as if she'd never been there. They kept their eyes glued to the surface for a few more minutes, but she was off, chasing the flash of a fish tail.

"What a beautiful moment," Leandro said.

Gwen's eyes remained fixed on the water, unable to let go.

"Ready?"

She nodded, but she wasn't. She willed the seal to reappear.

He cranked the ignition and the outboard whined. They sped past Hart's Island, a handful of boats still at anchor, a few beached by the retreating tide. People stood over a fire, drinking and laughing as they tended to hamburgers on a grill. Children lay on towels, asleep.

The lighthouse emerged from the haze as they rounded the corner, a white beacon, a swarm of tourists at the base looking upward, some with pants rolled up, feet in the water. A line of teens with camping equipment marched from the parking lot toward the woods, Parker's crowd headed to the campsite. Gwen resisted the urge to remind him: *Don't go swimming.* But he'd never hear her from this distance. She watched nervously as they disappeared into the woods.

When the boat entered the harbor, the tide was dead low. They skimmed over six inches of water, the bottom littered with broken shells and old bottles. Gwen leaned over the bow to ensure they wouldn't run into any wayward boulders on the way to the dock.

Leandro tied the skiff to the docking float and held out his hand to help her. "Thank you."

He smiled, pulling his sunglasses down his nose. "It was a lovely day, was it not?"

The ramp clanged as they climbed to the street, bodies pitched forward.

———

IN PERIWINKLE'S DRIVEWAY, Gwen peeled her thighs from the El Camino's vinyl seat and opened the door before Leandro could help, a strategy to avoid awkward goodbye handshakes or hugs. She shut the car door gently. "Thanks again," she said through the open window.

"Anytime, Cookies, anytime."

The El Camino rumbled away, rocking as the tires dipped into the potholes.

In the bathroom, the tub's faucet sputtered, disgorging a mixture of air and rusty water. Once the pipes caught their breath, she pushed the rubber stopper into the drain and filled the tub. She peeled off her sandy clothes, carefully avoiding her bandaged hand, and stepped in, sinking to her chin.

Steam rose from the tub and, with it, the smell of the ocean. The brine lifted from her pores, a cloud of salt and air hovering about her head. She inhaled deeply. She smelled like the sea, like sweat, like heat and metal. As if she had shed her Gwen-skin for the afternoon and followed the magical seal, chasing fish through the inky amnion water. She ran her good hand over the soft mound of her belly and hip bones, down her legs to her ankles. She even twisted her arm, palm to her back, searching her backbone for the rise of a fin, or the slip of scale.

Water changed things, Leandro had said.

She dipped her head under.

PART
TWO

FOURTEEN

THE STAINED-GLASS LAMPSHADE BESIDE THE BED CAP-
tured a sunbeam, stippling the ceiling and walls red and blue. Gwen raised
her uninjured arm and waved her fingers, shadow-dancing. What would
Leandro make of this ephemera, an artwork shaped by the dawn, his head
on the pillow next to hers? The thought caused her to sit up so quickly her
head spun, black spots peppering her vision. She threw back her sheet and
checked her ankle. The swelling was almost gone, the ache vanished. Leandro
had been right; seawater was a magical elixir.

She reached for her phone; time to bother a little bird.

Steven croaked, "Yes?"

"Feel like taking a walk?"

"Jeez, hon, what time is it?"

She checked her screen. "Six."

He groaned.

"Too early?"

"Definitely."

"If we wait, it'll be too hot."

"Ugh."

"Please? It's so pretty out now."

"You sound like Jess. He got up an hour ago. But, unlike some people, he let me sleep."

"Please?"

"Okay, okay. Be there in fifteen."

The coffee machine gurgling, Gwen opened the kitchen door to let in a breeze. A piece of paper fluttered to the ground. Smoothing it beneath her palm, she read:

Hi Gwen. Thanks for the food. That was nice of you. You asked if I needed anything. Could I have something to read? It gets a little noisy out here listening to my own thoughts. Shania.

Oh. Gwen smiled to herself. *A reader.* What would an adolescent girl like? She stood in front of the bookshelf and checked the titles. Robert Louis Stevenson? Gwen had devoured these when she was ten, so probably not. *A History of Hancock County*? Too boring. *Mariners and Mermaids, a Study of the Maine Coast in the Eighteenth Century*? Unlikely.

As if they had read her mind, the ceiling grumbled. "You're right," Gwen said. Exposure would ruin an old binding. That left the bookstore's section of used paperbacks, but it wouldn't open for a few more hours.

She propped the note on her father's copper-lined bar where she would see it after the walk.

When Steven pulled up thirty minutes later, she stood in the driveway, fully caffeinated and antsy.

He stepped out, holding out a foil-wrapped brick of banana bread. "For you," he said.

"Another one? I only just finished the first one you brought me!"

"I have to do something with my sourdough starter. You should see my freezer. English muffins, bagels. But people seem to like the banana bread best."

She put the loaf in the kitchen, pausing at the newly filled woodshed on the way back. The smell of freshly cut pine scented the sticky air. "Where did that come from?"

"Probably from the guy down in Bucksport who supplies most of the peninsula."

"But I didn't order it." A thread of anxiety wound up her spine. What did a cord of wood cost?

"Well, someone did."

Mrs. Condon's car rumbled toward them. She pulled up alongside and leaned out the window. "It's going to be a scorcher."

Gwen pointed to the shed. "You wouldn't know anything about that, would you?"

"Oh, sure. Donald dropped it off yesterday. He was concerned you'd run out."

"He shouldn't have . . ." Gwen bit her lip. How would she pay him back?

"Not to worry, dear. That can wait. Wood has to age a bit, you know. Hello, Steven. How's my boy?"

Steven rested his arm on the hood of the car. "Tired. Jess was up before the sun. He's working on that new house up near Tapper's Pond."

"The big one?"

"That's it."

She clicked her tongue. "Where are those folks from?"

"Colorado, I think."

"Won't be here much, I suppose."

"Probably not," Steven said.

"More money than sense." She shook her head. "Nice to have the work, though. Off to the old folks' home. Got to hold body and soul together." She waved her hand out the window as she pulled away.

By the time they reached the road, Gwen's back was drenched. The last time she'd checked her bank statement, her savings had dipped dangerously low. She pulled at her T-shirt to cool off, hoping to ease her mounting anxiety.

"So," Steven said. "Word is that you had a date yesterday."

She rolled her eyes, exasperated. Was that all Steven could think about? Her nonexistent love life? "No, I didn't, little birdie. He wanted me to help him check his artwork."

"Is that what they call it now?"

She stopped to take a sip from her water bottle. "Seriously. It wasn't a date. Stop trying to set me up."

"Okay, then, how was the not-date?"

"He's kind of a force of nature." *Swim with me, Cookies.* "Hard to say no to."

Steven grinned. "What exactly did you say yes to?"

"I set myself up for that one."

"Yes, you did." He laughed. "Hey, I think he's a fascinating guy. He's smart, engaged, kind. I really like him, even if he gets a bit obsessive about his art."

Climbing the hill, Gwen huffed. "He's doing a project with seawater and its effect on marine paint and metal. Alchemy, he calls it."

"Yeah, I heard. He does cool installation work, too. He re-created the lighthouse's interior in the middle of a Manhattan gallery a few years ago. Piped in the sounds of the surf and hauled in huge ropes and tackle, and then covered the floor in sea junk. Kelp. Dead crabs, too. It started to smell, and he refused to let the gallery clean it up. Created quite a stink." He laughed at his own joke. "I just love thinking about all those socialites in Jimmy Choos stepping over dried-up seaweed and rotting shellfish."

"I thought the panels were stunning."

"So is he, hon." Steven gently elbowed her side. "And I think he likes you."

"I doubt that."

"Why? You're smart and interesting."

She waved his comment away.

"And pretty."

She snorted. She'd had her shot at the fairy tale—the blissful period when she'd thought Guy would propose, and she'd let herself imagine the picket fence, the dog, the baby—but it didn't end well. What kind of idiot adult believed in happily-ever-after anyway?

They reached the top of the hill. A bundle of teens sat bleary-eyed on the side of the road, gear strewn at their feet. Parker lifted his head when Gwen called out.

"How was the campout?" she asked.

"Something was in the woods. It scared everyone so much, no one slept."

Steven said, "Are you sure it wasn't a raccoon?"

"A big fucking raccoon," one yelled. "With boots on."

A boy in a black T-shirt smacked his friend's arm. "Raccoons don't fucking wear boots."

"Hey—language," Parker said. He turned back to Gwen and Steven. "One of the girls went to pee and screamed. She said she saw Bigfoot. We made fun of her at first, but then we all heard it, branches cracking, like something was creeping around the campsite."

Gwen's eyebrows shot up. "Did you see anything?"

"Nah. Just noise. I mean, we might have worked ourselves up. We were telling ghost stories."

"That'll do it," Steven said.

A truck pulled up, and Walter Drinkwater waved from the cab. The kids struggled to their feet, grabbing backpacks and sleeping bags and slinging them into the back.

"Stay safe out there." Parker looked at Gwen, touching his finger to his nose.

She copied the gesture.

Parker grinned.

"When you've had some rest, we have an essay to finish."

"Yeah, yeah," he said, climbing into his father's truck.

"Such a cutie," Steven said as he turned and headed back down the hill. "Do you think you'll see him again?"

"He's still writing his college applications. So, yes."

"Not Parker, silly."

Gwen's phone buzzed in her back pocket. Steven watched her pull it out, grinning. When she saw Hugh's name on the screen, though, she let the call go to voicemail.

Steven touched her elbow. "Who was that?"

Gwen wiped her forehead with her sleeve. "Hugh."

Steven's mouth pursed.

"He's an old friend." Like Jess, Hugh remembered her as the person she'd once been. That kind of history could forgive a multitude of sins.

Steven looked unconvinced.

When they returned to Gwen's driveway, Steven took the last gulp of his water.

She held out her hand. "I'll refill that for you."

"Actually," he said, "you got anything with sugar? Someone woke me up too early."

"Banana bread, perchance?" Gwen pulled the door open.

"How's the hand?" he asked.

She wiggled her bandaged fingers. "Better."

She searched the countertop. No banana bread. "Huh," she said, opening the refrigerator.

Steven held up Shania's note. "What's this?"

Gwen froze, brain whirring. She wouldn't reveal Shania's secret until she knew why she'd run. She said, "Something from one of my students. I found it in my pocket."

"You bought your students books? Why didn't they go to the library?"

"Oh, you know. Gen Z. If it's not on Google or Wikipedia, they can't find it." She sighed. "Where the heck did I put it?"

"Put what?"

"The banana bread."

Steven clutched his throat. "Feeeed me, Seymour!"

"How about some candy?" She opened the drawer. "Ta-da."

"Wow, you like caramels," he said, peering in.

"I don't, actually, but Mr. Drinkwater gave them to me as a gift, and I didn't have the heart to throw them in the trash."

Steven held out his palms, smiling. "I'll take the rest. For emergencies only, of course."

"Deal." She put a handful in his palm.

He unwrapped one and popped it in his mouth, nodding toward the kitchen window. "What's that thing?" His voice sounded sticky, caramel caught in his teeth.

"A hot tub. I was going to ask Jess to cart it off, but Hugh says it'll cost—"

Steven snorted, interrupting. "Hugh? Whatever he told you, that's the special just-for-Hugh price. For you, Jess will haul it off for free."

"Are you sure?"

"Honey, I'm sure." He turned to leave. And stopped. "Hey, I'm not sure I mentioned this, but I have a side hustle as a photographer, and I wondered if you'd let me take pictures of Periwinkle."

"Periwinkle? Why?"

He shrugged. "I like old houses. They're filled with so many treasures—I don't mean valuable, necessarily, just a collection of things people love because they hold memories. Like that." He pointed to the copper-lined bar. "It's so charming, but it's not very practical. You have to polish it all the time and wipe up all the spills before the copper is damaged. Someone could have replaced it with a newer, shinier version, but no one did. You keep it *because of* the spills, because you remember the parties when you were having so much fun you forgot to clean it. And your Sailor's Valentine in the living room. Someone was in love and had that made. We don't know the couple or what happened to them, but it whispers to you, doesn't it? Like there's an aura around it. I think it's a Maine thing, hanging on to objects because they have that patina."

Steven stopped for a breath. "Anyway. Think about it."

"I don't have to think about it, Steven. You're welcome to photograph the cottage. Anytime."

He grinned. "Fabulous." On the way to his car, he paused at the garage. "Gwen, I think a critter got in here."

Trash was strewn across the dirt floor: wrappers, papers, plastic bottles, and the remains of the oatmeal she'd eaten for dinner two nights before. "No way," she said.

Steven grinned. "Raccoons. Or a yeti. You want some help?"

She rolled her eyes. *Fucking raccoons.* "I could have sworn I closed the door."

"Maybe you ought to lock it? Bears like garbage, too, you know."

"Grrr," she growled, grabbing a trash bag from beneath the sink.

The dust made her sneeze as soon as she stepped inside. Refuse was scattered across the dirt floor: plastic clamshell containers, bits of aluminum foil, a peanut butter jar mingled with food waste. She fumbled on the shelf for her mother's gardening gloves to protect her hands. Something fell to the floor, a T-shirt. Stooping, she came face-to-face with Anna Vale, *Mermaid Fest 1995, Dance with the Fishes*.

"What the . . ." She'd carefully folded and stowed it in the dresser weeks ago. And it was filthy, the collar stained. The scent of pine sap and body odor mingled with the cloying scent of old garbage.

Abandoning the trash bag, she returned to the house, shirt in hand. A worried bumping followed her up the creaky steps. In her old bedroom, the dresser drawers gaped open, her clothes in a heap on the floor.

Her mouth compressed into a thin line as outrage gathered. An offer to help did not mean the girl could break into Gwen's house and take things.

Her good hand was too grimy and sticky to touch the clean clothes. In the bathroom, the new bar of soap she'd placed by the sink had gone missing. Pulling aside the shower curtain, she found it in the bathtub. Both were streaked with something black.

"Ugh," Gwen yelled. She wrapped a towel around her hurt hand, pulled out the Comet and a sponge, and leaned over the side. The cast-iron lip dug into her rib cage. As she scrubbed the old porcelain, angry tirades scrolled through her brain. She was beyond done with entitled kids who took favors for granted and then walked all over you. They didn't want saving; they only wanted more. They took and took and took, and then, when they were done, they took your fucking job. Gwen knew this; she'd learned it the hard way, yet all it had taken was one more small, frightened face, and she'd ignored that hard-earned lesson. That wouldn't happen again. *Fuck it.* No more deliveries. No more anything. Shania could figure it out by herself.

By the time she was finished, Gwen's arm ached, and a bruise bloomed on her side. She threw the sponge in the sink. Once the clothes were folded and replaced, she dropped the filthy tee in the wash. Inside the open machine, the basin vibrated, the water slowly turning black. Humidity had forced the window open once again. She tried banging it with the heel of her good hand while the washing machine chugged, but it was hopelessly stuck.

Sighing, she gave up. She'd slid into the house through that window many times, stinking of cigarettes and risk-taking. Her friends had done the same, slipping through their own laundry room windows and side doors, relieved when they weren't caught. But the people they'd hidden from had been family, not the police, the danger only a likely grounding. Although breaking curfew had felt scary, it was nothing compared to whatever Shania faced.

She was probably terrified.

And she'd needed a shower.

Gwen's head fell into her hands, her anger evaporating through her fingers.

Stop, she reprimanded herself. Shania didn't need her help. She needed a parent.

The phone in Gwen's back pocket vibrated. She stared at the name for a few seconds before reading it. *Hugh*. Again.

"Gwennie," he said, his voice too loud. She held the phone away from her ear. "Glad I got you. Listen, I'm headed back up, and I hope you'll come for lunch today."

"Lunch?"

"You know, the midday ritual, generally eaten in the company of others?"

"I've heard of it." For Gwen, this usually involved a few slices of cheese or peanut butter on crackers straight out of the box.

"My niece will be in town with her sorority sisters. Please keep me company so I don't feel quite so old." He said it with a laugh.

"You're saying you need a chaperone?"

He laughed again. "I am. Being a teenager is catching. Next thing you know, I'll be sneaking beer from the downstairs fridge and thinking I need to stick it to the man."

"Hugh, you are the man."

"Exactly. You don't want me to dive off the bridge, do you?"

An image of Hugh returned, pounding his chest and jumping forty feet into white water, Gwen close behind. "God, no. Keep that shirt on. Please."

The washing machine kept scrubbing, brown soap bubbles popping.

"So, you'll come? Make sure I behave?"

"Not sure I can promise that." Staring into the filthy water, Gwen pictured the setup: a white tablecloth, white napkins, gold-edged plates, crystal, all spotless. So clean and organized. So beautifully predictable. "But sure," she said. "I'll come."

She held on to the image of Hugh's lunch as she finished cleaning the garage. Young women in flowered sundresses, the grass a perfect shade of green. A breeze blew the scent of his roses ashore. On Hugh's lawn, reality was sent into exile, all messes cleared away by invisible hands. Even his garage was probably spotless.

She stuffed the garbage bag into the metal bin before locking the door decisively shut.

Beside the kitchen door, her mother's sign, *Welcome to Summer*, dangled, the rope frayed. The flower bed beneath remained unplanted, the ground chewed up. Paint peeled from the dormer windows on the second floor.

She shut her eyes and sighed.

It took her thirty minutes to pull a comb through her matted hair before she could shower. Another hour disappeared in front of her closet as she tried to decide what to wear to Hugh's. Her favorite dress wouldn't fit over the bandage. Unwrapping her palm, she saw that the wound had scabbed. She wiggled her fingers. *Good enough*, she decided, and hung the dress on the closet door.

FIFTEEN

"WELL, HELLO, THERE, GWENNIE," PEARL SAID. THE
bookstore owner hobbled over, her dress brushing the floor. Gwen, not a
large person, towered over the shrunken woman whose white hair was pinned
to the top of her head.

Leaning over, Gwen wrapped careful arms around Pearl's bony shoulders.

"It is good to see you, girl," Pearl said, patting Gwen's waist. "What can
I do you for?"

Gwen pointed to the steps leading downstairs. "Going to browse through
the used books," she said.

Pearl waved her onward. "Let me know if I can help with anything. I'll be
up here, unpacking a shipment." She hauled a box from beneath the counter,
grunting as it landed on the wood.

"Can I help you?"

"*Pssh.* Go on. Been doing this for forty years, and I'll likely do this until
my time comes."

Books on maritime history and shipbuilding crowded the stairs. Gwen had
to step carefully to avoid the piles. At the bottom, the double-sized chair she
remembered from childhood still sat in the corner, hemmed in by stacks of picture
books. She sidled past multiple copies of Nancy Drew and the Bobbsey Twins.

The young adult section featured dog-eared fantasies of hollow-eyed zombies and beautiful vampires. At sixteen, Gwen had preferred the classics, Austen and Eliot and Henry James, enjoying how they made her brain hum. One month, much to her mother's amusement and Jess's bewilderment, she'd devoured the whole series of Anthony Trollope. It seemed unlikely that a kid born into the world of *Harry Potter* and *Twilight* would enjoy nineteenth-century literature. But maybe Shania was different. Maybe she would enjoy the long-winded sentences and awkward social rules. And, if not, at least she'd learn some manners. None of Trollope's characters would leave a tub unwashed and clothes all over the floor.

In the end, Gwen cast a wide net, choosing *The Picture of Dorian Gray*, *A Separate Peace*, *Dune*, and *The Fault in Our Stars*. Pearl charged her four dollars and told Gwen to come back soon. "I'll find you something special to read," she said, smiling. "There are some great biographies coming in soon."

At home, Gwen removed blankets and mothballs from a plastic bin and stuck insect repellent, toothpaste, and a jar of peanut butter inside, along with the books. *Hope you like these, Gwen. P.S. You should ask if you need a shower or some clean clothes. You left quite a mess. Also, don't take my banana bread without asking.*

She pulled on her sneakers and hiked into the woods, the bin bumping against her leg. A family of crows squawked when she found the clearing. One, the largest, hopped along a low branch, hissing. Gwen dropped the tub and raised her arms. "I'm not going near your nest, I swear." But he followed her almost the whole way back to the cottage, scolding whenever she stopped.

At the house, a card fell to the ground when she opened the screen. Janet Riggs's face, self-proclaimed "Realtor to the Peninsula," smiled at her in full color. She'd written *Call me!* in black Sharpie across the front.

Gwen crumpled it as she walked inside to change her clothes.

An hour later, she stood awkwardly at the edge of the pool at Ayr-y-Lee, Hugh nowhere in sight. A dozen young women in bathing suits lay on cushioned lounge chairs, wiggling their heads to the music piped into their ears. Oiled bodies gleamed in the warm sun.

A young man in a white polo shirt and khaki shorts passed out large plastic cups of ice water.

"Hey, Heather," one said. "How do you feel about a beer?"

"Too many calories," Heather responded without opening her eyes. "Tequila."

"Ooh, tequila." The first raised her hat brim and smiled at the man with the tray. "Can we have some tequila on the rocks with a little lime juice?"

"Of course," he said, turning to head back toward the house.

Five minutes later, the front door slammed and Hugh appeared, the young man with the tray a few steps behind.

Hugh kissed Gwen lightly on the cheek. "Happy summer."

Behind them, someone shouted, "Bottoms up!"

Hugh shifted his gaze. "Don't tell me you're drinking already?"

"We're on vacation!"

He gestured toward Gwen. "Please come say hi to my friend. I think she's been standing here for a while."

At this, they leaped up to shake hands with her, one after another. Bronzed and glistening, they looked like a composite creature or a many-limbed goddess, all rounded, dancing.

Heather, Hugh's niece, wore blue-tinted glasses that she lowered to look at Gwen. She took in Gwen's flowered dress, chosen to match Gwen's fantasy of a white tableclothed lunch on the lawn. "Cool," she said. "Vintage. Lisette likes retro, don't you?"

Her friend, wearing a white bikini and a belly chain, put a hand on her hip. "Geez, Heather. Are you still talking about the foulard headscarf? Come on. It's called *couture*." She rolled her eyes.

Heather leaned forward, smiling at Gwen. "She did look cool, but I like to give her shit."

Gwen laughed. "That's what friends are for."

"Come sit down," Hugh said. "Lunch will be out soon."

The table was set to the side of the pool atop slate tiles arranged in a herringbone pattern.

Only one of the young women put on a T-shirt. The rest came to the table in bathing suits, at ease with their bodies in a way that felt utterly foreign to Gwen. She hadn't tried on a swimsuit in years, unable to bear the sight of her belly, bluish beneath the department store's neon lights.

"You remember being young, don't you?" Hugh said. The young man who brought drinks poolside reappeared with several tequila glasses and a platter of lobster rolls.

Gwen took two.

Heather propped her chin on her elbows. "So, where do you live when you're not in Maine?"

"Here."

Heather's eyes widened. "Really? Like, full-time?"

Lisette grimaced. "Ouch. The winter. So much alone time."

Heather looked at her friend in the T-shirt. "God, Dana, you wouldn't last an hour." She turned to Gwen. "We once challenged her to shut up for ten minutes. We timed it. She didn't make it past seven."

They all laughed.

"I'm an extrovert," Dana said. "What's wrong with that?"

The young man came back carrying two opened bottles of white wine.

Dana turned her eyes toward the bay. "I mean, this place is pretty, but what do you do with no one around?"

"Same thing people do everywhere else," Gwen said. "Work and go to school. There's skiing and skating. And there are concerts." She repeated what Steven had told her a little defensively.

Heather grinned at her friends. "Oh my God," she said. "The Pan-Tones. We should one hundred percent go see them Labor Day weekend. It's the craziest thing, all the old barefoot hippies in their tie-dyed shirts dancing like they're at a rave."

Gwen bit down, listening to Heather describe the festival to her friends. The next event would coincide with Mermaid Days, the end-of-summer festival. *Dance with the Fishes.*

"It's delicious, Hugh," she said. The lobster was sweet, fresh, laced with a hint of mayo and tarragon.

"I'm glad you enjoy it," he said, pouring her a glass of wine.

The talk turned to majors and internships and starting salaries, the base figures so high that Gwen was startled. These young women would make more in a year than she'd made in her life. Heather wanted to follow her uncle into real estate development. "So much opportunity right now, you know?" she said.

Gwen finished her first roll and took a sip of wine, crisp, apple-tart. Once upon a time, she had been this eager, this certain that life held nothing but delights ahead. Molly's death had torn that veil from her eyes.

"Everybody happy?" Heather rose. "I'm headed inside for a sec. Anyone want anything?"

A chorus of "No, thanks" followed.

Gwen turned to Hugh. "How's it going in Portland?"

"Still behind schedule, but at least it's not a shit show anymore. Scott is down there on-site."

"And the project up here?"

"Nothing yet." He picked up the wine. "Want some more?"

"No, thanks. I'm okay."

"Come on," he said, pouring anyway. "You're on vacation."

He upended the bottle. The color matched the yellow flowers on her dress.

Heather shouted, "Hugh, your cell is ringing. You want me to bring it to you?"

He hopped up. "Sorry, gotta take this."

"It's Janet," she told him as he passed her in the doorway.

Heather returned to the table in a blousy shirt embroidered with sequins, a new glass of tequila in hand. "My uncle says you live near the lighthouse."

Gwen took a bite of her second lobster roll. "Right around the corner."

"Are you going to sell?"

Gwen coughed. "Sell? No."

"Oh, I thought someone said you were." Heather smiled. "My bad; I must have been thinking about someone else. Sorry." She turned her attention to her friends, her face flushed.

Gwen touched Heather's arm. "Why did you ask that?"

Heather shrugged. "I thought I heard my uncle say he didn't know your plans for the property."

Hugh had returned and sat back down. "I believe what I said was: I didn't know what her plans were for the *winter*."

"As I said, my bad." Heather leaned across the table. "Hey, Hugh, let's go for a boat ride."

He turned to Gwen. "Want to come?"

Gwen looked at her dress.

The decision made, Hugh stood. "Come on. We have sweatshirts aboard if you're chilly."

Plates and wineglasses abandoned for someone else to clear, they wandered to the dock, coolers and boat bags in hand. The young women giggled at private jokes as they took their spots, faces tipped to the sun.

With the bow pointed into the bay, Hugh gestured toward the houses on the harbor's edge. Most had been built over a hundred years earlier, before set-back regulations, their porches hovering over the rocks. "Those will be under-water by mid-century," he said. "It's already happening. See the foundations?"

The wooden supports sparkled with salt residue, evidence of the tide's reach.

"And it's worse in the winter. You'll probably get the ocean at your door come November."

"At Periwinkle? There's a berm."

"Won't matter if the storm's bad enough. The clock is ticking on everything built before the seventy-five-foot rule."

"You're saying that my cottage won't last."

"I'm saying you'll have waves up to the porch before long."

Gwen chewed on her lower lip. When she left North Carolina, climate change hadn't figured into her calculations.

As he angled the boat toward Hart's Island, sliding through the lobster pots like a skier down a slalom course, Heather lifted her head above the windshield. "Hey," she said, "can we go to that beach? Where we found all the sand dollars?"

"No." Hugh's tone was sharp. "It's private, and the owner gets upset if you go ashore."

"But—"

"We're going to Hart's."

Heather made a face before sliding back into her seat.

The boat slowed as they entered the cove. When they were a few feet offshore, Hugh told everyone to climb out.

"Throw us the noodles, will you?" Heather asked Gwen before jumping in.

Gwen ducked her head below and found the floats next to a stack of matching plush beach towels. The young women grabbed them, giggling.

"There's a path through the woods," Hugh said to Gwen. "Remember?"

"Of course." Gwen knotted her dress above her knees and took off her shoes. She inhaled sharply, stepping from the platform into the water. She waded carefully to shore, dress bunched in her hands.

Heather and her friends splashed and shouted, ducking beneath the waves and rising, sputtering, their heads shiny and slick. They didn't notice Hugh and Gwen wander off.

Hugh found the path along the pebbled shore, Gwen following closely. They passed through a field of wild grasses and rugosa, hips bright orange and bursting with seeds. An airplane flew far overhead in a pale blue sky whiskered with clouds. Ducking into the forest, they saw a handwritten sign propped against an old spruce tree pointing to the *Bathroom*.

"That's new," Gwen said.

"The island belongs to the Peninsula Conservancy," he told her. "The local day camp overnights here now."

The toilet seat leaned against a stump, a bucket waiting to receive it visible through the thicket. "That's one way to avoid poison ivy in unfortunate places on your body, I guess." Gwen laughed.

"It's disgusting," he snipped.

They climbed up a small ridge into the clearing at the top. At the center, they found their old firepit surrounded by logs hewn into rough benches. They sat, swatting at the occasional mosquito. Memories of firelight and dancing gathered fast and thick, accompanied by the smell of weed and cigarettes and burned marshmallows. In the shadows, Hugh danced with Aidan's cousin, an aspiring drama major from Portland. Jess held Gwen's hand, his thumb rubbing her palm. On the way back, night falling, Hugh cut the boat's engine, and they floated beneath the rising moon until Jess insisted it wasn't safe. Hugh had started the engine reluctantly.

"What was the music that summer?" Hugh stared wistfully at the firepit.

"Ricky Martin." Gwen knew all the lyrics and could sing them if asked. "Madonna, 'Beautiful Stranger.'"

He grinned. "It was the summer of gorgeous women." His face tanned, hair mussed from the boat ride, he looked the way he had back then. God, he had been so reckless, so unabashed. Just like the rest of them, sure that the summer would last forever.

Hugh leaned forward, hands clasped on his knees. He wanted her attention. "Gwen?"

Her head snapped up.

"It's hard to avoid, isn't it? I mean, you must think about it all the time." She looked away. "No."

He shook his head. "Man, I'll never forget that day. It was terrible for everyone."

"Somewhat worse for me, Hugh," she said.

"Of course. I just meant—well, there hasn't been a time since that I don't think about you and what you went through. I wish I could take that pain away."

"Let's not do this, Hugh." Everything about that afternoon was jumbled, indecipherable. She remembered hands on her shoulders, pulling, pulling, and a voice screaming.

He moved closer, his thigh inches from hers. "I just—"

132

"Please," she said, her vision wavering.

He put an arm around her shoulders and squeezed. His cotton shirt was soft, the muscles beneath taut, solid. He smelled of sunscreen and faintly of the spicy cologne he favored.

A moment later, he stood, eyes on a path. "Let's see where this takes us."

It led up a small hill thick with pine trees overlooking the bay. Hugh looked out, surveying, before striding back toward the beach and the sound of the young women playing.

Gwen waited, taking in the clouds overhead and the lapping waves below. Tangles of dried moss were twisted into the tree branches, clinging to the gnarled bark as if hurled there by an angry giant. Down underfoot, the roots looked arthritic, twisted, struggling to grip the earth. In winter, monster tides pulled at the soil from below while sheets of water and ice battered from above. Sometimes entire sections of land would slough off and drift out to sea, exposing the animals huddled in the hollow places, forcing them to flee or drown.

That might be her, crouched in her burrow beneath a mountain of blankets, hunched over a space heater, waiting for a nor'easter to blow Periwinkle from its foundations. She'd avoided this image, put on a show of bravado, a mask that slipped as she contemplated the toll such weather took on humans and creatures.

And if it was bad at Periwinkle, how would Shania fare in the woods? At least Gwen had shelter. Despite the sun on her shoulders, Gwen shivered.

Catching up to Hugh, she asked, "Theoretically, if I were to rent something in town for the winter, do you know how much that could cost?"

"Janet has some properties available. It's not expensive in the off-season."

"What is it with you and Janet? Do you work together?"

He laughed. "Whatever makes you think that? I just use her office for some contracts when I'm up here. It's easier than trying to find a notary or a Staples. She talks about her business because we're friendly." He put his hand on her shoulder. "Gwen, if you're worried about the winter, you could always stay at my place. I have heat. I'll pop in from time to time, but you'd mostly have it to yourself."

His empty house had many empty bedrooms, more than enough for her. Shania, too. Although by then Shania would hopefully be back where she belonged, and in school.

"Please let me help you, Gwennie. At least until you get yourself settled."

"That's an awfully generous offer, Hugh."

"No strings attached," he said. "It's what friends do, Gwen. Help each other."

In the cove, Heather and her friends had clambered back onto the boat. They muddled about, draped in the towels. One wrapped a sarong around her head, laughing. "It's couture!" she said.

"You're all Philistines," Lisette said.

"Hugh," Heather shouted to her uncle. "It's getting late."

"We should get back," he said to Gwen. "Just say you'll think about it."

She smiled. "I'll think about it."

On the way back to the mainland, she stood beside him, their hips and arms touching. His hands held the wheel lightly, slicing through the water with a practiced grace. The breeze blew her hair. Above, an osprey soared, riding the summer thermals, its beautiful wings outspread.

SIXTEEN

IN THE TOURIST HIGH SEASON—BEGINNING IN MID-JULY
and stretching until school resumed in late August—herds of buses ferried
people from Camden and Bangor to the lighthouse, spewing clouds of diesel.
Once disgorged, visitors clamored over the rocks, shouting to one another as
they scoured the shore for sea glass and shells and small wishing stones. Some
even wrestled with colorful lobster pots entangled in boulders, pulling them
free with cries of triumph. A few wandered farther afield. Steering clear of
the dangerous drop-off, they approached for a closer look at the small cottage
perched beside the ocean and the lone figure seated on the porch, barefoot,
computer on her lap.

One dared ask if Gwen ever listed the property on Vrbo. As she opened
her mouth to respond, the front door slammed behind her, shaking her chair.
The man scurried away, slipping and sliding on the damp rocks.

"Was that entirely necessary?" Gwen asked.

The Misses tapped the wall behind her head, an emphatic yes, and Gwen
laughed. Maybe she should warn trespassers: *Beware of ghosts, proceed at your
own risk.*

A black guillemot skittered across the water, diving for fish, unbothered
by Gwen or the Misses or the wayward tourists.

Gwen added her final comments to Parker's essay: *Great work* and *Consider removing an adjective here*. She'd email it later, using the library's Wi-Fi.

There, she thought, *Mr. Condon repaid*. A whole cord of wood cost way too much to accept as a gift, especially since the Condons had their own money woes. If only her credit card could be settled as easily. Even without the urgent care bill, it brushed dangerously close to her limit. Michaela had made no mention of salary when they spoke in May, but Gwen kept her fingers crossed that the offer would land close to the top of the salary range. This was likely what they would discuss at the meeting Michaela had requested last week. The email had been a little cryptic—*there are some things we need to discuss*—but Michaela had assured her months ago that her education made her a great candidate. Gwen felt hopeful as she drove to Ellsworth. For the first time in quite a while, the money worries abated. Someday soon, if she was very careful, she could pay down all that debt.

———

AT A DISTANCE, the Peninsula High School could easily have been mistaken for a warehouse. Fields surrounded the campus, no trees in sight. Above the worn concrete steps, a banner insisted that the *Future Begins Here*.

A blond woman, her ponytail askew, stood at the front door. "Gwen," she said, smiling, two dimples on either side of her mouth. Time had softened her; her hug felt like a downy pillow.

Gwen rested her chin on Michaela's shoulder. "Thank you," she said.

"Don't thank me yet," she said. "Come on in." Something about her tone made Gwen's stomach tighten.

The hallway smelled of disinfectant, the floor shiny with wax. Gwen caught glimpses of shuttered classrooms, bare corkboards, and clean blackboards. They passed a door plastered with colorful stickers. Daisies and rainbows competed with signs that read *It Only Gets Better* and a phone number for the teen suicide prevention line.

Michaela lifted her chin. "Counseling has been particularly slammed ever since the pandemic. So many kids came back to in-person learning with issues."

"The same was true in North Carolina, even at the college level."

"We had our special challenges, though. Only about a third of our students have an internet connection at home. So most of them had to use the public library alongside the adults trying to do their work. It got so crowded that the librarians had to meter people in, and the kids could only work online for an hour at a time. Some of them sat in the parking lot, trying to log on. It was a nightmare."

"How did you deal with it?"

Michaela sighed. "Well, we kind of gave up on grades after a while, focused on getting them to read and write, practice the math they already knew so they wouldn't take a step backward."

"A lost year," Gwen said.

"More like two or three, when you get down to it. I'm scared some of our kids will never recover." Michaela opened a classroom door. String instruments hung on the wall above music easels and precariously stacked chairs. At the front, a harp and some drums sat on a raised platform. "The band room," she said. "My 2017 class built the stage from scratch."

"Do you still play?" At boarding school, Michaela had been the star violinist in the music department.

Michaela shook her head. "No time. Four kids, husband always on the road."

They reached her office. Opening a file, Michaela talked about the student body, only about half of whom chose to continue their education after high school. Most of these attended community college or commuted to Orono. "This would be quite a change for you, I suspect."

"In some ways. But UNC is a state school strongly committed to teaching first-generation students."

Michaela sat back in her chair, her expression thoughtful. "So, remind me of everything you've done since Barnard?"

"I worked for a year in advertising, writing copy for a frozen food company. It was awful, so I went to grad school. I've been teaching undergraduates ever since."

"But you didn't finish the doctorate."

"No . . ." Gwen paused. The lonely hours at the library returned in a rush. The pages of notes grew longer and longer, the sentences more fraught, until she realized she had nothing to say. "I didn't."

"Have you ever taught high school?"

She shook her head.

"And you don't have a teaching certificate."

"You mean like a master's in education? No."

Michaela sighed. "You know I want to hire you, Gwen. You'd have been perfect for the AP lit position, but, when I offered it to you, I didn't realize that you didn't have the Ph.D. The state is currently very focused on credentials. I'm afraid I can't offer you the job."

Gwen's vision narrowed. The room stretched before her, impossibly long, Michaela's desk far away.

"I'm so sorry. I honestly had no idea this would happen when we talked last spring. I thought it was a done deal."

Gwen looked at her hands, tightly clasped in her lap. "Me too."

"Your department chair said you're quite good with the students and have an exemplary record."

"Phillip said that?"

Michaela nodded. "I've been racking my brain to think of a solution. Would you be interested in a different position? We could use a part-time person in the college guidance office. Our counselor is overwhelmed."

"I'm definitely not qualified to advise children." Gwen's voice sounded hollow.

"Not advising; help with the application process: transcripts and deadlines, SAT prep, that sort of thing. I'm afraid we can only fund twenty hours a week."

Would Walter let her bag groceries while Parker was in school?

Michaela shook her head. "If you're willing to get your certificate, we can revisit the lit position. I am afraid you might be overqualified for what I am offering."

"Well, there's not much I can do about that. I can't undo school."

Michaela put down the folder. "Let me talk to the board and I'll see what I can manage. We still have some time before school starts."

Feeling shaky, Gwen grabbed a stale donut from the tray outside Michaela's office on her way out. It tasted gross—too much sugar dumped on top of semi-stale bread—but at least it was free.

She drove back to town behind a dump truck shedding pebbles. These struck her windshield every few miles with a loud *ping*. She tried to pass, but its bulk blocked the view of the oncoming road for miles, so the sign at the edge of town took her by surprise. Just before the curve toward the lighthouse, she hesitated. The only thing waiting at the cottage was an open computer and a dark screen with no internet connection.

Instead of following the route home, she turned right, parking outside the new condominium complex. The putty-colored siding shone, impenetrable. Maybe Hugh was right: Gwen was a dinosaur, stuck in some image of a rural community that didn't accommodate old age or changing economic conditions. Maybe he should knock down those old Georgian homes and make way for a future that didn't include nostalgia.

Gwen knocked on Mr. Drinkwater's beige front door and waited.

"Coming, coming," she heard. A minute later, the door opened without a sound, no creaks or squeaks, just the clean whoosh of cool air.

"Gwennie," Mr. Drinkwater said. "How's the world treating my girl?"

She kissed his cheek. "Better now," she said.

"Come in, come in. Have you eaten anything today?" He held the screen open with his walker.

"I'm good," she said. "Why do you ask?"

"You've lost weight."

"Really?" But she could feel her hip bone through the pocket of her jeans. Guy would have been pleased.

In the living room, the television blared a soccer match. Parker sat on an orange lounge chair, forearms on his knees, his forehead creased in concentration.

"Look who's come to see us, young man."

Parker jumped to his feet. "Ms. Gilmore, hi."

"Gwen, please."

"Gwen." He touched his nose. "How's the garden?"

She leaned toward him. "Thriving, thank you very much. Bodies make excellent fertilizer."

He grinned, still standing, eyes straying to the television.

She patted his shoulder. "Sit, sit. Looks like you have important business to attend to."

"My team is losing. Blew it about twenty minutes ago." He seemed dismissive, but his eyes flicked back to the screen.

Mr. Drinkwater said, "This young lady and I are going to make some lemonade."

Parker hunched forward in the chair as if he could change the outcome through sheer force of will.

In the kitchen, Mr. Drinkwater handed Gwen a juicer made of pale green milk glass. He sliced lemons, carefully picking out the seeds, and passed the halves to her. She twisted the rind over the reamer, rubbing until she felt the bumps beneath her palm.

"So, missy, where have you been this morning?"

"At the high school."

Mr. Drinkwater poured the juice into a pitcher already filled with ice. "You gonna teach?"

"I'm both under- and overqualified, evidently." She took a deep breath. "I need a job, Mr. Drinkwater. Do you know if anyone is hiring right now?"

He turned on the tap and added an obscene amount of sugar. "Tough time, Gwennie. Summer folk will leave at the end of the month, and everyone cuts back then. What exactly are you looking for?"

"Pretty much anything."

"Bound to be something." Mr. Drinkwater leaned on his walker. "The glasses are above your head, dear."

Gwen poured the lemonade into glasses. Parker didn't shift his eyes from the television when she put one in his hand. He groaned as the ref blew a whistle and held up a yellow card.

Mr. Drinkwater placed a Thin Mint in her hand.

She held it, chocolate melting into her palm. She regretted each of the recent afternoons she'd spent with her nose in a book, walking on the shore, watching the clouds. She should never have counted on Michaela's offer.

Mr. Drinkwater leaned forward, smacking his lips. "You should eat that," he said.

She stuffed the Thin Mint in her mouth. It took several tries to swallow.

He handed her another. "That fella, the one who lives next door, I told him to go and see you a few weeks back. That terrible hot spell in July, remember?"

Gwen's shoulders lowered, and she smiled. Mr. Drinkwater had been the little birdie, not Steven. "He took me out on the boat."

"I think he likes you." He tapped his hand on his knee for emphasis. "You could do worse, you know. A man like that."

"I don't know." Right now she needed a job, not an affair.

Parker stood, his face inches from the television, his body tense. "Come on, come on," he muttered at the screen.

Mr. Drinkwater put down his glass, his expression serious. "There was a time when I was in trouble, too, you know. I was right wild back in the day, drank too much. But then I met Dora, and she said she wouldn't have me unless I got myself together. Her dad took a chance and offered me a job even though I sure as heck didn't deserve it. I worked my way up on the ferry and bought the store."

Parker bounced, arms gripped over his head. "Come on," he begged the television. "Come on."

Mr. Drinkwater patted her knee. "You're a good girl, Gwennie. You always were. You'll find what you need. And you're not alone anymore."

"Woooo," Parker screamed at the top of his lungs, jumping up and down. "Yes!" He turned, red-faced and beaming, to share his joy, but when he saw Gwen's face, he stopped. His arms fell. "But . . . Gramps, what did you say? You made her cry."

SEVENTEEN

PARKER AND MR. DRINKWATER TOOK TURNS AWKWARDLY consoling her, afraid the tears would start flowing again. When she finally stood to leave, they insisted on seeing her out.

At the door, Mr. Drinkwater leaned, one hand on the walker, and patted her arm. "Don't worry, Gwennie, we'll find you a job," he said, handing her a fistful of caramels.

"I'll talk to the other kids about sending you essays," Parker added.

"I'm fine, I promise," she told them, but their worried looks suggested they didn't believe her. They waved from the doorway as she started the car and pulled away.

She had nowhere else to go but home—and it was the last place she wanted to be. There was so much and so little to do, it was hard to decide where to start. Household projects abounded—the gutters needed cleaning, a shutter needed fixing, a curtain needed mending—but none of those would pay the electricity bill. She shook her head in frustration. Her retreat to Maine had led to a dead end, her path choked by state regulations and board requirements. What would she do now?

She drove around for an hour, past farms and small art galleries, summer-houses with neatly stacked rock walls and double-wides surrounded by discarded fishing equipment. A handmade sign directed her to buy local fish and produce from someone's garage. Cars with out-of-state plates choked the driveway.

At Bagaduce Falls, she pulled into the parking lot and found a spot away from the lunch counter where a harassed teenager was handing out lobster rolls to hungry patrons. She got out and walked to the shore. Brackish water from a pond on the other side of the road rushed beneath a bridge and cascaded over a slope of rock before disappearing into the cove in front of her. In the middle of the inlet, someone had arranged a whimsical trio of pint-sized sailboats, complete with mannequin children wearing life vests. The boats swung on their moorings, pushed by the waves, the puppets listing from side to side.

Gwen sat. Worries descended like gnats, buzzing about her head.

Even if Michaela found her a position—not a given, by any means—a part-time job would not support her. It wouldn't even pay for more wood once the weather changed.

Or the long-awaited hospital bill.

If she moved into Hugh's house to save on heating expenses, it would help, but his offer had not come with a job. And as Mr. Drinkwater had pointed out, not much remained open after October. The bookstore, the grocery store, the hardware store, and the retirement home were all that came to mind, and her Ph.D. coursework didn't prepare her to scan barcodes or track inventory or help the elderly. All potential employers would see the same thing Michaela had: overqualified and underqualified. All that education on her résumé useless. Less than useless.

Gwen sat for an hour before the kitchen closed and the teenager started slamming the take-out windows shut. "Need to put the chain across the parking lot," he shouted. She stood stiffly and returned to her car. The gnats followed her home, swarming. She got out of the Subaru drenched with sweat.

A note waited for her on the kitchen table. *Hi Gwen. I apologize. I never meant to upset you. I stepped into a bees' nest, and I treated the welts with pine*

144

sap and dirt. I had a hard time getting it to wash off in the ocean, so I used your shower. You're right; I should have asked. Ditto about the clothes. That was an asshole move. It won't happen again.

Thanks for the books. That Dorian Gray is some kind of hoe. Like one of those tech bros in the news, people so rich they think they are immune to consequences. Imagine living without any concern for others. I can't. Also, it occurred to me that the book works as a metaphor for social media, too—the disconnect between image and lived experience. Anyway, thanks. Shania.

Gwen reread the last few sentences, remembering the novel. The portrait, hidden away, grew to reflect the debauchery of the protagonist's life while the evil man remained young and beautiful, untouched by all he had done. She absentmindedly reached a hand to the white hair at her temple. As someone who presented the evidence of her fatal flaw for everyone to see, it would be a relief to stash guilt and worry in an attic somewhere.

———

A FEW DAYS later, as she scoured the want ads on her cell phone, Steven's smiling face filled her screen. "Hi," she said wearily.

"We're headed your way, girl. Meet us in the driveway."

"No, Steven, I—" This was not the time for a walk.

"You don't have a choice. Be there in five." He hung up.

She took a deep breath and closed her eyes. How was she going to muster the energy?

Minutes later, a loud beeping announced that Jess's truck was slowly backing down the drive.

Steven leaned out the passenger-side window. "Hellooo," he said. "We're here to take a hot tub off your hands."

"You're what?"

He jumped out of the cab. "Walter said you might need a little pick-me-up, so here we are."

"This is too much, Steven. I can't ask you to—"

He put a hand to her mouth. "Shush."

Jess maneuvered his pickup between the cottage and the garage and came to a stop. When he stepped out, he looked up at the sky. "It's gonna rain soon. Let's try to get this done before that happens."

Gwen turned to Jess. "Seriously, this is too much."

"Nah. Happy to help." He raised the vinyl cover and wrinkled his nose. "What happened here?"

Gwen looked over his shoulder at the sludge inside. "I had a small bonfire," she said.

Jess grinned. "And you didn't invite me."

Steven crooked a finger at Gwen. "I have a present for you." He led her to the truck, a childlike excitement in his steps.

Plastic trays of perennials and annuals were tucked between the seats. "Ta-da!" he said, hands outspread.

"Steven!"

"I thought it would make you happy."

"It does. It really, really does." She lowered her arms. "But I have to pay you back."

"Oh, please, it's a gift. Besides, it's so late in the season. They were all half-price and pretty picked over." The plants had all outgrown their seedling pots, tall stems towering over tight root balls, the lower leaves drooping.

Gwen touched a fingertip to a cobalt-blue delphinium petal. She hadn't let herself visit the plant sale, fearing what she'd spend. "Seriously, Steven. You are doing too much for me." She waved at Jess, who was crouched beside the hot tub, inspecting the underneath.

"This is fun. Plus, it'll really up your curb appeal."

Her smile lowered in distaste. "You sound like Janet. You know, she stuffed a card into my door the other day. Can you believe it? What an ass."

"Don't be so hard on her. You gotta admire her gumption, you know? She built that practice from nothing." He handed her a bag of compost. "And she pays my salary."

"You have to like her. I don't."

"Fair enough."

Jess hefted something from the truck's bed.

"What the hell is that?" Gwen asked, slightly alarmed.

He raised and lowered his eyebrows suggestively. "This is my friend Sawzall, and it can take apart pretty much anything."

Steven pulled on her arm. "Come on, Gwen. I'm not sure I want to watch this."

They unloaded the trays to the whine of the reciprocating saw. When the blade hit the hot tub, it became far louder than a woodpecker's hammer as it ground the plastic to dust.

"I hope you're wearing your respirator," Steven shouted.

The saw stopped, and Jess peeked around the corner wearing safety glasses and a mask. "You were saying, dear?"

Steven raised his hands in mock-surrender. "Just checking."

They carried the flowers to the churned-up beds, careful to keep the ungainly plants from toppling onto the ground. Steven arranged them on either side of the front porch and below the kitchen window, placing the tallest—bright red bee balm and golden daylilies—so that the petals would reach above the lower windowpanes. The shorter plants, oxeye daisies and dusty blue catmint, went in front.

"This is a deer salad bar," Gwen said, handing him pots.

Steven grunted as he dug his trowel into the dirt. "We're going to put up some temporary fencing to keep them out."

Every time the Sawzall stopped, Steven's head snapped up. "Jess? You okay?" he shouted.

"All good," Jess said, and the noise started again.

After an hour, the hot tub lay broken on the ground, a shattered blue eggshell spilling bits of yellow foam. "I could use a hand loading it up," Jess said.

They lifted each section into the waiting wheelbarrow, carefully avoiding the sharp edges, and pushed it up the ramp into the pickup bed.

Gwen fetched a broom to sweep up the crumbled insulation while small grubs and ants scurried away. When she finished, her face red with exertion, only a dark spot revealed where the hot tub had once been. The fireplace she'd built leaned against a fir tree at the edge of the forest, the logs falling from their scaffolding.

"Oh, mushroom," she whispered. "Your fort . . ."

Jess put an arm around her shoulders and squeezed.

"But at least that plastic monstrosity is gone," Steven said.

"I'm going to run to the dump before it closes. I'll come and pick you up in a bit," he said to Steven before walking to the truck.

Gwen followed. She reached for Jess's arm, which was hanging through the open window. "Thank you," she said.

His eyes crinkled. "My pleasure."

She watched the truck growl away, the big tires creasing the gravel.

Steven grabbed her hand. "Come on, let's finish this before the heavens open."

They rushed to plant everything as the lighthouse began to moan, heralding the approach of bad weather. They loosened the roots, coaxing apart the tightly woven knots, and spread them in the dark soil. If the weather held through August, the bed would spring to life. The hummingbirds might even return, green wings flickering in search of nectar.

Gwen bent over the last of the petunias, the musty scent filling her nose. Her mother had particularly loved their bright pinks and purples, and when the slugs chewed through the petals, she'd taken it personally. Beer poured into mouthwash cups had been her defense. The slugs were attracted to it, and overnight their bodies would turn to mush in the yeasty foam.

Fat raindrops started to fall as the last plants went into the ground. They gathered up the plastic trays and tools and dumped them outside the locked garage, racing to pull netting across the front of the beds to prevent any four-legged opportunists from devouring their work. By the time they finished, they were both drenched.

Steven chattered as she put on the kettle. Janet Riggs was making him crazy, constantly dashing out of the office, taking phone calls behind closed doors, making him run errands. He'd made four trips to Hugh's last week, ferrying heavy envelopes.

"Hugh's?" Gwen poured hot water over the tea bags. "Is he even here? I thought he was in Boston."

"Oh, he's here. Wouldn't miss high season when 'everyone' is in town and there's a cocktail party every night." Steven's voice was sarcastic.

"What is your issue with Hugh?"

"He treats me like I'm invisible, for starters. Jess, too. So much for old friends."

"Jess isn't in touch with Aidan, either."

Stephen frowned. "Well, that's a story."

"What story?"

"Not mine to tell, sister." He sighed. "You'd better ask Jess."

Jess's comment returned. *I had a little crush on Aidan.*

They took their mugs into the living room. The rain tapped the roof and sloughed onto the porch. The sea was a pale gray, the same color as the sky. Ribbons brushed across the water's surface, pushing the white-capped waves toward the shore and Periwinkle's protective berm. Mist crept through the room and settled on their skin.

"I'll light a fire," she said, closing the window. Her father's aged wood caught quickly. Gwen held her palms out, waving her cold fingers.

"How's the hand?"

"All healed."

"Did you make a follow-up appointment? Remember the nurse said you need rehab."

"The nurse said I *might* need rehab, and no, I haven't." She still didn't know what she owed the urgent care center for visit number one.

Steven bit his lip. Gwen could feel him debating whether or not to push the issue. *Please don't*, she begged silently.

He cleared his throat. "How much has this room changed since the house was built?"

"Not much at all." She plucked an old photo album from the shelf. "Here."

Inside, the silvered prints gleamed. They captured the same living room, colored in shades of sepia as if the cottage had been encased in resin.

"This is fantastic," he said.

"I know, right?" She switched on the lamp behind his head.

He turned the dark pages carefully. The earliest photographs were more faded than the rest, the inks rendered unstable by the climate and the passage of time. Miss Whitehead's spidery handwriting gave the date: *The site, 1920.* The images that followed documented every step of the construction, beginning with site-clearing. The foundation rose from the leveled ground, granite pillars held together with mortar. Carpenters appeared in overalls and work boots, wielding hammers and saws, hoisting trusses into the attic. The camera, held by Miss Gilmore, followed the men from spot to spot, focusing on their hands and shoulders, the strain of lifting beams into place. The Misses had occasionally helped, since one shot captured a feminine hand holding a floorboard in place.

"Look at those old gals," Steven said, shaking his head. "Fearless."

Miss Gilmore stood with her arm around Miss Whitehead, smiling.

"I can't wait to take pictures of this room," Steven said. "You know, the Historical Society has hired me to document some other old houses about to be torn down. I could use some help. Any chance you'd be interested?"

"I'm hopelessly underqualified, Steven."

"You don't have to know anything about photography. Just help me schlep the stuff, plug in lights, that sort of thing."

"In that case, I'd be happy to help."

"And would you consider writing some copy, too? They want notes about the history, the owners, the architecture, and so on. I can't pay you very much, but there might be more work once we finish this project."

Gwen drew back. "I don't know." This sounded a lot like a pity offer.

"I am going to have to hire someone regardless. And you have experience. Jess says you're a good writer."

"That was a long time ago."

"Please?"

Don't be proud, her conscience whispered. *Say yes.*

"Yes," she said aloud.

He closed the album, and an envelope fell from the back, clearly newer than the album but still decades old. He opened it with the same reverence. A handful of family photographs emerged.

"Look at you," he said, smiling at Gwen in braces. He stopped at the next one. A small girl stood at the foot of the porch steps, smiling. Golden curls, sun-kissed skin.

Gwen said, "Molly." In the following image, Molly approached the camera in her bathing suit, her face full of mischief. Gwen's heart twisted. This had been taken the year she drowned.

Steven said, "I'm so sorry, Gwen." He propped the picture on the coffee table where they could both see it. She rested her head on his shoulder.

A horn blast announced Jess's return. He walked through the back door wearing a raincoat and carrying a damp bag from the Black Anchor.

"Dinner," he said.

Gwen's stomach leaped.

"Mr. Drinkwater said you weren't eating."

"That's not true," she said as her belly gurgled.

Jess laughed. "It's a present. Just say thank you."

"Thank you."

"No problem. Be seeing you."

Steven and Jess ran to the truck through the rain. Opening the passenger door, Steven stopped and shouted, "Hey, do you want me to stick those in the garage?" They'd left the seedling trays piled by the door.

"It's locked. I'll do it in a little bit. When the rain stops."

The rain came in distinct waves, drops splattering the glass panes in the living room. She put another log on the fire and opened Jess's bag. The fries were cold, but she didn't care. She shoved a handful in her mouth and unwrapped the burger. She finished it in six bites. When she was done, she leaned back against the sofa, her stomach wordless with pleasure.

The rattle of plastic trays and furious barking from Mrs. Condon's dogs forced her to her feet. That raccoon was crawling over the plastic pots to get at the trash. Grabbing a raincoat, she decided she would give that nasty animal the scare of its life. "Shoo," she yelled, until, ten paces away, she stopped short, breath caught. A figure much larger than a raccoon had hands on the garage door, rattling and shaking the knob, trying to force it open.

"Steven?" She said his name without thinking. She could tell it was not him—too short, wearing a drenched hoodie three sizes too big, an overdressed scarecrow. The hands dropped, and the girl looked up. Gwen saw wide eyes set in a pinched face.

"I'm sorry. I'm so sorry," Shania said before turning and sprinting away.

Gwen, shocked, couldn't move. She stood frozen to the spot, water running from her raincoat's visor, until the Condons' dogs started to bark again.

EIGHTEEN

GWEN RAN TO THE EDGE OF THE WOODS, CALLING. TOR-
rential rain made it impossible to see. She stumbled off the drive, and her feet
sank into mud above her ankles. She had to hold on to her rubber boots to
lift her feet from the sludge. Lightning split the sky with a crack, and when
a branch fell within inches of her shoulder, she retreated to the cottage, out
of breath and rattled.

Her raincoat created small puddles on the kitchen floor as she struggled to
dial her phone. Thunder rolled overhead, shaking the rafters. In the distance,
the lighthouse horn called.

"Dear," Mrs. Condon said.

"Did you see anything near your house?"

"In this weather? I can't see two feet in front of my face in this mess." Her
calm tone didn't match the urgency in Gwen's. "Why?"

"I . . ." Gwen's voice trailed off. What could she say without revealing
what she knew? "I heard the dogs, and I thought there might be an intruder."

"Intruder? No. Likely that big old fox I seen carrying her kits into the woods."

"Guess I was wrong."

"Don't you worry." Mrs. Condon chuckled. "This isn't the big city, you know."

Gwen bit her lip as anxiety tightened its grip. The crime rate in Port Anna might be low, but the woods harbored perils equal to those in the big city. Trees fell, and sinkholes opened. Bears and moose wandered in search of food.

"No one is out there, Gwennie."

"Okay."

"Should I have Donald come down and check on you?"

Gwen held a hand to her forehead. "No, no, that's not necessary. I'll be fine, I'm just a little spooked."

"It is quite the storm. You call if you get nervous again, you hear?"

When she hung up, her brain whirred. In this weather, it would be impossible to go after Shania without risking injury to herself. She could only trust that the girl knew where to hide. After months of living in the trees, surely she had a safe place to shelter, a hollow place between boulders or the empty root ball of a fallen pine. One of those would protect her.

Wouldn't it?

Gwen pulled Sarah Orne Jewett's *A White Heron* from the shelf and opened to the first chapter. But her brain refused to follow the narrative, the words replaced by images of a girl in soaking-wet clothes. After five fruitless minutes, she gave up and began to roam the house, stopping to look out the windows. Early evening had given way to night. Because of the storm, the darkness was so thick she caught only her reflection.

After an hour, the rain slowed, pinging the windowpanes at longer intervals. In its wake, the wind picked up. Pine cones and small branches fell on the roof. The clatter refueled the adrenaline she'd only just put to rest. She went to the kitchen to turn on the kettle.

As she opened a box of Earl Grey, the back door rattled, and tea bags slid across the floor.

There was a face in the window. Gwen lunged forward, struggling to open it.

But instead of a cold, wet girl seeking shelter, Leandro smiled from behind the glass. "Cookies?"

Her eyes scanned the driveway behind him, as if she might catch a glimpse of Shania hiding behind the garage.

"May I come in?" he asked.

"Oh, sorry. Of course." She stepped aside.

He held up a grocery bag. "Situations such as this call for treats."

"Situations like what?"

"When one is having a bad week."

"I am not sure treats will do the trick. Maybe scotch."

He shook his head. "Alas, that I do not have. But coffee and chocolate chip ice cream might help."

She shut the door reluctantly. "Did Mr. Drinkwater call you, too?" she asked, taking two bowls from the cabinet.

Leandro put a napkin in his lap. "He said you might perhaps need a distraction."

"Did he?" She had more than enough of those. What she needed was a job.

"Has something happened?"

Yeah, she thought, *about a million things*, but he didn't need to hear any of them. She said, "A giant raccoon tried to break into my garage."

He raised his spoon. "Here is to the creatures that live in the Maine woods."

She touched her spoon to his, chocolate chip to coffee. "May they stay safe and dry in their dens."

Something hit the side of the cottage, and Gwen froze, her spoon in midair.

"I'll go and check," Leandro said.

She held out a hand to stop him. "That's not necessary. I'm sure it's nothing."

"Cookies, you are concerned. I will take a look."

He pulled open the door and stepped into the night. She sat unmoving, ears straining.

"A branch," he told her as the door closed behind him.

She exhaled slowly. *Where had Shania gone?*

Leandro pointed to the games on the shelf. "Do you play chess?"

"My father taught me when I was a child. I'm not sure I'm a very good opponent."

"Nonsense."

He followed her into the living room with the box, pausing in front of Miss Gilmore's portrait, his face inches from the canvas. "This is wonderful," he said. "It is painted with so much love. The way the light catches her hair." He held his pinkie out like a paintbrush, sweeping the hand downward. "And the neck. What is the word? The nape? As if it is waiting to be kissed."

"Miss Whitehead. She painted the landscape, too." Gwen pointed to a painting of an enormous boulder above the fireplace. In a field, the granite caught the light, sparkling, the wildflowers around it waving with joy.

"It is an erratic," he said. "This is what they call those rocks, the big ones, deposited by the glaciers as they melted."

With his words, the sun-drenched boulder seemed to shift, rotating its shadow face to look directly at Gwen.

"It is what I am," he said, smiling. "An erratic, tossed here, almost as far away as I can get from where I was born."

"And where was that, exactly?"

"In the northwestern part of Argentina. Do you know Salta?"

She shook her head.

"Ah. Well, my town is about an hour outside the city, near the Andes. It is very far from Maine."

They set up the chessboard. Outside, the wind continued to gust, occasionally pushing at the windows. The attic creaked as they traded moves in silence.

He slid the queen toward her knight. "You do not live alone," he said without looking up.

She watched his blue-flecked hands handle the piece she'd just lost. No wonder she was playing so badly, she was hypnotized. "Some nights are busier than others," she told him. "I think they might be curious about you."

He sat back in his chair, eyes glittering. "I am curious about them. Tell me."

"Even better: I can show you."

Game abandoned, they moved to the couch, his shoulder mere inches from hers. His soap smelled of something earthy and warm, cedar or sandalwood. For the second time that day, Gwen opened an old photo album. Leaning forward, Leandro ran long fingers through his white hair, pushing it aside as he leaned over the pages. The nape of his neck below the hairline was pale and clean-shaven.

He stopped at a portrait of a woman smiling, a mass of hair piled atop her head, her face crinkled and soft. She wore a toga and a crown, performing as Erato, the muse of poetry. Other women sat in a circle around her, clapping.

"Miss Whitehead," Gwen said. "And that"—she turned the page for him—"is Miss Gilmore." Black-haired and sharp-eyed, Miss Gilmore lifted her eyebrows, wary, less open to the world than her partner. She held her arms to her chest.

"Why do you think they remain?"

"Because it's their home," she said without thinking. But, of course, it had been Molly's, too, and Molly had never found her way back. Gwen preferred not to consider the reason why. She was either lost, adrift, or still too angry to return. Both options felt too terrible to contemplate.

"Perhaps they have work to do yet." He closed the album. "Or perhaps they wish to see the changes you will bring to their home."

"Changes?"

"You know, pick a new lamp, move that chair." He pointed to the tall wicker chair, the frayed caning causing it to lean.

"I don't want a new lamp. Or a new chair."

Leandro cocked his head. "Even granite alters its shape under the influence of water. We must, I think, expect change."

In the corner of the room, a lamp flickered and went out.

"Ah. The ladies disagree." He chuckled. "Perhaps they also think it is time for you to sleep."

"Sleep?"

"You have dark circles, Cookies."

She blinked as she realized how tired she was. "It's been a long day," she said.

"Then you must sleep. I shall stay here." He patted the sofa.

"What?"

"It is late. You have been nervous. I shall keep you company until morning."

She started to protest, insisting that the wind had stopped. She was fine. Really.

"Fine is not the same as untroubled."

"There is a bedroom upstairs. You don't have to be uncomfortable."

His eyes rotated, mesmerizing. "That is very kind, but I think the couch is best."

She fetched him a blanket and pillow, pulled on a nightgown, and crawled into her own bed. She fell asleep in minutes, lulled into unconsciousness by the sound of him breathing through the thin pine boards.

Pink streaks appeared in the morning sky just before six. She opened the door a crack, relieved to see Leandro still on the sofa, one arm thrown across his face, one foot on the floor. She pulled on a sweater—the temperature had fallen fifteen degrees overnight—and tiptoed past him, avoiding the creaky boards in the middle of the room. He snorted softly and rolled to one side when the coffee machine started gurgling.

She pulled on her mother's rain boots, grabbed an extra fleece, and went outside, careful not to let the screen door bang. Beneath the eaves, the rain had etched divots into the soil, and some of the new plants leaned sideways, in need of staking.

As she picked her way through low branches, boots squelching in the mud, water trickled from the leaves and splashed onto her head and shoulders. The chilly air raised goose bumps on her arms and legs. She should have brought more than a jacket for Shania; the poor thing was likely miserable and cold. The heat wave might return, but it wouldn't last long, September only two weeks away.

She found the plastic bin in the clearing where she'd left it, a box of protein bars still inside.

"Shania?" she called.

Songbirds chirped overhead.

"I'm sorry I frightened you last night."

A pine branch swayed as a squirrel jumped, sending a shower of water to the drenched ground.

"I didn't mean to lock you out. It won't happen again, I promise."

She turned in a circle, squinting into the dark green shadows, but there was no sign of a girl in a wet hoodie. Sighing, she put the fleece in the bin.

"Let me know that you're okay," she said to the still air, adding, "Please."

She made her way back, arms wrapped around her waist. The bottom of her nightgown was sopping wet when she reached the cottage.

"You are up early." Leandro leaned over the porch railing. "Are you making me breakfast?"

She dropped her hands to her sides. "I'm sorry. I really should, to thank you, but I don't have anything but coffee."

He raised a mug. "That I have already found. Although this"—he scrunched his nose in distaste—"is not South American."

"Folgers' best," she said. "Cheap and cheerful."

"Cheap, yes; cheerful, no." His eyes turned to the shoreline. "Look how still the ocean becomes after a storm. It is so placid today, one might be easily fooled into believing she is asleep."

Gwen shivered. "I think I need a warm shower," she said.

"Ah, I see. You are done with me now," he said, his eyes twinkling. "I will be off, my chivalrous deed now complete."

Her cheeks reddened. "Thank you for keeping me company."

He bowed his head. "I live to serve."

Before she could consider it, she reached for his hand. "You are very kind."

He smiled and gently squeezed her fingers. "You are most welcome." His warmth remained with her as the El Camino started with a deep rumble.

NINETEEN

GWEN SPENT THE MORNING AFTER THE STORM IN THE garden, staking the fallen bee balm and the sagging delphinium. Every few minutes, her eyes lifted from the earth to scan the woods, but Shania remained firmly out of sight. When the phone rang after lunch, the screen lit up with the letter *S*, and she jumped, swiping with a muddy finger. "Hello?"

Steven's voice responded, "Hey, girl," and her heart deflated.

"How was your night?"

"The storm did a number on our garden."

"Oh! Is it destroyed?"

She picked bruised daylily petals from the soil. "It looks a little sad, but I think it'll rebound in a few days."

"I wish I could come and help, but Janet is headed to Portland for the day, and she left me in charge."

"You're showing houses?"

"Oh, hell, no. She'd have to pay me a commission, and there's no way she's parting with a single red cent. I'm just answering the phone and handing her card to walk-ins."

"Good luck with that."

"Anything else happen during the storm?"

She could hear the cheeky smile in his voice. "Nope," she said. "And how do you know about last night anyway?"

"Leandro came by to pick up metal sheets from Jess. So, how was he? As a distraction, I mean."

She sat back on her heels. A dragonfly circled the rain-beaten petunias on gossamer wings. "Good company. We ate ice cream and played chess."

"And did he spend the night?"

She rolled her eyes. "On the couch, Steven."

He sighed. "Oh, come on, that accent! The hair! The man is deeply sexy. And I know you think so, too, because you look at him like he's dessert and you're starving."

Heat flooded her face. "Did you call for a reason?"

"Sorry, sorry, I'll stop." He laughed. "Would you mind if I photograph your cottage tomorrow? Ten-ish?"

With Steven, she'd learned this would mean ten thirty or eleven. "Don't be late," she said.

"Moi? Never."

With her phone stuffed in her pocket, she straightened the plastic deer fencing and returned the stakes and ties to the garage. She tied bungee cords over the garbage cans so that she could leave the door unlocked in case another storm swept through and Shania needed shelter.

At eleven thirty sharp the following day, Steven set a tripod in the center of the living room and LED soft lights around the edge. When he turned them on, they flooded the area, highlighting the dust on the coffee table that Gwen had failed to notice. She scurried to pull a rag from the laundry basket. When she returned, he was standing at the dining table, sorting a pile of shells she'd carried back from the beach. He arranged them into rows, a grid of slate-colored whelks interrupted by hollowed-out barnacles, a sand dollar, and a tiny crab claw. He placed a heart-shaped rock in the center. "There," he said.

"It looks like a meditation garden," she said.

He pointed across the room to the Sailor's Valentine. "I want to include

162

that in the pictures but it's hard to see from this angle. Can we take it off the wall?"

She removed it from its hook and handed it to him.

Under the light, the translucent shells looked even more fragile; the silk backdrop faded to a delicate pink. "From this angle, the shells don't look like intertwined hearts anymore," he said. "They're something else."

Gwen leaned in. "A whale fluke?"

"Or a seal's tail." Turning it over, he looked at the back of the frame. "Wow. Look at this."

She put down the cloth and took the piece in both hands. "*For Anna, ever thine, my love, 1875,*" she read aloud.

Steven met her eyes. "Anna," he said. "Doesn't legend say Anna Vale had a lover?"

"The story also says she had hair the color of the sea, eyes like the sky, and skin flecked with mica." She paused. "We know she existed, but the rest of the legend . . . who knows?"

The boards along the stairwell vibrated, barely audible, but Steven didn't appear to notice. He placed the mosaic on the bookshelf, propped against a row of books where it would be visible from the back of the room.

Standing at his shoulder, Gwen watched him check the image through the camera's preview screen. Even from a distance, it looked like the shells were moving, spiraling, pale pinks and blues twinkling. Steven nodded, satisfied, and pressed the button. When he checked his view screen, though, he frowned. He retook the picture.

"What's wrong?" Gwen asked as he repeated the exercise a third time.

Steven shifted the angle of the softbox light. "I'm getting a weird reflection," he said, staring once again through the lens. The camera clicked, and his frown deepened.

Gwen approached. "Can I take a look?"

He unscrewed the camera from the tripod. Enlarging the image on the screen, he pointed to the area near the Valentine. "There." A band of white light floated just above the bookcase, touching the octagonal frame. He scrolled through the rest. It was the same in each photograph, a prism hovering next to the mosaic.

Gwen recognized the stripe. The same phenomenon had appeared in the photographs the day she and her parents first met Periwinkle, a streak in the dormer windows.

"It's the Misses."

Steven rolled his eyes. "Oh come on. I love you but stay out of my shot!"

"Hey," Gwen said to the ceiling. "I'll put in another hot tub if y'all don't stop."

A loud crack in the attic joist made them both jump.

"Cats never do what you want, either," Steven said, an eye hidden behind the lens. The camera snapped once more. "Right." He sighed. "Let's see if I can do better if we switch vantage points."

They moved the equipment to face the porch, the ocean visible through the opened windows. Steven spent a long time trying to adjust for the sun's glare, but he was happy after he captured the first shot. "No ghosts," he announced.

They moved on to the kitchen. Steven gravitated toward the collection of rocks and feathers on the shelves and windowsills. He zoomed in for a close-up of a sage-green sea urchin. "God, the colors are incredible. And next to the dove-gray siding, wow. Love it."

The final shots were taken outside, with the camera at an angle to capture the ledge that dropped into the sea. The afternoon light gleamed on the damp rocks, the ocean beyond a startling shade of adamantine.

When he finished, she asked, "Can I see?"

"Of course." He handed her the camera.

In Steven's photographs, the shells on her table, the gull feather in the window, and the portrait of Miss Gilmore all looked enchanted. In spite of—or maybe because of—the white streak, the Sailor's Valentine glowed, ethereal. It presided over furnishings whose worn cushions and faded upholstery spoke of love and use. On the exterior, the tarnished shingles and the battered windows bore witness to a hundred years of storms, the cottage resolute and unmoving atop a granite foundation. "You see this place the way I do," she said.

Steven put a hand to his heart. "I'm flattered."

"Can I look at the rest?" she asked.

He nodded.

Clicking through his photographs, Gwen found libraries stuffed with books and old pottery, painted floors covered with braided rugs, and furniture scrubbed clean of paint. Old silver, weathered and dented, sat on kitchen shelves, and blackened woodstoves billowed smoke. Faded wallpaper and yellowed portraits filled walls, and driftwood crowded shelves. His images told a story she understood, a narrative of humans as custodians, temporary beings who lived on granite foundations destined to outlast them.

"These are wonderful," she said.

His face brightened. "Really?"

"Really."

"Jess thinks they're great. But, you know, he kind of has to. So please gush some more. My ego could use a little boost."

She smiled. "I especially love this one." The wide doors of an old boathouse opened onto a narrow cove, a tiny island visible on the horizon.

Steven put his hand to his heart. "God, that was a great place," he told her.

"Was?"

"They tore it down."

She pictured pine planks and shattered window frames in a heap on the ground. "What a loss," she said softly.

"Oh, hon, if I was that sad every time I saw an old house disappear, I'd never get out of bed. There's not much of a market for old ovens and pine paneling anymore. People want everything new."

In the following picture, an open closet revealed a child's red shoe, misshapen with wear, the buckle twisted. Gwen stopped breathing. Molly had worn a pair like this. One had remained behind on the rocks after the tide took the other.

Steven said, "I found that under a pile of schoolbooks."

She touched a finger to the screen. "There's a story here."

He smiled. "Why don't you write it?"

She started to tell him no, but the word stalled in her mouth. Instead, she heard herself say, "Can you email me these pictures?"

An hour later, her phone pinged. *Photos all sent,* Steven texted her with a happy-faced emoji. *Enjoy.* Gwen grabbed her computer and drove to town.

Unlike the clapboard homes that lined Main Street, the library was brick, a deep red punctuated by flat Georgian columns painted white. The cornerstone announced: *Est. 1862, Renovated 1992.* A handful of people sat on the steps, computers on their laps, their screens filled with images of gleaming cities, shiny cars, and shiny people.

Inside, a woman in a batik jumper read to a dozen toddlers in the children's section. At a long table, Gwen opened her email to find fourteen files, each stuffed with notes and images.

The first, labeled "Ashe House," opened with an image of a huge, late nineteenth century shingled residence stained an unusual dark brown, trim painted black. In the living room, the fireplace was covered in shells, some carved in bas-relief, and others actual mussels and clams cemented into place. The effect was clever, an archaeological record of fossils rising from floor to ceiling.

A close-up of the books in the study revealed a collection of architects' biographies and histories of architectural styles: Andrea Palladio and Robert Venturi, Stanford White and Charles McKim.

A nursery displayed wrought-iron beds, a small carrel, and a chalkboard in the corner—homeschooling old-style. Diaphanous curtains billowed, revealing the view all the way to Isle au Haut.

A picture of an attic stuffed with captains' chests and sheet-draped paintings followed. What Gwen wouldn't have given to look inside each latched box. She imagined old wedding dresses and veils, children's wooden toys, and embroidered linen sheets, all carefully stored in layers of tissue paper and never unpacked.

Who were the Ashes? she wondered.

At the research desk, she asked the librarian, who leaned on her elbows and nodded. "Let's check and see," she said. In the storage area, she unwound the library's compact shelves, revealing large cloth-bound volumes stored flat. "The records for that era will be here," she told Gwen. "Just leave the books on the desk when you're finished; I'll return them."

The faded ink on old deeds and newspapers told the story of the Ashes. Like many of their peers at the turn of the last century, they had been drawn to the peninsula for a summer experience that felt close to nature. Of course, that simplicity had only extended so far; they'd brought staff and supplies to ensure they could continue to live as they were accustomed—tea in the afternoon, dinners by candlelight at night. But unlike other summer playgrounds of the rich, Newport and Cape Cod, the Maine landscape wasn't as easily tamed, and the weather was far less predictable. Hence, they called themselves the "Rusticators."

Mrs. Ashe had designed the remarkable fireplace dominating the living room. An amateur archaeologist, she'd directed the workmen to copy details of her fossil collection and gathered the shells to affix to the chimney herself.

Port Anna attracts unconventional women, Gwen typed. She photocopied the most relevant passages and added them to the volumes spread across the library desk.

Steven's note told her the home had been replaced by a modernist building to house the new owners' impressive art collection. The loss made Gwen shake her head. This made her all the more intent upon describing the original Ashe home, a treasure of Arts and Crafts design, as if her words might return it to the living.

The next file was entitled "Monk's Cabin." A single caned chair sat before a rough-hewn desk. A small window opened onto a pond, the view partially obscured by branches, as if the inhabitants had wanted to remain hidden.

"I'm glad you're looking into this," the librarian said when she asked about the cabin. "Everyone else seems to have forgotten about our history."

The newspaper, published postmortem, confirmed that the shelter had been built to hide a disgraced priest. Hounded from his Augusta parish for a relationship with a married woman, the minister sought refuge in Port Anna. His detailed records of the natural world around him, found when his .

heirs went through his papers, became important documents for scientists studying plant life and climate in Maine. Gwen made a note to ask where these were stored.

The "In Town" file contained photographs of a Georgian two-story on Main Street, shaded by two ancient oak trees. Inside, the rooms were filled with Shaker furniture, the walls painted in shades of sage and cream, the windows without a single curtain. The photo of the child's shoe appeared in the middle, the red vibrant atop pale wood.

It took Gwen over an hour to locate the various owners and determine the renovation dates. The house had been a school when it was occupied by boarders, some as young as five. An advertisement in the paper extolled their *tried and true* teaching methods. Back then, corporal punishment was the norm. Gwen needed a walk around the building before she could continue.

All the homes Steven had photographed had been gutted or torn down, their contents shuffled off to the share-shed or the dump.

What had happened to that child's small shoe? The question felt urgent. She stopped walking, her mind whirring. She opened her phone and dialed. Steven listened as her words tumbled over one another, racing to the finish line. "This needs to be a book," she said.

TWENTY

AT THE CENTER OF A SMALL SLIVER OF LAND JUST ABOVE the high-water line, the tower rose as a solid mass, its walls pitted and salt-stained, battle-scarred in its defense against Maine's great enemies, the weather and the sea. In the lantern room at the top, the Fresnel lens rotated, both a beacon and a warning, ever moving.

When the lighthouse became a museum, tourists came to marvel at the intrepid who'd chosen to live on this tiny island, exposed to the mercurial moods of the Atlantic Ocean and cut off from the world for hours at a time. On the mainland side of the island, the sea withdrew every twelve hours, leaving the path exposed. On the other, facing open water, the ocean sloshed and heaved.

A sign posted onshore warned: *Check the Tide Schedule Before Crossing. The Water Will Rise as High as 14 Feet with Strong Currents. Swimming Is Prohibited. Please Note the Ferry Schedule Below.* The ferry, a pontoon boat that took fifteen minutes to cart twenty people two hundred yards, sometimes proved too frustrating for hot, impatient tourists. Every summer, a few ignored the warning and dove in. Sometimes, if the tide was high and the current strong, they never emerged.

In the empty parking lot, Gwen's heart beat erratically. She stepped out of her car when Steven pulled up beside her.

"You don't have to do this," he said.

"Yes, I do." *Yes, I do.* But her feet remained stubbornly stuck to the ground, refusing to move.

"Are you sure? I could go on alone."

"No, you can't," Gwen observed. He wore two backpacks, one attached to his chest, the other on his back, light poles in his hands. Gwen held on to the rest, bags of extension cords and light bulbs and several leather-bound books pulled from Periwinkle's shelves. The Misses had protested loudly until Gwen had sworn to return them unharmed.

She took a deep breath. "This is the only day it's closed to the public, and the tide is cooperating. We won't get another chance like this on a Monday for another month."

"Yeah," he said.

Boulders lined their route, damp and studded with barnacles. The old fear, long dormant, raised its head. She gritted her teeth and forced herself forward. "Let's go," she said. Seaweed, dark green and glossy, draped over the rocks as over the backs of small heads, faces buried in the sand. She swallowed bile and kept her eyes on her feet, choosing each step carefully. Although the tide was dead low, the rough path across the seafloor remained slick, the footing unsteady.

As they approached the island, a rock caught her toe, and she almost dropped the volumes cradled to her chest. *Stay calm, stay calm,* she repeated, inhaling slowly. Her shoes sank into the gravel, pulling her down, and, panic rising, she jumped the last few feet onto dry land. Despite the morning chill, a bead of sweat ran down her back.

Steven smiled at her. "You made it."

Gwen could only nod.

He forced the old skeleton key into the lock and shoved the door open. She exhaled as she felt the solid stone and plaster beneath her feet, the heavy thunk of the door as it closed.

Her eyebrows shot up as she registered the change in the almost unrecognizable room. The Doritos bags, beer cans, and the old futon were all gone.

So were the board games and the camp chairs. Any remnant of her behavior on that horrible day was now hidden beneath a heavy coat of white paint.

She put down the bags. It was colder inside, the thick stone holding on to the night air. As her hands found the pockets of her fleece, her fingers closed around a folded piece of paper she'd found squeezed into the screen door that morning. *I'm sorry I scared you, too.* Gwen had shoved it into her pocket on her way out.

The golden light of late summer crept through the high window, promising a warmth it didn't deliver. Gwen shivered. "The cottage has been freezing the past few mornings," she said. The seaweed had begun to fade, too, from a dark jade to straw.

Steven placed an oil lamp and several lengths of bleached rope on the central table. "It's always colder on the water. But don't worry; September is usually the nicest month. You have a little while before you'll really start to feel it."

"After all the years in North Carolina, my skin's too thin, I guess."

"You're worried about the winter."

"I am." She took a breath and said, "Hugh has offered his house."

Steven stood up abruptly, his silhouette haloed. "You can't be serious."

"Well, maybe?" She shifted her position to see his expression. "It's just for a few months. He has heat. And extra bedrooms."

He shook his head while he plugged an extension cord into the room's only outlet. The lights flickered and flashed, and his expression softened. "Hello there," he said.

"Anna? Or her father?" Gwen asked.

"I'd bet on Anna. She had more unfinished business." Steven turned to her, frowning. "Why would you want to be beholden to a guy like that?"

"Hugh doesn't expect anything," she said defensively.

"A man like that always expects something, Gwen."

"He's an old friend, and he offered me the use of his home. He told me himself, no strings attached."

"None that you're aware of."

"Why are you so hard on him?"

"You should ask Jess that question."

"Jess? What aren't you telling me?"

Steven bit his lower lip, uncharacteristically reticent. "Let's just say he has stories to tell."

"We all have stories. You don't get to be our age without them. Besides, it's not like I have a whole lot of options."

"Sure you do. You could stay with us."

"Steven, you are the kindest person I know. I really, really appreciate it, but I know you don't have room for one more thing." His photography equipment lived on the guest bed; the floor space was crammed with soft lights, umbrella diffusers, and lenses. "And there's the whole allergy situation," she added.

"Didn't Jess tell you he would insulate your walls?"

"Even if I said yes—which I won't, because you all have done me way too many favors already—I'd still need a woodstove, at minimum, if not a heat pump complete with ductwork. My pipes will freeze otherwise."

Steven shook his head as he set up the camera and tripod. "I hear you. I do. I wish there were another choice."

"I can't think of one. Can you?"

"Well, there's always Leandro . . ." His eyebrows lifted.

"I don't think so." Since the night on the sofa, Leandro had been working with his gallery in New York. He'd sent her random images of things, mostly cookies, glazed shortbread or chocolate chip. Yesterday, though, he'd texted a picture of a crack in the sidewalk and a single tiny flower, cornflower blue. "I barely know him."

"Too bad," Steven said. "He'd keep a bed nice and warm, I bet."

"For the millionth time," Gwen said, "I'm not interested." But she checked her phone anyway. Nothing from Leandro, but there was a new email from Michaela. *Would you be free to talk later? The position has been approved.*

She grinned, suddenly warmer.

Steven switched on the soft lamps, the white light mixing with the gold. Gwen ran her fingers down the wall, noting the texture, the bumps and ridges of the stone, the chisel marks still discernible beneath the paint. The blocks were cold, too, far colder than the air, as if they retained a vestige of the sea that had once washed over them.

Steven asked, "Can I have your books now?" He arranged them on the floor, an irregular, cantilevered pile. One volume, entitled *Hark, Hark the Sound*, leaned against the others, open to an illustration of a boat foundering at sea. The caption at the bottom of the image read: *Will no one rescue us?*

The camera clicked while Steven hummed softly. The room was utilitarian, almost barren, furnished only with a curved bed fitted to the wall and a long whitewashed table at the center. A black cast-iron woodstove sat in the corner.

He stepped away from the lens. "Let's ruffle it up a little. Make it look a bit more the way it did when the Vales lived here."

Gwen pulled down an edge of the gray-green comforter, exposing the tick mattress. "Does that help?"

He climbed halfway up the steps to look at the unmade bed beneath the window. The angle captured the loneliness of the job and the danger that lurked behind an expanse of unclouded sky.

Gwen pictured the lighthouse keeper at the table, hands busy mending ropes and lanterns; foul-weather gear spread out to dry, always waiting for the next shipwreck. When a boat foundered, volunteers rushed into the room, grabbing what they needed for the heavy wooden carts and dragging everything to the water. They cowered from the wind to strike the flint and light the rockets. With luck, the attached lines would strike the sinking vessel, and the sailors could pull themselves to shore. If a rocket landed on the water, the rescuers had to venture into the angry ocean, praying fingers and feet wouldn't go numb before they could save the stranded men, many of whom suffered from wounds and exposure. Sometimes, by the time they reached the lighthouse, only body warmth brought the hypothermic back to the living. It was said that Anna Vale had done this very thing to revive the man she loved. Yet how she'd hauled him to the lighthouse without help, wearing impossibly heavy gear, was a mystery.

Gwen said, "We need an old oilcloth."

Steven looked up. "Good idea. Do you think Ralph might have one?"

"Sure do, Gwennie," Mr. Drinkwater said when she called. "Come on down and get it."

She held her breath as she walked as quickly as she could across the wet stones to the parking lot. Mr. Drinkwater waited for her at the door of his condo in his slippers. He smiled toothlessly. "Knew this would come in handy one day," he said, handing her the coat, stained with use.

Gwen put it on. The sleeves reached her knuckles.

Mr. Drinkwater chuckled. "You'll have to grow into it, I guess."

Gwen thanked him, waving as she closed the car door. The jacket's scent filled the vehicle, a mixture of salt and oil and human sweat. The weight settled on her shoulders, the pressure comforting. Creases at the elbows molded to her arms. By the time she reached the lighthouse, she liked the feel of it. Somehow, it made the crossing easier. When Steven asked her to drape it over the end of the bed, the smell had settled on her clothing and hair.

Stepping out of camera range, she inhaled sharply. The photography lights had created shadows inside the coat that conjured a human presence, someone staring up at the window, sleepless, an arm thrown across the mattress, the other reaching for a lover's hand that would never come.

Steven hummed as he worked, the click of the camera a steady beat amplified by the rock walls.

They changed the position of the coat twice more, hooked across the back of a chair, draped on the stairs. Steven never lifted his eyes from the view screen.

After a half hour, he asked, "Would you take one of those lights to the lantern room?"

She carried the lamp up the narrow stairs that encircled the space, unlooping the extension cord behind her. The climb felt precarious, and she was vaguely dizzy by the time she reached the top. She pushed the light through the square opening onto the platform enclosing the lens and climbed up. Switching it on, she asked, "How's that?"

From below, Steven grunted, "Great."

She stood. The glass-enclosed space had a 360-degree view over the world, a stretch of fir trees, dark green and dense, on one side and the open ocean on the other. Port Anna's harbor sat to the south, a cluster of buildings and docks hugging the shoreline and boats bobbing on their moorings, a tiny settlement carved between forest and sea.

To the north, the ledge broke the expanse of water, small waves and eddies gathering around the thick mountain of granite just under the surface. This hazard was the reason for the lighthouse, a warning to sailors who misread their charts or whose boats had been blown off course.

From this vantage point, the steep drop-off at the edge of the island was hidden, the swirl of current and tide crashing into the rocks silenced.

Her breath fogged the thick glass window. A ferry chugged out of the harbor, its bow pointed toward Goose Island. A pair of common terns swooped past, headed out to sea. Up here, high above the ground, everything was visible, every boat, every storm. There would always be a warning when danger approached. Anna Vale had stood in this same spot, watching the horizon. For years she had done this, so patient. Only the daring knocked on her door, hoping for a glimpse of the woman said to be half sea witch.

A flash of red in the distance startled Gwen. A small figure was jumping across the exposed ledge, running toward the bend in the shore as if headed to Periwinkle. Gwen, startled, shouted, "Be careful," but her voice couldn't penetrate the thick glass. She pounded her palm on the window, but the sound went nowhere.

Steven appeared at the top of the steps. "What is going on?"

She stepped backward, dropping her hands. "Nothing."

He stared at her. "I don't believe you."

She took a breath. "If I tell you, you can't tell anyone else."

He made a cross over his heart. "I swear. Not even Jess."

She pointed. "It's Shania. The girl the cops were asking about in May."

He joined Gwen at the window. "I don't see anyone."

"She's gone into the woods."

"How do you know who it is?"

"Because I've seen her more than once."

"You're not serious." His face was lined with concern.

"I am."

"Have you told the authorities?"

"No." Gwen chewed a cuticle, eyes on the ledge.

"Someone is looking for her."

"There might be a good reason she ran away."

Beside her, Steven shifted from foot to foot. "Okay, granted. But listen to me: She shouldn't stay out there for too much longer. Think about it. Once the weather turns and the wind starts blowing . . ." He didn't need to finish. "Seriously, you have to tell someone. Social services. The sheriff's department."

Something closed in her chest at the mention of the sheriff, a word accompanied by sirens and screaming. "No," she said. She headed back downstairs, Steven following. "The sheriff won't help her. They'll pull some asshole move and scare her."

"Sometimes you have to be an asshole, especially with teenagers. What she's doing isn't safe."

"Other people live on their own in the woods. Your brother, for instance."

"He's a survivalist, Gwen. And he has a proper cabin, plus all the gear he needs to stay warm." Steven exhaled. "Honey, you can't leave her out there by herself. Think about it."

Gwen looked at the floor, trying to remember what she'd have wanted at fifteen.

"Also, hunting season starts up soon. Those folks go wherever the game is, and sometimes that's on public land. If she's living in the woods near here, it could be your land or it could belong to the Peninsula Conservancy. And, by the way, it doesn't really matter, I've seen men walk down your driveway in the off-season wearing camo, shotguns slung over one arm. You'd feel terrible if something happened. Call the cops. The local officers aren't bad, and they'll know what to do."

"I'll think about it," she said.

They packed up the equipment in silence. Gwen resisted the urge to run back up the steps and look for the girl again. She didn't want to incite another round of Steven's questions.

Once the tide lowered enough for passage, they slogged through the ankle-high water, holding lights and backpacks overhead, praying they wouldn't trip.

Steven kissed her cheek before climbing into his truck. "Thanks for your help," he said. "Now go call someone."

Gwen shivered, her sneakers filled with seawater. Back at the house, she hung the jacket on a peg in the kitchen. She half expected to find food missing from her cabinets again, but the peanut butter jar was still where she'd left it, and the candy drawer was untouched.

She put the leather-bound volumes on the table. The spine of *Hark, Hark the Sound* had come loose, the stitching frayed. She opened the cover and inspected the binding, wondering if superglue could repair it before the pages fell out. The mildewed paper and faded ink told a story of long winters in an unheated cabin.

Steven's warning returned. *You'd feel terrible if something happened.*

She picked up the phone.

But the sheriff didn't believe her. "Any chance you were seeing something?" he asked when she described the encounters.

Gwen exhaled, indignant. "Definitely not."

He sighed heavily, frustrated. "Lady, do you know how many crank calls we got about this back in May? Someone was certain they saw an alien spaceship carry her off, and someone else thought she'd seen her on a TV game show. I spent a whole day tailing a guy who was out with his niece, for God's sake." He chewed his dinner, smacking sounds audible through the speaker. "That girl is gone. Probably run off someplace."

Gwen's jaw tightened. "Shania. Her name is Shania."

"Yeah, right. Shania. Call us if you see her again, but my money's on New York City."

She was still annoyed when the phone rang, a Maine number on the screen. "Michaela," Gwen said, sitting up straight. "Thanks for the email."

"Listen, if you're still interested, we'd love to offer you the job in the guidance office."

"Oh," she said, deflated. Part of her had hoped that the board would reverse course and clear the way for the teaching job.

"Please don't tell me you've committed to something else."

"No. No. Sorry." A paycheck was a paycheck.

"Great. Come in on the Tuesday after Labor Day, and we'll show you the office and get your paperwork sorted."

"Would you mind if I continue to coach the kids who want help with essay writing?" Parker had sworn his friends would call, and the library had offered her the use of a conference room.

"Not at all. I'm sorry the other position didn't work out, but I'm glad you'd like to join the team. Aidan needs help."

Gwen paused. "Aidan Kemble? I thought he moved away."

"He commutes from Bangor. You know him?"

"I did. Years ago."

"Well, he'll be happy to see you."

Remembering their last encounter, Gwen wasn't so sure. She hung up with a sigh.

TWENTY-ONE

JUST BEFORE DUSK ON THE FRIDAY OF LABOR DAY WEEK-
end, Gwen sat in a line of vehicles inching toward the fairgrounds. Behind
a billboard advertising Mermaid Days, the top of a roller coaster crested the
tree line. Blue lights on the Ferris wheel winked between the branches, a
lighthouse warning of rocks ahead.

The fair would run until Monday, but Jess and Steven had sworn the first
night was the best—there was less trash on the ground, the rides were not yet
sticky with spilled soda, and a live band would play at eight.

"Leandro will be there," Steven had teased.

"Stop," she'd said. "I beg you."

The truck in front of her began honking at an old VW bug trying to
park in a bicycle-sized space. "Come on," the driver shouted, annoyed.
His companions, seated in the cargo bed, started yelling until the VW
driver gave up and banged a hard left into the driveway next door, where
a woman held out her hand for the ten-dollar charge to use her lawn as
a parking lot.

Gwen kept moving until she found a free spot and walked a quarter of a
mile to the entrance. Once through the entry tent, she stopped, overwhelmed.
The smell of popcorn and fried food thickened the air. Britney Spears and

Bruno Mars played at full volume, interrupted by calls to "step right up." A woman handed her an event pamphlet published by the *Port Anna Packet*, with *Mermaid Days!* printed in bold at the top. Gwen stuck it in her back pocket absentmindedly.

Carts rattled over the roller coaster's rickety tracks, and tweens screamed with joy, their arms in the air. Young men, voices raised with enthusiasm and too much beer, rolled past, headed to the booths that featured guns and targets. The *pop-pop-pop* punctured the rock and roll blaring from the luge slide and the pendulum drop.

"Hey, Gwen, over here," Jess shouted, waving. Soon he was at her side, Steven close behind.

Steven took her arm and pulled her forward. "Isn't it great?" he said.

Jess tilted his head in the direction of the beer tent. "Let's get in the spirit first."

Barkers shouted as they passed, encouraging them to take their places behind water pistols and basketball hoops. A round woman hugged an enormous pink bear to her chest, accompanied by a man with his arm wrapped tightly around her shoulders. Families clumped together in line for the Ferris wheel, the children carrying clouds of cotton candy on sticks.

Jess handed her a Miller High Life. "The champagne of beers," he said, touching the neck of his bottle to hers.

She tipped it back, the bubbly liquid tickling her throat.

"We have an itinerary," Steven said. "First the exhibit hall and then the skillet toss."

"The what?"

"Come on, you'll see."

They threaded through bodies bunched around ketchup-spotted picnic tables and a group of middle-aged women waiting for the restroom. A sign above the barn announced: *Maine-ly Goods*. Inside, they passed tables of candles and macramé, lacework and a collection of aprons in Christmas colors. Quilts hung from the rafters. At the back, in the agricultural section,

Jess lingered by the giant pumpkins. The winner, at 712 pounds, had a blue ribbon attached to its molten side. The sign beneath read *Kemble Family Farm*.

"Turns out I'll be working with Aidan," Gwen said. "We'll share an office."

Jess's eye twitched. "Tell him hi."

Steven took Jess's arm. They emerged from the barns beneath the grandstand.

"Let's sit up there." Steven pointed to the highest tier.

"Why not in front?"

Steven explained, already climbing, "One year a contestant released a skillet too early, and it went straight into the stands and took out a bench. Thank goodness no one was sitting in it."

"Seems a little dangerous."

"Oh, it is, my friend. Just you wait."

They found a trio of seats. A group of women lined up on the field, each with a ten-inch cast-iron pan. Some were dressed for this exercise in tees and sneakers, while others wore dresses and sandals as if they'd decided to sign up at the last minute.

"What do the men toss?" Gwen asked.

Steven laughed. "Oh, c'mon, you know men don't handle cookware. They watch."

The emcee announced the age categories: kittens, cats, and cougars. Gwen snorted.

The women approached the line one by one. Those with experience took practice swings before launching the skillet underhanded. Their pans arced through the air. Newbies, in contrast, tended to throw too close to the ground, burying the skillet in the sand.

Jess leaned toward Gwen, his arm on his husband's leg. "You should do this next year."

"Not on your life."

He grinned.

"Our next contestant is Michaela Vaughn," the emcee barked into his megaphone.

Gwen sat up.

"You got this, Ms. Vaughn," someone shouted from the stands.

Michaela hitched up her sleeves and took several steps backward. She let the skillet swing at her side a few times before running forward and launching the pan into the air. It landed an impressive forty-two feet from the throwing line. The crowd roared.

"Go, Michaela," Gwen said, genuinely impressed.

"She won last year, too," Steven said. "No one can top that."

They filed back down the wooden steps behind some chattering teenagers. "Man, that woman can throw," one of them said.

Jess tossed his beer bottle into the recycling bin. "It's just about time for the concert."

Steven turned to Gwen. "Classic rock, of course. Maine can't get enough of it."

On their way to the stage, Steven stopped for funnel cake. "I'm going to be paying for this for a month," he said, patting his stomach, but he took a big bite anyway. "Worth it."

Gwen followed suit. The hot grease burned her lips as she bit down, the dough dissolving in her mouth.

An announcement came over the audio system, "Ladies and gentlemen and children of all ages, welcome to the fifty-second celebration of Mermaid Days. Please give it up for our musical guests, our own local celebrities, Old Time Religion."

As the music started, the crowd moved as a single entity, a blob of humanity swept along by the beat.

"Hello there, Cookies." Leandro appeared at her elbow. The flashing lights of the go-cart ride behind him colored his pale hair green, red, green, red.

Jess shook his hand. "Good to see you, man," he said. "If I'd known you were back, I'd have offered you a ride."

"No need. I walked."

Gwen pulled her eyes away from him and took another bite. Sugar sprinkled down her front, sticking to her lip and chin. As she fumbled with her napkin, Leandro said, "Can I help?"

She handed him the plate and swatted at her front, sending a small cloud of white into the air.

"You missed some," he said, pointing at her face. "May I?"

He took the napkin and raised it to her mouth. When he touched her with it, a shock ran from her lip to her toes.

"There," he said, stepping back, and what was left of her funnel cake fell to the ground.

"Leandro," Steven said. "How was New York?"

Leandro stooped to pick up Gwen's lost treat. "Exciting, exhausting. The exhibit opened. There were dinners and people talking at me." He folded both plate and cake into a small package. "I'm glad to be home."

Steven's expression turned playful. "You were missed," he said, looking at Gwen.

Gwen's eyes widened. She stuck out her chin in silent warning.

Steven laughed and tugged on Jess's sleeve. "Come on, Jess, it's our song."

Once they left, Leandro turned his full attention to Gwen. "It is good to see you. I have thought of you often since we last saw each other."

"Thanks for the photos."

"My pleasure."

The band played an up-tempo version of the Rolling Stones' "You Can't Always Get What You Want." The dancers bounced as they shouted the lyrics. Leandro shifted his body as if he were longing to move, too.

Gwen said, "You don't have to wait here with me."

"Who else would I dance with?"

"I don't—"

"Dance. Yes, I know. So I will stand with you."

"Gwen?"

Gwen turned to find Michaela at her elbow. "Congratulations," she said, nodding toward Michaela's purse, where a miniature cast-iron pan labeled with a big number one was trying to escape.

Michaela laughed, stuffing it back in. "The kids think it's a hoot. Hey, well done on the story."

Gwen's forehead wrinkled. "Story?"

"Your piece about Anna. In the pamphlet. Didn't you get one?"

Gwen pulled it from her back pocket.

"Page two," Michaela told her.

The title was printed in bold at the top, "The Mermaid's Tale." Gwen blinked. Her story? *Her* story? "How . . . ?"

"So cool, right?" Michaela gushed. "Watch out, the editor of the *Port Anna Packet* is going to stalk you for more."

"I am so confused." It had been so long, she didn't recognize her own words.

Michaela patted her arm. "Gotta go now. My kids have moved on to the sobbing-hysterically part of the evening. But I'll see you on Tuesday."

Gwen nodded distractedly. Why had she written it that way, straight out of Brothers Grimm? *Long ago, far beyond the reach of living memory, the Gulf of Maine was a major highway leading to ports around the world, her waters so thick with sails that, on fine days, the horizon was hidden from view.*

Leandro said, "You are unhappy."

"This was written a long time ago."

He nodded, a small movement, barely perceptible. "Early efforts can be hard to revisit. Mine sit on a shelf where I can't see them."

As Gwen read, chewing her lip, Steven and Jess emerged from the scrum of sweating bodies.

"Well, that was something," Steven said.

Jess straightened. He mumbled something to Steven. "Hugh," he said, looking up. The group turned to find Hugh a few feet away, his attention laser-focused on Gwen and the paper in her hand.

Jess waved to them. "I'm headed to the beer tent."

Hugh spoke only to Gwen: "You saw?"

"My story? Yes."

"Crys insisted. I tracked down the journal—it's out of business, by the way—and let the *Packet* know there was no issue with reprinting; the copyright has expired. The editor was delighted."

"You did this?" Gwen asked.

"You're welcome," he said.

"But . . ." The granite shard buried deeply inside her chest worked itself loose. *Not good enough*, her undergraduate adviser had said. She felt utterly naked, skin stripped from her bones.

Leandro cleared his throat. "You published Gwen's story without her permission?"

"The publisher was defunct, and the *Packet* didn't ask." Hugh kept his eyes on Gwen. "I can't let your talent go to waste."

"But you also did not ask?" Leandro said, a note of warning in his voice.

Hugh turned to Leandro, smile gone. "Sometimes people need a little push."

Steven took a step backward. "Whoa," he said.

Leandro straightened his shoulders, his face dark. "Does she look like she wants pushing?"

"I'm *helping* her, asshole. This"—he pointed at the leaflet in Gwen's hand—"is what she should be doing."

"Ah. I see. You like to control, to make others do what you like rather than what they choose."

Hugh took a step forward. "I don't know who you are, prick, but this is none of your business."

Gwen put a hand on Leandro's arm, taking shallow breaths. People needed to stop looking at her. She said, "I know you meant well, Hugh. Thank you."

Leandro exhaled, exasperated.

"Hugh, hey, Uncle Hugh." Heather and her friends waved from the edge of the dancing crowd. They all wore cropped T-shirts and neon-laced sneakers, hair artfully disheveled. "Come on. Dance with us."

One of them raised her arms above her head and swayed her hips.

Hugh said to Gwen, "They polished off a bottle of tequila before we left the house, and I need to keep an eye on them. But don't worry; I'll check back in shortly." He disappeared into the crowd.

Steven touched her forearm. "You all right?"

"He's just trying to do me a favor." Everything felt distant, as if she were on the verge of floating away, lifted over the fairgrounds and to the lighthouse, where she stood vigil at the lantern window, Molly face down in the water below.

Leandro bent forward, his eyes on hers, and pulled her back into the present. "Breathe," he said.

Jess reappeared with another Miller Lite. He looked at their faces and took Steven by the arm. "We'll catch up with you two later," he said firmly.

Leandro said, "Perhaps I should also leave."

"No." Her voice was sharp. "I mean, please don't."

"I fear I am making you uncomfortable."

"No."

He pointed his beer toward Hugh's head, bobbing amid the sea of teenagers. "I am certainly making him uncomfortable."

"It's not like that."

"Of course it is."

"No," she said, stubbornly shaking her head. "He's an old friend."

"I do not think that is how he sees it, Cookies."

Anger spiked. "What would you know about it? You don't even know my name."

He stepped closer. His breath smelled of beer and something else, something sweet she couldn't place. "Your name," he said, "is Gwendolyn Shea Gilmore."

Her mouth opened.

"You are forty years old, recently of Chapel Hill, North Carolina. You are a writer who does not wish to make her art anymore. You tend to a garden.

You care about people, especially children. You worry that they will not be safe. You take care of your friends but not yourself. You love seals and birds and sand dollars, old houses, and rocks. You are afraid of strange noises but not of ghosts. You play chess badly. You like music, but you don't wish to dance. You love water but do not wish to swim. You hoard secrets. There is much more, and I would like to know."

She looked at the ground, trying to compose herself. "Anything else?" she said at last.

"You try very hard not to feel."

She exhaled a sharp burst. He was wrong about that. In the middle of the fucking fairgrounds, surrounded by strangers, she felt everything, every last thing, the granite shard slipping and sliding from rib to rib, slicing through her carefully erected barriers.

He pointed to the crowd again, forehead furrowed. "And that man, he sees a possession, not a person. A conquest."

She wanted to disagree, to say that Hugh didn't want her, but the words wouldn't come.

They stood there, nailed to the spot. The music wrapped around her, running over her skin, looking for a way in. He swayed ever so slightly. In response, her body softened. He placed both hands on her waist. His hips shifted from side to side and her legs responded. Her weight transferred from foot to foot, her knees liquid.

Without warning, the music stopped, replaced by the blare of a single voice: "Ladies and gentlemen, we are taking a short break, but never fear—we will be right back."

Leandro stepped backward. Her body buzzed.

Hugh emerged from the crowd. "Hey," he said. "The girls are ready to go. Half of them forgot sweaters. Would you like to come back for a drink?"

Leandro's eyes bored a hole in her, but he said nothing.

"No, thanks. I think I'll stay," she said.

Hugh paused, head tilted, as if he had something he wanted to add but changed his mind. "Right. I'll call you in the morning. C'mon, girls," he said, and headed toward the parking lot.

Gwen and Leandro remained silent until the band retook the stage. The silvery tones rolled across the grass like a concert just for them. In profile, deep lines etched his eyes and outlined his mouth. The white hair at his neckline looked so soft she wanted to press her mouth against it, feel the tickle on her upper lip.

"Red, red wine / Stay close to me," the leader singer crooned; the band played on.

Her hips moved, brushing his. Leandro pulled her closer.

His eyes were steady when he asked, "Cookies, would you like to go?"

She nodded, not trusting herself to speak.

They walked the quarter mile to her car. His scent filled the Subaru, and her chest tightened.

In Periwinkle's living room, she touched a match to the aged kindling in the fireplace. Within minutes, flames leaped, almost reaching the open flue. She turned toward him, every cell in her body jumping, each hair on end, so alive she could feel the blood rushing through her veins, pumping hard and fast.

He leaned in. "May I?"

"Oh God, yes."

His lips brushed hers. Goose bumps rose on her skin and rippled down her spine. He kissed her again and again, his tongue tasting of sugar.

When he pulled away, she reached for him, and it began once more.

He kissed her until she dissolved, utterly taken. Her hands found his chest, his waist, thick, firm; he caressed her back. She was melting and melting, dripping onto the floor. When his hand slid underneath the waistband of her jeans, she lost all cognitive function. Her skin burned, alight with him. His smell was on her hands, in her hair, in her lungs. She wanted to drown in it, disappear beneath the touch of this woodsy, solid man with the gentle, capable hands.

After a time, they moved to the bedroom. She stood at the foot of the bed facing him. He watched her, his eyes fastened on her face as she unbuttoned her shirt and shed her pants.

"Gwen," he said. He touched her.

Oh. The only word that would form. *Oh.*

The Misses gently closed the bedroom door.

TWENTY-TWO

IN THE MORNING, PRISMS OF LIGHT BOBBED ON THE
ceiling. "This is how I wake up every day," Gwen told Leandro. "The sun
dancing."

He stroked her arm. "Do you know why medieval churches adopted the
use of stained glass?"

She shook her head.

"It is a metaphor for God. As light passes through a colored window and
transforms what it touches, so God alters your soul." He placed a warm palm
on her chest.

She raised her face to his, running her hands over his back, down the swell
of his biceps, and the crest of his hip. Leandro was solidly built and broad, his
chest like a drum, so unlike Guy's cool, wiry frame. He touched her as if he
were playing an instrument. The hours disappeared in a miraculous jumble.
Skin to skin, they spoke of the sky and the clouds, the white-capped ocean,
their favorite books, colors of paint, and sea glass.

Eventually they got up to eat. He rummaged through her pantry and
freezer for several minutes. "Cookies," he said, "please tell me you eat more
than candy and peanut butter."

"Eggs," she said. "And toast."

He drove her car to the store for ingredients to make his specialty: curried shrimp and rice. As he beat olive oil into vinegar for salad dressing, the muscles of his forearm tensed and released like piano wires. He hated bottled dressing, he explained. "Vile stuff." He tipped the bowl in her direction. "You see how the oil emulsifies. This is also alchemy, no?"

Seated at the kitchen table, half-naked and wrapped in a blanket, she was sure it was the best salad she'd ever eaten.

———

ON MONDAY AFTERNOON, Labor Day, they sat on the ledge out front, shoulder to shoulder. The water shifted color as clouds passed overhead, silver to blue, gray, and navy. Driven by the wind, waves rose and fell, creased like corrugated metal.

"It reminds me of your paintings," Gwen said.

"My paintings." His face was thoughtful. "Many people assume that the alchemical process is magic, a miraculous change that arises from nothing. But that is not so. Alchemy also means destruction inflicted by fire and acid, compounds that utterly consume before they transform. It takes violence to create the elixir of life."

Gwen wrapped her sweater tightly around her torso.

"People do not like to consider that we hold so many contradictions inside. It takes a truth-teller, an artist, to reveal these things. Picasso once said, 'Art is the lie that makes us realize the truth.'"

She cocked her head. "What an interesting thought. That seems to me one of the differences between human experience and making art. We think we tell the truth, but what we say often conceals a lie." Guy had insisted, smiling, *I'm an open book, got nothing to hide.* And he was an oversharer—eagerly relating tales of youthful heartbreak and grad-school crushes—but the coldness at his center told another story.

Leandro turned to face her, his topaz eyes searching. "Tell me something true, Gwen," he said.

Gwen rested her chin on her knees. It took a few minutes to organize her thoughts. "I've always loved this place," she began. She spoke of her childhood, her adventures with Molly, crafting makeup of mussel shells and brick; of the family dog who dug up her mother's petunias, and the quest to find the fattest blackberries for jam. She told him how she held these memories too closely, so closely that people and places in her present often seemed unimportant or irrelevant. She ended with, "Part of me lives in the past."

He offered stories of his own, different from Gwen's. He described growing up in a large family, the constant bickering that disguised love, chess and soccer and other games, the meals his mother cooked, grilled plantains and chicken. Like Gwen, he'd lost his father—when he was a young man, living in London on an art scholarship. He couldn't afford a ticket for the funeral, and his brothers never forgave him. The truth, he told her, was that he could have found the money, but the fear of returning to a way of life he'd discarded kept him from trying. His career, his art, meant more to him than going home. "My art is more to me than anything else in this life."

He turned his hypnotic eyes to her. "I have accepted this ugliness about myself."

On the way back to the cottage, she picked the last of the summer heather. He ran a finger over the pale purple flowers. She took his wrist and held it to her mouth, feeling his pulse under her tongue.

Later, they lay entangled, watching the sun lower into the ocean. Her head was on his shoulder, nestled against the fold of his underarm. His hair smelled of the Maine woods, of fir and sea salt. She considered burying her nose in it.

He touched the streak of white at her temple. "Tell me about this," he said.

Deep inside of her, something unraveled, and, to her surprise, she told him everything, the whole terrible story: Molly bobbing in the water, the paramedics shoving at her tiny chest, her mother screaming, *How could you?* The morning after, she found the color drained from her hair—as if even her body blamed her for what had happened. When she finished, he held her in both arms. He said, "These are tears of love. So much love."

She wiped her face. "It's an old grief. It doesn't go away. Not really."

"It is the same, no? Love and grief. You cannot have one without the other."

She pulled his words in, gently holding them to her center. *Tears of love.* His heart beat in her ear, *thump, thump, thump,* so strong and steady, it seemed proof enough that broken things could be made whole again. He drifted into sleep, her arm across his body. His breathing deepened. From time to time, he made snuffing noises, and his fingers, wrapped around her waist, twitched, tickling.

Gwen closed her eyes, too. Her dreams were filled with blue: azure, turquoise, and aqua. Her fingers reached out, plunging into the shimmering mass, but it was too insubstantial and weightless, and she couldn't grasp it—not even the darkest shade of navy.

A crow's cry outside her window shook her from sleep. She opened her eyes to a moonless night. It was late, well into the witching hours. The bird called a wretched *caw* that sounded like a summons. She slid from the warm bed, shivering as she put on her bathrobe. Careful not to disturb Leandro, she opened the bedroom door. The handle clicked softly as she closed it behind her.

When she peered through the living room window, the crow looked at her. It sat on the porch railing, head twitching, lifting one claw and then the other.

Behind Gwen's back, someone sniffed. Gwen whipped around, startled.

Sitting on the couch, her shoulders hunched, Shania said, "I'm sorry if I woke you." Her voice sounded heartbreakingly young.

Gwen raised a palm to her mouth. She'd imagined this encounter so many times, but now she couldn't remember what she'd planned to say.

Shania wrapped her arms around her belly. "It was cold."

This broke the swirl of competing thoughts running through Gwen's brain. *How did she get in? Who should I call?* yielded to *She's freezing.* Gwen crossed the room, shifted the fire screen, and poked the cinders until an ember caught. She added wood, and the room warmed. "Better?" she asked.

Shania nodded. Stringy black hair fell out of the hood. She had a smudge on her cheek, and her lips were chapped.

Gwen sat on the edge of a chair facing the girl. "Are you hungry?"

Shania nodded again.

In the kitchen, Gwen pulled the remains of the dinner Leandro had made from the fridge and stuck it in the microwave, pulling it out before the machine could beep. When she returned to the living room with the tray, Shania was sitting next to the fire, her hands extended, the cuticles raw.

"Here," Gwen said. "Shrimp curry."

The girl's eyes widened. She ate hunched over, her face half-hidden by the hoodie. A miasma of DEET insect spray surrounded her.

Gwen waited. When the plate was emptied of food, the tray set on the floor, she asked, "How can I help you?"

"Help me?"

"The sheriff's department has been looking for you."

Shania's pinched features tightened. "Are they coming?"

"No." Gwen took a deep breath. "People must be worried."

Shania's jaw jutted forward, her eyes dark. "I'm not going back to Portland. I'm sick of foster care."

"But this is Maine. Bad things can happen out there." She gestured toward the woods.

"Bad things happen inside, too," Shania said.

"Sure." Gwen didn't want to imagine what this might mean. "But the weather is turning. It's going to get a lot worse. Frostbite, hypothermia, these things can kill you."

"I can take care of myself."

"Yes, you can. Wouldn't it be nicer to take care of yourself someplace warm, though?"

The bedroom door opened with a click, and Shania froze. Leandro stood in the threshold, wearing only sweatpants. "Ah, you have a visitor. Apologies."

Shania looked at Gwen, bewildered. "You live alone," she said, her tone an accusation.

"No. I mean, yes, that's just—"

Shania jumped to her feet. She ran to the door, yanked it open, and hurled herself down the porch steps toward the water. Just before the berm, she turned right, disappearing into the woods. Gwen called Shania's name into the night air until she realized it was useless.

Leandro put a hand on her arm. "That is the missing girl, yes?"

Gwen wrapped her bathrobe tightly around her body. "What do I do? Should I go after her?"

He shook his head. "No, let her be." He closed the door.

"She was hungry." Gwen pointed to the tray, the plate scraped clean.

"Yes, I am sure she is. Both cold and hungry. But you cannot force her to come in. You have to trust that she will do what she thinks is best. Come back to bed."

But Gwen stood at the door, her arms wrapped around herself, staring into the woods. A single question looped through her brain: *What if she doesn't?*

TWENTY-THREE

SLEEP PROVED ELUSIVE. EVERY SOUND LEANDRO MADE jerked Gwen into consciousness. Images of storms, trees falling, and silent hunters played on a loop, causing her heart to race. She tossed and turned and stared at the ceiling until her brain at last timed out, exhausted. When the alarm buzzed just before sunrise, it sent a shock wave through the room.

For the next twenty minutes, Leandro watched her run back and forth between the kitchen and the closet, shoveling toast in her mouth and gulping coffee. She'd made elaborate plans to steam out her clothes and buff her suede flats over the weekend, but none of that had happened because she'd spent the weekend in bed.

Leandro pushed his hair away from his forehead and pulled on his sweater. "Cookies," he said, "I thought today was an orientation."

"But I want to make a good impression," she said, buttoning her skirt. The waistband was loose, sitting too low on her hips, the hem below her knees. She should have taken it in, but it was too late now. "I want to look professional."

He grabbed her hand and pulled her toward him. "You look wonderful."

"I'll call you when I'm on my way home," she said.

He shook his head. "I'll be on a plane this afternoon. I'm off to Chicago today."

"Chicago?"

"And then Los Angeles. I have work in two group shows opening this month. There are meals and lectures. The gallery has also arranged a few site visits for commissions. One is in Toronto, and I cannot remember the others."

She pulled back. "Why didn't you mention this before?"

"We had other things to talk about."

But, her brain sputtered.

He said softly, "I did tell you that my work is at the center of my life."

"When will you be back?" She tried to keep the pique out of her voice.

"Not for a while, I am afraid. You are upset."

"Well . . ." She flapped her arms, at a loss for words. What had she thought? That the weekend would stretch into eternity? She looked at her feet. There was a spot on her shoe, and she'd forgotten to shave her legs. How the fuck had she let this happen?

"This changes nothing. I will return, and I will call you when I can."

This changes everything. "Of course," she said, and kissed him goodbye.

———

ON THE ROAD to Ellsworth, she gritted her teeth so hard her jaw ached. She'd vowed not to become attached again. She lectured herself: It was ridiculous to get this worked up over a three-day . . . Her mind stalled over what to call it. A fling? An affair? How had she developed these feelings so quickly?

She entered the parking lot behind a line of school buses. Students streamed from the opened doors into the building. She wiped her face and straightened her jacket. Time to get to work; she could feel sorry for herself later.

Michaela stood inside, greeting the students with "Welcome back," and

"Good to see you," and an occasional fist bump. They acknowledged her with chin raises and half smiles. A few muttered, monosyllabic.

"Gwen," Michaela shouted over the heads. "Do you know where you're going?"

Gwen shook her head.

Michaela pointed down the hall. "Room 180. That way."

Gwen followed the glassy-eyed crowd. When she spied *180*, she struggled to exit the herd, waiting for a break in the oncoming stream of bodies. Choosing her moment, she slipped quickly across the hall, careful not to disrupt the flow.

Aidan stood at a whiteboard, his back to her.

"Good morning," she said.

He turned. "Gwen." His blue eyes glanced at her before returning to his work.

"I'm so glad we'll be working together," she said. How had the young, openhearted boy she'd known become the resentful man in front of her?

"That way." He pointed. "There's a space you can use."

She stuck her head into the tiny, windowless room, the cement-block walls painted cream, the most soulless office she'd ever seen.

"And take this." He handed her a piece of paper.

"What's this?"

"All the kids who've signed up for some help with test-taking. I guess you made a good impression on Parker Drinkwater. I gather he told the kids you're a magician, whatever that means."

As she read the list, her mood lifted. There were fifteen names. It was a start. If they all asked for extra essay help, she might just survive the next few months.

"Don't get their hopes up."

"I'm sorry?"

"Don't make promises you can't keep."

Gwen couldn't decide how to respond. After a moment, she said, "I'm not leaving."

"Right." He turned away. "They're expecting you in the office. There's some paperwork, and you'll need a school email address."

"We'll be working together, Aidan. It would be great if we could start off on a good note."

He didn't turn around. "Who says we aren't?"

Gwen shut the office door behind her shaking her head.

———

MUCH LATER, CROSS-EYED from reading privacy policies and training modules, she followed the noise to the cafeteria. Once she was through the door, the noise was deafening. Trays clattered, chairs scraped, and students yelled. Michaela sat to the side, watching it all with amusement.

"They woke up," Gwen said, placing her meal on the table.

"Oh yes. Lunch is the escape valve for all that energy."

"It's infectious."

Michaela laughed. "These kids make me crazy sometimes, but you gotta love them."

Parker waved to them from his window seat.

Gwen said, "You sure do."

"How did you find Aidan?"

Gwen took a bite of salad and winced. Leandro was right, damn him. Bottled salad dressing sucked. "He's a bit . . . distant."

Michaela waited.

"He seems to think I'm planning on pulling out of here the second it gets hard."

"And will you?"

"This is my home now. Why is he so convinced I'm going to pull a runner?"

"Well, we've had some experience with transience recently. The pandemic brought a lot of folks from the city to the peninsula. They bought up every house and overwhelmed the schools. We had to hire more teachers, add desks, and so on, and then many left. It was a bit scary for those of us who've lived here our whole lives. City folks have different expectations. You should have seen the line outside my door. They wanted more AP classes and an honors program, things we can't afford to do. It pissed people off. And it underscored the locals' fear that our way of life is disappearing. Honestly, it was already happening before the pandemic: our kids don't stay in Maine after graduation, and jobs on the water are shrinking. Not all of that has to do with Covid—a lot of that momentum began before then—but change is coming awfully fast." Michaela shrugged. "And Aidan does have something of a chip on his shoulder."

"Oh?"

"Divorce, the wife kept the dog. You know the drill."

The bell interrupted their conversation. Michaela shooed stragglers from the lunch tables, waving to the cafeteria staff on her way out.

Gwen went back to the office. Aidan was gone, leaving sandwich crusts and a half-empty bottle of Diet Coke on his desk. She put a sticky note on his computer screen, *See you tomorrow*. On her way out, she thumbtacked a notice offering essay-writing help on the bulletin board below all the college recruitment posters. The halls were eerily quiet as she walked out the door, her heels tapping the tile.

She kicked off her shoes as soon as she walked into the empty kitchen. At four thirty in the afternoon, the shadows were already long, stretching across the narrow lawn and reaching into the living room. She stood at the window, feeling the warmth on her feet and calves and trying to decide what to do next. Solitude had been her friend these past few months and yet, in one weekend, it had turned into a stranger.

Just before bed, Leandro texted her. *Chicago is dreary and overcast but the lake is beautiful, a milky blue-gray.*

It was sunny today, she typed. *How was your flight?*

It was long, and I need some sleep. But before, tell me one true thing.

Gwen stared at the sentence. Her first thought was, *I miss you*, but she couldn't say that. Instead, she wrote, *Bottled dressing is truly terrible.*

Indeed it is, Cookies, he responded.

Gwen woke to frost on the windowpane. The last perennials in her flower beds were shriveled, the leaves curled. Before school, she cut them all back and added a layer of mulch to keep the roots warm.

In the afternoon, she trekked into the woods with more groceries and wool socks. Inside the bin, she found a note. *Thanks for the shrimp. It was really good. Any banana bread to spare?*

To Steven, Gwen texted, *Are you baking this week?*

A few minutes later, three emoji bananas appeared.

Gwen wrote to Shania. *I think I could part with a loaf.*

Later that evening, Leandro sent a photograph of the installation in Chicago, a huge white room filled with his ocean paintings. The silvery patina on the panels made them look like daguerreotypes, ancient and mysterious. The critics loved them, he told her. Every piece sold.

Once again, he ended the exchange with *Tell me one true thing.*

The sun looks like a giant orange orb exploding on the water, she wrote.

He returned with *Thank you.*

Over the next few days, fall settled in, cold burrowing into the ground. After school, she took more warm clothes, a loaf of Steven's banana bread, a tarp, and a heavy-duty sleeping bag from the L.L.Bean outlet to Shania's bin.

A murder of crows has adopted me, Shania had written. *Ever since I fed them pretzels, they bring me things. Missing any buttons?*

Gwen chuckled all the way back to the cottage.

Resting her feet on the hearth, she inspected the damaged book she'd taken to the lighthouse. Bracing the front and back boards of the fragile binding between her thighs to reduce any stress on the spine, she carefully opened *Hark, Hark the Sound.* She slowly turned the pages, quire by quire, to locate the one that had come loose. She found it toward the back. As she peered at the damage, yellowed papers, brittle with age, slid into her lap.

Written in Miss Gilmore's loopy hand, the letter was addressed to *Esther Hall, Department of History, Bryn Mawr College. July 1924.*

Dearest Esther,

The most extraordinary thing happened this morning and I confess that I am at a loss how to describe it. Nevertheless, I shall try to capture the details although I fear I shall fail to convey the import. As I dug in the dirt below the cottage steps—you know how the winter damages the flower beds—a man emerged from the woods beside the house, bedraggled, unshorn, his clothes filthy. I confess that my heart stopped when I saw him. In fact, his appearance was so unkempt and wild that I feared he wished to do us harm. My heart ran in every direction, and I stumbled as I got to my feet. Yet, when he spoke, his voice was so gentle, so soft, that my terror-filled imaginings dropped away. He held out a package. He said that he wished for me to take it, to keep this item, something very precious to him. He said that he did not have long. (Truly, his gaunt face and vivid coloring suggested he might be right.) "I have lived on borrowed time ever since she pulled me out anyway," he said. I asked his name as I took the bag from his hands. "Alexander," he told me, although he added that whatever others had called him in his youth had long ago ceased to mean anything to him. "I was a sailor once," he said. I looked at him, the weather-beaten face, the speckled arms, gnarled hands, and saw he told the truth. "What if you wish to reclaim your property?" I asked. His eyes drifted out to sea, clouded. "Miss," he said, "I will not. She's never coming back." He pointed to the box I held in my arms. "Keep it in memory of the love I had for her. For my dearest Anna Vale." Then he turned and walked back into the woods. I thought at first that I should follow but when I stepped from the ledge into the pine trees, I could no longer see or hear him. He left no footprints and no path. It was as if the trees had swallowed him whole. We opened the package when Judith returned from the store. Under layers of brown paper and cotton batting, we found a framed mosaic, an image of a heart crafted of shells, pink and coral and pale blue. It is a beautiful thing, truly, made with great skill.

The next few lines were illegible, the ink smeared.

. . . this object confers a blessing upon us, and upon our house. I am at
a loss, overwhelmed by the gesture, and by the magnitude of the gift.
We followed our hearts to this little village, in search of a place where we
could be together, live undisturbed. Judith had of course read your piece
and, convinced that a town named for a woman would demonstrate a
greater understanding of love's many manifestations than Philadelphia
society, persuaded me to drive for hours until we reached Port Anna.
You told me once that . . . [illegible] . . . Anna was no legend.

The letter ended abruptly, without Miss Gilmore's signature.

Gwen sat back in her chair. *Esther Hall.* Professor Hall's work on the history
of Downeast Maine had been a resource when Gwen wrote her short story
about Anna Vale. Hall had been the first and, for a while, the only historian
to take the legend seriously. Before 1920, everyone had dismissed it as a fairy
tale, a figment of popular imagination. Hall, the contrarian, had stubbornly
traced every mention of Anna, wading through mildewed archives, town
records, and musty newspapers to prove that she had been real and that she
had worked as a lifesaver and lighthouse keeper from roughly 1865 until 1880.

But Hall never established what had happened to Anna or why she vanished. Legend maintained that the man she'd rescued from a raging ocean,
her great love, left her to seek his fortune.

The letter Gwen held in her hands provided the only firsthand evidence
that he, too, had existed, returning to find her some years later. Judging from
the date at the top, he must have lived in the woods for a very long time,
surviving on whatever he found or killed, half-feral.

Gwen looked at the octagonal frame hanging on the wall. The shells caught
the firelight, glowing opaline. No wonder the Misses hovered nearby. The
Valentine was a testament to the beauty and fragility of human love.

She texted Steven. *Call me! I've found something amazing for the book.*

Waiting for his response, she held the letter to the light. In the illegible passages, drops of water had smeared the ink and buckled the paper. She tilted the pages right and left, looking for clues, depressions in the fibers that might reveal the missing lines of text, but the brittle paper, folded for so long, began to tear in the creases. When she placed the letter on the table, hastily refolding it to prevent further damage, there were caramel-colored smudges in the margins where Gwen's fingertips had already stained the antique pages.

TWENTY-FOUR

THROUGHOUT THE MONTH OF SEPTEMBER, THE PENIN-
sula erupted in a riot of color. Vermilion and canary-yellow leaves clung to the
branches, and mosses developed shades of mustard and brown. Blueberry bar-
rens, their fruit harvested, turned scarlet. Walking through the woods, Gwen
plucked golden chanterelles—miraculously blooming long past season—and
stooped to admire ruby-red toadstools. Clamshells emerged from clumps of
silvery grass, bleached blue-white. She stuffed these in her pockets, adding
them to the grid Steven had left on her dining room table.

The crows appeared as soon as she approached Shania's bin. *Caw,* they
warned, flapping their obsidian wings. *Someone's here.* Shania remained out of
sight, leaving handfuls of notes in the empty tub. Gwen brought them home
to read, spreading the array of intellectual delights across the kitchen table.

If you squeeze an earth-ball, it puffs a cloud of spores into the air.

*My crow family has two parents and two children, a perfect quartet. They all
defer to the mom, who follows me around like she's worried. Last week, they told
me a coyote was near, screeching until I stood up and chased it away.*

*The more leaves drop, the bigger the lichen grows on the tree bark. It spreads
across the raggedy surface and turns it pale gray.*

Ghost pipes have clustered roots that are covered in tiny hairs.

Everything provoked Shania's curiosity. Gwen added to the bin a volume from the used shelf at the bookstore: *Wild Plants of Maine: A Useful Guide.*

In return, Shania thanked her and asked for oatmeal and a second pair of gloves if she had any extras. Gwen gave up her own and wore her father's instead.

Gwen kept expecting a late-night visit or a request for shelter. But Shania didn't emerge, and, following Leandro's advice, she didn't ask. Not even when the temperature dipped again, and ice began to form on top of water puddles.

When Hugh called the first week in October, Gwen wore her polar fleece in the kitchen, her hands wrapped around a mug of hot coffee.

"Gwennie," he said. "How are you?"

"Okay," she responded, but she couldn't keep the shiver out of her voice.

"It sounds like it's getting chilly already. It's been beautiful here in Boston, sixties and sunny, but it's always a little cooler up north."

She poured more coffee into her cup. It was going to get so much worse, and she was so unprepared. The cord of firewood grew smaller every day.

"Look, I told the caretaker at Ayr-y-Lee to turn the heat on. There's a key waiting for you. You can go anytime."

"Thank you."

"Seriously, Gwen. Don't wait until your pipes freeze. The temperature will drop for real pretty soon."

She squinted at the thermometer out the kitchen window. Thirty-three degrees. *Shit.* She dumped the rest of her coffee down the sink.

That afternoon, she bought another plastic bin at Marden's and filled it with food, another blanket, and a camp stove she found in the laundry room. Just before she snapped it shut, she added her mother's well-thumbed *Birds of New England.* She wrote: *I closed the house for the winter, but I left the garage open. Leave a message, and I'll bring you whatever you need. If there's an emergency, talk to Mrs. Condon at the end of the lane. She'll help you.*

The path through the woods was harder to find through fallen leaves and pine needles. Submerged roots and rocks constantly conspired to trip her or twist an ankle. It was a relief to dump the heavy load in the clearing.

The bracken beneath the oak tree had turned a shade of butterscotch. She knelt to take a picture for Leandro. He would admire the tangle of stems and the curling yellow foliage. On her way back, she retrieved maple leaves from the forest floor. When she held them to the light, their fragile veins and capillaries looked like frozen rivers reaching for the sea. Soon the color would fade and the leaves would crumble. Like everything else that lived in the Maine woods, you either hibernated or died.

The thought brought her to a dead stop. An image of Shania's neatly stacked belongings arose, encircled by a family of crows in mourning.

Gwen turned around and hurried back. Reopening one of the bins, she added: *Please don't stay out here if you're miserable, we can figure something out.*

It took a few days to ready the cottage for the winter, stripping beds, folding towels, and closing the shutters. She carried her suitcases to the car while the Misses shook the rafters and slammed doors. No matter how much she reassured them that she wasn't leaving, they didn't believe her. When she unplugged the fridge, they retreated into sullen silence. "See you soon," she said aloud, forcing her key into the salted bolt. "I promise."

On the way to Hugh's house, she called Jess and asked him to drain the pipes. "Sure," he said. He didn't ask where she was going because—she realized—Steven must have already told him after their conversation at the lighthouse.

As promised, Ayr-y-Lee was unlocked, a set of keys on the front hall table atop the stack of pamphlets, her story printed on page two. A note from Hugh read *I had some extra copies made for you.* She held them to her chest as she walked upstairs.

She chose a bedroom at the end of the hallway, far from Hugh's. Feet curled underneath her, she sat at the convex window watching a working tug replacing the mooring balls with winter sticks that would not shatter if the bay froze. By the end of the day, the harbor bristled with them.

The water looks like a porcupine's back, she told Leandro, who was in Cleveland, meeting with curators.

In the evening, she took a warm bath, her toes stretched out in the long tub, bubbles floating into the scented air. Wrapped in a bathrobe, she sat in the living room, reading and editing her notes for Steven's book. No soft murmurs brushed the walls. No doors slammed. The house was a warm cocoon, the rugs plush, the comforters thick. The windows were so tight she couldn't even hear the wind. In the muffled silence, she stayed at her screen long after the sun set.

Over the next few weeks, Steven's book came into focus. She crafted a narrative that intersected with Steven's photographs. Together, these became a study of lost spaces and histories, ghost stories haunted by memory. Miss Gilmore's letter to Esther Hall—now carefully encased in a plastic sleeve—was the centerpiece.

With Steven's permission, she wrote to a New York agent she knew, a former colleague who had wisely ditched academia long before Gwen.

Words consume me, she told Leandro when he asked for *one true thing*.

Yes, he responded. *Art demands every ounce of your attention.*

In mid-October, the agent wrote back: *We're interested.* Gwen emailed a huge file with three chapters and two dozen images attached.

To celebrate, Gwen went to the bookstore. Pearl sat at her desk, peering at a computer screen through thick reading glasses.

Gwen asked, "Anything new?"

Pearl waved a hand at the shelf nearest the register. "Those came in last week. I'm told the biography is quite good, but I haven't read it yet."

Gwen flipped the volume over to read the reviews.

"Did the *Packet* reach you?" Pearl asked.

Gwen pulled out her phone but saw no unknown Maine numbers.

"The editor stopped by recently, asking me if I knew you. She liked the piece you wrote about Anna Vale, the one that was published for the fair, and wanted to talk to you about some more work."

"Really? Wow."

"That's what she said. Anyway, I told her how to get in touch. If she hasn't called yet, you might try her."

With the recommended biography in hand, Gwen returned to her car.

Gwen took out her phone and dialed. The *Packet's* editor picked up on the first ring. "I'm so glad you called," she said. "I heard through the grapevine that you're working with Steven Bowditch on a book about some of the houses that have been torn down recently, and it gave me an idea. Would you be interested in a monthly series devoted to forgotten people on the peninsula? I'm thinking around five hundred to seven hundred words each?"

"Sure," Gwen said, smiling.

"That's great, because I already have a title. I'd like to call it 'Those Who Wander.'"

Gwen pictured pilgrims walking away from home and family to follow ancient routes. Or hermits heading into the wilderness who cut ties with those they loved, severed links to their communities and disappeared. It seemed both awful and admirable: losing everything to find the divine. Or maybe the wanderer felt they had no other option. Maine could hide those who wished to disappear.

"I'm thrilled at the opportunity," she said to the editor, already making a list of questions for the librarian.

Now she had more work than she could reasonably manage. None of it paid well, but it was interesting all the same. The hours after tutoring sessions were spent bent over her computer screen working and reworking sentences. She'd forgotten how much joy this could bring.

After she left Hugh's in the morning, the noise at school jolted her system. Voices filled the hallway, bouncing off the walls. Bells rang, lockers slammed, and feet pounded the tile as students ran to class. It took a while to readjust.

Parker passed her in the hall, his dark head above most of the others', always surrounded by friends. He stopped by the office to ensure his transcripts had been mailed, but since he'd already finished his essays, he didn't book appointments with Gwen. Instead, he referred his friends.

"Parker made us," they said, eyeing her warily. "He said to ask you about what's buried in your yard?"

"Ah yes, about that," she said, dropping her voice. "You don't plan to miss any deadlines, do you?"

They giggled. "No, ma'am."

"Okay, then. See you Saturday at the library."

Many took longer to coach than Parker had. It could take a week before they landed upon a subject they enjoyed or were at least willing to explore in a thousand words or less. Some chose topics related to the sea, lobstering, pulling mussels from slimy ropes, or scallops from mesh bags. Others wrote about the land, the task of organic farming in greenhouses without electricity, raising goats for milk, and selling produce at the summer farmers' markets. A few described internships at the Ellsworth Hospital, their trips abroad, or the challenge of belonging to an immigrant family in a state wary of strangers. One had lost her father to gun violence after one of his nights of drinking. The freshness and awkwardness of their voices followed her home.

She told Leandro, *The defining moments of our lives happen before we turn 18.*

So true, he wrote from Toronto.

In the third week of October, the agent Gwen had contacted sent a contract. She and Steven polished off a bottle of wine to celebrate, and Jess had to drive her back to Hugh's. He waited until she stepped through the front door, but he didn't come inside.

A few days later, the editor of the *Packet* called to rave about Gwen's first installment in the hermit series. "I think you struck a chord," she said. "When do you think we can see the next one?" Gwen couldn't stop smiling, even when she managed to spill half of her coffee on her blouse before work.

At school, Aidan remained aloof. In the first few weeks, she'd tried to rebuild their connection, certain they had something in common. She offered anecdotes, the fox she saw crossing the school lawn, an interesting piece she'd read in *The Atlantic*, and the accident that wiped out power to most of Port Anna—although she neglected to mention that it hadn't affected Hugh's house, since he had a generator. Aidan said little in response, and soon Gwen stopped trying. He nodded at her in the morning and mumbled a careful goodbye in the afternoon.

One Friday, though, he poked his head into her office. "They're calling for snow," he said. "Be careful driving."

"I will," she said, surprised.

"You didn't get much practice in North Carolina, I imagine."

"As soon as I saw a single flake, I went home. People are idiots behind the wheel down there."

"That's what I thought. Anyway, nice work with those kids. They're getting their applications in on time, and that's a first. Also, their essays are definitely improving."

Maybe their relationship was, too? She crossed her fingers. "Thanks," she said.

In the morning, she woke to a gray sky, gray water, and white ground. She stood before the living room's huge bay window and watched the flakes gently dust the lawn. When the sun came out, everything sparkled.

She wrote Leandro, *An inch of snow fell last night, and the ground is crusted with sugar.*

From JFK Airport, he texted back, *I hope to be home soon.*

The deliveries through the woods became challenging. The oilcloth coat kept her warm, but its weight made progress difficult. She felt like she carried an extra person on her back, a burden pushing her feet deeply into the cold, damp earth. After years of living in the South, Gwen didn't own snow boots, and her mother's galoshes had developed a leak. She returned to Hugh's with wet feet and a sour mood.

Her own discomfort led her to ask Shania, *How are you?* repeatedly. Despite all the layers of clothing she'd left for the girl, she couldn't imagine how Shania managed to stay warm. She pictured frostbitten ears and chapped fingers. *Please let me know when you're ready to come out of the cold.*

But Shania insisted all was well. *Saint Stylites lived on a column, and people sent him food in a basket. I guess I kind of live like that.*

Gwen looked up Saint Stylites at school. He'd climbed a pillar in 437 CE and remained there for thirty-seven years. Others followed, believing that the mortification of their bodies would ensure their salvation. Had Shania chosen exile to atone? Gwen had assumed she was running from something. But maybe she also had a voice that whispered, *How could you?* in her ear.

This idea gnawed at her all morning, and she arrived at lunch unsettled.

She found Michaela in the cafeteria, one eye on a table near the door. A lone boy dressed in black, eyes red-rimmed, hunched over his meal.

"I think there might be drugs in the house," Michaela said, her voice low. "The brother was arrested last week."

"Jesus." Gwen exhaled. "Poor kid."

"He's not the only one who's struggling. We have one student who came to us from an island offshore. She lost both her parents. Can you imagine? An island of literally twenty people, and two are shot, a third wounded? So far, she seems to be coping. But you never know. I might have to call social services."

Gwen chewed the inside of her cheek. She asked, "What about runaways? What do you do with them?"

"Depends. Sometimes they go back home. Most end up in foster care. However, if the kid is determined to stay on their own, nothing works. They just keep bolting. I'm licensed as a foster parent, but"—she shook her head—"once we had our own kids, I couldn't take the heartache anymore."

Gwen walked back to her office, a cloud of sadness following in her wake.

TWENTY-FIVE

BY THE END OF OCTOBER, THE CARS FILLED WITH LEAF peepers vanished, lines at the grocery store dwindled, and the road to Ellsworth emptied. Some mornings, Gwen had the whole route to school to herself.

No birds sang as she hiked to Shania's bins, many having migrated south. White light revealed shades of gray on tree trunks and granite, and overhead the branches wrote dark calligraphy in the sky. In the stillness, Gwen could hear her own heart beat.

It is beautiful out here now, Shania wrote. *The woods have been stripped to the bone. Like an old person when the skin is transparent and you can see into their soul.*

How did this fifteen-year-old know so much? It boggled the mind.

Hugh called. "I'll be there on Friday," he said. "It's the closing dinner at the Inn. My treat."

Another boozy dinner? She started to object when he added, "Jess and Steven are coming, too."

"I'd love to," she said to Hugh.

THE BUZZ OF conversation greeted them as they approached the dining room. On the way to the table, Hugh waved to a couple near the door and stopped to pat an older man on the shoulder.

"Headed back to Palm Beach soon?" Hugh asked.

Gwen waited awkwardly beside him, scanning the room for Jess and Steven. They nodded from the corner table, Steven's face tense.

The old man wiped his mouth. "The plane is coming on Monday."

"I'll see you on the water next summer, then."

Hugh took Gwen's elbow. As he steered her toward the corner, her eyes met Aidan's, seated at a nearby table. "I see the robber baron has returned," he said, scowling.

"Aidan." Hugh held out his hand.

Aidan made no move to take it. Hugh shifted to Aidan's dinner companion, an older woman. Her eyes switched anxiously between Aidan and Hugh. "Nice to see you, Mrs. Kemble," Hugh said.

"Don't talk to her," Aidan barked. A few diners turned in their direction.

Hugh returned his hand to his pants pocket. "Business is business, Aidan."

"And corporations are people, too. If we're talking in clichés, Hugh, then let's say, 'Boys will be boys,' and 'Assholes will be assholes.' None of those phrases excuse what you did, you piece of shit."

Hugh's hand tightened on Gwen's arm. "Let's go. Some people never grow up."

"Be very careful, Gwen," Aidan said as they walked away. "He's a viper."

Steven pulled out a chair for her. She sat as Jess thanked Hugh for the invitation. Hugh waved his hand. "It's nice to have old friends back together," he said. "Hope you saw your old 'buddy'"—Hugh made air quotes with his fingers—"over there. Jesus, has he got a chip on his shoulder."

Jess dropped his eyes, and Steven shifted in his seat.

"Hello, Mr. Fox." The waitress placed a martini in front of Hugh and passed out menus.

Hugh, engaged with the wine list, took a sip, seemingly unaware of his rudeness to the server. The rest of them studied their menus as if for an exam.

As soon as the waitress reappeared to take their order, Hugh said, "What would you recommend?" The relative merits of each dish ensued, followed by various wine pairings.

Gwen stopped listening and closed her menu.

Steven tapped her arm. He whispered, "The literary agent called when you were at school yesterday. An editor is interested."

She raised her eyebrows. "You're kidding."

"I think we should call it *The Lost House*."

Hugh lifted his gaze from the wine list. "What's this?"

Jess said, "Gwen and Steven are writing a book."

Hugh smiled, satisfied. "Another piece about mermaids?"

Gwen straightened, irritated. "It's nonfiction," she said. "Focused on the peninsula, some local homes and their histories. Steven's photographs are the inspiration."

"Really?" Hugh said, surprised.

"He takes pictures of houses," Gwen offered.

"I am aware. Janet uses them in her brochures. I just didn't realize he did this outside of business hours," Hugh said.

The waitress tapped her pencil to her pad, waiting for Hugh to decide. His eyes returned to the pages in front of him. "Well, then you'll want to photograph Ayr-y-Lee. It's a perfect example of Maine shingle style," he said. "Couldn't ask for better."

Steven and Gwen exchanged a glance. Steven said, "Maybe."

Jess cleared his throat.

Hugh snapped the wine list closed. "Great." He ordered a bottle of red and a glass of white. "The lady prefers it," he explained.

Gwen started to protest, "I'll drink whatever—" but Hugh cut her off with "Nonsense."

The appetizers arrived: carrot soup with shaved fennel, followed by steak for the men and halibut for Gwen. The sauce was creamy and buttery, fried shallots sprinkled on top.

In the awkward silence, Jess said to the table, "The *Farmers' Almanac* reports it will be a hard winter."

Hugh looked up. "You believe that?"

"They're usually right."

Gwen, relieved, said, "So it wasn't just me? It's been unusually chilly this fall?"

"Well, I wouldn't say that, necessarily," Jess said.

Steven offered, "She's not used to the cold yet. Give her a year and she'll be fine."

"Not if she stays in that house," Hugh said.

Beneath the table, Steven's leg bounced. Gwen couldn't think of anything else to say. The conversation felt mandated, everyone just trying to get through the hour.

Between bites, Hugh ran through his list of work for Jess over the coming months. He was particularly concerned about the seawall along the edge of his property. "But," he added, "wait until the ground freezes so the Bobcat won't damage the lawn."

Jess nodded.

"Once it snows, plow first thing after the storm. Gwen has to get to work."

"Yep."

They skipped dessert, Jess explaining he had an early morning. On the way out, Gwen glanced toward Aidan's table, breathing a sigh of relief when she saw it was empty.

In the parking lot, a brisk wind rattled the bare branches. Gwen stuffed her hands in her pockets. Steven and Jess both kissed her cheek as they said goodbye and thanked Hugh once more for the meal. They practically ran to the car.

At Ayr-y-Lee, she gratefully accepted a second glass of wine. Hugh stepped outside for wood.

Music played, piped through hidden speakers. All the songs dated to the nineties, the soundtrack of her high school years. She knew every lyric by heart. "Great playlist," she said as he placed logs on the grate. "Did you make it yourself?"

"All I listen to," he said. "Can't stand the new stuff."

He sat down next to her, his knee brushing hers. The crease down his pants leg was sharp, raised above his lean thigh, a mere inch from her faded black jeans. She carefully shifted to the edge of the sofa. He was so absorbed in his lecture about the rising price of Sheetrock and metal that he didn't notice.

He shook his head, bemoaning the falling work ethic of employees, and poured more into Gwen's glass. The silvery wine slipped down her throat. The fire popped and spat, embers breaking off, edges aglow. She smiled when she thought he expected her to, making noises of agreement, but his words all ran together. Hugh liked to make money, and everything had a price tag, from the cord of wood outside to the glass in her hand.

"A Zweifel enoteca series will set you back close to one hundred a stem," he told her.

"Ah." The word *enoteca* rolled from one end of her brain to the other.

"I'm boring you."

"No, you're not," she said, sitting up straight.

"Yes, I am." He set down his glass. "You're right, of course. It's late." He kissed her cheek and sauntered upstairs. She exhaled, relieved. Leandro had read the situation incorrectly; Hugh didn't want anything from her. This could have been the *one true thing* of the day, but it sounded too snarky to say, *I told you so*. Instead, she wrote: *The light was dark gold today*.

Still in Berlin, Leandro typed, *Ah, Maine*.

She had been meaning to ask when exactly he planned to return. Ever since she moved into Ayr-y-Lee, the memory of their weekend had drifted out to sea, pulled by an unseen current. She went for hours without thinking about him, his face blurry when she tried to call it up.

In the morning, she found Hugh in the kitchen, nursing an espresso. A pan soaked on the counter, bits of yellowed egg floating on top.

"I'm headed to Portland in an hour, but I'll be back a few days before

Thanksgiving. Would you like to drive to Boston with me for the holiday? Heather has decided she doesn't want to fly home and so my sister is coming east."

Gwen stuck a tiny cup beneath the machine's spout and pushed "brew." "That's so kind of you, but Steven and Jess already invited me."

"Too bad," he said, and returned to his iPad. If he was annoyed, it didn't show.

Liquid dribbled into her waiting mug. She blew on it as she opened her laptop and checked her email.

"I'm glad you're staying here," he said, breaking the silence. "I always worry something will happen when I'm not around. The caretaker only stops by once a week, and it's just not enough. Things can go wrong in a heartbeat in these old houses."

"This one feels pretty solid."

"I did a lot of work on it—replaced all the pipes and the wiring—but stuff happens. A true nor'easter can do a lot of damage."

Gwen had never experienced a nor'easter, but she'd read about them—the hurricane-force winds that ripped trees up by the roots and tore shutters from windows. Looking out the window toward the harbor, she said, "It seems pretty sheltered here."

"True." He added, "Not like your place. Your cottage takes storms on the chin. It's a miracle it's held up as well as it has."

Gwen focused on her computer screen. In between the junk mail, student requests for transcripts and test prep filled her inbox.

In her Gmail inbox, she found a message from the urgent care center, "Request for payment." She opened it and inhaled sharply.

"What is it?" Hugh said.

"Nothing," she said. *Shit, shit, shit.* The email said they'd sent her a bill weeks ago. She'd never seen it. Maybe it had gone to junk?

"Gwen?"

She smiled half-heartedly. "Everything's fine."

"Seriously, Gwen, you can tell me."

She looked at the screen, the big number floating at the bottom of the email. "It's the urgent care bill." The X-ray alone had cost several hundred dollars, the total close to three thousand dollars. *Three thousand!* Her stomach lurched. How much did she have left on her credit card?

"Let me help you."

She shook her head. "No, you're doing too much already."

"Gwen. I'm good with money."

"Oh, I know that."

"Tell me what you're doing with yours."

"What money?"

"Didn't your parents leave you anything?"

"My father's money disappeared when my mother entered the Alzheimer's unit."

"Anything left?"

"A little." She told him.

He whistled. "Other assets?"

She shook her head.

He leaned forward, elbows on his knees, hands clasped. "You have the house. The land."

"Periwinkle? You know that's not for sale."

"What I meant is, you could get a loan. A reverse mortgage, essentially."

"From a bank?"

He sat back. "Well, there's no need to involve an institution. They'll just suck you dry. I meant me. I could write a note and lend you the money. You can pay me back on your own schedule. I won't even charge you interest."

"Hugh, that is way too generous."

He waved a hand dismissively. "I've done it before."

"I don't know, Hugh." She chewed on the inside of her mouth, thinking. She heard her father's voice, *Friends shouldn't borrow money from friends.* But the number typed at the bottom of the hospital's email might as well be in flashing red neon lights. Why had she let Steven take her to urgent care in the first place?

"Think about it," he said. "Do some number-crunching and let me know if you'd like to proceed. No rush."

She swallowed. "That's a very generous offer, Hugh."

He brushed her hair behind her ear before kissing her cheek. "I'll see you in a few weeks," he said.

As his car pulled away, she picked at her sleeve, worrying at a thread that had come loose. The dynamic between them had changed, and she couldn't get a handle on it. Too antsy to work, she wandered around the house, looking out the windows.

The weather was worse today. The waves, white-tipped, broke on the pier. A seal lay on a rock in the middle of the harbor, its back sprinkled with snow, watching gulls glide overhead. The gusts of wind were so fierce that their wings strained, barely able to control their flight path.

She straightened the pillows in the living room and retrieved the wine-glasses from the coffee table. Hugh's pan still sat on the counter, unwashed. She pulled out a steel wool pad and scrubbed until it gleamed. Once the dishwasher started up, an alto hum, she had nothing left to clean. Still restless, she checked each room, remaking beds and checking the taps, until finally, in the midafternoon, she pulled on her hat and coat.

As soon as she stepped outside, the damp chill slipped inside her collar, seeking bare skin. *How long does it take to get used to this?* she wondered, tucking her chin. Her shoulders hunched to her ears, she walked toward the road.

The number on the medical bill nipped at her heels. She was cornered, and, at the moment, Hugh's offer was the only way out. A mortgage on Peri-winkle would give her a cushion. She could stop worrying, pay off her debt, and maybe even outfit the cottage for winter. The idea pulled at her. Money worries had weighed on her so much recently that it had become a sort of white noise, barely noticeable but always there, constant, grinding. To have thousands of dollars in the bank would silence it for good. The relief of that promise felt immense.

And yet. *And yet.* She'd owe Hugh. Really owe him.

She took a deep breath and considered the other side of the argument.

Hugh wanted to help. How many times had he said that in the past few months? Too many to count. *Why* was a little bit of a mystery. Maybe he saw the offer as amends for having witnessed her grief, a weird sort of reward. Because he'd seen it all, hadn't he? He had dared to stay with her, to try to comfort her even if there was none to be found. Throughout that whole summer, Jess had sworn, *I'll always be here for you*, and yet, when the worst had happened, Hugh was there. *Hugh*. Not Jess.

A truck carrying a load of salt flew past, spraying her pants with half-frozen mud. "Shit," she said. She'd planned to wear these to school this week, and now there would be a dry-cleaning bill.

She turned around, the sleet at her back. She was so sick of the fear, the mess, the dirt, the worries that dogged her every step. Hugh's offer could make it all go away. She could start over with a clean slate. The loan, she told herself, didn't need to cover Periwinkle's full value. Depending upon what it's worth, she could only mortgage part of it. She could pay him back quickly. She picked up the pace, a half jog.

When she returned to the house, breathless, cheeks shining with sleet and excitement, she texted him, *Okay. Thank you.*

He responded, *I'll have Janet draw up a contract.*

TWENTY-SIX

A FEW DAYS LATER, AS THE ESPRESSO MACHINE CHUGGED liquid nectar into the waiting cup, three messages lit up Gwen's phone, all from Mrs. Condon.

There's a strange truck parked out front, dear, she wrote.

This was followed by, I sent *Don up there to check it out.*

Then, *The guy says you sent him?*

Gwen shook off the morning's quiet and raced upstairs to put on some clothes. Once she was in the car, the Subaru's heater struggled to do its job, blasting lukewarm air at her face. "You must be hibernating, too," Gwen said, shivering. The steering wheel was so cold she pulled down the sleeves of her shirt to keep her hands warm. She parked behind a white truck in her driveway and stumbled toward the front of the house.

A man in an orange-and-yellow vest stood on her lawn, looking into the woods, a pencil in his mouth and surveyor's tape in his hands.

"Hello?" Gwen said.

He took the pencil from his mouth. "Hello," he said.

"Who are you?" she demanded.

He looked surprised. "Janet Riggs sent me to mark the boundaries. It won't take long. The last survey was a year ago, so I just have to double-check my work."

What the hell? "I own this land, and unless the town sent you, I don't need a survey."

"You do if you want a fair market price."

"And why would I need that?"

He looked at her like she was insane. "To sell it."

"Sell it?" Her brain began screaming, *What the fuck?*

"Lady"—he sighed—"Janet Riggs sent me out here because she's your Realtor."

Gwen's mouth fell open, rage choking her words. Finally, she sputtered, "She most certainly is not."

He raised his hands in resignation. "Look, I just do what I'm told by the person who pays my bills. She told me to come down here and survey your land. You need to take it up with her." He put his pencil back in his mouth and returned to his tape.

The Subaru's wheels spun as Gwen gunned the engine. She had never understood the expression "seeing red" before, not until now. She shouted at the driver in front of her, a blue-haired old woman taking her time making a right turn, and immediately felt guilty. It wasn't the woman's fault Janet Riggs was a motherfucker.

A white Lexus sat in the real estate lot. Gwen parked beside it and slammed the car door. The office was still locked, but Gwen pounded on the jamb until a dazed Steven appeared.

"Hi, Gwen," he said, unlocking. "Everything okay?"

"Is Janet here?"

"She just walked out, headed that way." He pointed toward the cars.

"Thanks," Gwen said, and ran back down the front steps.

"Hey," she shouted as Janet emerged from the back of the building. "Who the fuck told you to send a surveyor to my house?" Gwen's breath came out in puffs, clouds that bubbled and faded in the cold air.

Janet's smile remained in place, her lips carefully outlined in red. "Well, dear, Hugh tells me that you need an appraisal for a mortgage. I asked my guy to go out there as soon as possible."

Gwen blinked—*an appraisal.* Of course she needed an appraisal.

"Did Hugh not mention that to you?"

"No, I . . ." Her anger dissolved, replaced with confusion. She braced a hand on the Subaru to steady herself.

"This is all part of the process, dear." Janet's face was immobile, a mask of pleasant, ingratiating agreeability. "I guess Hugh forgot to mention that."

"I guess he did."

Janet patted Gwen's arm. "Well, you'll be glad we did it in the end. It will help with property valuation. Now, if you don't mind, I am off to Bangor."

Gwen moved away. "Of course," she said. "So sorry."

"No worries, dear."

"But wait," she said just before Janet shut the door. "Why was a survey done last year?"

Janet's smile stretched. "Last year?"

"The surveyor said he'd been out there last year."

"Ah, of course. I forgot. When the Peninsula Conservancy bought the land surrounding the lighthouse. It abuts yours, as I am sure you know. Now, I really do need to leave."

Gwen stood back, watching Janet drive off, head still awhirl. *You're an idiot*, she told herself. Hugh was trying to help, and she'd flown off the handle. The fading adrenaline left a metallic taste in her mouth.

"Gwen." Steven waved to her from the door. "You want to come inside? There's coffee."

"No, thanks." She didn't want to talk to Steven. He'd just think she was an idiot, too. Because she was. "I should get back. I have essays to read."

"Okay. Well, you probably shouldn't stand out there much longer without your coat. You're shivering."

Gwen looked down. Her knees were trembling. "I'm okay," she said, teeth clacking. The shaking continued all the way to Hugh's. Even after she got to school, wearing two extra layers, the pit of her belly still quivered as if it thought something was coming for her.

TWENTY-SEVEN

WITH THE APPROACH OF WINTER IMMINENT, TIME ITSELF seemed to slow. Herds of deer crossed the lawn without hurrying, nosing at the icy grass; chubby porcupines lumbered behind. Gwen found herself slowing, too. She stood at Hugh's bay windows for long stretches, watching sea smoke drift across the water and frost the trees. Swamp rose berries appeared on the shoreline, a pop of bright red against the slate-gray ocean, and in the harbor a thin crust of ice floated on the surface, bits of which slid together like pieces of a jigsaw puzzle. It was all far more beautiful than she could have imagined.

When she opened the front door to leave Ayr-y-Lee, though, her lungs tightened in protest. She cranked the car's heater to the highest setting, with little effect.

"Come on," she begged the slow-moving school buses at the edge of the parking lot, her breath clouding the windshield. She started to shiver. "Come on," she said again as the kids ambled across her path.

The car door rattled when she slammed it. "Sorry," she muttered. The Subaru might be old and cranky, but it had gotten her all the way to Maine in one piece. Trotting toward the school building, she tried to remember the last time she'd taken it in for service—a year at least, but it certainly could have been longer. After her mother died, her grief-scrambled brain hadn't done a great job of keeping track of details like that.

Her office felt overheated and stuffy, yet the warmth took a long time to reach her fingers and toes. By lunchtime, she had yet to remove her fleece jacket. She stood at the plate-glass window in the cafeteria at recess, watching the students play soccer and basketball in shirtsleeves. Parker's cheeks shone bright pink.

"Don't they ever get cold?" she asked Michaela.

"They're kids," Michaela said. "And it's probably thirty-five degrees outside. You're not sick, are you?"

"Not quite a Mainer yet."

"It can take a while to get used to it, I'm told," Michaela said. "Aidan tells me you're doing a great job. I wondered if you would be willing to come in an extra day a week and help with writing tutorials. Our learning specialist splits time between several area schools, and she's too busy to give us any more time."

Gwen smiled gratefully. "Of course. I'd love to." A paycheck was a paycheck.

"Great. I'll let HR know." Michaela squeezed Gwen's arm. "Maybe you'll warm up by the time you get in the car."

"Sadly, I think the car's the problem."

Throughout her afternoon appointments, Gwen fretted. Maybe the car just needed some fluids, like the windshield wipers. Or, and this seemed more plausible, she hadn't run the car quite long enough to warm the engine. It had been below twenty when she left Port Anna, after all.

On the way home, the temperature a balmy thirty-nine degrees, she turned away from Port Anna toward the Ellsworth waterfront, where rows of commercial warehouses and enormous shellfish tanks lined the river. Across the street, package stores alternated with offices serving the homeless and the addicted. A semi rumbled past, running the red light. Gwen kept driving, praying the heater would finally start to work. After a half hour, though, the vents still blew nothing but cold air. She pulled into the lot by the town dock to fiddle with the knobs. She turned them all down and then back up to high. This exercise had no effect. Maybe the system needed a reboot, like a computer. She turned everything off and waited.

The afternoon sun gleamed on the river, melting the morning's ice puzzles. She tucked her hands into her armpits. A pair of mallards swam upstream, unfazed by the temperature. The female shook her tail, briefly revealing the clever layer of down that prevented heat loss.

Gwen turned the car back on and returned to the main road, cold air blasting.

The mechanic at Port Anna Motors shook his head. "Something crawled under your hood," he told her. "Chewed some wires and left a mess behind."

"You mean, like a mouse?"

He shrugged. "Sure. Chipmunk, maybe."

A gust of wind whipped through the harbor. She gripped her arms to her chest. "What will it cost to fix it?"

"Have to check on the parts."

"Do you have a guess?"

His face twitched as he calculated. "Like to run you about five hundred," he said after a minute.

"Five hundred?" Her voice rose half an octave.

"Aye-yuh."

Maybe she could live without it. The commute was blessedly short. If she kept the vents turned off and wore a lot of clothes, it would be bearable.

The mechanic shrugged. "You could chance it, but there's no telling what other wires that rodent ate through. The damage could be pretty bad. I'd hate to see you stranded on the Ellsworth road in the snow."

Gwen nodded, defeated.

"We'll give you a call when we need you to bring the car in. We are a bit backed up right now."

"Thanks," she said to the mechanic. To the car, she said, "Shit," and smacked the steering wheel as if it could have prevented the animal from taking refuge inside the heating ducts. The hard plastic hurt her sore palm. It continued to throb as she turned into Hugh's driveway.

Once inside, she felt better, soothed by the silence and the effortless warmth. She sat at the kitchen table for an hour, toggling between bank accounts. No matter what she did to the numbers, there wasn't enough for a new car heater. Closing her eyes and praying some new idea would occur to her didn't change anything, either. Once again, it seemed Hugh's offer was the only logical way out.

She opened her computer and wrote, When can I sign?

An answer arrived fifteen minutes later. Anytime. I am glad, Gwen. You won't regret it. Her breath loosened, her gratitude overwhelming. Janet will bring the documents to the house tomorrow, and you can have your money by the end of the day.

Her burden lifted, she felt lighter, almost giddy. She went online to pay her urgent care bill. It would completely max out her credit card, but once the loan hit her account, she could pay off the balance. And replace the car's wiring. For the first time in years, she'd owe nothing. Her final celebratory act was a call to Jess.

"Let's winterize the cottage."

There was a pause on the line. "Are you sure? That's a nontrivial sum, Gwen."

"I'm sure."

At dusk, she opened a bottle of Hugh's chardonnay, one she pulled from the back of the fridge. "Cheers," she said, raising a glass to the approaching darkness. "It's good to have rich friends."

In the morning, Janet rang the doorbell. "Here you go," she said, passing over a brown envelope.

Gwen thanked her and started to shut the door.

"Hugh asked me to wait," she said, and stepped into the foyer.

"I can drop them off."

"Oh, it's no trouble." Janet followed her into the kitchen.

Gwen asked, "Would you like a coffee?"

"Goodness, no." She smiled. Her white teeth gleamed.

How does she do that? Gwen wondered. She must invest in whitening strips.

Gwen opened the envelope and pulled out a sheaf of papers.

"I'll get myself a glass of water," Janet said.

"Please, go ahead," Gwen said distractedly. A jumble of words and phrases she didn't recognize filled the pages. The clauses and subclauses led in circles, and her brain refused to follow. She had to restart at the top, chewing her lip to stay focused.

"Can I help you?" Janet stood at her shoulder.

"It says that the agreement ends in a year."

"Yes. But it is also renewable." She pointed to the bottom of the third page. "I believe Hugh mentioned that to you?"

"And what does 'Automatic Termination and Acceleration' mean?"

"Don't worry about that. That's only if you miss a payment, and that's not going to happen, is it?" Her red lips stretched across her face. "You are only repaying the principal, no interest at all. Hugh is a very generous man."

Gwen pointed at the bottom of the page. "It needs to be notarized."

Janet pulled a bag from the depths of her purse. She said, "That's what I'm here for." She held out a shiny silver pen and removed the cap. "You don't have anything to worry about."

Gwen took it and signed.

PART THREE

TWENTY-EIGHT

AT THE UPSCALE COFFEE SHOP IN ELLSWORTH, A TWENTY-something barista in a knit hat and a sweatshirt that read *The Maine Grind* slowly poured frothed milk into a waiting paper cup and drew a heart on the top. It was so artfully done that Gwen felt a little guilty forcing on a lid, foam oozing through the hole.

"Have a great day," Gwen said, opening the door, eager for her first sip of vanilla latte. It tasted like victory, like a flush bank account and friends who loved her. The treat glided down her throat, warmth blooming despite the curdling November chill in her car.

Aidan looked up and smiled when she stepped into the office. "You have a mustache."

"I've decided to stop shaving," she said, wiping her lip. A familiar glimmer of boyhood shone in his eyes as he chuckled. They hadn't had time to chat in almost a week. "How is your mum?"

He glowered. "That jackass completely spoiled our evening at the Inn. Mum insisted we leave, even though we always eat there for the closing dinner."

"That's too bad." She cocked her head. "I know Hugh's not easy, but he never used to bother you this much."

"It's a long story, Gwen." He shifted his attention back to the computer screen. "Just be careful."

What was there to be careful with? "Of course."

"And don't ever do any real estate deals with him."

"You think the school pays me enough to invest in real estate?" She put her coffee down on her desk.

Aidan was still talking. "And that fucking partner of his, Janet. She's just as bad as he is. She'd do anything to get her hands on waterfront property."

Gwen turned. "Wait. What did you say?"

He repeated himself.

"Is she in business with him?"

Aidan nodded. "Oh yes."

"I thought . . ." Her words stumbled. "Hugh said he just used her office when he wasn't in Boston."

"Nope. They are fully intertwined. They built the condos in town and the apartments on the Ellsworth road. I see her face all over the . . . well, it's not a restaurant anymore."

The hair rose on the back of her neck. "Your family's place?" On their way to Port Anna, her family had stopped there twice, back when Molly still sucked her thumb. Like all the other diners seated at picnic tables, they'd ordered steamed lobster, clams, and blueberry pies as big as her whole face. She'd met Aidan on the second visit, serious-faced, dragging a lobster car from the water. She'd grabbed the rope to help, pulling until the floating plastic bin surfaced with its cargo of blue-green creatures, squirming and alien.

"Not anymore. Not thanks to Hugh."

"Your family sold to Hugh?"

"No, we never sold. We worked with a bank, when the lobster market crashed in '08. Mum and her brother leveraged the property. It took a while, but things were coming back. Then the pandemic hit, and Mum refused to apply for a PPP loan. The bank manager was working with us so we wouldn't default when we couldn't make the payments."

"What does this have to do with Hugh?"

"He bought the note! The bank sold it to him. And I was so happy, because was my old friend, always reliable, always generous. A good guy, I thought. In fact, he had us—Mum and my uncle—sign a new contract. We'd pay only the interest, and the terms were renewable, a deal better than any bank could offer." Aidan snapped his fingers. "Six months later, he calls the note. We couldn't pay it. Fucker said, 'Sorry, sorry. I have my own bills.'"

"They foreclosed."

"I talked to him. Begged him. Hugh promised to keep the restaurant open. He said Mum and my uncle could keep working there and buy it back." Aidan took off his glasses and rubbed his eyes. "I didn't mean to take it out on you, Gwen. It's just that I see Hugh and you and Jess, and it feels like he got everything. That the world rewards him for being a lying, conniving piece of shit."

Gwen's stomach churned. "Aidan, I've got to go."

"I upset you," Aidan said. "That was too much."

"No, I—I'll be back in an hour, I swear."

Steven answered the door of the real estate office. "I was just about to call you. Listen, we—"

"Where is she? Janet. Is she here?"

"She's in Bangor. Listen—"

"Do you know how to get in touch with her? I have to cancel that contract."

"Contract? What contract?"

"A loan! On Periwinkle." Dread mounted, filling her chest.

Steven closed his eyes. "I could lose my job for this."

"For what?"

He walked to Janet's desk, picked up a fat envelope, and handed it to Gwen. "I swear to God, I didn't know, Gwen."

"Know what?" She pulled out pages printed in blue ink, architectural renderings stamped with the logo for Fox-Finnigan Enterprises, Hugh's company. When she unfolded the renderings, she saw a series of shingle-style cottages aligned on lots facing the ocean. "I don't understand."

"Look at the last page."

The survey at the bottom of the pile showed how the developers planned to carve the land into eight sites, some with swimming pools and hot tubs. Notations indicated an old, twisted driveway that needed to be reworked. Steven pointed to a faint outline close to the shoreline. "That's what they will take down to build this," he said.

A small rectangle faced the ocean, a semicircle of lawn out front. It could only be Periwinkle.

"I don't understand. I'm not selling the cottage. He gave me a loan."

Steven looked sick, his face pale. "But the house is the collateral, right?"

"Yes."

He waited.

"He thinks I'll default?"

"You need to talk to Jess." His expression shifted from caution to anger. "Goddammit, I told Jess not to get involved with Hugh, that sneaky fucker. But Jess kept insisting that we need the money, we need the money. And he charges Hugh double, so somehow that makes it worthwhile. And meanwhile the shithead is pumping Jess for information about you. I think you need to talk to Jess." He dropped his head into his hands. "I'm so sorry."

Gwen barked, "Stop it, Steven. I don't have time for this. Where is Jess?"

"In Orland, I think."

She stumbled to the parking lot. The phone shook as she dialed. "I need to talk to you," she said as soon as Jess picked up.

"I'm working on the house on Tapper's Pond."

"The one you built last summer?"

"The very same."

The road flew by as she passed every car. She couldn't make sense of it. If Hugh meant to loan her money, why did he have plans for her land? Those drawings would have taken weeks to produce, at least. Probably months. Then she remembered the surveyor's words: he'd marked the boundaries before.

"Shit," she screamed at the windshield. "Shit, shit, shit."

Jess stood in the driveway when she pulled up, his hands stuffed into his jean pockets, shoulders up to his ears.

"Why the hell does Hugh think he will get my land?"

He winced. "We'd better go inside."

She followed him through the front door and into the sparsely furnished home that still smelled of Sheetrock and new paint. He led her to a pair of chairs facing the water. Gwen glanced up the steps.

"The owners are back in Colorado," he said.

Gwen wrapped her arms around her ribs, holding on to herself. Jess watched the breeze-ruffled pond shimmering in the late morning sun.

"Let me guess. He wants to finance a mortgage on your house."

"Yes." It sounded like a shout, too loud in the empty room. "He has blueprints."

"Son of a bitch." He shook his head. "Okay. Grant you, I don't know everything, but he's done this before."

"Aidan's family." Gwen cut him off. "But why does Steven say I need to talk to *you?*"

He cleared his throat. "What happened to them is all because of me and my big mouth."

"Tell me."

"Hugh came up here during the lockdown. I guess he was lonely or whatever, bumping around that big old house, and he called me. I kept him company and sat outside with him near the firepit. He talked a lot about the old days and the trouble we used to get into. I guess I mentioned that Aidan was in a world of hurt. His family business was in trouble, and he was scared that they'd lose it. I don't remember exactly, because Hugh just kept pouring."

Now that Gwen considered Hugh's hospitality, it always seemed to involve alcohol—drinks that others finished, but he didn't.

"Next thing you know, Aidan's uncle has a call from the bank. They tell him that Aidan's old friend has bought the note. Hugh had tracked down the mortgage and assured the manager that he planned to work with the family. Of course, the bank was happy to take the loan off their books; they had a gazillion similar situations to manage. Aidan was happy, too. He called to thank me for putting Hugh up to it." He leaned forward, elbows on his knees, eyes on the floor. "Then Hugh calls the note. He knew that the family couldn't pay, and he called the note."

"It's the Portland marina project, isn't it?"

"Yep."

Her jaw tightened.

"Because of me, he knew the family was in trouble, and all he had to do was a little research to find out how bad the situation was and which bank would have mortgaged the property."

"And what did you tell him about me?"

He put a hand on his heart. "Nothing, I swear. I swear. He read your mom's obituary, and he asked if you were okay. He wanted to know if you had a boyfriend or a husband or kids. I told him I didn't know. I thought he was interested in *you*, not your property."

Gwen stared out the window toward the glassy lake, the banks slushy with ice. To be fair to Jess, it wouldn't have taken a genius to see that she had trouble paying her bills. She drove a beat-up old car and lived in a cottage she couldn't afford to heat. And Hugh had been patient, gaining her confidence, constantly assuring her he was her friend. All he'd needed to do was sit back and wait for something to dig the financial black hole a little deeper.

She clenched her fingers. It would have been easy to blame Jess, but she was the one who'd messed up. Steven had tried to tell her that Hugh wasn't to be trusted, and she'd ignored him. She'd clung to an image of a shared past, their teenage friendship but also, more importantly, because Hugh was beside her as she screamed over her sister's dead body. He'd stepped in when Jess had run. It took adulthood to understand how awful it would have been for Jess, too, but at the time, watching him leave had only compounded her terror. She'd wanted Jess's arms around her, but it was Hugh who'd held her as she tried to breathe into her sister's mouth. Hugh had been the one to stroke her back and whisper, *Ssh, ssh*, as the EMTs loaded Molly into the ambulance. Hugh had been there, his eyes wet in sympathy. "He was such a kind person," she said.

"He's not the kid we used to know," Jess said.

Bile stung her throat.

"Only one thing matters to him, and that's business." Jess shook his head. "He never apologized to Aidan. Or to me. He only calls when he wants his driveway regraded or a pipe mended. Or his fucking seawall fixed."

Jess turned his head abruptly to look at her. "You didn't sign anything, did you?"

Gwen nodded weakly, too sick to speak.

He dropped his head in his hands. "Shit."

The sob she'd held back reached her throat. Through the tears, she croaked, "I don't know what to do."

He shut his eyes. "Okay, back up, what are the terms?"

"A year, no interest. He said it's renewable."

Jess took a deep breath. "Right. He did this to Aidan. This means that if he doesn't renew in a year, you'll owe the entire sum plus interest. They call it a balloon payment."

Gwen's chest tightened. She'd already paid off her massive credit card bill. At six percent interest, she'd need to win the lottery to repay it all if Hugh called the loan. "Aidan's family only had six months."

"Did it say anything about late payments?"

"The acceleration and termination clause? Yes."

"I'd bet my last dollar that he has language in there that says if you miss a payment for any reason—and I mean by even one hour—the collateral is his."

"So I just need to pay it on time. Every month until I figure this out." She chewed the inside of her cheek, thinking. "Am I going to need a lawyer?"

"I don't know. But I do know this: Fighting him will be easier if you're living on-site. There are laws about evicting people, which might buy you more time."

Gwen took a deep breath. She'd move back in. There was no way she could remain at Hugh's now anyway.

"And I promise to help you. Steven is clever with real estate law, and I will park my backhoe in your driveway if I have to. I swear I will not let this happen a second time."

Gwen shook her head. "It's not your fault."

"Yes, it is, Gwennie. You've seen Aidan. He's changed. We still grab a drink from time to time, but he doesn't trust me anymore. And I can't say that I blame him."

From across the pond, a chain saw whined as it bit into wood.

Jess wiped his face with the back of his hand. "That night at the firepit cost me a friendship I care about. And I can never take it back. Please don't tell me it will cost me yours, too." His face looked years older; deep grooves lined his forehead, crow's-feet at his eyes.

"It will not, Jess."

"Good," he said quietly. And again, "Good."

The chain saw stopped. Men shouted as the crown of a tree fell, a loud crack followed by a thud she felt in her bones.

TWENTY-NINE

IT DIDN'T TAKE LONG FOR GWEN TO SHOVE HER CLOTHES
into bags and stuff them in the trunk of her car. She peeled out of the driveway, eager to put as much distance between herself and Ayr-y-Lee as possible.

The empty road curved around the harbor. The trees, stripped of their
leaves, revealed the houses beneath, square-lined and solid. Smoke rose from
chimneys and curled into the frosted air. Inside, people worked and talked,
read and cooked, sheltered from harm.

Jess and Steven had offered their spare room, but she'd begged off, using
the cat as an excuse. She craved solitude, an empty den where she could lick
her wounds. She had no idea how to manage the cold, but she'd figure it out.
People survived worse.

The closer she got to Periwinkle, the clearer Hugh's deception became.
In the harsh glare of a November afternoon, his solicitousness and repeated
reminders of their connection had been such obvious ploys. All those weeks
she'd spent in his home had somehow worked a spell, muffling her senses,
clouding her vision, lulling her into complacency. His money had slipped
into her bloodstream like a drug, one that wore off as soon as she pulled into
her own driveway. And now that it was gone, she was raw and aching. But
at least she could think.

A thin veil of clouds rolled across the sky. Inside the cottage, the milky light made everything feel colder. Gwen lit a fire and sat on the flowered love seat, her body too heavy to move. Her eyes shut against gathering tears.

How had her life gotten so fucked up? Once upon a time, she'd dreamed of a writing career and a family. She'd planned to travel across the globe to the pyramids, the Andes, and the Great Wall of China and send back articles to *Forbes* and *Vogue*. Instead, she'd stepped into middle age as a washed-up teacher on the edge of bankruptcy. *How had this happened?*

But, of course, she knew the answer. It happened because Jess had called that long-ago afternoon, and she'd said, *Yes, come get me*, before the words were even out of his mouth. She'd pulled on her favorite T-shirt, fluffed her hair, and had run to the door.

Take me with you? Molly had begged, her freckled face wrinkled and pleading. *I want to play.*

Not now, mushroom, Gwen had replied without even looking at her sister. *Mom is in the garden. Ask her.*

Molly had stamped her foot. *No*, she shouted. *I want to be with you, Winnie!*

Maybe when you're older.

I'm old enough, Molly pleaded. *I want to be with you.*

But Gwen had needed to dash that hope if she wanted to spend the afternoon with Jess. So she'd said something awful, something she should never have said. *We're going to the lighthouse. You can't come if you can't swim.* And then she'd turned away before she could see her sister's tears, climbing into the cab of Jess's truck.

Heedless of the hours that passed, consumed by the fire in her belly, she'd pressed her body to Jess's, her lips on his. When the air in the lighthouse grew too close and the futon too sweaty, they went outside to swim. At slack tide, the water was calm and unmoving, placidly awaiting the shift that would drag millions of gallons back out to sea. They lowered into the water on the mainland side, unable to separate. Dizzy with desire, their bodies as slick as seal pups, they moved through the shallows until they dropped over the lip of the ledge into the deep-water side. Gwen let the ocean close over her head, still gripping Jess's hand. With the other, she held on to a fissure in the rock face. Periwinkles and sea stars in shades of pink and red clung to the granite and a sea urchin waved its spines. Releasing her hold, Gwen wiggled pale fingers, too. Jess, grinning, pointed upward. They rose for breath, sputtering. Jess leaned forward to kiss her again, his mouth salty and cool. Her body loosened, and her legs wrapped around his waist. *More, more, more*, ran through her brain as she pulled him closer.

Something bumped Gwen's back. She turned. A buoy severed from its tether and covered in pale seaweed floated behind her. She went to push it away when Jess cried out, a guttural sound. The horrified look on his face forced her to look again.

"No," Jess said as he scrambled back into the shallows. "No!"

Gwen stared dumbly at her sister's small head bobbing in the water, the strands of gold turned dull, thick with salt, her eyes staring into the dark below.

"Help me," she screamed to Jess's retreating back, her hands hooked under her sister's armpits, pulling her toward shore. But it was Hugh who appeared from the parking lot and helped pull her from the water. Hugh had held her when the paramedics finally came. Hugh had whispered, "Shh, shh," as she screamed. No one else.

How could you?

Her mother's voice surrounded her still, the tone so fresh she could have been in the room, two decades later.

Shame curdled Gwen's stomach. "I'm sorry," she said aloud.

She inhaled very slowly, waiting for the Misses' response. They said nothing.

"Goddammit," she shouted, reaching for the closest thing she could find— Robert Louis Stevenson's *Treasure Island*—and hurling it across the room with all the force she could manage. It hit the wall with a crack and landed on the floor, splayed open, the spine broken. She held her breath, heart racing. Still, nothing creaked, not a whisper in the walls or a shift in the ceiling; only the relentless throb of the sea slid through the cracks in the walls, as if the Misses, like her mother, could no longer bear to look at her.

She pulled a pillow to her face and screamed. It still smelled of Leandro, a warm cedar. She held it to her nose. *Cookies*, he called her. As if she were a treat, something desirable, something that made the mouth water and the spirit happy.

She picked up her phone and texted him her one true thing: *I miss you.* No gray dots appeared. It was probably the middle of the night in Berlin.

Hours passed, Gwen staring at the flames as they consumed log after log. She pulled on a second fleece and two more pairs of socks, but the cold burrowed into her skin. Her fingers turned blue. She pulled on gloves and brought blankets into the living room, nesting in front of the fireplace. The faint crackle followed her into sleep.

Much later, the darkness outside absolute, her phone pinged. She fumbled in the covers to find it. *I'll be home on Friday.* She held the screen to her chest for the rest of the night.

———

FIVE DAYS LATER, she waited in her car outside Leandro's condo, sitting on her hands. Nine weeks was a long time to wait for someone. The door to Mr. Drinkwater's unit opened, and he stuck his head out. She rolled her window down and waved.

He said, "Come on inside."

"That's okay."

He opened the door wider. "You can sit by the window if you like. Come have some tea with me."

She turned off the car.

In the kitchen, he pulled a tangle of tea bags out of a canister. "I liked your article in the *Packet*. Going to do another?"

"Yes. Do you have a story for me?"

He lit the stove under the kettle. "You know, when I was a boy, down near Owls Head, there was a house we passed every day on the way to school. Never saw a light or anything moving behind the curtains, but every year the pile in the yard got bigger and bigger."

"Pile of what?"

He smacked his gums. "Ah, you name it. Toys, farm equipment, cans of paint, old bedposts, things that should have gone to the dump. It was all arranged as if someone planned to use it. But they didn't, and the piles got bigger until someone complained and the town condemned the property. A man was living there, hidden away behind stacks of newspapers and canned goods. When he came out, he was all hunched over, couldn't stand up straight anymore because his house was so full of stuff."

Gwen pictured it, windows dark behind shredded curtains and peeling paint, grass sprouting between rusted lawn mowers and a child's hobbyhorse in the yard.

He handed her a cup. "There was so much junk; they made a bonfire in his yard. Turned the big pine tree black."

She held the mug by the handle to keep from burning her fingers. The liquid scalded the tip of her tongue.

He said, "You never know what people are hiding." He nodded his head, agreeing with himself. He turned to face her. "I find it's best to tell folks what's on your mind."

She heard a car rumble, and the El Camino slid into the spot out front.

Mr. Drinkwater put a hand on her shoulder. "Go on, now."

She kissed him on the cheek and ran out the door.

Leandro stepped out. Exhaustion lined his face, but he smiled when he saw her. "Cookies," he said.

She buried her face in his neck. He mumbled words into her hair and kissed her temple. She couldn't let go, even as they walked into his house. "It is okay, Gwen," he said gently, unlocking the door.

Once inside, he pulled her close. She pressed her forehead against his breastbone, breathing in his warmth. They held each other in silence. "You were gone so long," she said at last.

He leaned back to look at her. His eyes revolved, flickering green and brown. "This is the life of an artist."

"I thought artists spent hours in the studio."

"Yes, but then they must peddle the work. There must be buyers so that the studio rent can be paid."

She swallowed this.

"It's what I do. I come, and I go."

Gwen looked at the floor, where a patterned rug covered a beige carpet. Exuberant flowers in shades of rose and blue burst from thorned vines in the wool beneath her feet.

"But I am here now, Gwen."

It's not enough, her heart screamed.

"Shall we?" He pointed to the kitchen. "I haven't eaten all day."

She followed him in, sitting at the table as he shuffled frozen containers, each carefully labeled.

"Chicken piccata?" he asked. His shirt gaped at the neck, revealing the groove at his throat, a sprout of white hair beneath.

"Delicious," she said, her mouth dry.

He took off the top and put the casserole dish in the microwave. The hum filled the kitchen, soon followed by the aroma of butter and white wine.

They sat at the table and laughed. He told her stories of his tour, of the collectors who asked crazy personal questions about his childhood, his love life—this made Gwen sit up a little straighter, wondering how he'd answered—and his immigration status. He'd delivered more than a dozen lectures, endured seminars with pretentious MFA and Ph.D. candidates, and eaten too many terrible meals in bland hotel rooms. "Or perhaps it was bland meals in terrible hotel rooms," he said.

When the microwave beeped, he served them both a heap of sautéed chicken on a bed of noodles, flecks of capers scattered across the top. She shoved huge bites into her mouth as if she'd never eaten before.

"And you? What has happened to you while I was away?"

"The students are delightful. The book is going well. I wrote an article for the *Packet*."

"This is wonderful news. Why didn't you say anything?"

Why hadn't she? "I don't know. Maybe because it's just a small-town paper?"

He leaned forward, his expression serious. "Do not dismiss your work. Just because the circulation is small does not mean what you say is not important. I never think about how many will see what I do. It is the making that matters."

She was quiet as his words settled.

"And how are your ghosts?" he asked.

"I think they're hibernating. Or maybe just ignoring me." She dropped her head. "I've done something terrible . . ."

"Ah?"

"I'm serious, Leandro."

"What is this face? You are seeing someone else?"

"No. God, no."

"You are moving away?"

"No. Well, maybe. I took out a loan against my house."

"This is not so terrible."

"Well, the person who loaned me the money expects me to default."

"And has this happened yet?"

She shook her head.

"Then I think we should go to bed now and worry about this in the morning. There are always solutions."

She took his hand and followed him up a flight of stairs. Leandro flipped on a light, and Gwen's mouth fell open with astonishment. The beamed ceiling rose double height, crisscrossed by wooden trusses that made the room look more like a barn than a new condominium. Large charcoal drawings were pinned to the walls: landscapes and water studies, branches of fir trees resting on boulders, and roots splitting ledges like greedy fingers reaching into the earth.

Papers covered the floor, a mosaic of photographs, pages torn from books, and yellow sticky notes. "Come," he said, gesturing toward the bed at the center of the room.

Gwen laughed. "How?"

"Like this," he said, demonstrating. He walked on the balls of his feet, carefully choreographing a path only he saw. She followed, trying not to disturb anything.

"Stop there," he told her when she was a few feet away. He took her shoulders and turned her. A large drawing of a seal stared at her with black eyes.

"Oh," she said, hands clasped at her chest. There were seals all around her. One sat on a rock, throat lifted. Another extended a flipper, testing the air. Two nostrils poked through the water's surface, opening and closing as the whiskers twitched. Gwen approached, zigzagging through the drifts of paper. The animal's sleek fur shone as it leaned from a ledge to gaze at its own reflection. There were streaks of white at the temple.

She looked back at Leandro.

He smiled.

Below the seal drawings, a woman, captured in profile, stared at the ocean. She turned to the viewer, her expression lost. Gwen had an impulse to reach out and comfort the sad person, but, of course, it was her.

"Is this how you think of me?" she asked.

"At times, yes. But, also, like that." He pointed to another, much larger, image. Gwen stood poised, her powerful body preparing to dive. Like the seal, she looked at her own face in the rippled water, her chin dipped low, her back split open to reveal the seal beneath.

Gwen inhaled very slowly.

He came to her and ran a hand the length of her spine, a single finger, seeking the seam. And he found it, slowly unzipping, until she shed her skin.

Her backbone continued to tingle the next morning. Over coffee, and a bagel pulled from the depths of Leandro's magical bottomless freezer, an electrical current slid up and down its length. It made her shiver from time to time. When Leandro saw this, he asked her if she was cold, should he turn up the heat? No, no, she assured him. "I'm just happy."

He touched her cheek with his fingertips. "I must go to the store," he said. "Would you like to come?"

Of course she would. She didn't want to leave his side.

The door of Drinkwater Provisions tinkled as they pushed it open. Parker, behind the counter, grinned when he saw them.

Five days had passed since Gwen had last left food for Shania. Dried fruit, nuts, two loaves of bread, and a huge hunk of cheddar went into her cart alongside more fuel for the camp stove. Cans of beans, a can opener, Cheetos, Doritos, and a bag of Milky Ways followed.

"You eat like a child," Leandro said. His basket was filled with fruits and vegetables and a carton of milk.

"It's not for me," she said.

He raised his eyebrows but didn't ask.

When she was almost to the front of the line, she remembered bottled water. She hefted a huge jug onto the counter.

"Got well trouble?" Parker asked.

"The water is cut off at Periwinkle."

"You're staying at the cottage?"

"I am."

Parker leaned over the counter and whispered. "Are you part Yeti? You can trust me. I won't tell."

"Only on my mother's side. My father was a polar bear," she whispered back.

"Good thing. In a month or two, you'll need that fur coat."

Watching Parker ring her up, she took a slow breath. The situation was not sustainable, she knew that, not least because she had no running water, and her pipes were too exposed to turn it on. Everything would freeze and burst within days. But at the moment she didn't have any other solutions. Leandro had a nice bathroom. And when he left again—her heart zinged the moment she admitted this to herself—she could hit up Steven and Jess to use theirs. The school gym had showers, too. She'd be fine.

A dazzling yellow sun warmed their backs as they loaded the groceries into the car.

"You'll need a hand with that water," Leandro observed. She slid next to him as they rounded the hill toward Periwinkle, their thighs touching. He lifted the jug onto her kitchen counter and nodded at the bags of groceries in her hands. "What shall we do with those?"

"Would you like to come with me to deliver them?"

"Ah," he said. "You take them to the girl."

He followed her across the ledge and into the woods, the ground crunchy with frost. "You do this all the time?"

"Once or twice a week."

"You are feeding a wild being who might not wish to be domesticated."

"Maybe. But I don't want her to suffer, either."

At the bottom of one empty bin, she found: *Hi Gwen, did you know that chickens are the closest living relatives to the T-Rex? Also, can I have a book about math? Like a history of math?*

I'll see what I can do, Gwen wrote back, adding, *Back at the cottage now. You're welcome anytime. I mean that. Anytime.*

Leandro helped her stuff the supplies inside, arranging each bag and box so that it could all fit.

They walked back quietly, hand in hand. Horsetail clouds drifted above them, the sky crystalline.

At the cottage, Leandro said he must go. He needed to unpack and do laundry, answer emails, and organize his studio. The gallery had called and he would leave again for New York in the evening.

She had work, too, she assured him. The next installment in the series for the *Packet* was due soon.

He kissed her on the mouth, and her body melted. "I will see you in a week or so, yes?"

On her phone, she found sixteen unanswered emails in her inbox, most of them junk, but one was from Janet Riggs, letting Gwen know she'd filed the documents. The woman used way too many exclamation marks. And another from Hugh's caretaker, asking her if she'd left the keys on the front hall table by mistake.

Gwen responded curtly, *No mistake. I've moved out.*

The phone rang an hour later, Hugh's profile picture on the screen. "Gwen? What's going on?"

"I can't stay there."

"I don't understand."

"The balloon payment," she said. "You know what that means, but I didn't. You fucking lied to me, Hugh."

"But I told you I'd renew the loan. You don't have to worry."

"I don't believe you."

His voice slowed, honeyed. "Gwennie. You know you can trust me. I only have your best interests at heart."

"Is that right?" She wanted to add, *Because I've seen the pale outline of my demolished home on the survey, the ledge carved up, the woods razed.*

He switched tactics. "Where are you? Can I see you?"

"At Periwinkle."

"You don't have heat, for Christ's sake."

"I'm perfectly fine."

"Look, I can drive up tomorrow and we can discuss this. I'll be at the house by noon."

"There's nothing to talk about."

"I don't understand. I've done you a favor, and now you're acting like this?"

Gwen chose her words carefully. "I work with Aidan, Hugh. I know what you did."

His voice rose an octave in outrage. "I helped that family. They were almost bankrupt, for fuck's sake. If I hadn't bought them out, they would have drowned."

"How dare you!" Anger swarmed her chest. She shouted, "How dare you! You of all people . . . Is that what I am to you, Hugh? Another *drowning* victim?"

"Gwen, I apol—"

"No. Fuck you, Hugh." She ended the call.

THIRTY

MORNING BROUGHT A TOURMALINE SUNRISE, DARK
green streaked with rose. Gwen lay curled in front of the dying fire, half-
buried beneath five blankets and a quilt. Out the window, a lone gull circled.
The rest of its flock had left weeks before in search of warmer temperatures.

"I think that makes us the stupid ones," Gwen said.

The chill hit her right away. On her way to the kitchen, she tiptoed in
sock feet, the floorboards creaking loudly. Half-frozen water from the jug
dribbled into the coffee machine while she bounced in place, rubbing her
hands to keep warm. When she couldn't take it anymore, she put on the
oilcloth coat. The weight of it calmed her nerves, and after a minute she
was warmer. She took a deep breath and splashed a cupful of water on her
face, flinching.

Before he left, Leandro had insisted she could stay at his studio, but
she'd turned him down. She'd made this uncomfortable bed, and now she
had to lie in it. He'd nodded as if he understood. On his way out the door,
he'd promised to return in a week at most. No more than two.

"Sure," she'd said sadly.

The coffee machine hissed before releasing a stream of hot liquid into the

257

carafe. Mug clutched between icy fingers, Gwen returned to the fire. Fresh logs dumped on top of glowing embers caused sparks to rise, drafted upward into the dawn light.

The first payment to Hugh was due by five o'clock at Janet's office. The check was ready to go, safely sealed inside an envelope on the kitchen counter. It was the only reason she needed to leave the house today.

Steven's careful arrangement still filled the dining table, a grid of shells and stones. She pulled the heart-shaped rock into the center, fingering the soft edges and the rougher crystal band around it. An hour passed and then a second as she arranged and rearranged the whelks into spirals that fanned outward, a nautilus in shades of yellow, creamy white, and slate blue. Unlike the pearled translucence of the Caribbean shells in Anna's Valentine, the whelk walls were thick and dense. Sturdy. Like a Mainer, it would take effort to break them.

She nestled each element between dried mosses in hues of sage-green and ash. When she finished, she went to look for rubber cement. As she rummaged through the art cabinet, a voice shouted, "Miss Gilmore?" This was followed by banging loud enough to shake the house.

Gwen peered out the kitchen window.

A woman had her fist raised to hit the doorframe again just as Gwen opened the back door.

"Yes?"

Dressed in a blue uniform, the woman wore a name tag: *Nan Richoleau, Town of Port Anna, Code Enforcement Officer*. She said, "I'm here to do an inspection."

Gwen frowned. "An inspection?"

"You received a notice two days ago."

"No, I did not."

The officer nodded at the ground. "Right there."

Gwen bent down and pulled a half-hidden envelope from beneath the doormat. A pink sheet of paper announced: *Notice of Intent to Inspect within 48 hours.*

"My office received a report that this dwelling is unsafe and needs to be condemned. Please let me in."

"What report? This house isn't unsafe." *What the fuck?*

"I still need to inspect the property."

"And what if I refuse?"

"I'll come back with the deputy. And you don't want that."

Gwen opened the door.

The woman walked into the kitchen, notepad in hand. The radio at her waist crackled. She pressed a button. "That's right. I'm inside," she said. The response was unintelligible. She looked at Gwen. "I'll be walking through the residence, ma'am. I'll need you to keep your distance."

Gwen stepped back. She tore at a cuticle, blood pooling in the nail bed as the woman looked at the ceiling, the windows, the walls. She opened the cabinet under the sink and checked the laundry room, occasionally scratching words on her notepad.

Gwen followed, still sucking on her bleeding finger. The inspector took in the makeshift bed in front of the fire and looked at Gwen, eyebrows raised. "You're not winterized."

Gwen crossed her arms in front of her chest. "Nope."

"You might want to think about that," the woman sniffed. She checked the window casings and the doorjamb before crossing to the center of the room. The floor creaked loudly under her weight. She looked at her feet, shifting from side to side. The boards sank as she did this. "Huh," she said, writing. She disappeared into the bedroom.

Gwen paced, anger rising. *Unsafe dwelling.*

The woman reappeared. "The attic that way?"

"The door is in the ceiling upstairs," Gwen told her.

The inspector climbed the steps. Minutes later, Gwen heard the crank of the attic pull chain.

Gwen took out her phone and punched a number. As soon as the line connected, she said, "Holy shit, Hugh. You called the code enforcement officer? You told them my house should be condemned?"

After a beat, he said, "I did."

"Fuck you."

"Gwen, you can see through the walls!"

"It's none of your fucking business."

"Of course it is. You're behaving like a crazy person, living in a broken-down cottage without running water and pretending like everything is fine."

"Everything *is* fine, Hugh."

Hugh groaned. "Listen to me. This is not okay. You have debt, and you have a job that barely pays minimum wage. I am offering you a lifeline, Gwen."

"You just want my land, Hugh."

"Is that what you think?" He ground his teeth in frustration. "Why do you have to make everything so difficult? God, you're infuriating."

This gave her pause. Guy had said that: *Why do you make everything so hard?*

"Ma'am," the inspector said from the middle of the room.

Gwen said into the phone, "I have to go." She cut Hugh off mid-outrage.

"You're going to need to pay attention to that roof," the inspector said. "There's some leakage in several places, and water is seeping in. That can cause all kinds of issues. I'm headed outside now."

Gwen opened her phone and searched YouTube for roofing videos. How hard could it be? She watched the blue wheel spin on her screen and chewed her mangled cuticle, when a pair of crows landed on the porch railing. They opened shiny beaks and screamed, *Haw, haw.* Over and over, they yelled, raucous, demanding. "Not now," she barked.

"Hello," a young voice said from the other side of the door.

When Gwen threw it open, the largest crow flew from the railing to the door, beaded eyes on Gwen.

"Hi," Shania said. She looked smaller and paler than the last time they'd seen each other, her dirty hair pulled into a hair band. Gwen recognized it as one she had left for her weeks ago. She probably should have left shampoo as well—although, on second thought, Shania had no use for it now that fresh water was frozen.

Gwen opened the door wider, heart sinking. "Come on in." Shania's timing couldn't be worse.

Shania went straight to the fire. She dropped to her knees and held out reddened hands, her black eyebrows knit together in concentration.

Gwen sat on the edge of the blue sofa. "You got the jacket I left?"

"Yeah. Thanks. I didn't think I needed it today. It was warm until the wind picked up."

"I've been worried. It's cold and we are weeks away from winter."

"The Inuit people live in subzero temperatures for most of the year." Shania rotated her position.

"They also have fur-lined coats. Are you hungry? I can make you some eggs."

"That shrimp thing was really good."

"I didn't make that. Leandro did."

Shania's face twitched. "You can't really cook, can you? My mom was the same."

"Not really." Gwen inhaled and asked quietly, "Where is your mom?"

"Gone." A dark look crossed the girl's face.

"What about your dad?"

"Don't have one." Shania went to the bookshelf, running her fingers down the spines. "Guess what I learned," she said. "There is such a thing as immaculate conception. It's called parthenogenesis. Komodo dragons do it." She held curled fingers to her face and snarled.

Gwen blinked.

"Yeah, sorry. That was supposed to be funny. I guess Komodo dragons aren't really funny, since they practice cannibalism and their bite can kill people. Maybe I should have said a sand flea instead."

"A sand flea."

"Yeah. Another species that can spontaneously reproduce. There are others. Am I boring you?"

"Not at all."

"I don't have a filter. People say that to me. It's worse when I'm nervous. I just talk and talk until someone shuts me up."

"I don't want to shut you up. But I would like to know your story."

"You want to know why I ran. The short version is: Portland wasn't working anymore."

"Why?"

"Let's just say there was a noxious cloud in my foster household that went by the name of Buddy."

"Is that when you came up here?"

"Not right away. I spent a few weeks with other kids under a half-built complex down by the water. But then the owners got pissed because we kept tagging the site, and the cops came in."

"Tagging?"

"You know, spray-painting stuff on the sidewalks and the I-beams."

"Stuff like what?"

"*Capitalist Pigs Live Here. How Many Species Will Die for These Rich Assholes?* Also, my personal fave, *Get Off Our Lawn.*"

Gwen's mouth opened in surprise. "You were living below a marina?"

"How did you know?"

Gwen grinned. "Doesn't matter. What happened after the cops came?"

"Another kid was worried what would happen if the cops caught me. He gave me money, and I took a bus to Bangor. Then I hitched a ride into town."

"Why here? Why not Florida? California? Someplace warm."

"Who wants paradise? Not me." She laughed.

Gwen waited.

"Dunno. I guess I read about the lighthouse and Anna Vale and how some think she's still out there, in the water, keeping everybody safe." Shania lifted her narrow shoulders and shrugged, trying to make it look casual, but Gwen knew the signs, the desperation lurking behind the girl's bravado. This was serious business. Shania had come looking for a savior.

"It turns out it's a legend. Stupid of me to believe it anyway," Shania said. "Anna Vale is dead and buried. Hightailed it out of here, just like my mom."

Gwen bit her cheek. Long before Alzheimer's had claimed her, Gwen's mother had drifted away, too.

Shania took a breath. "You said I could come anytime. So . . ." Her eyes narrowed as they focused on the window behind Gwen's head. "There's someone in your driveway," she said.

The code enforcement officer, covered in dirt and cobwebs, stood outside, writing. When Gwen opened the kitchen door, the inspector looked up.

"Miss Gilmore. You have a serious issue with your foundation. Two of the pillars beneath the house no longer support the beams. I thought that might be the case when I felt the sag in the living room floor. There's about a four-inch gap." The woman tore a yellow sheet from her notepad and held it out. "You have ninety days to complete these repairs before the town takes action."

She looked past Gwen's shoulder.

Gwen followed her gaze. Shania stood behind her, fury etched into her face.

"Does that child live here?"

"No . . ." Gwen started to explain, but she didn't know how to finish the sentence.

"As I said, you have ninety days." She turned her back and marched toward the road, her stride purposeful, officious.

The paper in Gwen's hand quivered.

"That was bullshit," Shania said.

Gwen inhaled a shaky breath. "It's not her fault. A guy I used to know wants my land, and this is his strategy to get it."

Shania left the room and returned a moment later with a picture frame in her hand. "Him?" she asked, pointing to Hugh as a teenager.

"Yes. How did you know?"

"I've seen him before."

"When?"

"Last spring, when I was living upstairs."

"Jesus. Of course." He'd been planning and plotting for months. Gwen looked up. "Wait. You *lived* here?"

Shania bit her lower lip. "The window was open, and I needed a place to sleep. I thought the place was abandoned, but you came back in the middle of the night."

The memory of Gwen's return was murky, clouded with exhaustion and sorrow. It had taken a while to force her key into the salt-encrusted lock. Her eyes had closed the second her head touched the pillow, but just before she was swept under, she'd heard the whisper of feet padding down the stairs. At the time, she'd assumed it was the Misses.

Shania was still speaking, emphatically pointing at Hugh's picture. "There was a woman, too, with teeth like this." She spread her lips. "I'd like to see her smile like that at a chimp. It would eat her face off."

"Janet Riggs. A Realtor." Gwen shook her head.

"She knocked again when I came by to shower. I'm sorry about the tub, but she scared me. I thought she was going to break down the door." Shania looked at the photograph again, her sharp eyes narrowed. "You think he might have bribed her to say that about your foundation?"

"Shit," Gwen said. She grabbed the oilcloth coat from the dining room chair.

An eighteen-inch opening between the ground and the wall was just enough for Gwen to squeeze through. As she army-crawled in, the depression beneath the house deepened. The flashlight on her phone illuminated the darkness. It caught tiny rodent bones, and a desiccated bird's wing wrenched from its socket. Shivering, she swept the light across the top of the pillars. In some places, the mortar was cracked, crumbled bits of cement littered the ground. Gwen scooted along. As she approached the center, she found what the inspector had described: a noticeable gap between two pillars and the floor above. The beams bowed, seeking support. Splinters bristled from the cracks in the boards. She reached up and pushed as if the pressure would make them snap back into place. They didn't budge.

Gwen shut off her flashlight.

Periwinkle's foundation was failing. Was there a video for "How to fix a house that's falling into the ocean?" Even without checking the web, Gwen knew the project would require heavy equipment—a concrete mixer, at least. And some sort of jack to hold the cottage up. And she would need help, people bigger and stronger than her. Also, money. Money she would owe to Hugh. She lowered herself onto the dusty ground littered with shriveled spiders and worm casings. Above her, the house pressed down, a weight too heavy to bear. She should have stayed in North Carolina.

Frigid air forced itself into the crawl space. It nuzzled her neck and grabbed her ankles. Her thoughts slowed to a crawl until there was only one left: *I'm out of options.*

Periwinkle would disappear. The Misses' carefully chosen beams would splinter like toothpicks when bulldozers tore through the walls. Drills and sledgehammers would shatter the ledge to make room for swimming pools, and chain saws would carve up the woods, leaving gaping holes in the canopy and ruts in the earth. And when the work was finished, no one would remember the cottage the Misses had built. No one except Gwen, and by then she'd be long gone, too.

THIRTY-ONE

TWO SMALL, BOWED FEET IN BEATEN-UP HIKING BOOTS
appeared at the side of the house. Shania bent down to look at Gwen, her
pinched face squeezed with concern. Her oversized hoodie gaped at the neck,
revealing bird bones at her collar, so fragile they could snap in a strong wind.
"Can you come out now?" she asked.

Gwen wiped her face with icy fingers. "Why?"

"I want to talk to you." Shania's voice sounded small.

"Now is not the time."

"But . . . you said I was welcome anytime."

Cold snaked up Gwen's arms and legs. It found the pocket between her
neck and collar and slithered in, down her spine toward her waist.

"Gwen?"

Numb, Gwen didn't answer. The air wrapped around her like a blanket.
If she could just stay where she was, hidden in the half-frozen ground, she
could disappear, and all of this would go away. She squeezed her eyes shut
and imagined this with a ferocity that shocked her. She would dissolve, molecule by molecule. The foundation's boulders beneath her rotting cottage
would topple over and crumble, and the ocean would drag it all out to sea,
scattering her bones.

A wailing, deep and low, shattered the spell. Gwen sat up, and her head smacked a heavy crossbeam, knocking her backward. A second moan sounded, fainter this time. It occurred to Gwen that it might have come from her own mouth. It took long minutes to crawl from beneath the house. When she emerged, she called, "Shania?" But no one answered.

Staggering into the kitchen, she found a note on the kitchen table. *You said I was welcome.*

Gwen crumpled it in her hand. She had nothing to offer Shania, nothing at all. She should never have said otherwise.

Her body shook. She sat in front of the dying fire, unable to find the energy to fetch more logs. The goose egg on her forehead pounded her skull.

Hours passed. At nightfall, she opened the empty fridge. Her stomach ached, and her head reeled, on the verge of nausea, making a trip to Drinkwater Provisions necessary. She checked the time, and as she did, the world came to a crashing halt.

She had forgotten to deliver Hugh's payment.

Her tires squealed as she tore out of the driveway. Maybe, she thought, Janet was still at the office, going over ledgers or pamphlets, crafting her next pitch, but the windows in the Riggs Real Estate office were black. Gwen rang the bell, just in case. No one answered.

She dialed Steven. "Can you open up for me?"

"I'll be there in ten," he said.

"Jesus, what did you do to yourself?" Steven said when he arrived. He placed gentle fingers on her forehead.

Gwen winced. "Crawling under the house."

"Ouch. I have Advil."

She shook him away. "I'll be fine."

They left the check on Janet's desk. Steven warned, "She locked up today, so she'll likely realize your check is late, but maybe she'll cut you some slack. I'll see if there's anything I can do."

Gwen nodded as if she could believe in Janet's good intentions.

She spent the weekend on edge, jumping at every noise, the house creaking, the crash of waves, the fall of acorns on the tin roof. The yellow warning notice screamed at her from the kitchen table, *ninety days* in bold lettering. She didn't touch it; she couldn't even look at it. Even if Janet accepted the late check, Gwen would have to spend even more of Hugh's money to fix the cottage, adding another set of zeroes to the sum she already owed. And all of it would come due at the end of the year if he enforced the late payment clause. Plus interest.

On Monday, the alarm barely roused her, and when she finally got up, her muscles ached. The bruise on her forehead was still black. Ice packs didn't seem to help, Tylenol barely made a dent. Her brain throbbed, a dull background noise that beat with every step she took.

Aidan was startled when he saw her. "What on earth?"

"I can't even begin to explain." She sat down heavily.

Aidan's concern deepened. "I think someone should look at that."

She gently shook her head. Speaking hurt too much.

"Not even the school nurse?"

"No." She pressed cool fingers to her eyelids to ease the pain.

"What happened, Gwen?" he asked quietly.

She whispered, "I'm going to lose my home."

Aidan said nothing for several long minutes. When he finally spoke, he asked, "Is there anything I can do?"

"No." She felt his hand on her shoulder.

"Was it Hugh?"

She nodded.

His breath hissed between his teeth. "That . . ." His grip tightened. She placed her palm on top of his. They stayed this way until the school bell rang.

The kids politely looked away from her forehead, their eyes locked on their papers. With college testing approaching, more and more had begun to attend her seminars. Too sore to move, she sat as she coached them through essay writing and ran drills for time management. They took notes, heads bent, tongues caught in teeth. Gwen reminded them to keep their language clear and to check their punctuation and sentence structure. She heard herself recite these rules, wondering why anyone would take direction from her. She knew nothing about anything except literature, and look where she'd landed. If she could forgo her meager salary, she'd tell Michaela to find someone else.

At lunch, Michaela pointed to Gwen's head. "Um?"

Gwen shrugged it off, saying she'd stumbled, but Michaela raised an eyebrow, skeptical. She reached across the table. "Something's off. You can talk to me."

But Gwen just shook her head. She couldn't bring herself to admit her lapse in judgment, her financial stupidity.

Michaela persisted. "I'm your friend."

As a last resort, Gwen offered, "Leandro's gone."

Michaela sat back in her chair, a relieved smile on her face. "A new relationship. When you've been married as long as I have, it's kind of a blessing when they leave you for a little while. You can take over the bed. No one wakes you up snoring or farting." She squeezed Gwen's hand. "He'll be back soon," she assured her.

Gwen smiled thinly and went back to work.

Aidan nodded toward her office door. "You have a visitor."

Parker bounced from his chair when she walked in, but his expression changed abruptly when he saw her face. "Oh, that looks gnarly."

"Just a bruise. What's up?"

He bowed dramatically. "My thanks to the grand high witch of Port Anna," he said. "I got in early action to Orono. And guess what? The soccer coach wants to talk to me."

"I'm so happy for you," she told him.

On his way out, he turned. "Grandpa wants to know if you can come for Thanksgiving."

"Tell your sweet grandfather thanks, but I already promised Steven and Jess." Steven had insisted that because Gwen had spent so many years in the South, she should know how to make sweet potatoes. No matter how many times she'd told him that this was not the case, he wouldn't listen.

"As long as you don't spend the day by yourself."

"I won't." Or maybe she would. A day in bed didn't sound so bad. Steven could make his own damn sweet potatoes. Janet could help him.

Before she left the building, she used the gym shower and filled plastic gallon jugs with water. It took courage to step into the cold afternoon with wet hair, and even more to sit on the Subaru's vinyl seat. Twilight hovered over the school parking lot, sunset only an hour away.

By five o'clock, the woods outside the kitchen window were impenetrable, Vantablack. She heated soup in the microwave and washed it down with slushy water from one of the jugs. Once dinner was over, she stared into the flames, empty-headed, waiting for Leandro to text. *One true thing*, he asked.

She was all out of truths. She wrote, *Please come home.*

When the weekend arrived, she pulled on her boots and the oilcloth coat and hiked into the woods to drop off more supplies for Shania. She left cans, camp fuel, and a note: *I'm sorry about your last visit. Please let me know if you're all right.* But she didn't offer help.

On her way back to the cottage, the pain in her forehead traveled to her neck. She swallowed three Advil before bed.

THIRTY-TWO

"YOU REALLY SHOULD GO TO THE DOCTOR," AIDAN repeated the following day. When she ignored his observation, he said, "Listen, I am happy to help you strategize a way out of your predicament. There must be something."

"I can't imagine what, Aidan. I signed the note. And there's an eviction notice on my kitchen table."

"I have a lawyer friend who would be willing to look at the contract."

"I can't pay them."

"I understand. But, if it's okay with you, let me see what I can do."

She nodded. *Don't get your hopes up*, she told herself.

At lunch, she remained at her desk to avoid Michaela's questions. Her appetite was gone anyway. Red pen in hand, she marked up an essay. The poor kid loved semicolons but had no idea how to use them. As she struck through an entire paragraph, the phone rang.

"I'm at work," she told Steven. *Go away*, she thought.

"Look, I know you're angry. But I've been researching; if Periwinkle is named a historic property, they can't tear it down."

"What?"

"I googled it. You can apply, and if you're chosen, the cottage will be protected. It also means you get tax credits, and you can apply for special loans for upkeep and so on."

"How long would it take?"

"About a year. Maybe a little more."

The dimples in the concrete walls of her office resembled lunar craters. She stretched out a hand but misjudged the distance. Her fingers wouldn't reach—at least, not unless she pushed her heavy desk across the tile floor.

"Gwen?"

"I don't have that kind of time," she said, and hung up. She had less than three months to fix the cottage or the town would condemn it, and less than a year to wiggle out of the loan.

At home, a series of birdcalls interrupted Gwen's work. The calls were frantic, outraged. Seconds later, a barred owl landed in a tree, weighting the branch to the ground. At once the other birds scattered in terror, a flurry of dried leaves and feathers. The owl turned her head and looked at Gwen with obsidian eyes.

"What is it?" Gwen whispered.

The bird stared, unmoving. A breeze ruffled her feathers, revealing the pale down underneath. Her talons clutched the branch, each claw sharpened, dangerous.

Gwen pressed her nose to the glass. The owl cocked her head, a jerk to the right, and, with a single beat of outstretched wings, lifted away, rattling the tree.

Below the window, among the frozen roots, Gwen found a single striped feather. She placed it on the dining room table next to her collage. The brown and gray stripes echoed the color scheme of the shells as if they belonged together. She lifted a few unglued whelks and nestled the feather between the rows, tucking the quill and adding a dollop of rubber cement. Her valentine would join Alexander's on the wall, an offering to a lost love, his for Anna, hers for her family. Both would go down with the house.

The Misses had been quiet recently. Gwen dreaded the moment they woke up to bulldozers and jackhammers. It would be best if they went in their sleep.

She dotted glue on cardboard, holding the last shells in place until it hardened.

The scrape of gravel in the drive announced Mrs. Condon's arrival. She stepped inside, wiping her feet on the mat. "I brought you some things." She pulled snow boots from a plastic shopping bag. "You shouldn't go walking in the woods without a proper pair."

"Mrs. Condon, that's too much. I can't accept those."

"Don't be silly. They're just sitting at the back of my closet, getting no use at all." She pressed them into Gwen's arms and held out a white tube. "For the bruise," she said, pointing at Gwen's forehead.

"How did you know?"

"Aidan Kemble called me. He was worried about you. Hold still." She squeezed the clear gel onto her fingers and gently dabbed it on Gwen's blue-and-black forehead. "Arnica," she said. "Put it on as much as you want. It's homeopathic, whatever that means."

"Thanks," Gwen said. *Please leave.* "I should tend to the fire."

Mrs. Condon smiled. "Go right ahead." She followed Gwen into the living room.

Defeated, Gwen stepped over her piles of blankets and pillows and dropped three big logs onto the embers.

"Will you look at this," Mrs. Condon said, lifting Gwen's spiral of shells and moss. "Just like your sister."

Gwen picked the bedding off the floor and began to fold it. "Can I get you anything?"

"No, dear," she said. "I just came to check up on you. Don and I were wondering how you're doing. I can't imagine it's any fun without heat and all."

Gwen turned to poke at the fire, urging it along.

"You can always come up the road and stay with us for a bit. You don't have to suffer, you know."

Yes, I do, popped into Gwen's brain. "I'm responsible for my situation, Mrs. Condon," she said, needlessly rearranging logs, unwilling to meet Mrs. Condon's level gaze. How could she tell her what she'd done? Because the Condons lived down the lane, Hugh would surely make her and her husband's lives unpleasant.

"You know," Mrs. Condon said after a minute. "Your mother came back here the fall after your sister passed. After she dropped you at that boarding school."

Gwen straightened.

Mrs. Condon nodded. "She didn't want to see anybody. She wrapped her arms around herself like she was in a straitjacket, but I invited myself in. I guess I have a habit of that." She chuckled. "Anyway, I asked her—same as I asked you—how she was doing. And you know what, she sorta said the exact thing you just did."

"What?"

"She said she was responsible."

"Responsible?"

Mrs. Condon moved a jumble of pillows aside and sat heavily on the flowered sofa. "To be honest with you, she didn't make much sense. She rambled on and on about Molly and how she was to blame. I kept saying it was an accident, but she acted like I wasn't even there, not even in the room. She kept saying, *How could you, how could you.*"

"She meant that for me," Gwen said. "I left Molly."

"No, dear, I'm sorry, but no. At the end of that afternoon, I understood. Your mother said she hadn't been paying attention; she was so wrapped up in the garden, concentrating on other things. She was distracted. She saw your sister walk to the water, but she didn't follow. She was so sure that Molly would never step foot in the ocean that she didn't go after her. Not even when she heard a splash. She thought it was a seal. And then, to make matters worse, you, young as you were, you had to find her. It broke your mother's heart, thinking about you pulling that little body out of the water. All her fault, she said."

Gwen arranged and rearranged this in her head. It didn't make sense. "She never said that to me."

"It can be hard to talk about the things that hurt the most. She didn't want you to see her pain. She thought the boarding school was the right answer."

"She sent me away because she couldn't stand to look at me."

"That school was to protect you. To keep you from listening to the fights between her and your dad."

Gwen's hands flapped like fish out of water. "But . . ." Words refused to form.

Mrs. Condon stood. "Well, you sit with this for a spell, and then you decide what to do." She reached for Gwen's shoulder and squeezed. "Our door is always open to you. And Steven and Jess may have made some mistakes, but they are your friends. They love you, Gwen."

So Mrs. Condon already knew. Of course she did. No one did anything in this town without May Condon knowing about it. Gwen started to apologize just as Mrs. Condon walked away. "See you later, Gwennie," she said. The kitchen door opened and closed.

The living room, once so familiar, looked foreign, as if she had blinked and someone had rearranged all the furniture. Her legs buckled. The flowered sofa caught her. She dropped her head into her hands. She and her mother had each played a role—and their guilt had only hardened with every passing year. After the funeral, they'd never mentioned the accident again. Engulfed in shame, neither had dared. Eventually, even uttering her sister's name had become impossible, the unspoken prohibition in effect until her mother's death. And, because they'd been so afraid, they'd never spoken of Molly's life, either, her warmth and creativity, her laughter and resilience. Molly's room had remained untouched, but her name never again crossed their lips.

How could you? The phrase, transformed, floated, looking for a place to land. It had been Gwen's for so long that there was a hollow place left in its absence, an emptiness that felt like a relief but also sorrow.

Why had her mother never told her how she'd felt? She'd died, lips still mouthing, *How could you?* They could have shared their pain, cut it in half.

If only they'd had more courage.

THIRTY-THREE

GWEN GAVE HERSELF OVER TO GRIEF UNTIL HER EYES grew raw and her stomach emptied.

When the tears stopped, she remained curled on the faded sofa in the middle of a living room that had witnessed so much. And yet, somehow, nothing had changed; no furniture had been reupholstered, and no lamps had been rewired. Not a single cushion had been moved. Even the books—the Misses', her father's, and hers—had remained in the same places on the shelves for over twenty years.

Now, because of her folly, it would all land in a heap at the dump.

Sorrow crested and broke once more. The Misses awoke. They fussed, a murmur in the walls. "Shh," Gwen said. "Go back to sleep." They didn't need to know what awaited their beloved cottage yet.

Aidan pretended not to notice her puffy face, but he brought his lunch into her office.

Gwen couldn't manage a conversation. "I'm terrible company."

"Me too," he said as he bit into his peanut butter and jelly.

Two weeks later, after the worst had passed, she called Mrs. Condon. "Thank you for telling me what I needed to hear," she said.

When Mrs. Condon finally spoke, her voice sounded rough. "No charge, dear."

———

THE DAY BEFORE Thanksgiving, a few hours before Leandro's flight touched down in Portland, Gwen packed a suitcase. Before she left, she called Mrs. Condon to tell her where she was going, adding, "Please don't worry."

"I see," Mrs. Condon said, asking no questions.

Gwen shoved her bag into the Subaru and drove to the Black Anchor for takeout. Paper turkeys in pilgrim hats were taped to the deli case in honor of the upcoming holiday. The man behind the counter was in no rush, carefully packing soups and salads into plastic containers.

Gwen stood in line behind Pearl. "Hi there," she said, tapping the older woman on the elbow.

"Gwen." Pearl smiled. "I'm glad I ran into you. Did you find the book on mathematical history you were looking for? I did some research, and I think I know where to turn. There's a textbook called *The History of Calculus*. I can get a used copy for you. It won't cost you much."

"Thanks, yes."

"Did I hear you might be selling your house?"

Gwen started to ask where Pearl had heard this juicy bit of gossip and stopped herself. It didn't matter; it would happen regardless. "Maybe." Janet hadn't confronted her with the late payment yet, but Gwen expected it would happen sooner rather than later.

"Oh dear." Pearl shook her head. "That would be a tragedy." She took her bag from the counter and turned to go. "Well, have a lovely Thanksgiving."

Gwen advanced to the front of the line and placed her order. Waiting, she checked her phone to see if Leandro had texted. Nothing yet. She plucked a bag of potato chips from a wicker basket in front of the deli case and placed it on the counter. Her phone pinged. *Almost there.*

Once her order was ready, Gwen grabbed everything and raced out the door, nearly knocking Mr. Condon, who was just entering, off his feet.

"Careful, there, missy," he said, recovering.

"Sorry," she shouted, already halfway to her car. She sped up the hill, praying the sheriff wasn't parked around the bend waiting to dole out his quota of tickets.

The late-afternoon sky was pale gray, the ponds patched with ice. Smoke rose from chimneys and rooftops. Once night fell, Periwinkle would be cold, so very cold and empty, the conditions in the deep woods even worse. She pushed an image of the shivering girl away.

Leandro waited at his door. He opened his arms, and she stepped inside.

"Gwen," he said into her hair.

"I brought dinner," she said. "Black Anchor's finest."

She tossed the salad with Leandro's dressing and warmed the chicken soup on the stove. The smell filled the kitchen as they ate potato chips straight from the bag. When the soup was ready, he ate quickly and returned to the stove for more. "Best meal I've had in a week," he said.

He pushed his empty dish away and said, "Should we go upstairs?"

He'd cleared a wider path into the room for her. She stopped at the edge of the bed, facing her portrait, her seal body half-hidden under her skin. Summer seemed like a million years ago, a foreign country she could never revisit.

"What is it?"

She shook her head. "I don't know where to start."

He nodded, eyes grave.

"I'm so tired," she said.

He pulled her sweater over her head and unzipped her jeans, a hand on her waist as she stepped out. He handed her a T-shirt and lifted the duvet so she could crawl in. She curled under the covers, her cheek on the smooth cotton. He climbed in beside her.

"What is true, Cookies?"

She said, "I got so much wrong, and . . ." She'd cried so many tears in the past few days that she was desiccated, completely unable to imagine crying anymore. But when she put her head on his muscled shoulder and inhaled his warmth, she started again. "It ruined everything."

"Gwen," he breathed.

She kissed him, his lips salty with her tears. She wrapped her legs around him, chest to chest, her mouth on his. When he entered her, she gasped and pulled him even closer; their bodies knitted together so that she could no longer tell which was hers. In the dark of his room, the stars visible through the skylights above their heads, they floated, weightless in the vastness of space, moving so slowly it felt as if this could go on forever. And it almost did. Almost. Eventually, they slid apart by inches. She stroked his cheek. He held her until she fell into a well, cushioned and silent.

————

THE SMELL OF browning butter and onions woke her in the morning. She pulled a sweater over Leandro's T-shirt and wandered downstairs. He stood over the stove, a wooden spoon in his hand, sausage, sage, and breadcrumbs mounded on a cutting board nearby.

"Good morning," he said. "There is coffee. Not the cheap, uncheerful stuff."

She filled a mug, laughing. "What is this?" She nodded toward the stove.

"It is Thanksgiving, and I am in charge of the stuffing. We are expected at two o'clock."

Her heart sank. "I'm supposed to make sweet potatoes." After her conversation with Mrs. Condon, she'd neglected everything.

Leandro brushed the hair from his forehead and smiled. "With marshmallows."

"Steven mentioned it?"

"He did."

"I should go to the store." Drinkwater Provisions would be closed. Hannaford's in Blue Hill would be the closest option, a grocery chain filled with last-minute shoppers, all grumpy because they'd forgotten the garlic or burned the pie crust.

"I have already done that."

How did she get so lucky?

She spent the next hour wrestling with the monster sweet potatoes, mashing them into an orange paste, melting a lake of butter. Leandro coached her to add salt, a grind of pepper, and some maple syrup. After she dumped the heavy glop into a baking dish, she opened a bag of mini marshmallows. She arranged them in a spiral in imitation of the valentine she'd left on Periwinkle's dining room table. When she finished, she slid it into the waiting oven. Twenty minutes later, the marshmallows began to bubble, and butter spat over the edge of the pan.

Leandro threw her a chef's kiss. "Perfection," he said.

She placed the hot dish on the counter beside his perfectly browned stuffing. "I'm going to go change," she said. Digging through her bag, though, she couldn't find her favorite blue shirt.

"I have to go to Periwinkle," she told him. "Back in a jiff."

———

COLD HAD SETTLED into the cottage walls and floor, everything frozen and still. She dropped her purse on the empty kitchen table. It took her a minute to notice that the paper with the ninety-day warning was missing.

"Hello?" she said to the air, expecting an answering thump or an angry creak. She walked into the living room. Someone had moved her valentine to the edge of the table. "Miss Gilmore? Miss Whitehead?" she asked the rafters. No one responded.

Shivering, she dug through her closet until she found the shirt she wanted.

"Hey," she heard behind her back. She whipped around, her heart racing.

Shania stood in the doorway in Gwen's oilcloth coat.

Gwen put a hand to her sternum. "You startled me," she said.

"You were gone."

"At Leandro's."

"When are you coming back?"

"I'm not."

Shania watched her, her expression wary. "Something's going on."

Gwen sat on the edge of the bed. "I can't stay here, Shania."

"Because it's too cold for you."

Gwen slowly shook her head. "No. Because they're going to condemn the house."

Shania crossed her arms over her chest. "The asshole."

"Yes, the asshole. And you need to think about your exit strategy, too."

"Fuck that."

"I can help you talk to your social worker."

Shania's eyes sank deeper into their sockets. "I thought we were friends. You said I could come to you. You said I could stay here."

Gwen sighed. "That was before. Things have changed."

Shania turned her head, her jaw clenched. "I'm not leaving."

"Who's going to bring you food? Who's going to make sure you're okay?"

"I can take care of myself."

Shania wiped a sleeve across her face. Her fingernails were bitten to the quick, and dirt encrusted her cuticles. She looked impossibly young.

Gwen softened her tone. "I know it's confusing. But I was outmaneuvered by someone a lot smarter and more experienced than I am, and because I didn't do what he wanted, the cottage will be condemned. Even if, by some miracle, it isn't, the house needs massive repairs that I can't afford. I owe a huge amount of money I don't know how to repay, and right now, my only resource is this land. If you have any ideas, I welcome them. But"—Gwen shook her head—"there is just no way you can stay here. I have to sell. Once they tear the cottage down, the developers will come for you. They will chase you out of the woods and report you to the sheriff for trespassing. Your absolute best recourse is to let me help you negotiate something with foster services. I have a friend who knows the system. We can help you."

"No. Fucking. Way." Shania wouldn't look at her.

Gwen sighed. She'd done all she could. "Look, it's Thanksgiving. Would you like to come to dinner?"

"It's a stupid, made-up holiday. The whole story of the pilgrims and the American Indians is a myth. White people stole from the Pequot and the Ogunquit and the Wabanaki, taking what they wanted. It's not a holiday; it's

America's original sin. Besides bringing hundreds of enslaved workers across the ocean, of course."

"I don't think I should leave you alone right now."

Shania lifted her chin, defiant. "What do you care?"

"Fine. Suit yourself," Gwen said. In the bathroom, she downed a Claritin—Steven's enormous cat always wanted to cuddle—and hastily dabbed foundation to the lingering yellow-green on her forehead.

As she was leaving, Shania sat cross-legged on the blue sofa, an open book on her lap and the oilcloth coat beside her. Gwen added logs to the grate and lit the paper below, carefully replacing the fire screen afterward. She started to say, "Make yourself at home," but Shania had done precisely that more than once. "You'll be okay?" she asked instead.

Shania, her face hidden behind a curtain of black hair, didn't look up. "Whatever."

Gwen got in the car, frowning.

———

STEVEN MET HER at the door in an apron emblazoned with a giant turkey. He put a drink in her hand. "A Pumpkin-tini," he said. "My own creation."

"It's great," she said, after taking a sip.

"Of course it is." He walked across the kitchen and picked up the yellow notice from the code enforcement officer. "Aunt May brought it with her. You never said anything." His voice sounded outraged.

So much for privacy. Mrs. Condon must have gone over to check on the house once Gwen left.

Steven waved the paper. "Is this why you've been acting so weird?"

Jess appeared in the doorway, the Condons at his shoulder, a phalanx of grim faces. He asked, "Who reported the cottage? Was it Hugh?"

She nodded.

Jess's eyes darkened. "That fucker."

"Jess, goodness," Mrs. Condon said.

"Jess's right." Mr. Condon shook his head. "I wouldn't trust that Fox man to do the right thing unless you paid him. His papa was the same."

Leandro opened the back door and stepped inside. He bent forward and kissed Gwen's cheek. "It is an intervention, yes?"

"They're telling me Hugh's an asshole."

Steven opened the oven door and put in the sweet potatoes and stuffing. "He's a ruthless person, regardless. But that"—he nodded toward the violation paper—"is beyond the pale. I had Jess call the code enforcement officer."

"You did what?"

Jess lifted a shoulder. "I went to grade school with Nan. She says that a notice of intent to fix is good enough. If you show her that some progress has been made, she said they'll work with you."

Gwen shook her head. "That's so kind. But I signed the loan agreement. And I don't have the money to fight this in court."

Steven handed plates to Leandro, who carried them to the table. "We are going to put our heads together."

The room wavered. *It's too late*, she thought. There was nothing any of them could do, but they were all smiling expectantly, so, instead, she said, "Thank you."

Leandro kissed her ear. "You see how you are loved."

"Enough mushy stuff," Steven said, removing his apron. "Dinnertime."

They held hands as Leandro offered grace to the God of Many Names. Dishes were passed, and plates filled. Steven complained that Jess had left the turkey in too long, but Gwen thought it was amazing. There was cranberry sauce and gravy, mashed potatoes, a heap of stuffing, and green beans. When her sweet potatoes made the rounds, Steven didn't take any.

"Steven?" Gwen said, holding out the spoon.

"Oh, I hate them."

"But you asked me to make them."

"So you wouldn't pull a runner and decide to stay in bed all day."

Gwen's mouth opened. Was she utterly transparent?

286

Jess whispered, "There are no secrets in Port Anna. Not even your innermost thoughts are hidden."

Laughter rippled across the table. An hour into the meal, the sun started to set, orange at the horizon, with a glow that filled the room. Mr. Condon pushed his chair back and folded his arms across his belly, hands tucked into his armpits. There were crumbs in his beard.

"Hard to believe weather is headed our way," Steven said, pouring more wine.

"Have you heard the forecast?" Leandro asked. "That storm looks like a monster."

Jess added, "Supposed to dump a foot or more."

"Gwen's first nor'easter, and it's a humdinger," Mrs. Condon said. She looped a stray hair back into her bun.

"I've lived through a hurricane or two," Gwen said. Once, creek water had reached the front door of her graduate student housing. But that was more than two hundred miles inland, and, in Maine, a storm would bring snow and ice, too.

Jess pointed to the far horizon. "I bet it starts before we go to bed tonight." With this, the lighthouse horn started to sound. Goose bumps broke out on Gwen's arms.

As if she'd seen, Steven's cat jumped into Gwen's lap, purring. Her heartbeat tickled Gwen's thigh.

Steven grabbed empty plates and stood. "Anyone for coffee?"

Gwen nudged the cat to the floor. "I should head back. I'll take the rest of the sweet potatoes with me." Shania might eat them.

"No," Jess yelled from the kitchen. "Not all of them."

They cleared the table and set the pans to soak. Leandro held her waist as Steven filled plastic tubs with leftovers, shaking his head. "We could feed the peninsula."

"And your banana bread has taken over the freezer," Jess said. "Can't you find something else to do with that sourdough starter? How about some English muffins for a change?"

Steven stuck out his lower lip in a pout. "Everyone likes my banana bread! It's tangy."

Leandro said into her ear, "I'll drive."

"Do you mind?" She should have said no to that last glass of wine. Everyone hugged good night at the door, even shy Mr. Condon, stomachs and hearts full.

When they reached the car, the wind had picked up, lashing the trees. Pine cones and leaves fell on the windshield, and branches smacked the road.

Gwen nuzzled Leandro's neck. "Periwinkle, please."

He raised his eyebrows. "You cannot be serious. This is absurd—" He stopped his diatribe. "Ah, the girl is there."

The car bounced as they ran over a tree limb. "Cookies, you should not stay in that house if the weather is dangerous." His voice was grave. "You must call, should you need me."

"I'll keep the phone in my pocket," she promised. As she closed the car door, the lighthouse horn sounded, a bass note to the high-pitched roar of the wind.

"Hey," she called out. "I'm back." A strong gust pushed at the cottage, bending the exterior walls. She put the leftovers on the counter.

Shania came into the kitchen, a quilt wrapped around her shoulders and the damaged copy of *Treasure Island* in her hand. Her face and hands were clean. "Smells good," she said.

Gwen stuck a plate heaped with food into the microwave. "How's the book?" she asked.

"Good. I've read it before."

They sat together at the dining room table. Gwen waited, expecting Shania to dump anger and frustration into Gwen's lap once more. But instead Shania started to ramble, mouth half-filled with food. "This is delicious, but it makes me feel a little guilty. Gaggles of turkeys used to walk past my camp, calling to the little ones to keep up. Did you know that the turkey was supposed to be the national bird of the United States? We could have had a majestic creature with a beautiful fantail, smart, hardworking, and family-oriented. Instead, we ended up with a scavenger that eats rotting flesh."

Gwen listened, nodding. Shania had a lot of opinions and a very nimble mind. *Avid*, Gwen thought, *that's the word*. Also, resilient, empathetic, and smart. She'd been through so much—endured hardships Gwen couldn't begin to understand—and yet here she was, eager and funny and trusting. What this child couldn't do, given half a chance. God, she could rule the world with a brain like that. Gwen shook her head in admiration.

"What?" Shania said, mouth full. "Am I talking too much?"

"No, not at all." This kid needed to be in school, not wandering alone in a forest.

Shania pushed her plate away, her sharp little face breaking into a smile. "I guess scavenging isn't so bad."

Gwen picked up the plate, scraped clean. "I'm glad you liked everything."

"Did you cook it?" Shania asked from the living room as Gwen stuck the utensils in a tub of frigid, soapy water.

"Just the sweet potatoes," she said, drying her cold hands.

Gwen returned to the living room. Shania's face was still, her eyes far away. Her fingers brushed Gwen's collage of shells and feathers. "You made this?"

Gwen nodded. "For the house."

Shania looked at her hands. "Please, can't I stay?" she whispered. "I won't bother you, I swear. You'll never even know I'm here, just like last summer."

Gwen took a breath. "Shania, this is not negotiable." She tried to sound patient, but she heard the frustration leaking into her voice.

"There must be something you can do."

"Well, there isn't. Look, I am not trying to hurt you . . . Truly, I'm not. I've fucked myself more than anyone, but no."

"Then take me with you."

"I can't." For the foreseeable future, Gwen would sleep on couches, dependent upon her friends' forbearance. "You should be in school." Someone needed to care for this girl, someone settled and stable, someone with experience handling runaway teens, someone who wasn't Gwen.

"Why do you get to say what I should or shouldn't be doing? You don't know anything about me."

"Well, I know you can't keep doing what you're doing, Shania."

"I don't want to go anywhere else or be anywhere else. I don't want another shitty foster family. I want to be with you."

I want to be with you. The words sank like a stone into the pit of Gwen's belly. "You need someone who can look after you."

Shania's eyes filled. "You can do that."

"No, I can't." She couldn't even take care of herself.

"Please."

Gwen was sick of the conversation. What the girl proposed was impossible. "Shania," she said with finality, "I am not your mother."

Shania's mouth hardened, lips compressed into a thin line. Her fingers curled around the heart-shaped rock at the center of Gwen's shell collage.

"What are you—" Gwen reached out to grab Shania's wrist.

But Shania had already torn the stone from the cardboard. With a scream of rage, she hurled it across the room with shocking accuracy. The rock found its target, striking the center of the Sailor's Valentine with a crash. The old glass disintegrated. Shells shattered and fell in a shower of pale pink and blue.

Gwen froze, shocked. The beautiful, precious relic offered to Anna, her mother's favorite piece, was destroyed. By a girl who had no idea what this meant to Gwen, to the Misses. Rage shot into her mouth. "How could you?" she screamed.

Shania's eyes widened, frightened. She bolted for the door, leaving it wide open behind her.

THIRTY-FOUR

COLD AIR AND BLOWING SNOW POURED INTO THE ROOM. Gwen, furious, slammed the door shut so hard the wall rattled. The Valentine's black frame lay cracked open on the step, the heart-shaped rock still inside. Broken glass and splintered shells dusted the floor below.

Gwen reached careful hands underneath the shattered mess and picked it up. On the table, she removed the rock. When she sifted through the shards, looking for anything that might remain intact, her fingers snagged on a piece of yellowed paper beneath the torn silk. She pulled it out gently and uncurled it. The brown ink, protected all these years from the sun, remained vivid.

My dearest Anna. I returned for you, but you had gone. I pray one day you will see this and know I was ever thine. My regret is profound. I should never have left. You are what I desire most, what I have always desired most, in this sad world. All I want is you. Only you. Alexander.

Grief flooded the room. *Only you.* The phrase echoed. *All I want is you. I want to be with you.*

Inside Gwen's chest, something cracked. She grabbed the oilcloth coat from the sofa and threw open the door. The wind yanked the handle from

291

her grasp, sending the screen crashing into the wall. "Shania?" she called into the dark.

Pine tree branches whipped from side to side, and in the distance the lighthouse howled. Gwen squinted into the darkness. Out front, the ocean churned, waves breaking over the ledge. Snow and ice slapped her cheeks.

"Shania!" she shouted. The wind screamed across the rocks, and Periwinkle's shutters rattled. Halfway down the steps, she slipped, the wood already iced over. From the porch railing, crows yelled, their feathers on end.

"Shania," Gwen called again, her voice swallowed by the storm. The sea sent fingers over the berm, splashing into her yard, trickling beneath the house.

Gwen took the path toward the woods, but before she ducked into the trees, a crow landed in front of her, its beak opened wide. The bird shrieked and hopped, forcing her backward. Something caught Gwen's eye just as she raised her arms to chase it away. A shape moved in the middle of the raging water.

Shania stood on the second ledge, the open, raging ocean at her feet. The water splashed upward, hungry.

Gwen ran across the icy grass, tripping on the mounded rocks of the berm. Hands out to steady herself, she scrambled up. The ice reached her core, slowing her progress.

"Shania," she called. Her voice cracked.

Waves slammed the ledge, sending spray high in the air. Foam landed on the girl, frigid, salty rain, but Shania didn't flinch.

Seawater splashed Gwen's shins as she waded into the surf toward the first ledge. She yelled again, but the wind carried her voice away. She leaned forward, gripping the rock face. Her foot found a boulder but, as she pulled herself up, it shifted and she was knocked off balance. Her knee landed on the barnacles that hid beneath the seaweed, sharp as knives. Hot pain clashed with cold numbness, making her whole body tremble. She pulled herself out of the rising water with numbed fingers.

Using her hands and knees, she crawled across the ledge until she reached the drop-off. Between the two ledges, the ocean churned. Gwen gathered her strength and jumped, landing with her torso on the flat rock. Despite the numbing cold, she felt the blow to her ribs and side. She clamped her fingers around grooves in the stone, fighting the slip of seaweed and the pull of the waves. She gritted her teeth, held on, and rolled onto the sloping expanse.

The girl turned.

Gwen sat up and slid forward using her heels, arms outstretched. "Come on, please." Her ears hurt, a deep ache. "This is dangerous."

Shania didn't react. She watched Gwen with wary eyes.

The air in Gwen's lungs felt like shards of glass. How could Shania just stay there in the frigid water, unable to feel her feet? The cold stabbed, relentless, penetrating clothes and skin. Gwen's stomach shrank, cleaving to her ribs, the shivering nearly uncontrollable.

A wave rose and smashed into the girl, and for a moment, Gwen couldn't see. When her vision cleared, she saw Shania had edged down the slope, closer to the open ocean.

"No!" Gwen scooted forward. "Please, no." Her voice quavered, the shivering so violent she could barely control her limbs. "Please come back. Please."

Shania said, "I broke it."

Gwen edged closer until only a few feet separated them. She reached her hand out, trembling. "Don't do this."

Shania's face crumpled. "I ruin everything." Her wet hoodie was weighted down, exposing her clavicle.

"I promise it's okay. Just come back."

Gwen's hands opened and closed, looking for something to hold, but everything was off-kilter and unstable. A wave formed behind Shania, a black mountain rising. Reaching forward, Gwen tried to scream, but the sound was lost in the wall of water that hit them both. The shock of the cold took Gwen's breath. The sea grabbed the heavy oilcloth, a million hands that yanked and tugged. It wanted her, and she hadn't the strength to fight. She sank, her mouth full of salt water, Shania's hoodie clutched in her closed fist.

Seaweed brushed her face and neck as she fell. Caught in the undertow, they twisted, the cotton of Shania's sweatshirt rotating around Gwen's biceps until Shania's limp body was next to hers. It was black and quiet beneath the waves. It would be so easy, so very easy, to stop fighting and give in to the darkness. Their bodies swayed. For a moment, it was all she wanted, this drifting peace, this silence.

But when Shania's leg flopped against Gwen's, *Fight*, she screamed at herself, *she has to live*. She kicked once, twice, a third time, and their heads broke the surface. Gwen strained to orient herself, but the waves were too high, the water too rough, and she couldn't see anything. She spun around, eyes stinging. The cotton hoodie stretched, and Shania's body started to slip. Gwen's hands wouldn't tighten. Water splashed Shania's slack face. *Please*, Gwen pleaded. *Help*.

She screamed, "Help," the sound stolen by the waves. She screamed again, helplessly, as the great crests and troughs of the water lifted and lowered, tossing their bodies. Through the splatter of snow and salt, the lighthouse beam swept overhead, but she couldn't tell which direction it came from. "Help," she whispered.

Something nudged her side.

A seal's black eyes looked into Gwen's. Part of her recognized that this wasn't possible; she must be dreaming, adrift in the hallucinations brought on by hypothermia. But she blinked, and the seal was still there, its mottled brown face only inches away. It looked at her as if it knew her.

The animal turned.

Gwen couldn't make sense of it, but she kicked her feet and swam behind the seal's sleek head. Somehow keeping her grip on Shania's hoodie, Gwen battled the sea, white water breaking over their faces. She couldn't see the shore and had no idea where she was going, but she kept moving.

There was a low bark as the seal leaped from the water onto the rocks. Gwen, buoyed on the crest of a wave, landed, too, still clutching the girl.

She knelt on the rocks, her breath ragged, wind and snow cutting through her skin, reaching for her heart. At her knees, Shania's face was white and still. *No, no, no*, her head screamed. She locked her arms around the girl's rib cage and pulled her upright. When Gwen stood, eyes flicking to the ocean, the seal had gone. The lighthouse's white beam revealed nothing behind a curtain of blowing snow.

THIRTY-FIVE

IT TOOK A LONG TIME TO DRAG SHANIA UP AND OVER THE berm and across the lawn. Once they reached the stairs, Gwen sat and pulled Shania into her lap. She scooted upward, one step at a time, Gwen holding Shania's body to her own until they reached the cottage door. Gwen threw it open, carried Shania inside, and placed her gently on the floor.

Wind and snow poured into the room.

When she turned to close the door, a crow flew over her head and landed on the mantel. It squawked once, twice, beaded eyes on the girl lying motionless before the fireplace.

Shania was crumpled, unmoving. Her head listed to the side, fingers curled, feet pigeon-toed. She was breathing, but only barely.

Gwen's teeth clacked so hard she thought they might shatter. Her brain wasn't working very well. *Think, think, think.*

Panic rose. With a sob, she dropped to her knees, reciting the guidelines she'd memorized in sailing class three decades ago.

Wet clothes off.

She yanked off the heavy coat and stripped herself, then Shania. Without her oversized hoodie and baggie jeans, the girl looked even smaller, her bones sharp. Small scars etched her torso. Gwen couldn't think about what this meant as she dried the girl's still body.

Add warmth.

She put a log on the fire and grabbed all the covers from her bed. A blanket went on the floor, Shania on top of it. Gwen wrapped a towel around the girl's wet head and ran to the kitchen for Mr. Condon's Mylar blanket. She threw a quilt around her own shoulders and wound her shirt around her bleeding knee.

The Misses moaned. Their distress amplified the noise of the storm outside. The wind howled around the cottage; snow and ice tapped the glass. And beneath it all, the lighthouse horn bellowed.

Check extremities.

She took Shania's hands and feet from beneath the Mylar blanket. The tips of her fingers and toes were white, two an ominous black, and her lips were blue. She needed a hospital, and Gwen's car was still at Steven and Jess's.

Leandro. She turned in a circle, looking for her phone, before she remembered it had been in her pocket when she went into the ocean.

Her chin dropped to her chest. The lights flickered and died; the power lines must have been blown down. On the mantel, the crow hopped from foot to foot, feathers gleaming in the firelight.

Despair crept into the room and squatted in the corner, plotting what would happen next. Water shed from the oilcloth coat spread across the pine floor in puddles. Gwen looked into Shania's still face and knew what she had to do.

THIRTY-SIX

HOURS PASSED. THE STORM BEAT THE HOUSE, FISTS PUM-meling the siding. Branches cracked and fell, followed by trees. The lighthouse called for help that wouldn't come as they lay wrapped in Mylar, Gwen atop Shania, quilts and blankets covering them both. Their limbs aligned, arm to arm, hip to hip, heart to heart. The girl felt like ice; the chill cut through skin, a knife, and yet Gwen stayed where she was, offering what little warmth she had. She shut her eyes and listened to her own breathing, counting, counting, and then to her heartbeats: One, two, one, two. The ball of muscle thumped her chest so hard it hurt. A distant echo came from Shania, an answering beat, and Gwen doubled her focus, one, two, one, two. But the storm out-side intensified; the screen door banged; the crow, talons digging into the mantelpiece, shrieked. Gwen's body jumped in response, and the synchrony of heartbeats was lost.

Fighting tears, she began to speak, words the only defense she had left. She told a story taken from the dreams she'd once had, an offering of all her abandoned plans to a girl who had yet to live.

"You will travel," Gwen said, "Paris and Istanbul and Marrakesh. You'll climb the Eiffel Tower and drink café au lait, visit the Hagia Sophia, and float over the caves of Cappadocia in a balloon. You will learn to speak Spanish and hike through the jungle to Macchu Picchu. Then you'll board a creaky train and venture south to the wilds of Patagonia, where blue whales migrate to calve. You'll brave the wild ocean to see them breach, the large barnacled bodies rising above the surf, mouths open, crashing down. You'll dip fingers into the Nile and eat by candlelight in a tent. You'll ride a camel that spits and honks across desert sands, sun in your eyes and a smile on your face."

The vision unfurled, a magic carpet that swept them away, far from the battering outside and the fear hovering nearby. Together, they soared and floated, drifting, mesmerized by Gwen's descriptions of light refracted in a glass of champagne, the breeze at a river's edge, and fine grains of sand spilling from folds in jeans.

"You'll wear out your backpack. The soles of your hiking boots will fall apart. Your skin will freckle, and your clothes will smell of sweat by the time you stop."

The world, Gwen told Shania, would be hers to explore. And then she would come home, to Port Anna. The words slipped from her mouth before she could reflect whether this was something she should say, and yet, as she uttered them, she was seized with a fierce sort of joy, a desire that gushed from her core, a sensation so powerful, she was unable to fight it.

They'd sit together in this room, Gwen said, one on the blue sofa, the other on the love seat, and read until the sun went down. At dusk, they'd head to the beach to watch a shooting star tear across the sky. They'd make a wish. Afterward, they'd fall asleep, Gwen downstairs and Shania upstairs, snug inside Periwinkle Cottage. The image grew so real that Gwen could taste it, sweet and warm, a vision of family life that hadn't been hers in a long, long time.

Shania would be safe, Gwen said over and over again. She would go to school and learn and do homework at the kitchen table. She'd have boyfriends and girlfriends, and a pet lizard or a turtle that would eat berries right out of her hand. She would be loved.

Gwen would learn to cook. How hard could it be? Of course, Shania would laugh at her first attempts, but eventually she'd learn. When they came home at the end of the day, there would be roasted chicken and meat loaf, mashed potatoes and green beans. No more peanut butter or protein bars.

Shania would never worry about her next meal again. She would be cared-for and attended-to. "You will be loved," Gwen repeated. This became a mantra, uttered over and over until the words became her breath.

Close to dawn, a weak sunrise crept into the room, the assault outside finally at an end.

Gwen sat up. There was a slight flush to the girl's arms and legs. Gwen brushed hair from Shania's face. Shania stirred. Gwen lay back down, wrapped her arms around the young girl, and closed her eyes. The lighthouse horn fell quiet at last.

Almost immediately, the seal's black eyes emerged from the darkness of sleep. They sought Gwen's, whiskers twitching. Gwen had so many questions, but before she could ask, *Who are you? Where did you come from?* the seal was gone, vanished into the deep water.

"Cookies?"

Leandro leaned over her, a worried expression on his face.

"What has happened?"

"Shh." She put a finger to her mouth. "Let's go to the kitchen."

"Why is this in the house?" he whispered, pointing to the mantelpiece. The crow stared at them both, blinked, and shifted shiny eyes to the girl, sleeping peacefully.

"It followed us inside."

They crept past Shania and into the kitchen. Gwen started the coffee. Out the window, snow lay a foot deep, mounded on the trees and rocks, the sun achingly bright.

As she poured coffee into two mugs, the quilt slid from her shoulder, exposing the dark bruises on her ribs.

Leandro said, "You look as if you have been in a war."

"No. Just the ocean."

"What?" His eyes widened. "But it is too cold. That water could kill you."

"Well, it didn't. Either of us."

From the other room, they heard Shania say, "Gwen?" Her voice was hoarse.

Gwen raced back. Shania sat, a dark head emerging from a mountain of blankets. "I thought you'd gone."

Gwen knelt beside her, pressing a hand to the girl's forehead. She felt warm and flushed but not too hot. "How do you feel?"

"Everything hurts."

"Can you move your hands and feet for me?"

Shania wiggled her fingers. Some of the fingertips were dark.

"Leandro is here. He was worried."

Shania drew back.

"He's here to help, Shania."

Shania's eyes searched Gwen's face, and then she pointed at Gwen's cup. "Can I have some?"

Gwen scurried back to the kitchen, where Leandro stood with his back to the sink. He leaned in as Gwen filled another mug. "She needs a hospital, Gwen." He kept his voice low. "She could have pneumonia."

"I know. But the sheriff will come once we say her name. What if they take her away?"

"You can call Michaela Vaughn while we drive," Leandro said. "She will know what to do."

Leandro waited, pacing, while Gwen talked to Shania.

"I'm fine," Shania insisted. But when she tried to prove it by standing up, she fell. "Oh," she said. She reached for Gwen's arm, gripping so hard Gwen winced. "They'll take me back to Portland."

"No, they won't," Gwen promised, hoping she was right. "I won't let them."

She found some Shania-sized clothes in her old chest and helped her get dressed. When she tried to brush Shania's hair, pine sap and salt from the dried ocean water stymied her efforts. She finally gave up and pulled the mass into a rough approximation of a ponytail. Standing back, it was terribly messy but, she decided, still a solid first effort.

Leandro was careful. He spoke softly, reassuringly. Since Shania's boots were at the bottom of the Atlantic, he pulled the car up to the back door and carried her over the snow. With a single cry, the crow followed them outside, sweeping over their heads into the trees. It landed on a branch, scattering snow, and watched the car pull away.

En route, Gwen used Leandro's phone to call Michaela, who promised to meet them at the hospital. Leandro drove slowly, careful with the turns. The main roads were already plowed, but in some places a layer of ice slicked the blacktop. It took more than an hour and a half to reach the hospital, twice as long as it should have.

Michaela arrived minutes after they did, her face puffy from sleep.

"We got you out of bed," Gwen said. "I'm so sorry."

"Don't be silly." Michaela's eyes were on the girl, hunched in a wheelchair. She crouched. "Hi there," she said. She introduced herself before asking questions. Shania answered, her fingers tightly gripping Gwen's arm.

"Why don't you two come on back with her?" the nurse asked Gwen and Michaela after they finished the intake forms. "The waiting room is that way," she told Leandro.

Gwen followed behind Shania's wheelchair down a hallway that smelled of disinfectant.

Doctors came in and out of the room. They all examined Shania, frowning at the old scars, the fresh bruises, a cut on her head. "She needs some tests," one said when they were finished.

The social worker arrived, an androgynous person with thick glasses and a thin tie. Their backpack was stuffed with papers, and they took notes as they talked to Shania. Gwen watched quietly, studying the worry lines on Shania's pinched face.

When the nurse came for Shania, the social worker put a hand out. "Why don't you let Ms. Vaughn go with her?" they suggested.

Michaela went down the hallway, fingers on Shania's shoulder.

The social worker had questions. How long had she known that the girl was living on her own? Did she try to contact the authorities? How had she come by her injuries?

Gwen answered slowly and politely, grateful that Steven had talked her into calling the sheriff weeks ago. It made her seem like a responsible adult, not someone who would neglect a child's welfare.

"Ms. Vaughn says you wish to be the guardian. Is that right?" they asked.

Gwen took a deep breath. "I do."

The social worker looked up from the chart. "It's a long road."

"I have boots," Gwen said.

The social worker stepped into the hallway to make calls. When the door opened again, Gwen leaned forward expectantly, hoping Shania was being returned to the room. But a nurse entered instead, a smile on his face. "Great work reviving her. Old school, but I like it."

Gwen smiled back.

"It won't be too long now. When the doctors are done with her, we will come for you."

Gwen found Leandro in a corner of the waiting room. He insisted that she also needed attention. "Your knee is a mess."

"They're just going to slather it in Neosporin. And charge me hundreds for it."

He sighed. "Very well. Then I shall attend to it." He went to the car and returned with a first-aid kit. His hands were gentle as he cleaned the salt from her swollen knee, covered the gash in lotion, and wrapped it in gauze.

When he finished, Gwen cupped his face in her hands and kissed his beautiful mouth.

An hour later, they were summoned to Shania's room. Michaela sat at the end of the bed, watching the girl sleep.

The doctor gathered them all in the hallway and explained that they'd like to keep Shania overnight. Gwen protested, but the doctor insisted. They needed to be sure her body temperature and heart rate were stable. As a licensed social worker, Michaela could stay, but since Gwen was not a relative or a guardian, the doctor suggested it might be best if she went home for now.

Gwen's eyes filled. "What if she wakes up and panics?"

Michaela put a hand on Gwen's arm. "I'll make sure that she knows you're coming back. Get some rest."

"I could stay in the waiting room."

"You cannot help her, Cookies, unless you get some sleep," Leandro said.

Gwen, resigned, went to say goodbye. As she bent over to kiss Shania's forehead, the girl whispered, "You're going to learn to cook?"

"You bet," Gwen said.

"Ha," Shania said as she drifted away again, snoring softly.

THIRTY-SEVEN

CLUMPS OF SNOW SPACKLED THE ROAD TO PORT ANNA.
The sun dazzled. Gwen leaned her head on Leandro's shoulder, her eyes at
half-mast. "The world is showing off," she said.

"That it is, Cookies."

Her body curled into his.

"We are here," he said softly as they pulled into Steven and Jess's driveway.
A foot of snow covered the Subaru. Steven came to greet them as they swept
it off. "What happened to you?" he asked as she limped around the car.

"It's too much to explain right now," she said.

They both waved to Leandro as he pulled away.

"Well, you missed the excitement here, too. Hugh came by."

"Oh no. What did he want?"

"To yell at Jess."

Gwen swore under her breath as she walked to the house. The cat jumped
from the couch and ran to her. "What did he say?" she asked.

Jess looked up from his iPad, reading glasses balanced on his thin nose.
"He called Aidan. Aidan cussed him up one side and down the other. I gather
he called him a 'usurious son of a bitch.'" Jess laughed. "But he also told him

you two had not discussed the marina deal. So Hugh figured out it was me. He thinks I misrepresented his 'contribution to the community.'"

"I'm sorry," Gwen said. The cat slid between her legs, a grapevine step, purring.

"I'm not. I'm glad I could speak my mind. He won't send any more work my way, but we'll figure it out."

Steven said, "Who knows, maybe our book will sell a million copies, and we won't have to work again."

"Here's hoping." She gently pushed Miss Kitty aside and turned to leave.

Jess said, "Hey, Gwen?"

She stopped.

"I'm so sorry. I know why you trusted him." His voice cracked as he shook his head. "I should never, ever have left you alone that day. I don't know what came over me. I—"

She held up a hand. "Stop." She wrapped both arms around Jess's broad torso. "You were scared, that's all. We were so young, so, so young. You have always been a good friend to me. Couldn't ask for better."

Jess wiped his face on his sleeve when she released him. Miss Kitty followed Gwen to the door.

As she stepped out, Steven pushed a loaf of hot banana bread into her hands. "Stress-baking," he told her. "Call me later?"

"Definitely." She laughed. "Well, once I get a new phone. Mine went for a midnight swim."

"Well, that sounds like a story I need to hear," he said, waving.

Gwen, unsure of herself in the snow, drove very slowly.

There were fresh tire tracks in Periwinkle's driveway that led to Hugh's polished car. He was pacing in front of the cottage, wearing a down jacket so shiny it looked like it was coated in oil. She took a deep breath before she stepped out, banana bread clutched to her chest.

"What do you want, Hugh?"

"I want to talk about this."

"Hugh, I—"

He cut her off. "I've only ever wanted to help." He stepped toward her, a hand reaching for her shoulder. "You know that."

She shook him away, woozy with exhaustion. "I really would like to get inside." All she wanted was to gather clothes and nap in Leandro's wide, white bed until the hospital said she could see Shania.

He wiped a hand across his face. "Goddamnit. I'm not trying to scam you or cheat you. It's a good deal. You'll have financial security. Think about it: You won't have to worry anymore. Shit, you won't even have to work. You can write if you want, and you'll never have to deal with this wreck again." He gestured toward the cottage at his back.

Periwinkle's screen door was caught in a snowdrift, the frame bent. Inside was a disaster: quilts, blankets, and wet towels in a heap, and the Valentine shattered. Gwen's weariness reached her core.

"Hugh . . ." She stopped as exhaustion caused her to sway.

He took her elbow, steadying her. "I can make sure you're safe."

Gwen bit her lip. *Make sure you're safe.* Despite her fury, that phrase hooked something inside her chest and tugged. He knew her weakness. Because, of course he did; Hugh was an excellent salesman. Driving to Maine, she'd entertained fantasies of a moated castle, a place so detached from the world that nothing could ever hurt again. And here it was, the opportunity for just that thrown at her feet: a life of cushioned splendor, numbed contentment, the thing she'd once craved with all her heart.

"Gwennie?" Hugh looked hopeful, smiling as if he'd broken through and she'd come around. He reached out a hand and placed it on her shoulder. "What do you say? Let me take care of you."

Through her open coat, the banana bread warmed her chest.

Her fingers tightened, and the heat spread. "No," she said.

"No . . . ?" He choked a little.

"No."

"But why?"

"Because I have this," she said, smiling as she held up Steven's misshapen loaf.

Unexpectedly, she giggled. There was no way to explain it to him—even if she had the words, Hugh would never understand—but she was filled with joy, so much of it that it bubbled into her throat. It burst from her fingertips and up through the top of her head, and tears rolled down her cheeks.

"I'm sorry," she tried to say. "It's just . . ." She waved her hand. "You can't give me . . . this," she said. All her plans had gone awry, and yet she had banana bread.

Coming to Maine, she'd thought she would live on solid ground, knowing exactly where she stood, never needing to adjust her weight or get her bearings. The bedrock of her adult life had been forged on this peninsula, the grief and regret upon which everything depended. This was the one thing of which she was certain.

At least, that's what she'd thought.

There had been flaws in her logic. Granite crumbled. Foundations failed. Grief morphed and changed shape. And sometimes, the most broken of hearts could be repaired. Somehow, alone on her ledge, everything she'd ever needed had swept in and found her. *Tears of love*, Leandro had said to her. In the middle of grief, there were also gifts: a smushed loaf of banana bread from a friend who knew she forgot to eat, the caress of a man covered in blue paint, and a skinny girl's indomitable spirit.

The story wasn't quite as she'd scripted it—there would be no picket fence, no travel, no brilliant career. And yet, standing in the gravel driveway of her damaged, haunted house, looking out over an expanse of brilliant white toward a blue, blue sea, she also knew this: she was exactly where she wanted to be, a part-time counselor and essay tutor living in a shack by the ocean, smack in the middle of her very own messy, painful, uncertain life.

"I'm sorry, Hugh," she said as she wiped her cheeks.

He grabbed her arm. "You're not making any sense. Don't you know how much you need me?"

"Maybe. But I don't want you, Hugh."

His face hardened. "Let me remind you: you signed the fucking paper. You owe me. This place is mine now."

"At the moment, Periwinkle still belongs to me." She peeled his fingers away. "Now get off my lawn."

"No, no, no." He shook his head, incredulous. "This isn't how it ends. You can't just walk away."

She turned and went inside without a backward glance.

THIRTY-EIGHT

DECEMBER ARRIVED, AND DARKNESS DEEPENED. IN THE weeks before Christmas, a feeble sun emerged for an inadequate six hours, and even the moon hid its light. Gwen spent her days groping through what felt like constant twilight, reaching for familiar landmarks without finding any. It was one thing to walk away from Hugh with a cocky fuck-you attitude, and another thing entirely to wriggle out of a legally binding document.

As anticipated, Hugh called the note a week after Gwen kicked him off her lawn, citing her failure to submit the first payment on time. She had ninety days until she would owe everything she'd spent, plus the interest. The *tick tick tick* of a countdown clock followed her to school and punctuated her dreams.

After some hours at the library, she learned that there were squatters' rights laws in Maine, but her status as such was tenuous. The path to foreclosure was set, and her attorney, a college friend of Aidan's, didn't see a solution. Unless a miracle happened, the cottage and the land would soon belong to Hugh.

The Misses, fully awake, gave in to despair. Cabinets slammed, boxes overturned, and the walls cracked and snapped as they pounded invisible fists in frustration.

Gwen escaped to Leandro's. Before he left again, this time bound for London, he insisted she move into his studio, and she'd gratefully accepted.

Staying at Periwinkle had become increasingly untenable, both emotionally and physically. Since her plunge into frigid water, her hands remained stiff and sore, and the slightest drop in temperature would cause her to shiver. From Shania's doctors she learned that it would take time to resolve, although some of the residual effects of frostbite might be lifelong.

Shania's symptoms were worse. The tips of her ears and several fingers remained stubbornly discolored, and her nose and chin turned white within minutes of exposure. Although she didn't complain, she wore gloves throughout the school day, a hat pulled low.

Between appointments with students and her lawyer, Gwen spent hours on the phone with various state agencies, trying to secure Shania's guardianship. Until Gwen was approved, they decided that Shania would live with Michaela. It had seemed like a great solution at first: Michaela had the training to manage a traumatized teen, and she could take Shania to school every day. But Shania quickly chafed at Michaela's demands.

"Why does she have to nag me?" she complained to Gwen. "*Make your bed, wash the dishes, do your homework, did you do your physical therapy*"—she imitated Michaela's voice. "I know how to take care of myself. I've been on my own for years. None of those foster situations ever took care of me."

"She's not being unreasonable, Shania. She's trying to help you."

Shania ground her fists into her eyes. "And there are all these little kids. They make so much noise! One of them plays their radio nonstop. I can't take it." After her months in the woods, unaccustomed to human voices or loud music, Shania's ears hadn't adjusted. She begged, "Can't I stay at the studio with you?"

"That's not how this process works. You know that. We have to wait for the pencil pushers to sign off."

This resulted in a slammed door as a furious Shania stormed from Gwen's office.

"What on earth was I thinking?" Gwen said at lunch, her head in her hands. "I can't do this."

Michaela smiled. "Yes, you can." She coached Gwen through the arcane bureaucracy, cutting through much of the red tape. Gwen suspected that her help came partly from friendship and partly to get her house back. Shania might be small in stature, but she made her presence known.

Just before Christmas, a call came granting Gwen temporary guardianship. There was still a long road ahead—more forms, references, home visits—but, for now, Shania could live with Gwen on Tapper's Pond. Jess had arranged it with the owners, who needed a live-in caretaker to accept furniture deliveries and let in the electricians.

The house was lovely, nestled in the woods, the walls painted shades of ivory and gray. Teak windows overlooked the frozen pond. But, since it was half-empty, every noise was amplified. Their footsteps sounded like elephants, and their voices ricocheted on bare walls.

"Sorry, sorry," they said as they bumped into each other in the kitchen. Shania left the refrigerator door ajar, and the washing machine—which Gwen liked to run at night—kept her awake. Gwen liked the living room shades closed; Shania preferred them open. Shania hated pasta, and Gwen could cook little else. They tiptoed past one another, trying to learn the steps to a dance neither of them knew.

When she was overwhelmed, Shania took to walking out the front door without closing it. The first time this happened, Gwen stood on the lawn and yelled for her to return, but Shania did not respond.

In the house, Gwen stood anxiously at the bay window, watching her circle the pond, her crow family, which had somehow found her here, following overhead. She held her breath when Shania disappeared into the brush, exhaling minutes later when she reappeared. Rounding the path, Shania stopped to gaze upward into the canopy, running her fingers across a birch's papery bark. She wrapped her arms around an old oak. The forest, Gwen realized, felt more like home to Shania than the house on the pond. Small wonder she preferred the company of trees.

When Shania returned a half hour later, once again failing to shut the door, her eyes were bright. Her chin, though, was too white, and her fingers numb. Even when they were held under warm water, it took too long for the feeling to return.

Gwen pleaded with her to stay indoors until the weather improved.

Shania looked directly at Gwen, her brown eyes serious. "I am a dendrophile."

Gwen sighed. "Maybe just cut it shorter next time? And please remember to close the door."

On Christmas Eve, Shania returned from her walk early. "Come with me," she said.

She led Gwen to a snapped-off crown of a fir tree, the casualty of a recent storm.

"What do you think?" Shania asked.

"It's perfect," Gwen said.

They pulled it back to the house and stuck the trunk into a bucket filled with stones. Gwen found a red towel to wrap around the base. After dinner, they ate popcorn and drank hot cider while Gwen taught Shania how to cut out paper snowflakes to decorate their makeshift Christmas tree. That night, as she lay in bed staring at the ceiling, it occurred to Gwen that they hadn't bumped into one another once that day. *Progress*, she thought, *that's progress*.

In the morning, rays of sunshine, amplified by the glassy pond, flooded the first floor. It was so bright in the kitchen that Gwen had to put on her sunglasses to make pancakes, squinting to read the box's fine print.

"You can close the blinds if you want," Shania said, yawning, before she devoured an entire stack drenched in syrup. Afterward, her chin still sticky, she found her gifts under the tree: a copy of the *The History of Calculus* and a pair of battery-operated, heated gloves.

"For your walks," Gwen said. "So you can stay out longer."

Shania looked at the torn paper and frowned. "But . . . I don't have anything for you."

Gwen pulled her brand-new phone from her back pocket and grinned. "Why would I need anything else?" she said. And she meant it. Mostly.

Eight more weeks, and the cottage would be Hugh's. Dwelling on the loss, though, dragged her away from Shania, from her students, from the project of rebuilding her life without ghosts, and so she forced her brain away from the grieving Misses.

"Let's get dressed," she said. "Steven and Jess are expecting us for lunch."

Steven greeted them at the door in a red Santa hat. "Jess is no fun. He won't dress up."

Jess put an arm around Steven. "You look cute enough for both of us."

Christmas carols played in the living room. White lights, wound through the vintage toys on the mantel, twinkled and flashed.

"Eggnog?" Steven passed a nutmeg-scented glass to Gwen.

"Ooh, I can smell the rum." She laughed.

Shania held out her hand, grinning.

He raised his eyebrows. "It's pomegranate juice for you, missy."

"Yoo-hoo," Mrs. Condon called from the kitchen door. "Mrs. Claus is here." She entered the living room carrying an armful of presents. Mr. Condon trailed behind, frost in his yellowed beard.

Jess leaped to his feet. "Let me help you."

"May!" Steven cried. "We said no gifts this year!"

"Oh, pooh. Let an old woman have a little fun." She handed the packages to Jess and sat down next to Shania. "Everyone needs something to unwrap, especially when there's a young 'un with us."

Mr. Condon pulled a rickety wooden chair from the dining room and placed it beside the sofa.

Steven stood. "Take my seat, Don."

"Perfectly fine right where I am," Mr. Condon said, lowering himself with an "Oof." The spindly legs creaked under his weight.

Mrs. Condon sat beside Gwen on the couch. "Sure are missing your fella."

"Me too. It's hard to turn down an invitation to spend a holiday with brothers you haven't seen in twenty years, though." Leandro and his siblings had agreed to meet in Miami to repair their rift. Leandro had left with hope on his face and, at Gwen's insistence, a bottle of scotch and the last remaining box of Thin Mints in his luggage.

Jess placed a gift in each lap. "One, two, three," he said. "Unwrap."

The sound of tearing paper and delighted *oohs* filled the room. Mrs. Condon beamed. She'd knitted a sweater for Shania, cream with a pale pink trim. Shania hid her face behind it. "Thank you," she said softly.

317

Jess opened his package to find a red scarf, and Steven received a Bundt pan. "In case you want to branch out from loaves of banana bread," Mrs. Condon said. "Coffee cake is good."

Gwen held her gift in her palms, a framed black-and-white photograph of Periwinkle taken just after it had been built. The Misses stood on the lawn in white linen dresses, wide-brimmed hats shading faces awash with joy.

Mrs. Condon patted Gwen's knee. "Sure wish I could give you the real thing."

Gwen inhaled, nodding. She didn't trust herself to speak. Three generations of Condons had cared for the cottage; it was as much a part of their family as hers.

"Who wants more eggnog?" Steven stood up, filling the silence with bustle. He'd tried every angle to fast-track the historic property designation, calling legislators and preservation societies across the state, with no effect. After the last fruitless call, Gwen had told him to stop. "You've done all you can," she'd said.

Mr. Condon cleared his throat and sat forward, his chair creaking ominously. "Sure have enjoyed those stories," he said to Gwen. Somehow, the once-silent Mr. Condon had found his voice. "Even sent a copy of the *Packet* to my sister in Michigan. She keeps asking for the next one."

"I'm working on it," Gwen said. The article about Anna's lover remained unfinished, stalled at the moment he walked out of the woods and handed over his Valentine to Miss Gilmore.

Mr. Condon raised shaggy eyebrows. "You're writing about the man who lived behind the lighthouse?" he asked. "My dad saw him from time to time. Big bushy guy, wild-looking." He extended his arms to indicate a tremendous head of hair.

"His name was Alexander," Gwen said.

Miss Kitty slid past Gwen and curled into Shania's lap, purring. Shania buried her face in the cat's fur.

"How about that?" Mrs. Condon said. "Donald's dad always swore that he was Anna's sailor."

Gwen's eyes widened. "That's so interesting. I found a letter that says the same thing."

"What, now? A letter?" Mrs. Condon put down her eggnog and leaned toward Gwen. "About Anna?"

"Yes, written by Miss Gilmore."

"My goodness."

Steven said, "It's in the book, May. You can read all about it when it's published."

"Well, I hope you show the original to the ladies at the historical society. If it concerns Anna Vale, they will want to see it."

Steven's face brightened. "Could it help save Periwinkle?"

Gwen put a hand on his arm and shook her head. "It's time to stop," she said. Change came with a cost. If Periwinkle had to go, maybe that was how it was meant to be. She had a room full of people who loved her. What more could she ask for?

Steven turned to Gwen. "Stop being so Zen. It's admirable and all, but I'm not ready to give up yet, okay? May, would the letter help us?"

Mrs. Condon leaned back into the couch. "I wouldn't know about that."

Mr. Condon slowly shook his head, his palms folded beneath his armpits. "The Misses aren't going to let that place go without a fight."

Jess leaned forward, forearms on his knees. "If you want to stop Hugh's project from moving ahead, we need something more than a letter. Something tangible that would make the land unusable or unsellable. We already know that it percs for wells and septic because of the survey, so he can build half a dozen houses there if he wants, and the lots are deep enough to accommodate a seventy-five-foot setback." He sighed. "I wish I had another idea. But a letter is not going to get the results you hope for. It's not enough."

Steven's jaw jutted forward defiantly. "Then what would be enough?"

Jess threw up his hands. "I don't know: artifacts, remains, that sort of thing."

"What do you mean, exactly?" Steven asked.

"Years ago, I was part of a crew on a project that couldn't go forward because the bulldozer unearthed American Indian relics and a bone. They called it a burial site 'of archaeological interest,' and it brought the work to a dead stop."

Shania turned her attention from Miss Kitty to the group and sat up. "Burial site? You mean like a grave?"

Everyone turned.

"Yes," Steven said. "Like a grave."

Shania smiled. "I know where it is."

"You see?" Mr. Condon raised his arms in triumph just as his chair collapsed to the floor.

THIRTY-NINE

MR. CONDON ADMONISHED THEM TO STOP MAKING A fuss as he limped to the door after lunch. "I'm not too concerned," he said when Jess suggested he might need medical attention.

"That little bitty chair." Mrs. Condon shook her head. "Jess told you not to sit in it."

"Did nothing of the kind," he huffed.

"Oh yes he did, mister." The Condons bickered all the way to the car. "You just wanted to sit next to our Gwennie. Stubborn old coot."

Steven, laughing, handed out parkas and gloves. "Shall we take a post-prandial walk? Perhaps through Gwen's woods?"

"We shall," Shania answered, stepping into the back seat of the Subaru beside Steven. Jess sat up front with Gwen.

On the drive, Gwen's mood alternated between hope and resignation. In the weeks since Hugh called the loan, she'd run her hands over every square inch of the cottage: the walls and floor, the fireplace, every stick of furniture and artwork. *I will miss you*, she'd said, her heart split in two. *Go in peace*. But now, faced with a potential lifeline, all that hard-earned resignation evaporated, replaced with a wild, furious hope.

"Explain this to me again, Jess," she asked.

"As I said, I only know about this from another project I worked on. But that house was never built. When they found out the land was essentially worthless for development, the owners tried to sue, but there was some clause that made it impossible to get their money back."

Gwen's breath clouded the car window. They passed the Congregationalist church, a handful of people clustered at the front door, wearing down coats and mittens. The bells rang out in celebration, and Gwen's heart lifted in response. If Shania was right, and there was a grave, it would certainly slow him down. And, maybe, just maybe, she could negotiate. If Hugh wanted to punish her, though . . . well, then the outcome wouldn't change. She shut her eyes. Why, oh, why had she told him get off her lawn? The eggnog flip-flopped dangerously inside her stomach.

Jess, Steven, Gwen, and Shania all paused at the forest's edge to zip up jackets and pull hats down. Shania held up her battery-powered gloves. "I feel like a cyborg," she said.

"Lead on, bionic woman," Steven said.

They stepped from the ledge into the cushion of snow-covered pine needles, following the path Gwen had cut months before. Shania's crows squawked overhead, their wings starkly black against the turquoise sky.

"Are they always with you?" Steven asked Shania.

She shrugged. "They don't come into the school building." For the next fifteen minutes, they learned about the cognitive abilities of the corvid family. Crows and ravens recognized faces and built strong attachments. "I used to feed them," Shania explained. "So we're friends."

They came to a clearing, where the half-buried stove stuck out of the snow. Jess stopped and turned in a circle. "What else is here?" he asked.

"I'm not sure. I was so anxious that I'd trip over that rusted old thing that I didn't explore." She kicked the toe of her boot into the crusted ice.

"I wonder . . ." Jess looked thoughtful.

Gwen exhaled sharply. "You think this might have been Alexander's campsite."

"Maybe."

Shania veered away from Gwen's path, leading them into the thick brush. They trudged uphill, where the trees grew closely together, fir and spruce and clumps of aspen. In places, they had to turn sideways to pass. Shania held branches aside for her followers. At the top of the hill, they stopped. A lean-to covered in a green tarp huddled beside an erratic boulder, a small camp stove underneath. One of the supports leaned sideways, weighted with ice. Shania shook the plastic free of its burden and straightened the branch.

"This is where you lived," Gwen said.

Shania nodded.

Inside the shelter, a depression lined with leaves, blankets neatly folded at the foot, suggested a bed. Books were stored inside a clear plastic bin nearby. Gwen recognized the spine of her mother's *Birds of New England*. Shania unsnapped the lid and pulled it out.

"I've missed this," she said.

Steven stomped his feet. "You stayed warm out here? Snaps to you, girl. It's colder than a witch's tit."

"A witch's tit?" Shania looked confused.

Jess shook his head. "Don't listen to him. He says strange things sometimes."

"Okay." Shania shrugged. "This way." She turned and ducked under the low branches of a cluster of fir trees. On the other side, the path headed downhill.

Shania wound silently through the trees. In comparison, the rest of them sounded like a herd of bison, heavy-footed and clumsy. Small pines and slender branches snapped as they made their way toward a half-frozen stream. Steven lifted his leg over a piece of granite, split in two by a massive pine, sliding to his feet on the other side. Gwen, wary of falling, held on to tree trunks to help herself down the slippery rock.

"Hey, girl, slow down," Steven called ahead to the sprite of a girl moving gracefully over the uneven ground.

Shania grinned. "Slowpokes," she said, but she waited for them at the bottom of the ravine. A waterfall rose up the opposite slope, transformed into jagged lengths of ice, shimmering stalactites tinted blue and green.

"Would you look at that," Steven said.

Shania stepped aside to reveal a moss-covered headstone planted beneath the ragged bark of an old river birch.

They read the inscription in silence. *Alexander, Beloved of Anna Vale. Called to His Maker, September 1932. May He Rest in Peace.*

"Oh shit," Steven said. Then he tilted his head back and whooped.

FORTY

GWEN'S ONLY PUBLISHED STORY, "THE MERMAID'S TALE," embellished the widely circulated story of Anna Vale. As the nineteenth century waned, the great schooners of the Maine coast disappeared. Months passed without a shipwreck, then years, as Anna's skin slowly thinned to transparency. Children sometimes returned from the lighthouse with tales of a ghost singing to the seals, their bewitched black eyes fixed on her face. Adults smiled indulgently; none thought to check on the lonely keeper whose only love had left her.

One spring night, the horn blared an unexpectedly loud warning. The residents hid while rain lashed windows and wind tore shingles from rooftops. Days later, when the townspeople emerged, they found the lighthouse door ajar and the building abandoned. Anna had disappeared.

The romantics among them claimed her sailor had come for her at last, while others believed she'd returned to the arms of her sea-goddess mother. Some even insisted she swam the waters still, a pale gray seal with eyes like pitch. Lobstermen and recreational sailors both reported sightings at the ledge beyond the lighthouse.

Thus, the story of Anna and her lover became myth. Because history recorded so little of Anna's existence—and nothing at all of her lover's—it had been easy to transform their lives into fiction. But no real human ever stepped so lightly on the world, leaving nothing of themselves behind. The living wade through the vast remains of those long gone, the dregs of things worn or eaten or used or held, and so it stood to reason that vestiges remained.

A wave of sadness swept over the group standing silently at Alexander's grave site. Gwen removed her glove and ran her hand over the stone. If Anna's story ended on a magical, wistful note, his felt far more tragic.

"Star-crossed lovers," Steven said quietly. "Isn't that what they call it when fate conspires to keep them apart?"

Gwen nodded. She imagined that the Misses had hoped for a different ending, too. They kept Alexander's gift safe, stowed at the back of their closet, hoping Anna would step from the sea and he would return to claim his Valentine. One morning, though, after a long, sleepless night, they pulled on their rubber boots and traipsed into the forest, calling his name. They found him beneath the river birch, empty eyes fixed on the sky. They buried him there next to the stream, placing a granite stone at his head. At the cottage, they removed the Valentine from its frayed parcel, the shells gleaming as if they'd just emerged from the seabed, and placed it on the wall, an ode to the fragile promises of love.

Once they died, though, Alexander's memory faded, his name slowly erased from the headstone by lichen and moss. That is, until one day, fifty years later, a skinny girl hiding in the woods stumbled across it.

"The crows brought me," Shania explained. "They like it here."

"I understand why," Steven said, his face tilted into the shaft of sunlight falling through the branches of an ancient oak.

Jess smiled at his husband's bright face. He reached for Steven's hand. "Let's go, love," he said. "We have work to do."

As they retraced their steps back to the cottage, Shania wrapped an arm about Gwen's waist. "I think Anna is still lifesaving," she said softly.

Gwen could only nod, the knot in her throat too thick to allow words.

Gwen's first phone call after the holidays was to Nan Richoleau, the code enforcement officer. A week later, Nan arrived with a representative of the

State Historical Commission, who followed Shania past the campsite to the grave. Although neither of them said much at the time, the commission later sent two more people to inspect the forest floor. They gently lifted rocks and raked through pine needles. Bundles of cloth and shards of pottery rose from the earth, halting any plans for development until further notice.

"You can fight me," Gwen told Hugh. "But you'll never make money off my land."

Their lawyers agreed to the payment schedule as originally proposed. Hugh would still get his money; if she couldn't pay, the historical site, with its protected land, would belong to him.

In April, once the snow melted and the temperature rose, Gwen and Shania returned to the cottage. Shortly afterward, archaeologists were dispatched to excavate the area. They hauled in generators and tents, widening the trail to the site. Yellow tape marked the area under review, and a careful grid was laid out. Gwen watched them hike past her kitchen window every morning, and waited for the Misses to protest. They did not.

Throughout the spring and into early summer, relics emerged attesting to Alexander's many years of solitude: a pewter cup and plate, shredded blankets and clothing, a set of knives still carefully boxed, and a ragged Bible. A small pile of animal bones and ash identified his trash heap. Clues of his existence were scattered through the woods beyond the cottage, a trail that led from the lighthouse through the woods to Periwinkle.

When the archaeologists paused to catalog their finds, Shania, during summer break from school, peppered them with questions. What made a bit of stone or an end of frayed twine significant? What was so important about the splintered wooden shaft or bit of cloth? The scholars patiently explained the potential of each tiny remnant and what careful analysis could reveal about it.

"We are trying to get a picture of how Alexander lived," they said. "Where he traveled, who he knew, that sort of thing."

A month into their work, they dug up journals, their bindings warped, the ink-streaked pages illegible. Shania peered over their shoulders.

"Oh. That's too bad," she said.

"You'd be surprised what we could still get from things that seem ruined," one assured her. "Even the ink itself is important."

Shania trotted back to the cottage. She opened the closet in the back hall and carefully pulled a box from the shelf.

Gwen appeared in the doorway wearing gloves and safety glasses. Under Jess's guidance, she was slowly insulating the cottage, blowing foam into the attic joists and walls. She frowned. "What are you doing?"

Shania hitched a shoulder toward the woods. "They said that every detail can tell them something important. I thought maybe . . ." She paused, blinking. "Maybe they could learn from this, too."

Gwen took in a long, slow breath. Stored in the box, the Sailor's Valentine was beyond repair, its frame twisted, the silk lining torn, and most of the shells shattered.

Shania lowered her shoulders. "I'm sorry," she said. "I'll put it back. You've already given away so much."

They had already packed up all of Gwen's teenage artifacts—the beer bottles from nights on Hart's Island, tickets from concerts she had attended with Jess and Aidan, and old beach treasures scavenged after long winters—and thrown them in the trash. Shania had removed Gwen's posters and thumbtacked a series of Leandro's drawings to the walls, images of the coastline, rough boulders covered in barnacles and hunks of seaweed. Gwen hadn't been so sure it was a great idea to wake up surrounded by pictures of the water and the rocks that almost took her life, but Shania had gazed at the pictures, mystified. "They're beautiful," she'd said. "And he made them for me." So they stayed.

When they'd first opened the door to Molly's old room, Shania had hung back. "You don't need to do this, Gwen."

But Gwen had shaken her head, determined. "It's time." Twenty-four years was long enough to mourn. Molly's old toys and books, even the tea set, went to the donation center. Gwen kept only the hairbrush and the doll salvaged from the beach, stowing them in the captain's chest under her bedroom window. She no longer needed a shrine to hold the memory of her sister.

The Misses had not protested, apparently ready to stop grieving, too.

Shania held out the box now. "I'm sorry," she said again. "Put it back."

The ceiling creaked, insistent, and Gwen's eyes filled. She wanted the Valentine to stay in the cottage, to return to the hook where it had always been, but that wasn't possible. And it was not what the Misses wanted.

Gwen exhaled, nodding. "You're right. The archaeologists should have it. It's of no use to anyone sitting in a closet."

She stood at the window and watched as Shania stepped from the ledge onto the path, the box clutched to her chest. Above her, the attic sighed.

Shania told Gwen later that the scholars were delighted. They had a colleague interested in the trade routes from Maine to the Caribbean, and the Valentine's shells could help reveal where Alexander's boat had taken him. Maybe even suggest why it had taken him so long to return to Port Anna.

Throughout the long, warm summer, the archaeologists dug ever more deeply. Layer after layer of sediment piled up, and far older artifacts than Alexander's surfaced, some tentatively dated to as early as 1000 CE. They told Gwen the ongoing work could take years to complete. With this news—aired on Portland's Channel 5 live from Port Anna—Hugh and his partners threw in the towel and vacated the sale.

"Janet is beyond pissed," Steven informed Gwen with a grin. "But there's nothing she can do."

Later, in the cottage, Gwen turned on the music and coaxed Shania into dancing with her on the far less creaky living room floor. Jess had arrived in June trailing a concrete mixer. While Shania took her end-of-year exams, Gwen and Jess repaired the foundation. When the work was complete, the old pine boards felt solid as Gwen and Shania jumped and whooped to the Beach Boys.

By the end of August, with a book advance for volume two of *The Lost House* and, with Steven's help, a renegotiated hospital bill, Gwen repaid the last of what she owed Hugh.

"Go fuck yourself," she whispered into the mail slot at the post office as she sent the final payment.

The seventy-degree days stretched well into September, the sea and sky an unusual shade of ultramarine. The grass stayed green; leaves refused to fall. When October arrived, only the fading light signaled the approaching winter. Gwen had plenty of time to finish caulking the windows and help Jess with the pipes. A ballooning number of tutoring sessions paid for the first installment on a heat pump.

In November, cold air finally slid in, forcing the scholars to abandon their work for the winter. Gwen turned on the heat, smiling. No more sleeping on the floor in the living room, no more shivery mornings, no more peeing in a jar. Money remained an issue—how to manage Shania's future college tuition kept her awake at night—but as she stood at the cusp of her second Maine winter, everything looked different.

In the afternoons, Gwen and Shania walked across the school parking lot together to the car, Shania bent under the weight of her heavy backpack. On the way home Shania fiddled with the car radio, switching between stations, all of which played classic rock.

"You'd think fifty years of Creedence Clearwater Revival would be enough. But nooooo." She drew the word out into a song.

"Come on, CCR is timeless."

Shania snorted.

"You're going to miss the oldies, I predict." Gwen had promised Shania a new phone at the end of the school year, and then Shania could play what she wanted. "Then what will you have to complain about?"

"Your cooking," Shania said, grinning.

"Come on, now. Give a girl a break."

"Kidding, kidding. Not every woman needs to cook. Hey, did you know it used to be illegal for women to dress in men's clothes? We learned that today in English class. Willa Cather liked to wear pants, which was an issue for her." Shania voiced her outrage throughout the length of the Ellsworth road.

As they rounded the bend to town, Shania switched topics from women's studies to environmental science. Her teacher had asked them to gather water samples from the bay. Did Gwen think Mr. Drinkwater might give her a pass for the ferry? The water quality was surely quite different offshore than it was in the harbor.

"We can ask," Gwen said. "I'm sure it's not a problem." Demand dropped dramatically in the off-season, and Walter, like his father, had a soft spot for Shania, the little lost girl with the gap-toothed smile.

They passed the *For Sale* sign posted by Janet Riggs outside of Hugh's property. Gwen had thought briefly about calling him when it appeared last month, but she'd decided she didn't want to know why he chose to list his home. Steven had told her the asking price was ridiculous.

Gwen slowed as they approached their driveway. In the winter, the deer sometimes walked brazenly down the middle of the road in search of food.

"What's for dinner?" Shania asked, once again attending to the radio dial. Gwen had tried to tell her that reception was impossible this far from the tower, but Shania persisted.

"I thought I'd try to make chicken piccata." Leandro had texted her the recipe from New York, promising it would be super easy.

"Yum," Shania said. "When is he coming back again?"

"In a week or so." Leandro remained busy, consumed by his work. He was fully present when in town, texting when he was not. And, to her great surprise, this was okay with Gwen.

They unloaded the car, and shed their heavy coats and boots in the back closet.

Gwen opened the fridge.

"Want some help?" Shania asked, dumping her backpack on the kitchen table.

"I've got it. You go ahead." Gwen frowned as she reread Leandro's directions on her phone. How did one zest a lemon? She took out a knife.

"Hey," Shania said. "You're doing great."

Gwen looked up. "*We're* doing great."

Shania's small, pinched face softened. "Yeah, we are, aren't we?" The frostbite had left a faint scar on her chin and it was more pronounced when she smiled. Several of her fingers still suffered from occasional numbness, too, although Shania never complained. Other reminders of her past were more worrying: nightmares that didn't end right away once she woke, and temper tantrums that lasted too long. Shania's social worker and her counselor insisted these were normal, given what she'd endured, but they also promised that, with time and patience, she'd improve. Youth was in her favor. The stretches between outbursts had begun to lengthen, and her sleep was improving.

Shania shouldered her backpack. "I'm headed up, then."

"I'll let you know when it's ready."

"Okey dokey." Shania bumped up the steps to Molly's old room, her study space. After school, she would sit at the desk, Gwen's old headphones on, feet tucked underneath her, body swaying a little to the tinny music.

Downstairs, at the dining room table, Gwen opened her computer. Images of interiors for Steven's second book sat on one side, notes for the ongoing *Packet* series on the other. Her editor had even made noises about expanding the hermit project to book length.

A thump above Gwen's head caused her to raise her eyes. Habit told her it was the Misses fussing, but it wasn't. It was Shania, moving about the room. Or maybe she'd dropped a book. As quiet as the Misses had been over the summer, careful not to frighten Shania, it took until Labor Day for Gwen to notice she'd heard nothing from them in weeks. At first Gwen had blamed the silence on all the changes to the cottage, the insulation in the walls, the new heat pump, Molly's emptied room. Surely, she'd thought, they'd return as they always had, full of opinions. So she'd waited, ears carefully attuned, confident they would make themselves known when they were ready. But they didn't. Not when she moved the furniture around upstairs, not when she replaced the rug, and not on Labor Day when they usually grew agitated in anticipation of their abandonment. They didn't even surface at Thanksgiving, on the anniversary of Shania's rescue. She and Shania returned from dinner at Steven and Jess's and listened, patiently holding their breath, but only the wind outside brushed the house.

The Misses had left. Perhaps, Gwen thought, their work at an end, they'd moved on to some other sphere or dimension. Maybe they swam with Anna.

Maybe they, like Alexander, had returned to their Maker. Gwen liked to imagine that they were at peace wherever they were, but it was a loss, one among many. They'd kept her company when she'd most needed it, assuring her she wasn't alone, even when she thought she deserved to be. When she'd been ready, they'd coaxed her back into the world. If only she'd had the chance to thank them and say goodbye.

Now, carefully peeling the skin from a lemon, she heard only her own breath and the faint rustle of the wind through the woods outside the kitchen window. Night spilled into the room.

"Gwen," she heard. This was followed by Shania clomping down the stairs at top speed. "Outside. We have to go outside." She threw open the door and rushed onto the porch.

Gwen joined her. They stepped from the lawn onto the berm, gazing down at the water.

A blue-white moon, aglow, hovered at the edge of a glossy sea, the light so bright it cast shadows. Below, on the second ledge, a seal turned, its rounded head lifted on narrow shoulders. Shining eyes stared from a mottled face. The whiskers twitched, and Gwen said, "Oh," in astonishment.

Although this animal often appeared in her dreams, she'd convinced herself the episode wasn't real. How could a sea creature know to guide a disoriented human to the shore? It seemed like something out of a fairy tale. And yet, here it was, Gwen's brown-furred, freckled, wet-eyed savior.

The seal's mouth curled upward as if smiling as another, much larger seal rose from the water, too. The coloring was different, a pale gray that was almost white. Steam curled above their heads, a wisp of moon reflected in their dark eyes. The sound of their collective wet breath carried across the water. The four of them, humans and seals, remained in place, unmoving, watching each other. After a moment, the larger head sank, disappearing beneath the surface without a trace. The smaller, mottled seal turned and locked eyes with Gwen once more. Something passed between them that Gwen couldn't name, something enormous that was at once grief and gratitude and joy. And love. Mostly love. It rose, an enormous wave, and engulfed them both.

"Oh," Gwen said again, very softly. Her eyes filled. *Molly*, she thought. *Oh, Molly.*

A small hand slid into hers.

"She's back," Shania said as the little freckled seal slid from the ledge, splashing into the waiting water. Ripples spread across the still ocean.

Gwen whispered, "I don't think she ever left."

They stood together, motionless, hand in hand, as moonlight spread across the sea, reaching for the shore. It crept across the ledge and, slowly stretching, at last puddled at their feet as if revealing a path only they could see. Even the air around them was filled to overflowing.

ACKNOWLEDGMENTS

I owe a great debt to my parents, who bought a small summer cottage when I was very young. Wildflowers grew along the foundation in the summertime, and winter left salt deposits on the shingles that glittered in the sun. The tidal pools out front provided hours of entertainment, and mysteries abounded in the deep woods behind. Thus began my lifelong love affair with Maine. I am deeply grateful for its many gifts—the bounty and diversity of the land and seascape as well as the fascinating, complicated people who call it home. Thank you for firing my imagination and filling my soul.

The town of Port Anna is fictional, but the character of Anna Vale was inspired by a book entitled *Periwinkle* found on a shelf in my parents' cottage. Although long out of print, the story told of a young girl who lived in a lighthouse and rescued drowning sailors from raging seas. I have a vivid memory of the illustrations—and the volume's antiquated prose—but I can no longer remember the author's name. If any reader should find a copy, please remind me.

The book written by Gwen and Steven was inspired by *The Maine House* and its sequel, *The Maine House II*, created by Maura McEvoy, Basha Burwell, and Kathleen Hackett. I know of no more-accurate depictions of Maine's charming architecture than these two volumes, and I encourage all readers who responded to Periwinkle Cottage to have a look.

Extraordinary thanks are also due to Rick Richter, my wise, ever-smiling, and cheerful agent, who first thought Gwen's story should be told, and to Tim O'Connell, my brilliant editor, whose enthusiasm for this book humbles me. Working with you has been one of the highlights of my life.

The entire team at Simon & Schuster made the production process a delight. Thanks are especially due to Anna Hauser, editorial assistant extraordinaire; the copy editors, who caught all the slip-ups and inconsistencies; and the designers, who made this book more beautiful than I could have imagined.

I am deeply grateful to Peter Behrens and the members of the seminar taught at Hollyhock on the island of Cortes in Canada. It is safe to say that I would never have had the courage to write a single fictional word without you. Lucy Buckley, I am so glad you insisted we attend. Thank you for holding my hand when I needed it.

To Alpin Geist, the most devoted and sympathetic of writing partners, I cannot imagine any project without you. To Kerry Cullen, who deftly helped move the project along. To Mason Howard, my dear friend, who stepped in at a crucial moment and offered insightful comments.

To 2U (you know who you are), your friendship means the world. Special thanks go to Constance Costas and Hampton Carey for their early reads and valuable support.

To the Wine-boxers, thank you for holding me in the light. Your friendship is a beacon in dark times.

To Melissa, Laura, Molly, Vicki, Melody, and Margaret, you're the best cheerleaders anyone could ever ask for.

To Dani Strauss, thank you for describing your love of trees in such a beautiful and poetic way.

To Wendy and Jack Brown, whose generosity and kindness during the writing of this book and at so many other moments besides have been life-sustaining.

To my sister, Alice Gray Stites, my most resolute supporter, my closest friend, and my lifelong companion. Your conviction that art can heal the deepest of wounds matches my own. May you see this story as a small offering.

ACKNOWLEDGMENTS

Our brother, Bo Gray, left us way too soon, just as this book was in production. His lovely photographs reflect our shared love for the brave and rugged coast of Downeast Maine. I feel your presence everywhere.

To Emory, Kelley, and Charlotte, I am grateful for your patience, sympathy, and enduring enthusiasm. You believed in me even when I doubted myself. And to my Leo, you are the rock upon which my foundation rests. I love you more than words can say.

ABOUT THE TYPE

The body text of this book is set in Adobe Garamond, a digital revival typeface designed by Robert Slimbach for Adobe Systems. Slimbach was inspired by a sixteenth-century roman type crafted by Claude Garamond and an italic type by Robert Granjon. His aim was to replicate the elegance and even maturity of the original Garamond, renewed for digital use.

Playfair Display, the font used for the title page, was created by Danish type designer Claus Eggers Sørensen in 2011 and updated in 2017. Its influences can be found in mid-to-late eighteenth-century typefaces such as Baskerville, and it is typically considered a transitional serif font. Playfair Display is ideal for titles and headlines due to its subtle elongation and high-contrast strokes.

ABOUT THE AUTHOR

Libby Buck earned a Ph.D. in art history from the University of North Carolina at Chapel Hill. She and her husband share three daughters, an English cocker spaniel, and an abiding love for the great state of Maine. *Port Anna* is Libby's first novel.